CHAMELEON

'*Chameleon* is a *Casablanca* for the 21st century. Burnell writes with verve and assurance about the unsavoury realities of international terrorism. Where he really excels, however, is with his characters. Not only are his two protagonists convincingly complex and three-dimensional, but they also share a love story which is as moving as it is passionate.'

Boris Starling, author of *Messiah*

Also by Mark Burnell

Rhythm Section

CHAMELEON

Mark Burnell

HarperCollins*Publishers*

HarperCollins*Publishers*
77–85 Fulham Palace Road,
Hammersmith, London W6 8JB

www.**fire**and**water**.com

This paperback edition 2002

This novel is entirely a work of fiction. The names,
characters and incidents portrayed in it are the work
of the author's imagination. Any resemblance to actual
persons, living or dead, events or localities
is entirely coincidental.

A catalogue record for this book
is available from the British Library

ISBN 978-0-00-651338-4

Set in PostScript Linotype Meridien by
Rowland Phototypesetting Ltd,
Bury St Edmunds, Suffolk

I would like to thank Lydia Grishaeva and Nikolai Morgunov in Moscow, and Marjaliisa Björkbom in Helsinki. In particular, I am grateful to Toby Eady and Susan Watt for their ceaseless assistance from first to last. I count myself lucky to have had them at my side. I would also like to thank Larry Ashmead in New York for his continuing support.

To Isabelle with love

The only indecipherable code in the world is a woman.
Leo Marks
Special Operations Executive

PARIS

The rhythm of the windscreen wipers was hypnotic. The rubber blades squeaked against the glass, smearing rain left and right. James Marshall leaned forward and peered at the brasserie on the other side of the street. The clock on the dashboard said it was five to two. He checked his own watch – it was marginally fast – and lit a cigarette. The caller had given him the address, the time – two o'clock – and a reminder not to be late. That had been half an hour ago at a pay-phone at the Gare du Nord.

The other phone call – the one that had caught him at home the day before yesterday – had come out of the blue. And out of the past. He'd recognized the voice instantly. A simple job that paid cash in hand; that had been the offer. Good cash, too, considering how little work was involved. He wouldn't even have to leave Paris. At first, that had made the proposal all the more attractive.

Would he consider acting as a courier? Nothing fancy, naturally, just a fetch-and-drop, as a favour from one seasoned veteran to another.

Of course, he'd said, he'd be delighted. There had been times in the not-so-distant past when he would have considered such a job beneath him, when he would have been offended by the offer. James Marshall, the courier? The errand boy? Now, he was as

1

grateful for the opportunity as he was for the money.

He instructed his Tunisian taxi driver to drop him on avenue de Friedland, from where he walked back to rue du Faubourg Saint Honoré. The rain was growing stronger. And colder. A lead sky darkened everything. The driver of a delivery van attempted a U-turn in front of the brasserie. The vehicle stalled. He tried the ignition twice. Nothing. He slapped the steering wheel and tried again. Still nothing. A woman in a navy Mercedes saloon held open her hands in exasperation. The van driver shrugged. The traffic staggered to a halt. Headlights sparkled, exhausts wheezed.

Marshall tried to ignore the tightness in his stomach, the tightness that suggested it would have been better to ignore the money. He wished he was home. His chilly, damp, single-room apartment in Saint Denis had rarely seemed so appealing. He crossed the street, meandering through stationary vehicles, and entered the brasserie.

Half a dozen customers congregated around a curve of copper bar. A waiter took his damp raincoat and asked if he was alone but he was already moving into the dining room. Oleg Rogachev was in the far corner, at a table by the window. Marshall recognized him from the photographs he'd studied; built like a bull, a moustache like a slug, silver hair cropped to a spike. His collars and cuffs were tight to the skin, accentuating fat hands and fat face. He wore a charcoal silk double-breasted suit.

Rogachev looked up from his plate – pig's trotters and spinach – and nodded towards the seat opposite. The man sitting next to him was a stranger but not a surprise; a translator, Marshall assumed. Rogachev

2

spoke no English and had no reason to expect Marshall to speak Russian. As it happened, he'd been fluent for thirty years.

With only a slight accent, he said, 'In Britain, we have a saying. Two's company, three's a crowd.'

Rogachev raised an eyebrow. 'This is Anatoli.'

'I hope neither of you will be offended if I ask him to leave.'

There was a frosty pause. Then Rogachev said, 'I'll see you back at the hotel.'

Anatoli rose from the table and left. Marshall sat down. Rogachev pushed his plate to one side, hailed a waiter and gesticulated with chubby fingers. A clean glass arrived. Rogachev waited until the wine had been poured.

'I hope your people recognize the risk I'm taking.'

'They do.'

'Then I hope they'll show their appreciation.'

'They will. But only unofficially. They're keen to stress this and they're sure you'll understand their reasons.'

Marshall looked out of the window. Gridlock, a crescendo of car horns, teeming rain. When he looked back, he noticed the small device next to Rogachev's glass. It resembled a travel radio but had no aerial or display. The Russian felt for a switch on the side. He saw Marshall's expression and said, 'It jams directional radio microphones. It emits violent electronic signals, casting a five-metre protective shield. Anybody trying to listen to us will hear only static.' He smiled slyly. 'Even though I'm not here, it's better to be careful.'

Hence the delay in naming the rendezvous, Marshall supposed. In the old days – in *his* day – these types of precaution had been routine. Naively, he'd imagined things would be different now. He wondered where Rogachev's friends and enemies thought he was. Moscow? Yekaterinburg? Miami?

'What have you come to offer me?'

Marshall took a sip from his glass. The red tasted bitter but the effect was welcome. 'It's possible that the investigation into Weaver Financial Services will come to nothing.'

Rogachev pulled a face, unimpressed. 'That is possible anyway.'

Marshall shook his head. 'There's something you don't know. Weaver's links to Calmex in Lausanne have been established. Arrest warrants are being prepared as we speak.'

The small, piggy eyes narrowed slightly. 'Go on.'

'If you accept our offer, the Weaver directors will still have to be replaced. That is non-negotiable. The company would also have to pay a small fine for a lesser misdemeanour. It's better if the investigation comes up with *something*.'

'What else?'

'On the plus side, your assets would cease to be frozen. Also, your status as *persona non grata* would be revoked on the understanding that you do not try to enter the United Kingdom for a period of six months.'

A waiter came to clear plates and refill glasses. Rogachev ordered two espressos and the bill. 'You should know that the reason I've decided to come to an arrangement with you is not for my own advantage. That is merely – how would you put it? – a bonus.' He reached into his pocket and produced a gold Sony Mini-Disc which he placed on the table between them.

'I'm a wheat trader, not a criminal. The people who are exploiting my commercial network are renegades. They are a threat to everyone.'

'Of course.'

'I want that distinction understood.'

'Naturally.'

He tapped the Mini-Disc. 'It's essential they never discover the origin of this information . . .'

'I understand.'

'. . . because that could lead to complications. The kind of complications where everybody suffers.'

Marshall tried to ignore the threat. The espressos arrived. The Russian added sugar. Outside, the congestion caused by the delivery van had escalated. The driver was now standing next to his vehicle, arguing with half a dozen people. Some of those inside the brasserie had turned to watch the commotion.

Rogachev spoke softly. 'The courier will arrive at Heathrow Terminal Two from Budapest on the third of April. Malev flight MA610.'

Marshall took a propelling pencil from his jacket and began to write notes on a small pad. 'What's the name?'

'You get the name when the flight leaves Budapest. I don't want him intercepted in Hungary.'

'What's he bringing?'

'Plutonium-239.'

'From where?'

'MINATOM. I can't be more specific.'

MINATOM was the Russian Atomic Energy Ministry, a vast department which had a history of not being specific.

'How much?'

'One thousand five hundred grammes.'

'What's he bringing it in?'

'A suitcase with a shielded canister inside.'

'Concealed or loose?'

'Loose, we think.'

'How pure is it?'

'Ninety-four per cent.'

'Anything else?'

'He may be carrying quantities of Lithium-6.'

'How much?'

'We don't know. Probably two to four kilos. Maybe nothing.'

'Do you know the target?'

'No.'

'What about the end user?'

'Unidentified.'

Rogachev glanced at the notes Marshall was taking. Bread, sugar, bacon, olive oil, kilos and grammes, pounds and ounces; it appeared to be a conventional shopping list. When they were finished, Rogachev paid in cash, leaving an extravagant tip. They collected their coats and stepped outside. The rain was heavier; there was a flash of lightning, a five-second pause and a rumble of thunder that was almost inaudible over the chorus of screeching horns. The soaked van driver was shouting. Rogachev erected an umbrella. He seemed amused by the scene in front of him.

Marshall was thinking ahead. The disk, the drop in Montmartre, then back to the Gare du Nord. From a public pay-phone, the London number that he'd memorized, the message relayed, then back to Saint Denis, perhaps stopping off at a café for a cup of coffee. Or something stronger. Then tomorrow, the delivery. A plain brown envelope, he expected. Full of francs . . .

It wasn't thunder. It was louder than that. And sharper. The liquid that splattered across his face wasn't rain, either. It was hot.

The umbrella slipped from Rogachev's grasp. A gust of wind carried it away. Another deafening crack and he was spinning. Marshall didn't move. Shock insulated him from what was happening around him. Time slowed to a standstill. He had no idea where the source of the noise was. He saw faces turning in the rain, hands rising to mouths, eyes widening. Nobody was paying attention to the van driver any more. Rogachev fell forward, smacking against the car at the kerb before collapsing to the ground. He left blood across the white bonnet. Rain diluted it pink.

Curiously, Marshall found himself thinking about the good old days.

1

She's eighteen months old. Two years ago, she was twenty-five years old.

They made love slowly but it was a hot afternoon and soon their bodies were slick. Laurent Masson was a tall man with no fat on his sinewy frame; dark-haired, dark-skinned, dark dirt beneath his fingernails. When she'd first seen him, Stephanie had thought he looked slightly seedy, which she liked. She, by contrast, had never looked more wholesome, which she also liked. Plump breasts, the curved suggestion of a belly, a dimple in the soft flesh above each buttock. She'd allowed her hair to grow; thick and dark, it fell between her shoulders down half her spine. Summer sun had tanned her normally pale skin, a healthy diet had improved her complexion.

The first-floor bedroom was small; a high ceiling, floorboards worn smooth, two tatty Yemeni rugs, a narrow double bed with a wrought-iron frame. On one wall, there was a mottled full-length mirror. On the opposite wall, there were six sepia photographs of Provence's brutal beauty.

Masson was on his back, Stephanie above him, his body between her thighs. Slowly, she rocked back and forth, trailing her fingertips across his chest and stomach. Neither of them spoke and there was no hint of a breeze to cool them. When she came, she closed her eyes, dropped her head back and bit her fleshy lower lip.

Later, Masson smoked a cigarette, rolling his ash onto a dirty china saucer. Stephanie stood by the window, naked and damp. Her gaze followed the land, falling away from the farmhouse, across the vineyard and the dirt track that bisected it. The vines shimmered in the heat. Somewhere at the bottom of the valley, screened by emerald trees, there was the road. To the right, Entrecasteaux, to the left, Salernes. Beyond either, the real world.

'Last night, the dogs were barking all down the valley.'

Behind her, Masson shifted, the bed-springs creaking. 'They kept you awake?'

She nodded. 'Some were howling.'

'You should have spent the night with me.'

'Actually, I liked it. It sounded . . . sad.' She crossed her arms. 'Sad but beautiful.'

'Will I see you later?'

'If you want to.'

'Do *you* want to?'

'What do you think?'

'I don't know. I never know what you think.'

'Lucky you.'

Laurent leaves. From the yard, I watch his old Fiat lurch along the track, kicking up clouds of golden dirt. When the dust has settled, I go inside and make tea. The kitchen is cool and dark; a stone floor, terracotta walls, a heavy oak table flanked by benches. Bees murmur by the small square window over the sink. French windows open onto a terrace. A blanket of greenery laid over wooden beams provides dappled shade.

Behind the house, olive trees are organized along terraces that climb the hill.

The farm belongs to a thirty-five-year-old German investment banker who was transferred from Frankfurt to Tokyo eighteen months ago. Initially, I rented it for six months through an agency in Munich. That was just over a year ago; I'm seven weeks into my third rental period. The roof leaks in places, some of the plasterwork is crumbling, the windows and doors are ill-fitting. But I don't mind. In fact, I prefer it this way. It feels more like a home. Then again, how would I know? I've lived in too many places to count but not one of them has been a home.

When the tea is ready, I take it outside. The fragrance of summer is as strong as its colour; scents of citrus and lavender envelop me. I love days like this as much as the severer days of mid-December, when fierce winds scrape the harsh landscape, when rain explodes from pewter clouds that seem only just out of reach. Then, the dusty track turns to glycerine, cutting me off from the road. I always enjoy the artificial isolation that follows.

There is a large fireplace in the sitting room and a good supply of logs in the lean-to behind the outhouse. For me, there is a childish comfort in being warm and dry as I listen to the storm outside. I was raised in north Northumberland, close to the border with Scotland. Wild weather was a feature of my childhood. More than a mere memory, it's a part of me.

That's the thing about me, I suppose. I'm a collection of parts that never adds up to a whole. With me, two plus two comes to five. Or three. Or anything except four.

As far as the people around here are concerned, I am Stephanie Schneider, a Swiss with no parents, no siblings, no baggage. I live off a meagre inheritance. I spend my days *reading, drawing, walking. I came from nowhere and one day I'll return there. That's what's expected by those who gossip about me. Apparently, I've slept with a couple of men in the area – surprising choices, some say – and now I'm seeing Masson, the mechanic from Salernes. Another outsider, he's from Marseille. The local word is, it's a casual relationship.*

This happens to be true. It's because I can't cope with commitment. Not yet – it's too early for me – maybe not ever. But I am making progress.

I read my book for ten minutes – The Murdered House *by Pierre Magnan – and then lay it to one side. From where I'm sitting, I can see my laptop on the fridge. There's a fine layer of dust on the lid. It must be nearly a month since I last switched it on. In the beginning, it was two or three times a day. Slowly but surely, I'm severing my ties to the old world. With each passing day, I feel increasingly regenerated. But this process has not been without its setbacks.*

The first man I had an affair with after moving here was a doctor from Draguignan named Olivier. I should have known better; he was very good-looking, always a danger sign. We met in Entrecasteaux during the firework display to commemorate Bastille Day. He was charming and amusing, so I started seeing him, which was when he changed. Sometimes, he would be jealous, at other times, indifferent. When I walked into a room, it was impossible to know whether he would say something wonderful or cruel. He was not interested in equilibrium; we had to be soaring or falling. And if we were falling, there would be reconciliation so that we could soar again. For someone of my age, I've had more than my fair share of highs and lows. The last thing I needed was Olivier's amateur dramatics.

The night we separated, I drove to his house in Draguig-

nan. The previous evening, he'd come out to the farmhouse. He'd arrived two hours late. The dinner I'd cooked had spoiled but he couldn't bring himself to apologize. We had sex – it was coarse and uncaring – and in the morning, between waking and leaving, he managed to insult me four times without even realizing it. Not that I minded; I was already over him. I phoned him later that morning and said I would come to his house and cook for him again, and that I'd appreciate it if he was on time for once.

He was only an hour late. I put the plate before him – beef casserole in a red wine sauce – and filled our glasses.

'You're not eating?'

'I ate when it was ready,' I told him. 'An hour ago . . .'

He shrugged and began to fork food into his mouth. I watched in silence as he finished the plate and took some more. When he finally laid his knife and fork together, I rose from my chair and dropped his spare keys onto the table.

'I've taken my spare set back. Here are yours.'

He looked down at the keys, then up at me. 'What is this?'

'What do you think?'

'Some kind of joke?'

I resisted a cutting retort and simply shook my head.

A frown darkened his face. 'What are you saying, Stephanie?'

'You drink with your friends but not with me. You fuck me but won't kiss me.'

He sat back in his chair and sucked in a lungful of air. 'So – '

'So nothing.' I didn't want to hear a second-hand apology. 'It's over.'

'Wait a minute . . .'

'Why?'

'Why?'

'Yes. Why? Why wait? Why waste any more time?'

'Can't we at least talk about it?'

'My mind is made up.'

'What about me?'

I think I smiled at him. 'Exactly.'

'What does that mean?'

'You know. And if you don't . . . well, it makes no difference.'

I picked up my car keys, which were lying on the draining board beside the sink.

'Stephanie . . .'

I turned round. Given an opportunity, he couldn't think of anything to say, so I said, 'One last thing, before I go.'

'What?'

'Did you enjoy your dinner?'

He looked confused. 'What?'

'It's a simple question. Did you enjoy it? Yes or no?'

He shrugged. 'Sure, I guess. It was fine . . .'

I walked over to the swing-bin beside the door, stuck my arm inside, found the empty can and tossed it to him. 'You're a spoilt child, Olivier. For someone with some intelligence, your behaviour is moronic.'

He glanced at the label. 'Dog food?'

'Not just any old dog food, darling. Premium quality dog food.'

'You gave me dog food?'

'I wanted to do something that would make you understand.'

'Understand what?'

'How you've made me feel over the last few weeks.'

Stranded for a reply, all he managed was: 'You said it was beef casserole!'

14

'It was. Made with dog food. Beef heart and something else, I think . . . it's on the label.'

The colour drained from his face. I couldn't tell whether it was rage or nausea.

'You lost interest in me but you lacked the courage to tell me.'

'That's not true.'

'Are you seeing someone else?'

He faltered. Then: 'No.'

'You are, aren't you?'

'No.'

I didn't want an apology, just a slither of honesty. 'Come on . . .'

His expression hardened. 'Okay. If you have to know . . . yes.'

The change of heart was too abrupt. It left me more uncertain than before. I had the feeling his admission was a lie, designed to hurt me while he still could. Either way, I no longer cared. It was typical of Olivier not to see that.

'Well,' I said, unable to resist the cheap shot, 'that would explain the drop-off in your sexual performance, I suppose. Recently, you've been dismal.' Before he could respond, I went on. 'The point is, you don't feel anything for me and I no longer feel anything for you, so what's the use?'

Outraged, he rose to his feet and jabbed a finger at me. 'I can't believe this! You . . . you're . . .'

He frothed, spluttered and, eventually, found his insult. He called me frigid. A frigid Swiss bitch. It sounded so helpless and absurd – so castrated – that I should have felt a pinch of pity for him. But I didn't. Instead, I laughed and Olivier, his anger now complete, threw a slap at me.

What happened next was automatic. I feinted to my left, ducking outside the arc cast by his arm. I intercepted his hand,

15

crushed the fingers into a ball and twisted it. All in half a second. I heard his wrist crack, felt two fingers breaking. As he sank to his knees, I let go of him, took a step back, spun on one foot, lashed out with the other and broke three ribs.

The next thing I remember, I was standing over him. I was silent. The only sound in the room was Olivier's breathing. He was gurgling like a baby. There was blood on his face, there were fragments of teeth on the floor.

In some ways, I think Olivier recovered quicker than I did. It certainly crushed my complacency. I had come to believe that I'd purged that part of my past. Now I know better and don't take anything for granted. Violence is a part of me and probably always will be. I was manufactured to be that way.

After Olivier, there was Remy, a professor of economics from Toulouse who was taking a year-long sabbatical in order to write a book. That was nice. Older, wiser, more civilized, for a while the whole affair seemed more in keeping with my new frame of mind. But after three months, he started to talk about the future, about a life in Toulouse. The first hint of permanency was the beginning of the end.

Now, there is Laurent. I told him at the start not to expect any commitment.

'I've only been divorced for three months,' he replied. 'The last thing I need right now is commitment. I just want an easy life. Some good times . . .'

Which is how it has been, so far. He's bright, witty, kind. He's wasted as a mechanic in Salernes. Then again, who am I to speak? After all that's happened to me, I could live this way for years and not grow bored with it. I don't know what the future holds and I don't care. For the first time in my life, I'm happy with the present. Doing nothing and being nowhere seem perfect.

These days, when I think of 20 January 2000 and that tiny room on the second floor of that run-down hotel in Bilbao, I think to myself, was that really me?

She spent the afternoon at one end of the highest olive terrace, sketching the ruined shepherd's hut at the farm's edge. She made four drawings from two vantage points, ink and charcoal on paper. There was a constant hot breeze. By the time she returned to the house, she felt the sun and dust on her skin. She left the drawings on the slate worktop, drank a glass of water, refilled it and went upstairs.

The free-standing bath stood at the centre of the bathroom on heavy iron legs. The rusted taps coughed when turned. Stephanie pulled her linen dress over her head, dropped it onto the scrubbed wooden floor and lowered herself into the water. Through a circular window, she watched the vineyards turning blue in the evening light.

A steam shroud rose from the surface. She closed her eyes and the present made way for the past: an airless top floor flat in Valletta with a view of the fort; the crowded lobby of the Hotel Inter-Continental in Belgrade; Salman Rifat pouring olive oil onto her skin; a bout of dysentery contracted in Kinshasa; TV pictures of pieces of wreckage from flight NE027 floating on the North Atlantic; the message on the screen – *I have work for you, if you're interested*; Bilbao.

Eighteen months ago, these memories would have provoked panic. Now, Stephanie felt calm in their company. She accepted they would never go away but the further she moved away from them, the easier it became. She was starting to feel disconnected from them. In time, she hoped she might almost believe that they belonged to someone else.

The door onto the street was open. Masson's apartment was in a narrow side street off the main square in Entre-casteaux. A first floor with high ceilings, patches of damp and rotten shutters that opened onto a shallow balcony. The bedroom was at the back, overlooking an internal courtyard that reeked of damp in the winter. During the summer, it was a humid air-trap.

Masson was barefoot, his hair still wet from his shower. He wore faded jeans and a green cotton shirt, untucked and badly creased. Like his apartment, he was a mess. It suited him.

They ate chicken and salad, followed by locally produced apricots. The sweet juice stained Stephanie's fingers. Later, they went to the bar on the square. Small, stuffy, starkly lit, it lacked charm, but Masson was friendly with the *patron* and Stephanie had grown to know the people who went there. There was a TV on a wall bracket in one corner, a European football tie on the screen, a partisan group gathered in front of it. Behind the bar, there were faded photographs of a dozen Olympique Marseille teams, all taken in the Stade Vélodrome. Children scuttled in and out of the bar, some dressed in the white and sky-blue football shirts of *l'OM*. It was quarter to midnight by the time Stephanie and Masson returned to his apartment. A little tired, a little drunk, they made clumsy love.

In the morning, Stephanie woke first and went out to collect fresh bread. When she returned, Masson was making coffee, smoking his first cigarette of the day.

'Are you busy tonight?'

'Yes.'

He turned to look at her. 'Really?'

'You seem surprised.'

He looked back at the ground coffee in the pot. 'Not really. It's just . . .'

'Just what?'

'I don't know . . .'

'It's okay, Laurent. I'm not busy.'

Uncertainty made way for a lopsided grin. 'No?'

'I just don't want you to take me for granted.'

'How could I? I don't even know you. You tell me that you have a temper but I've never seen it.' Stephanie grinned too. Masson let it drop, as she knew he would. 'You want to come here again?'

'Why don't you come out to me?'

'Okay. I'll be finished in the garage at about six thirty, seven.'

When Masson went to work, Stephanie climbed into her second-hand Peugeot 106 and drove back to the farmhouse. She parked beneath a tree and left the windows rolled down. Despite the cool dawn, it was already a hot morning, a firm wind among the leaves and branches. The lavender bushes were clouds of bright purple that whispered to her as she climbed up the stone steps to the rough gravel beside the terrace.

It wasn't anything she saw or heard that made her stop. It was a feeling, a tightness in the chest. Just like her reaction to Olivier's slap, it was an instinct she couldn't rinse from her system. She stood still, held her breath and felt her pulse accelerate. There was no apparent reason for it; no door forced, no window broken, nothing out of place. She waited. Still nothing. She told herself she'd imagined it. But as she took a step forward, she heard a noise. A soft scrape, perhaps. One hard surface against another. The sound was barely audible over the wind. It could have been the gentle clatter of a branch on the clay tiles of the barn, or the creak of a rotten shutter on a rusty hinge.

The memory triggered the response. The mind functioned like a computer. Gathering information, analysing it, forming strategy, assessing risk. She felt herself begin to move, directed by a will that didn't seem to be her own.

She hummed a tune to herself as she strolled round the farmhouse to the back. To look at, a girl without a care in the world. Behind the house, she shed her shoes and clutched the drainpipe which rose to the roof gutter. When she'd moved in, it had been loose. During her first week, she'd bolted it to the stone wall herself.

She began the climb, the surface abrasive against the soles of her feet, the paint flaking against her palms. She was out of practice, testing tissue that had softened or tightened, but her technique remained intact. She pulled back the shutter – always closed, never fastened – and made the swing to the window, grasping the wooden frame, hauling herself up and through, and into a tiny room that the leasing company had fraudulently described as a third bedroom.

She paused on the landing to check for sound but heard nothing. In the second bedroom, which overlooked the courtyard at the rear of the house, she opened the only cupboard in the room, emptied the floor-space of shoes, pulled out the patch of mat beneath and lifted the central floorboard. Attached to a nail, there was a piece of washing line. At the end of it, there was a sealed plastic pouch, coated in dust and cobwebs.

For all the serenity of the life she'd made for herself, it had never occurred to Stephanie to dispense with her insurance. She took it out of the pouch. A gleaming 9mm SIG-Sauer P226. In the past, her gun of choice. She checked the weapon, then left the bedroom.

The staircase was the worst part, a narrow trap. She eased the safety off the SIG and descended, her naked feet silent on the smooth stone. On the ground floor, she moved like a ghost; the sitting room, the cloakroom, the study.

The intruder was in the kitchen. She felt his presence at the foot of the stairs but only spied him when she peered through a crack in the kitchen door, which was half open. She saw a patch of cream jacket, some back, a little shoulder, half an arm, an elbow. She tiptoed inside. He was facing the terrace entrance, his back to her. He was standing, as if expecting her. Perhaps he'd heard the Peugeot park; he couldn't have seen her approach from the steps, not from any of the kitchen windows, and yet he seemed to know that she most often entered the farmhouse via the terrace.

Stephanie managed to place the cold metal tip of the SIG's barrel against the nape of his neck before he stirred. When he did, it was nothing more than a gentle flinch. He made no attempt to turn around or to cry out with surprise. That was when she recognized the clipped, snow-white hair.

'Hello, Miss Schneider.' And the clipped Scottish accent. 'Or should I say, Miss Patrick?'

2

You tell yourself it *can't be true. For once, you're honest with yourself but your first reaction is denial. It has to be a mistake. Your mistake, somebody else's, it doesn't really matter. Any excuse will do when you can't face the truth about yourself.*

Everybody has a talent. This is what the cliché tells us. I think it depends on what you regard as a talent. When the lowest common denominator determines the threshold for that talent, almost anything can count; having a nice smile, being a good liar, not succumbing to obesity. Personally, though, I reject the idea that everybody has a gift. It's rather like saying 'art is for the people'. It isn't. It's for those who can appreciate it and understand it. It's elitist. Just like talent.

Most people have no particular ability. Mediocrity is the only quality they have in abundance. I should know. For a long time, I was one of them. But that was before I discovered that there was an alternative me, that there was another world where I could rise above the rest and excel.

It's one thing to discover you're exceptional. It's quite another to recognize that what makes you exceptional is unacceptable. What do you do when you finally see who you really are – what you really are – and it's everything society rejects? You tell yourself it can't be true. That's what you do, that's the first thing. And maybe it's what you continue to do. But not me. I'd already lied to myself for long enough. When the moment came, I stopped pretending I was someone

22

else and chose to be the real me instead. I chose to be honest.
Brutally honest.

'How are you, Stephanie?'

Slowly, he turned round, his face emerging from her memory; ruddy skin stretched tightly across prominent bones, aquamarine eyes, that white hair. He was wearing a cream suit, a dark blue shirt open at the throat, a pair of polished black slip-ons.

'I heard the rumours, of course. That Petra Reuter was back. Naturally, I didn't believe them. But when it turned out that there was some substance to them, I assumed that someone had hijacked her identity in order to protect their own identity. Just as you once did.' He squinted at her, perplexed, offended. 'It never occurred to me that it might actually be you, the *real* Petra Reuter.'

Alexander was a man who believed mistakes were made by other people. That was why he was staring at her so intensely. He was looking for an answer.

'I was sure that once you vanished, I would never hear of you again, let alone see you. But for more than two years, you *were* Petra. The question is, why?'

Stephanie said nothing.

'And then you stopped. About eighteen months ago, wasn't it? No reason, no warning. Again, the question is, why?'

Alexander. A man with no first name. A man she'd spent four years trying to forget.

'What's the matter? Cat got your tongue?' He took a packet of Rothmans out of his jacket pocket. 'How unlike you.'

Stephanie couldn't help herself. 'Fuck off.'

23

She'd wanted to stay silent. Now, Alexander had his reaction. 'That's more like it.'

She jabbed the gun against the bridge of his nose. 'Get out.'

'Are you familiar with the phrase "act in haste, repent at leisure"?'

'Are you familiar with the phrase "I'm going to count to three"?'

He didn't even blink.

'You rented this property through the Braun-Stahl agency in Munich. You bought your Peugeot from Yves Monteanu, a dental technician from St Raphael. Did you know that his father was a Romanian dissident? He used to publish an underground pamphlet in Bucharest each month. All through the seventies and into the eighties. A brave but foolish –'

'One.'

'No, I don't suppose you did,' Alexander concluded. 'But that would be because you didn't do as much research as we did. You know what we're like, though, how thorough we are. For instance, I know that you rarely stray further than Entrecasteaux or Salernes. I know you have a checking account with Crédit Lyonnais that receives fifty thousand francs a month. Which seems a lot, considering the life you're leading. Each month, it's from a different source that vanishes as soon as the transaction's complete. A neat trick – one day, you'll have to explain it to me. I also know that you're having a relationship with Laurent Masson, a car mechanic from Marseille. I assume you know that Masson has an ex-wife . . .'

'Two.'

'. . . but I wonder whether he's told you about his

criminal record.' Stephanie was betrayed by her expression. 'I didn't think so.' Alexander took his time, making a play out of plucking a cigarette from the packet. He tapped it on the lid. 'He's a car thief. Three convictions to his name. Last time out, he got four months inside. That was when his wife decided she'd had enough. She moved out. Took everything with her; furniture, carpets, curtains, the lot. You can imagine his surprise on the day of his release when he got back home. Mind you, it must have made it easier just to walk away ... there being nothing to walk away from.'

Stephanie increased the pressure of metal on skin.

Alexander met her stare fully. 'Three?'

There was a moment where she could have done it. In her mind, there was nothing but static. It was fifty-fifty. She felt that Alexander sensed it too, yet he hadn't backed down.

She eased the safety on. 'What are you doing here?'

When she pulled the gun away, it left a pale, circular indentation over the bridge of his nose.

'I guess Masson thought he'd come to a quiet little town like Salernes – or Entrecasteaux, for that matter – where nobody'd bother him. Where he could start to build a new life for himself. Just like you. Right?'

There was a briefcase on the kitchen table. He opened it and produced an A4-sized manila envelope, which he handed to her.

'Take a look.'

Inside, there were about twenty photographs, half of them in black-and-white. The first was of a school playground, five girls in uniform, aged seven or eight. They were playing, laughing. From the grain of the print, Stephanie could tell that the photographer had used a zoom lens. For a few moments, the significance of the shot wasn't apparent. But then she saw.

It was the hair that fooled her. Brown and thick, it was almost waist-length. Four years ago, it had been cropped short. She was tall, too, taller than the girls around her. As a four-year-old, she'd been small for her age. Now, she'd caught up with her school friends and surged ahead. The facial features began to chime; Christopher's nose, Jane's eyes. The girl at the centre of the photograph was Polly, her niece.

'I don't believe you've ever seen Philip, have you? The last time you saw your sister-in-law she was pregnant with him. We were standing on the road overlooking Falstone Cemetery. Your family were burying you after your fatal car crash. Remember?'

Stephanie ignored the barb. There were five photographs taken on a beach. Bamburgh, perhaps, or maybe Seahouses. Those were the beaches Stephanie's parents had taken them to as children. They'd remained popular with Christopher and Jane and their children. She saw James and Polly running through ankle-deep surf, Christopher with his trousers rolled up to the knee, Philip on his shoulders, tiny hands in his hair. It looked like a windy day. As she remembered them, they always were. There was a golden retriever in two of the shots. She wanted to know if it was theirs but knew she couldn't ask. The final photographs were taken at their home, overlooking Falstone; Christopher rounding up sheep in the field below the paddock, Jane captured in the bathroom window, unfastening her bra, unaware. Stephanie recognized an implied threat when she saw it.

She put the prints on the table. 'I imagine there's a point to this.'

'Been to Paris recently?'

She said nothing.

'What do you know about James Marshall?'

'Never heard of him.'

'How about Oleg Rogachev?'

'No.'

Alexander finally lit his cigarette. 'Ever heard of a man named Koba?'

'No.'

'Another Russian.'

'I would never have guessed.'

'Not even when you were Petra?'

'No.'

'I have a proposition for you . . .'

'Not a chance.'

'You haven't heard it yet.'

'It doesn't matter. I'm not interested.'

'You will be. So why don't you sit down and listen?'

She remained standing.

Alexander looked bored. 'I'm not leaving until you hear me out.'

'Then get on with it.'

'You have no right to expect any leniency from me, you know. You belonged to Magenta House. You still do. The last four years count for nothing. You should bear that in mind when you consider my proposition, which is this: one job in two or three parts –'

'No.'

Alexander continued as though he hadn't heard her. 'Afterwards . . . well, you'll be free. You won't have to see me again. A pleasure for both of us, I'm sure.'

'No.'

'Stephanie . . .'

'You don't understand. I can't work for you again.'

'You mean, you won't.'

'I mean, I can't. I've changed.'

'We've all changed. Some of us more than others. But no one changes quite like you. Changing is what you do best, Stephanie. And once you've changed into Petra Reuter and taken care of business, you'll be free to change back into who you are now. Or anyone else you might want to be.'

'Didn't you hear what I said? I'll never work for you again. I'd sooner be dead.'

Alexander took a long, theatrical drag, then exhaled slowly, smoke spilling from his nostrils. 'I don't expect you to agree. Not here, not now. You have your pride. But when you manage to put that to one side, you'll see that this is a good offer.' He picked up the photographs from the table. 'It's Monday afternoon now. I'll expect you at Magenta House by the end of the week.'

'You must be out of your mind.'

His shrug was dismissive. 'You seem to have made a good life for yourself here. Why ruin it? Why go back on the run? Which is what you'll have to do. Think about it. You can set yourself free.' He was about to put the photographs back into his briefcase but changed his mind. 'I'll leave these with you.'

'You don't really think you'll see me again, do you?'

'Were you really going to shoot me?'

'Yes.'

'But you didn't.' He headed for the terrace, then paused. On the slate worktop, next to the sink, were the drawings she'd made of the shepherd's hut the pre-

28

vious afternoon. He picked one up and examined it. 'Yours?'

'Get out.'

He dropped the sketch back onto the pile with casual contempt. 'You should stick to killing people, Stephanie. That's where your real talent lies.'

'I'm retired.'

Alexander smiled. She wasn't sure she'd ever seen him do that. He said, 'You're twenty-seven. You're too young to retire.'

Stephanie watched Alexander walk down the track towards the road. She hadn't noticed a car on her return from Entrecasteaux. Perhaps he had a driver nearby. She didn't wait for him to fade from view.

You can make a home for yourself, you can make a life for yourself, but don't make anything for yourself that you can't walk away from in a second.

There was no need to think. The procedure was self-activating.

She collected a paring knife from a kitchen drawer and went upstairs to her bedroom. Beneath her bed, there was an old leather suitcase with brass locks. She opened it and slit the stained fabric lining near the bottom, so that the contents would not be damaged. A German passport in the name of Franka Müller and two thousand Deutschmarks. That was enough to get her to Helsinki. There, in a safe-deposit box at the 1572 Senaatintori branch of the Merita-Nordbanken on Aleksanterinkatu, the ingredients of Franka Müller's life awaited collection; keys to a rented bed-sit in Berlin that was paid for monthly by direct debit to a management agency, a birth certificate, a valid American Express card, a German driving licence, personal bank records. A dormant but complete identity.

She opened the cupboard to the right of the bed and stood on a chair so that she could reach the back of the top shelf. Behind an old shoe-box, there was a small black rucksack. Everything was already packed; some underwear, socks, a pair of trainers, a pair of black jeans (now probably too tight), a couple of T-shirts, a sweat-shirt, a thin grey anorak with a hood. Also, a wash-bag containing a few toiletries and a medical pack that included sutures, disinfectant and painkillers.

Stephanie looked at her watch. It was only ten thirty. Traffic permitting, she'd be at Nice airport by twelve thirty. From there, one way or another, she'd make sure she was in Helsinki before the end of the day. Tomorrow, once she'd gathered the rest of Franka Müller, she would have the whole world in which to lose herself. Tomorrow, there would be no trace of Stephanie Schneider left on the planet.

Seven fifteen. Masson entered the kitchen from the ter-race, as he sometimes did, and stopped. On the floor, there was smashed crockery, shattered glass, cutlery. The wooden chair that had been next to the fridge was broken. Not just a slat here or a leg there, but destroyed.

He shouted her name but got no response.

In the sitting room, books had been torn from their shelves and hurled about the room. A turquoise china vase lay in pieces in the cast-iron grate. He ran upstairs to the bedroom; untouched, she wasn't in it. Back in the kitchen, he noticed blood for the first time. A trail of glossy drops led through the back door and vanished into the coarse grass outside. He looked up and saw her sitting beneath an olive tree, legs dangling over a stone ledge.

'Stephanie!'

She'd been ready to leave before Alexander had reached the road. But she hadn't. She'd hesitated. Now, she found she couldn't remember quite why. An hour had passed. Her mind had drifted. She'd been perversely calm. Later, she'd walked among the vines, and among the lemon trees on the steep bank that rose to the east. Sometime during the afternoon, though, the psychological anaesthetic had begun to fade. First there was sorrow, then incandescent fury.

'Your hand,' panted Masson, as he reached her and dropped to her side, 'what happened to your hand?'

Both hands were in her lap. The left was lacerated over the back and across the knuckles. Sharp fragments protruded from dark sticky cuts.

'What happened?'

She had no sequential recollection of the passage from late afternoon into early evening. The black rucksack was by the front door. She couldn't remember putting it there but she did know that Franka Müller's passport and Deutschmarks were tucked into a side pocket.

'Should I call the police?'

She shook her head.

He began to protest but stopped himself. 'You need to see a doctor.'

She saw herself spinning like a dancer. A whirlwind of fury, striking out at anything, her vision blurred by tears of frustration and rage. She wasn't sure what she'd hit but the pain had been cathartic. As she knew it would be.

*   *   *

They turned off the main road, Masson's Fiat creaking over the winding track. The headlights flickered on the vines, bugs dancing in weak yellow light. Neither had spoken since leaving Salernes. There were four stitches in the back of Stephanie's left hand. The smaller cuts and grazes had been picked clean and disinfected. She'd declined the offer of painkillers.

They entered the kitchen. Masson's eyes were drawn to the one thing he'd missed earlier: the gun by the sink. Stephanie watched him pick up the SIG and turn it over in his hands. She saw anxiety creep across his face.

'Is this yours?'

She could see that he desperately wanted the answer to be no. 'Yes.'

'What are you doing with a piece of hardware like this, Stephanie?'

'Don't ask.'

'I am asking. Just like I'm asking what happened here.'

'I can give you answers, if you want. But they'll be lies.'

'You owe me more than this.'

'I don't owe you anything,' she snapped. 'No commitments, remember?'

'Don't you think this is different?'

'I think we all have our secrets, Laurent. Pieces of the past that are better left in the past.' She let him consider that for a few seconds. 'What do you think?'

He turned away from her. 'I think I'll start to clear up some of this mess.'

She reached out and put her good hand on his arm. 'Not now. It can wait.'

They ate bread and cheese. Masson opened a bottle of wine. They sat at the table on the terrace listening to the chorus of cicadas. When they'd finished, he cleared away their plates and returned with coffee and a dusty bottle of Armagnac. She said she didn't want any. He said it was medicinal, so she relented and he poured an inch into a dirty tumbler.

When she'd decided not to run, she hadn't had a reason. It had simply been instinct. Now, she saw why. Alexander had been unarmed. Subconsciously, that fact had registered. No gun, no accomplices, no protection at all. Under the circumstances, an incredible risk. She could have killed him in a moment. He would have had no chance at all. Hindsight prompted the question: why?

Masson poured a glass for himself. 'Look, about before. If you don't want to talk about it, that's okay. But if you do, you can trust me.'

'I know.' She gathered her tumbler in both hands and stared at her stitches. 'Someone came to see me today.'

'Who?'

'A man from my past.'

'What did he want?'

'A bit of my future.'

'What are you going to do?'

'I don't know yet.'

Masson avoided eye contact and made a show of picking at a thread on the seam of his trousers. 'That gun . . . I mean, if you're in some kind of trouble . . . if you need help, there are people I used to know who . . .'

'I know.'

He looked up at her. 'You know what?'

'Why you're a mechanic.'

'I'm sorry?'

'I know you like cars, Laurent. You like them a lot.'

They sat in silence for a minute before Masson spoke again. 'Anyway, like I was saying, I know some people who –'

'It won't make a difference.'

'Well, if you change your mind . . .'

'Thanks.'

He lit a cigarette. 'The people in those photographs in the kitchen. Who are they?'

Stephanie shrugged. 'Just a family I used to know.'

The struggle lasted through Tuesday and Wednesday. She barely slept, barely ate. Sometimes she panicked, sometimes she was almost catatonic. All her arguments seemed circular; her new life was worth fighting for, worth revisiting the past for, except nothing was worth that, nothing except the chance to leave it behind permanently.

On Wednesday, she spent the whole day in the hills, beneath a fierce sun, among the jagged rocks and thorny bushes. She could run, she knew that. And perhaps she'd stay ahead of Magenta House but for how long? If she stopped, they'd find her again. She saw now that it would only be a matter of time. And even if they didn't find her, the possibility would linger. No matter how hard she tried to pretend it hadn't, the threat had always been there.

More than anything, she wanted to stop running. The life she'd created for herself at the farmhouse had taught her that, if nothing else. Ultimately, she didn't know where she was destined to settle. But that didn't matter. It was the act that was important, not the location. To abandon the dream was to let Alexander win. That had been the insurance against the risk he'd taken in approaching her unarmed. He hadn't offered his word as a guarantee because he knew she'd reject it – there could never be trust between them – but perhaps the risk had been a gesture of good faith.

By dusk, her feet were blistered, her skin burnt, her mind scorched.

The pretence was over, the memories resurrected. That night, she couldn't sleep. Repulsion, fear and anger kept her awake. Later, at dawn, there were moments when she almost convinced herself that it wouldn't be too bad. *It's just one job.* But she knew that wasn't true. Eighteen months of a real life had seen to that. No amount of effort would ever reclaim the edge she'd once had. Despite everything, that made her happy because it made her human.

Magenta House. An organization that doesn't exist, run by people who don't exist. An ironic consequence of the modern era. In a time of greater openness, somebody still has to get into the sewer to deal with the rats.

I don't know how many assassins Magenta House operates – four or five, I should think, perhaps six – but I do know that I was unique among them. They were simply trained in the art of assassination. I was trained for more. Operating under the alias Petra Reuter – a German student turned activist turned mercenary terrorist – I was taught to infiltrate, seduce, lie, eavesdrop, steal, kill. I learnt how to withstand pain and how to inflict it.

It's been four years since I vanished and I've been running ever since, first as Petra, then as me. Even now, after more than a full year living here, I'm still on the run. Alexander's terms represent an opportunity to stop.

On paper, it's an easy choice. One job buys any future I want. But I've changed since I stopped being Petra. I think I'm becoming the person Stephanie Patrick should have been. And that's the problem. She might be difficult and selfish – she might be a complete bitch – but she's not an assassin. Not like Petra, who was never anything else.

I find myself thinking about people like Jean-Marc Houtens, Li Ching Xai, John Peltor, Zvonimir Vujovic, Esteban Garcia. Like Petra Reuter, they are names without faces. I wonder what they're doing at this precise moment, wherever in the world they are. Petra's was never a large profession. Sure, you can find a killer on a street corner in the run-down district of any city. You can even find self-styled assassins relatively easily; in the Balkans, or the Middle East, you can't move for enthusiastic amateurs. But those of us who formed the elite numbered no more than a dozen. Our backgrounds were diverse but we were united by the quality of our manufacture.

I used to imagine meeting other members of the club. I pictured us around a table in a restaurant, trading industry secrets, putting faces to names, assessing the competition. I'd hear gossip from time to time. Usually from Stern, the information broker, who'd offer a morsel in the hope that I would pay for something juicier. For instance, I know that former US Marine John Peltor was responsible for the Kuala Lumpur car-bomb that killed the Indonesian ambassador last year. And that Li Ching Xai was the one who murdered Alfred Reed, founder of the Reed Media Group, in Mumbai in May 1999. A five-hundred-yard head shot in a stiff crosswind, according to Stern.

When I was Petra Reuter, none of the concerns of Stephanie

Patrick affected me. Nor did any of the issues surrounding my profession. I didn't worry about morality. I worried about efficiency. I didn't worry about the target. If I was offered the contract, he or she was already dead because if I didn't accept the work, somebody else would. When I looked through a telescopic sight, or into the eyes of the victim, I never saw a person. I never thought about the money, either; that came later. Instead, I was always thinking . . . would any of the others have done this better than me?

As any female in a predominantly male profession knows, you have to be better than the men just to be equal with them.

Thursday morning. Stephanie watched the sun come up from the terrace. It was chilly for a while. Later, Masson appeared, a cup of coffee in his hand, stubble on his jaw.

'So, you're going, then?'

'You saw the bag?'

'I saw what you're leaving behind.'

'Meaning?'

'The clothes you've left in the cupboard – well, I wouldn't take them either.'

'They wouldn't fit you.'

'You'd be surprised what I can get into.'

'The image in my mind is not a pretty one.'

He grinned, then said, 'Look, are you sure you know what you're doing?'

'To be honest, not really. But I know what will happen if I don't go and that's something I can't face. The last year and a bit has been really good for me but before that, well . . .'

'What?'

She sighed deeply. 'For a long time, it was a bad time.'

'You're not the only one,' he said, in a tone that was sympathetic rather than confrontational.

'I know.'

'What did you do?'

'You don't want to know.'

'Stephanie . . .'

'Just like I don't want to know about your convictions for auto-theft.'

For a moment, he was stunned. Then he shook his head. 'You knew?'

'Not until the other day. But that's the world I was in. I knew things I never wanted to know. Saw things I wish I could forget. For months, then years, I drifted from one bad hotel to another, from one country to the next, and the things I did . . . they were . . .'

She faltered and he put his hands on her shoulders. 'It doesn't matter.'

Looking at Masson, she felt helpless. 'Laurent, I'm sorry.'

'It's okay.'

'Are you sure?'

'I'm sure.'

'I should have said something.'

'No. I don't think so. We've had a good time, just the way it's been.'

She couldn't bring herself to look into his eyes. 'True.'

'I always knew it wouldn't be forever with you. That was part of the attraction.'

'Thanks very much.'

'You know what I mean.'

She nodded. 'I am planning on coming back, though. If I can . . .'

He took her right hand in his. 'Let's not talk about it. Let's sit here and drink coffee in the sun. We can pretend you're going away and that you'll be back for the weekend. I'll cook something special for you. We'll make love, drink too much wine. And we'll do the same thing the day after, the week after . . . and before you know it, summer will be gone and it'll be autumn.'

3

Stephanie had never imagined that the sight of Brentford would trigger any kind of emotion within her. But there it was, a tightening in the chest. She pressed her face to the window as the aircraft ducked out of the clouds. Terraced streets, crumbling tower blocks, storage depots. Her first sight of London in four years and she hadn't missed it at all. What she felt was not some misplaced sense of nostalgia. It was anxiety.

She took the Underground into London, changed from the Piccadilly Line to the District Line at Gloucester Road, rising to the street at Embankment. It was hot and humid, the sky a dirty grey smudge. Tourists swarmed around hot-dog stands, the smell of fried onions corrupting the air. Across the Thames, the Millennium Wheel turned slowly. Stephanie slung her rucksack over her shoulder and entered Victoria Embankment Gardens. Through a veil of leaves, she saw Magenta House; a network of company offices housed within the single shell of two separate buildings. The main entrance was on the corner of Robert Street and Adelphi Terrace, where she recognized the thing she liked most about Magenta House: the brass plaque by the front door. Worn smooth by years of inclement weather and pollution, the engraved lettering was still legible. L.L. Herring & Sons, Ltd, Numismatists, Since 1789. She glanced up at the old security camera above the door. On the intercom next to the plaque, she pressed the button marked Adelphi Travel.

The voice was terse and tinny. 'Yes?'

'I'm here to see Alexander.'

'Alexander who?'

'Very funny.'

'I think you must have the wrong –'

'I don't know what I'm supposed to say. It's been four years.'

'I'm sorry, madam, but –'

'And you can drop the "madam" thing.'

'There's no one of that name –'

'Just tell him Stephanie Patrick is here.'

Inside, the reception area was as she remembered it. On the wall to her right, there was a polished wooden board listing the names of companies. Some existed, others didn't, and the relationship between them and Magenta House was as complex as the maze of corridors and staircases within the building. She remembered a few – Galbraith Shipping (UK), Truro Pacific – and saw others that were new: Galileo Resources, WB Armstrong Investments, Panatex Ltd. A bored-looking woman sat in front of a ten-year-old computer terminal, playing Hearts, smoking. Middle-aged beneath a crumbling mask of make-up, she was designer-shabby. Just like the security camera over the front door, the worn carpet and the faded blue-and-grey striped wallpaper. Each was a brick in the façade behind which Magenta House hid. Stephanie knew there were miniature security cameras concealed within the lights over the paintings, that the quaint front door was actually grenade-proof, that the weary harridan had a fully-loaded Glock attached to the underside of the table.

She spoke out of one corner of her mouth, the cigarette wedged in the other. 'Down the hall, take the stairs and –'

'I know the way.'

Margaret Hornby, Alexander's secretary, was not at her desk. Stephanie opened the door and saw him standing by the window.

'Don't you believe in knocking?'

'I don't believe in anything. Not any more.'

'You're too old to play the teenage rebel, Stephanie.'

'But too young to retire?'

She didn't think anything had changed; the shelves crammed with leather-bound books along opposite walls, the Chesterfield sofa, the parquet floor and the Persian carpet, the antique Italian globe in the corner. She remembered how disappointed she'd been to learn that it wasn't a tasteless drinks trolley.

'What happened to your hand?' asked Alexander.

'I cut myself flossing.'

He let it pass and moved away from the window. Curiously, on home ground, he seemed more cautious.

'You've made the right decision, you know.'

'It had to happen some time.'

He slid an envelope across his desk. She picked it up and felt keys inside. There was an address on the front. Alexander said, 'This is where you'll stay. It's a furnished rental. We start on Monday morning at nine. That gives you the weekend to get settled.'

Stephanie smiled without a trace of humour or warmth. 'That's going to take more than a weekend. That's going to take years.'

*　　*　　*

The two-bedroom flat was on the top floor of a five-storey Victorian red-brick building on Bulstrode Street, just off Marylebone High Street. The communal entrance hall was dust and junk mail. The staircase grew narrower and darker with each floor. The locks on the front door had been changed. Inside, the air was still and stale. Stephanie dumped her rucksack in the hall and opened windows in a futile attempt to encourage a cleansing breeze.

The floors were sea-grass, except in the kitchen and bathroom, which were tiled. The walls were all painted off-white and the windows had blinds, not curtains. She ran a tap in the bathroom; there was hot water. In the kitchen, the stainless steel fridge was cool but empty. She looked through the cupboards. Nothing except a jar of Marmite and half a bag of long-grain rice. The main bedroom had a low double bed, a mattress as hard as concrete, and a pristine white duvet.

In the sitting room, there was a TV in one corner, a black leather sofa, a table with a top that was a large disc of etched glass. There were paperbacks on the shelves, CDs in a rack, framed black-and-white prints of pouting models down one wall. Definitely a man's flat, Stephanie decided, but a real man? There were some framed snapshots on the mantelpiece above the Victorian fireplace. She picked one up; a shot of a pretty girl with long, light brown hair. She was smiling. Stephanie turned it over, released the clip and opened the back. The cosy, family photo had been culled from a glossy brochure. She examined the paperbacks. Not a single crease along a single spine.

Stephanie recognized the signs; the clumsy, artificial

human touches that only served to underline the place's cold sterility. Pure Magenta House.

After the rank heat of a Monday morning rush hour on the Underground, the cool air conditioning of the subterranean conference room was welcome. The walls and carpet were the same dark grey as her T-shirt. There were sixteen screens set into the wall on her left, in a four-by-four arrangement. At the centre of the room, there was an oval cherry table with ten chairs around it, black leather over graphite frames.

'Hey, Stephanie.'

Stephanie turned round. Rosie Chaudhuri was standing in the doorway. She was slimmer than four years ago and it made her look younger. She wore a tight dark red knee-length skirt and a black silk shirt. Her lustrous black hair was gathered into a thick ponytail.

'Rosie.'

'I'm sorry to see you again.'

'Me too.'

They smiled at each other.

'Can I get you anything? Coffee? Tea? A ticket out of here?'

'Sounds good.'

'You look well.'

'So do you.'

When Alexander entered the room, Rosie left, taking the warmth with her. He sat at one end of the table, Stephanie sat at the other. There was no small talk. He pressed a button on a silver remote control and a single picture appeared over four screens; a black-and-white portrait of a dour-looking man with a long face, a craggy brow and thinning hair swept over the scalp from one ear to the other.

'This is James Marshall. A former SIS employee who came to work for us and then retired early.' Alexander shifted awkwardly. 'Unfortunately, he developed a drink problem that ... well, it got out of hand and affected his reliability.'

'I can't imagine how that could've happened working here.'

'In the past, he'd proved to be an effective field operator. Which partly explains why, out of some misguided notion of loyalty, we continued to employ Marshall on an informal, part-time basis. It was a mutually beneficial arrangement; he got a little extra cash to supplement his disgraceful pension, we got someone we could rely upon for the odd job that was better handled by an outsider. Which was why, in April, I chose Marshall to run an errand for me in Paris. It seemed perfect since he chose to live in Paris after leaving us.'

Marshall's face was replaced by some footage from a security camera. Run in slow motion, it showed a man moving through a customs hall before being beckoned by officials. The footage then froze to focus on him; tall, with sandy hair slanting across the forehead down towards the left eye. The next images were stills; head-and-shoulder shots from the front and side.

'Hans Klepper, a Dutch career criminal based in Amsterdam, heroin his speciality, all of it through Indonesia, the routes secured by influential friends bribed in Jakarta. The video footage we've just seen was taken at Heathrow on December the sixteenth last year, as Klepper stepped off a flight from Baku. Acting on an SIS tip-off from Moscow, but originating in Novosibirsk,

45

customs officials intercepted Klepper, who was travelling on a false Belgian passport. Being well aware of Klepper's reputation, they expected to find him carrying heroin. Instead, they found Plutonium-239. Seventeen hundred and fifty grams of it with a purity of ninety-four per cent. Do you know why that's significant?'

Stephanie shook her head.

'Anything above ninety-three per cent purity is weapons-grade. What's more, you only need about eight kilos of it to make a nuclear weapon. Klepper was carrying the Plutonium-239 in protective canisters inside two suitcases. He was also carrying quantities of Lithium-6, which enhances bomb yields, even though it's not radioactive itself.'

'What's a heroin dealer doing with nuclear material?'

'The obvious question.'

'What was Klepper's answer?'

'He didn't have one. He died.'

Stephanie raised an eyebrow. 'There and then?'

'Within an hour.'

'How?'

'Heart attack.'

She glanced at the stills. Klepper looked as though he was in his late thirties or early forties. 'Heart attack?'

Alexander nodded. 'Artificially induced. Klepper would've known that once his case was marked for examination he was in trouble. He'd have known that in the custody suite he'd be stripped and searched. The postmortem revealed a pin-prick on his left wrist. An examination of his clothes and effects revealed a Mont Blanc pen that had been adapted to act as a syringe, attached to a cartridge of chemically doctored Alfentanil. The pen acted as a delivery device, like those gadgets used by diabetics. As a weapon, it was not unlike the umbrella tip used on Georgy Markov, the Bulgarian dissident, here in London in September 1978.'

The slow-motion footage resumed. Klepper approached an examination bench, hauled both cases onto it and handed his passport to an official. Then he reached inside his jacket pocket and took out his Mont Blanc pen. The most mundane action imaginable. He appeared to adjust the pen, holding it with one hand, twisting with the other. He was looking the officials in the eye, giving silent answers to their silent questions. They never noticed the jab. Discreet but firm, he never flinched.

Stephanie shook her head. 'Without a care in the world.'

'Or maybe with *every* care in the world.'

'But to be so casual about it?'

'Perhaps suggesting that he was under the impression that he was injecting himself with something else. Something that would provoke a reaction but which wouldn't kill him. In any event, it's unlikely we'll ever find out what he thought he was doing.'

Stephanie continued to look at Klepper. 'Still, no great loss, I suppose . . .'

'We now know that he was the first of five couriers, two of whom were UK-bound. We don't know about the other three. We do know that the action was abandoned after his death but SIS was unable to discover the target or the identity of the end users. As for the suppliers of the Plutonium-239, the intelligence community looked no further than the former Soviet Union. One name emerged. Or rather, an alias. Koba. But that was the end of the line. Until March. Then, out of the blue, SIS were contacted by Oleg Rogachev, head of the Tsentralnaya crime syndicate, an organization that has been strongly linked to nuclear smuggling in the past.'

'How was the contact made?'

'Through a Kazak investment company. Almatinvest. They have an office here in London but the contact was made through their Moscow office. An Almatinvest representative got in touch with the British Embassy on Rogachev's behalf. The request was for a secure face-to-face with a senior SIS official. The job of evaluating that request fell to Roger Stansfield, a man I know personally. He concluded that the approach was *bona fide*. The representative said that Rogachev wanted to give SIS Koba's real name.'

'What did Rogachev want in return?'

'Nothing.' Alexander saw her expression change. 'I know what you're thinking. But maybe fingering Koba was some reward in itself.'

'Or maybe Rogachev saw SIS coming and figured that he could get them to eliminate a rival on his behalf, at no risk to himself. Koba probably doesn't even exist.'

'That thought did occur to Stansfield. Which was why he didn't want anyone from SIS involved. Not directly.'

'So he asked you.'

'Exactly. The plan was simple enough. Masquerading as a senior SIS officer, Marshall met Rogachev in Paris. At the meeting, Rogachev was supposed to hand over a disk containing information on the terrorists, the end users and the couriers. The two men met at a brasserie on the rue du Faubourg Saint Honoré. As far as we know, the meeting went to plan. However, as they stepped out of the café . . .'

Alexander changed the picture. There were two bodies lying face-down, one splayed across the pavement, the other crumpled in the gutter. The blood looked black. Although Stephanie was looking at the screens, she could tell that Alexander was staring at her.

'No disk was recovered from either body. Nobody recalls the assassin frisking either man. It's possible the disk was removed later. It's also possible that the disk had already been lifted – perhaps in the brasserie. The only thing we know for sure is that it's now in the possession of George Salibi.'

'Never heard of him.'

'A Lebanese banker. Lives in New York. Founder of First Intercontinental.'

'How does he fit into this?'

'The way he fits into everything else. Money. God knows how he got hold of the disk but you can be sure he'll use it.'

'How?'

'He'll auction it or use it as leverage. Either way, the disk is now currency. And that's not a situation we can tolerate.'

'Salibi's a target?'

'The disk is a target. If Salibi gets in the way . . . well, that's his problem.'

'So that's the job, then? The disk.'

Alexander's glance was scathing. 'James Marshall's murder cannot go unpunished.'

'Sounds a bit Old Testament to me.'

'It's not purely a question of revenge. It also sends out a message. Then there's Koba. We don't know whether Klepper's consignment of Plutonium-239 was destined for Britain or whether it was merely in transit. And because we don't know, we have to assume the worst. That being so, we need to find out who Koba is, who he's supplying and what their target is.'

'And then?'

'As long as Koba's alive, he's a threat. The problem is, if we simply wanted to find *a* Koba, that would be easy. There are plenty to choose from. But we need to find *the* Koba.'

'I'm not with you.'

'There's a tradition of Russian criminals adopting aliases. The original Koba was a Georgian robber who protected the poor from their oppressors. A sort of Caucasian Robin Hood, if you like. The legend has lasting appeal. Criminals today are still calling themselves Koba. Even Stalin fell for it, adopting the name while he was robbing banks in Georgia at the beginning of the twentieth century.'

'So you have no idea who you're looking for.'

'On the contrary. We've narrowed our Koba down to two. By the time you're ready, we'll know which one he is.'

'And what if you don't?'

'There's always the fail-safe option.'

'Both men?'

'There would be no other way to be sure.'

'Cute.'

'Believe me, the world wouldn't miss either of them.'

'Which makes it okay?'

'If you spared yourself the pretence of a conscience, you'd see that it makes it better.'

Stephanie couldn't be bothered to argue the point. 'Could Koba have killed Marshall and Rogachev?'

Alexander shot her a withering look. 'I don't know. You tell me.'

'What do you mean by that?'

He looked back at the images of the dead men on the screen. 'There was one assassin, two shots per victim. Neither had time to react. In the panic that followed, the assassin escaped easily. There were witnesses but their accounts varied wildly. It was raining hard at the time. It was a dark afternoon. The killer was dressed in black or blue or grey, and wearing some kind of dark jacket with a hood to obscure the face. An anorak, maybe. There might have been an umbrella for extra cover. Physically, we have almost nothing to go on. A slim build, between five foot six and six foot tall – let's say five foot nine, for the sake of argument. In other words, about your height.'

With the conference room lights dimmed, part of his face was hidden in shadow. She could see the flickering screens reflected on his eyeballs.

'Might have been a man.' He held her gaze completely. 'Could have been a woman.' Alexander leaned into a cone of pale light. 'Is any of this starting to sound familiar?'

Stephanie was incredulous. 'You think *I* had something to do with this?'

'There's a rumour going around . . .'

'You're out of your mind.'

'Really?'

'If you provided me with the date, I could probably tell you.'

'Let me guess. Masson would vouch for you. *I was with her the night before and the night after.* But from where you live, Paris is a day trip.'

'You're serious?'

'Always.'

'You can't prove it, though, can you?'

Alexander's smile was cold. 'I don't need to. You're the one with something to prove.'

The hijack at Malta was my last job for Magenta House. In the chaos of its aftermath, I vanished. That should have been it. Instead, for the next two and a half years, I was Petra Reuter, more than I ever was before. Life imitated art and I became the professional assassin.

Today, sitting in this room, I can look at the way Magenta House originally transformed me into Petra Reuter and I can understand that process, even though I'm repelled by it. What I don't understand is why I chose to embrace her so completely once I was free of her. Alexander doesn't understand it, either. Which is why he's wondering whether I killed Oleg Rogachev and James Marshall. Two years ago, I wouldn't have hesitated, as long as the contract was right. So why not now?

I can see where this is leading. I need to find the culprit in order to prove that it's not me. Although Alexander says he needs Koba and the disk, what he really wants is the Parisian assassin. He craves revenge because he feels responsible for Marshall's death and this is the only way he can deal with that. Somebody else must pay. A life for a life. That's what Magenta House trades in.

'You chose to learn Russian. Why?'

'For professional reasons. I was led to believe there'd be plenty of work for me – for Petra – in Russia. Or at least from Russian criminals.'

'And was there?'

'Actually, no. I never took a contract from a Russian, although I came into contact with quite a few.'

'Where?'

'Serbia, Cyprus, Latvia. In Paris and Zurich, too.'

'Who led you to believe that learning Russian might be a good idea?'

'Stern.'

'You were in contact with Stern?'

The surprise in his voice was, itself, a surprise to Stephanie. 'Yes.'

'Do you know who Stern is?'

'Of course not. That's the whole point of him.'

Stern, the information broker. A man who existed only in the ether of the Internet, trading secrets and rumours for cash. Some said he was Swiss, others thought he was German. Or Austrian. Or even American. Like Alexander, a man with no first name. Or perhaps with several. Stephanie had always called him Oscar when they communicated. It had been his suggestion but she'd never believed that was his real name. He might once have been a spy although no one could agree for whom. Others said he'd been a journalist, or a mercenary. Stephanie had heard a theory that Stern didn't exist at all, that he was a collection of people. Or perhaps a single woman.

'Tell me about him.'

'After Malta, I scanned all the old websites looking for messages for Petra. I didn't expect to find anything but there he was, casting into the dark. I replied and we began to correspond, both of us cautious at first. Eventually, he told me he had work for me, if I was interested.'

'How did your relationship evolve?'

'We came to an arrangement. I agreed to let him act on my behalf. Essentially, he became my agent. It worked well because it meant I never met the client face-to-face. And no one ever met Stern. Everyone's anonymity was protected. Stern used to joke that it was a perfect example of practical e-commerce. He said the Internet was invented for people like us.'

'Sounds as though you two were made for each other.'

'It was a relationship with no downside.'

'You paid him, I suppose?'

'He took fifteen per cent of the fees he negotiated on my behalf. On top of that, he offered other services, which I bought separately.'

'Such as?'

'Information, general or specific. Or reliable contacts in strange cities. That kind of thing.'

'You never worried about that?'

'Not unduly. If anything happened to me, he stood to lose money. And Stern hates to lose money.'

'Don't we all?'

His tone took her by surprise, so she stayed silent.

'You know what I'm talking about, don't you?'

She knew perfectly well. 'No.'

'One million and eighty thousand dollars, give or take some loose change.'

Stephanie felt herself harden. 'I earned that money.'

'It belonged to us.'

'It belonged to Petra.'

'Petra belonged to us.'

'Petra belonged to nobody. Not then, not now.'

The colour began to drain from Alexander's face. 'You *will* return it.'

54

'Are you a betting man?'

'Petra was our creation. You were playing a part. Nothing more.'

'What about after Malta?'

'We're talking about money earned before Malta.'

'Well, guess what? Before Malta, after Malta, I don't give a toss what you think. I was Petra. I've *always* been Petra. If you want the money, sue me.'

4

The first week is *the worst. Some mornings, we talk in his office. On other mornings, we use a briefing room, or an office I've never seen before. It's just the two of us. He makes occasional notes on paper, taking care to prevent me from seeing what he's written. We break for lunch – an hour usually – then continue until five or six. Spending so much time alone with him is a form of claustrophobia.*

At first, the questions are general, as he establishes a chronological order for everything that happened after Malta. I don't mind that so much. Later, when he grows more specific, focusing on detail, I start to lie. Not all the time, only when it matters. I give him some dry bones to pick over, but I won't give him my flesh and blood.

'You're wasting your time,' I tell him on the fifth morning. 'You have no idea whether what I'm telling you is the truth.'

'Believe me, I'll find out.'

'Only if I let you.'

Which, on occasion, I do. Despite a general instinct to give him nothing, there are some exceptions. I want him to know that the Petra I became was better than the Petra that Magenta House created. When I describe how I infiltrated Mario Guzman's fortified villa overlooking Oaxaca and then silently assassinated the Mexican drugs baron, I can hear the pride in my voice. Alexander pretends not to have noticed. And I'm happy for him to know how I lived in a shattered storm drain in Grozny for almost a week, before taking the single sniper's shot that killed Russian General Vladimir Timoshenko.

I should feel too ashamed to boast about such things but I don't. Not when I'm with him. Instead, I feel pleasure. That's the corrupting effect he has on me.

At the end of each day, I try to leave my anger at Magenta House but it's almost impossible. Another gruesome rush-hour ride on the Underground, a few groceries from Waitrose, an evening in front of the TV, a night of fractured sleep. I miss Laurent and the sound of the dogs barking in the valley. I miss the murmur of the cicadas, the scent of lavender and a glass of wine on the terrace.

On Friday afternoon, Alexander says, 'Stern handled all your financial affairs, did he?'

'He's an information broker, not my accountant or banker.'

'But he negotiated your contracts?'

'Yes.'

'How much money did you make through him?'

'That's none of your business.'

'I'm making it my business.'

I shrug in an off-hand way. 'A lot more than I took from you.'

Alexander looks absolutely furious.

I smile slyly. 'A lot more.'

We move into the second week. Sometimes I'm moody and silent, sometimes I'm ready for a fight. We argue several times a day, which brings out the worst in my vocabulary. On Thursday afternoon, we have a stand-up row in his office. I storm out, slamming the door behind me. I don't slow down until I've left the building. Rosie Chaudhuri catches up with me in Victoria Embankment Gardens.

She approaches me as though I'm a dog that bites.
'Stephanie?'

I'm pacing but I've got nowhere to go. 'What?'

'You okay?'

'What the fuck do you care?'

'Hey . . .'

'What is this? Good cop, bad cop? Are you going to sweet-talk me, then run back inside and tell him what I tell you?'

'Is that what you think?'

It wasn't. 'You work in there, don't you? For him . . .'

She looked disappointed, not cross. 'I thought you knew me better than that.'

I take a deep breath and let it out slowly. 'Christ, Rosie . . .'

'It's okay.'

I put my hand on my forehead, shielding my eyes. 'No, it isn't. I'm sorry.'

At the weekend, I decide to strip the flat. I'd sooner it was bare than cluttered with someone else's idea of personal touches. I take the pictures off the walls and dump them in the storage room in the basement. I empty the photos and paperbacks into black bin-liners. I sift through the CDs to see if there's anything worth keeping. It's a collection of chilling mediocrity; Michael Bolton, Mariah Carey, Whitney Houston, Elton John. Not a decent song between them and the rest. I reject all thirty-four albums in the rack.

I spend an hour of Saturday afternoon in Daunt Books on Marylebone High Street, where I buy a few paperbacks of my own. On Sunday afternoon, I buy half a dozen CDs at Tower Records on Piccadilly Circus, including two Garbage albums and Felt Mountain *by Goldfrapp. In the early evening, I watch* Wonder Boys *at the Prince Charles cinema on Leicester Square. When I come out, I go back round to the front and pay to watch the next film on the bill,* Buena Vista Social Club.

Wednesday afternoon. The febrile humidity of morning had made way for rain. They were sitting in Alexander's office. Two windows were open; the downpour drowned the sound of traffic on the Embankment.

Alexander lit a Rothmans and said, 'Tell me about Arkan.'

Arkan and his paramilitary Tigers. Stephanie's skin prickled. 'What about him?'

'There was a rumour that Petra Reuter killed him.'

'I never read that.'

'It wasn't in the papers.'

Stephanie tilted back on her chair. 'Arkan was a dog. Not a tiger. And he died like a dog; he was put down, not assassinated.'

'Did you kill him?'

Stephanie closed her eyes. It was 15 January 2000. Arkan – real name, Zeljko Raznatovic – was striding through the lobby of the Hotel Inter-Continental in Belgrade. For a fraction of a second they'd looked at one another. It had been his last fraction of a second. She'd used a Heckler & Koch submachine gun and had aimed for the head because Stern's sources had said that Arkan would be wearing a bullet-proof vest. Which turned out to be true. Three of the bullets she fired found the target.

'Eye-witnesses spoke of two assassins. Who was the other?'

'It doesn't matter. He's dead.'

Stephanie saw something in Alexander's reaction. Surprise, distaste, consternation? She couldn't tell. He said, 'The contract came through Stern?'

'Yes.'

'With no indication of the client's identity?'

'Not at first. Stern described the job as domestic.'

'How did you interpret that?'

'Slobodan Milosevic.'

Alexander reflected for a moment and then nodded. 'I agree. You never met Milosevic, I assume.'

'No. But I met his idiot son, Marko.'

'How did that come about?'

'Stern set up a meeting with an intermediary. I travelled from Belgrade to Pozarevac –'

'Milosevic's home town?'

Stephanie nodded. 'I met the intermediary – a Belgian named Marcel Claesen – at Bambi Park. It's a kind of sick amusement park that Marko Milosevic built.'

'And he was there?'

'Yes. With Malizia Gajic.'

'Who?'

'His partner. They had a child together.'

'Did she have any connections that you know of?'

'Only to a plastic surgeon who evidently believed the bigger the breasts the better.'

'What about Marko?'

'He thought he was a businessman.'

'But you didn't?'

'I thought he was as thick as elephant shit. He had a peroxide spike for a haircut and wore a lot of Tommy Hilfiger.'

'Did he appear to know the Belgian?'

'In a manner of speaking. They were talking but I got the impression that Claesen was embarrassed to be seen with Marko.'

'Do you think Marko passed on the information to Claesen?'

'How do you mean?'

'Was Bambi Park simply the rendezvous or was Marko in the loop?'

'I doubt it. I mean, Claesen was the intermediary. If Marko had been involved, he could have just given the information to me himself. There would have been no need for Claesen.'

'Yet they clearly knew each other. Suggesting previous associations. Perhaps involving other members of the family?'

'That's what I thought.'

'Then what?'

'Claesen and I drove back to Belgrade and he provided me with the information.'

'Which was what?'

'Where to pick up the weapons, where to meet the second gun, what Arkan's schedule was.'

'Why did you pick the Inter-Continental?'

'It was nice and open, plenty of scope for panic.'

'Did you kill the bodyguard, Momcilo Mandic?'

'No. I focused on Arkan. The second gun scattered the protection. And everyone else.'

'There were suspects arrested, I seem to remember. A man called Dusan Gavric, who was wounded.'

'Getting shot doesn't make him guilty. It makes him unlucky. Or careless. Having said that, I wouldn't have fancied being in his position *after* he was arrested . . .'

'Petra's name was linked to other murders in the region. What about Pavel Bulatovic?'

'No.'

Stephanie remembered the details clearly, though.

The federal defence minister of Yugoslavia had been eating at the Rad restaurant in Belgrade, an establishment that looked onto a football pitch. The gunman had fired his Kalashnikov through the window in three concentrated bursts, cutting across the room in a diagonal, before using the pitch as his escape route. Following so soon after Arkan, Stephanie had wondered whether both assassinations had been ordered by the same individual.

'What about Darko Asanin?'

She'd heard the name, a former Belgrade criminal. 'No.'

'Anybody else I should know about from that part of the world?'

Stephanie smiled coldly. 'Arkan isn't enough for you?'

I can't face the Underground. It's a foetid evening. Businessmen sweat into their shapeless suits. I walk beneath Hungerford Bridge, along Victoria Embankment, past the Ministry of Defence, towards Westminster Bridge. Gradually, the noise of the traffic, of the aircraft overhead, of the multitude around me, begins to recede. In my mind, it grows darker, cooler. The open spaces restrict themselves to four walls until I'm in a cramped room in a small hotel. There is a narrow bed with a thin mattress, a single wooden chair between a cupboard and a chest of drawers.

I'm lying on the bed, staring at the ceiling. I'm cold but I'm perspiring. I look as though I'm saying something but there's nothing to hear. I don't notice when I urinate, soaking the lumpy mattress. I only move when I know I'm going to vomit. But I react too slowly. I fall to my knees and throw up onto the floor. My back arches as I retch, and when it's over

I collapse onto my side and roll myself into a ball. I don't know how long I stay there.

January 20th, 2000, Bilbao. Five days since Belgrade, five days since Arkan. Three days since I arrived in Bilbao and checked into this black hole. I was only supposed to be here for thirty-six hours. The arrangements were not complicated: pick up the package at the post office, use the new identity to travel to Rabat and then discard it, spend a week relaxing in Morocco as Delphine Lafont – the identity I used to enter Morocco ten days ago – and then return to Paris, as scheduled. Simple, clinical, perfect. Pure Petra.

At first, there was an overwhelming lethargy. My muscles turned to lead, my blood cooled. I imagined it congealing, turning black. With it came a sense of dread. Creeping up on me, smothering me. For two and a half years, I had functioned without fear. In my pursuit of mechanical perfection, I turned anxiety into caution, pain into penalty. I wanted to feel nothing, no matter what I did. And whatever I did, I wanted to do it with ruthless efficiency. I thought I'd eliminated doubt and chance from Petra Reuter's life.

Now, lying on the floor, drenched in sweat, my head a sandstorm of emotion, I know that I've snapped. For two days, I've been unable to eat or drink. My body has rejected everything I've put into it. My body and also my mind. I can see that in some ways I'm rejecting myself. Seen from another perspective, however, I'm rejecting an intruder.

Later, I told myself that this was the moment I chose to stop being Petra Reuter. But the truth is, my body had already made that decision for me. Two and a half years of Petra had poisoned me.

She didn't recognize the room, which now belonged to the Thurman Mining Company. Through the window, she saw the monumental Adelphi Building on the other side of Robert Street. One wall of the office was covered by two huge maps, one of Brazil, the other of Mongolia. Small areas on each had been staked out in blue, black and red ink. Lists of hectares had been pinned next to selected areas. On the desk, a paper Brazilian flag sat in a mug that had *Ordem e Progresso* stencilled around it. There were framed photographs on the wall beside the window; miners in hard hats at the mouth of a mine, men in short-sleeved shirts in front of a wasteland of felled forest, the horizon smudged brown by smoke.

The door opened. A skinny man in khaki combat trousers and a blue Nike T-shirt entered. His light brown hair was clipped short. He wore glasses, the grey frames with a matt finish, the lenses with a tint.

'Hey, Steph. Sorry to keep you waiting.' Stephanie stiffened; the familiarity of strangers had always had that effect upon her. His accent sounded mildly Lancastrian. He offered a hand. 'Martin Palmer.'

She didn't think he looked any older than she did, which – with the exception of Rosie Chaudhuri – made him the youngest person she had seen at Magenta House. Palmer had a grey nylon satchel slung over his left shoulder. He took it off and sat in the swivel chair behind the desk, relegating her to the plastic seat opposite. He produced a pad of paper and a pencil, and then apologized for not being able to offer her coffee.

She said, 'I've never seen you before.'

He looked coy. 'I'm new.' He offered her a conspiratorial smile that she didn't reciprocate. 'I've got a few questions I need to ask you. It's just routine.'

'What kind of questions?'

'Personal, mostly. If that's all right?'

'What are you, a psychologist?'

'Something like that.'

'You look nervous.'

'Well, I'm not.'

'I didn't say you *were* nervous. I said you looked it.'

Now, he looked embarrassed. 'Do you mind if we start?'

The balance shifted, Stephanie shrugged. 'Sure. What do you want to ask me?'

'Well ... let's see. You've been coming in here for ... what is it? Three weeks?'

'And two days.'

'For debriefing?'

'That's not what I'd call it.'

A soldier had once told Stephanie that debriefing was therapy. That it helped him to come to terms with the things he'd had to do – and the things he'd had to see – during active undercover service. Each mission had always been followed by intense analysis; what went wrong, what went right, the lessons for the future. Some of the scrutiny was technical, some of it personal. By the end of the process, he'd always felt mentally exhausted but, crucially, he'd also felt that no element had been overlooked, that every aspect had been examined and rationalized in the minutest detail. And that no matter how draining the experience, it had left him better equipped to cope with his memories.

Stephanie understood what he'd meant but did not feel the same way. As the soldier had pointed out, to succeed as therapy, it was important to place one's trust in those conducting the sessions. Over three weeks, the more Alexander probed, the more violated she'd felt, and the more she'd reacted against it. From sullen silence to outright hostility, she'd felt unable to stop herself.

Palmer jotted something onto the pad. 'What are you doing away from here?'

'How do you mean?'

'In the evenings, for instance.'

'I just stay in the flat. I buy something to eat on the way home, cook it, watch TV, read a book.'

'You haven't gone out at all?'

Only once, during the second week, after a long day lying to Alexander about a contract she'd taken in New York. She'd felt she needed a drink so she'd stopped at a bar on St Martin's Lane. She'd picked a small table by the door and watched the pavement traffic for half an hour, letting alcohol soften the ache. The place had been busy, the after-work crowd unwinding; groups at tables and around the bar, laughter, gossip, cigarette smoke.

He wore a cheap pin-stripe, she remembered. Thick around the waist, growing a second chin. Pink cheeks and ginger stubble. He emerged from a crowd at the far end of the glass bar, a pint in one hand. He offered to buy her another drink. She smiled and declined but he sat down opposite her.

She said, 'I'm waiting for someone.'

He grinned, revealing smoker's teeth. 'Me?'

Stephanie said nothing.

'Seriously, love, sure you won't have another?'

She glanced at his group. 'Am I part of a bet?'

'Don't worry about them.'

He was slightly drunk. She could smell the beer on his breath.

'I'm not worried about them.'

'I'm Charlie.'

'I'm not interested.'

When he offered his hand, she took it, rolled the fingers into the palm and crushed the fist against the table-top. He sucked air through his teeth, his eyes widened and perspiration sprouted instantly across his pale forehead. Stephanie felt as though she was watching someone else hurt him. But when she thought of how she'd turned on Olivier, she was filled with self-disgust. She let go of him and he sprang up from the chair, backing away from her, bumping into other customers, muttering something she couldn't hear.

Martin Palmer was waiting for an answer.

Stephanie said, 'I'm not much in the mood for partying at the moment.'

'Are you drinking?'

'What?'

He kept his eyes on his notes. 'Are you drinking alcohol?' Now, he looked up. 'At night, when you go home?'

Beneath the anger ran a current of sadness. 'Not enough.'

She was aware of her defences rising, which made her aware of how quickly they'd been lowered. Not by Palmer's crafty questions – she was surprised by his clumsiness – but by something within her. She recognized the feeling. It was the desire to unburden herself. But Palmer wasn't the right confessor. For two hours, they talked. There were many questions she wanted to answer honestly but couldn't, not to him. To have done so would have been to cheapen the truth.

She was disappointed, then frustrated and eventually bitter.

'Let me see,' Palmer murmured. 'This Turkish arms dealer, Salman Rifat. According to Mr Alexander, you told him that you had to sleep with Rifat in order to gain his trust and earn yourself access to files he kept at his villa.'

'Sleep with?'

Palmer looked annoyed by the semantic distinction. 'Have sex with.'

'What about it?'

'Well, how did you feel about that?'

'How did I feel?'

'Yes.'

'Sore.'

He blushed. 'That's not what I meant.'

'I know what you meant,' Stephanie snapped. 'But sore is what I felt. And do you know why? Because Rifat had a dick as thick as your wrist and there wasn't a part of me he didn't like to force it into. And I let him do that to me because that was part of the job.'

Palmer tried to convey control and began to scribble notes. 'Fine. I see. Okay . . .'

'*Okay?*'

He winced. 'Sorry. I didn't mean it to sound like that.'

'What did you mean it to sound like? Compassion? Comprehension?'

'Look, I'm trying to help here . . .'

'Let me tell you about Salman Rifat. He's an arms dealer. A charmer. A monster. And he has his pleasures.' She hesitated, then looked at her feet. 'His favourite thing was to make me strip for him, usually in a living room, never in a bedroom. While I stripped, he'd tell me to do things and I'd do them. But the end was always the same. He has this estate in Greece. It produces olive oil. And wherever he is in the world, he has these small bottles of home-made olive oil with him. Dark blue glass, a miniature cork in the top. What he liked to do most was to make me bend over something – the back of a sofa, a table – and he'd pour a little of this oil onto the centre of my spine. He liked to watch it run over skin. That was his thing. He'd tell me to move this way or that. And the more turned on he became, the more aggressive he became. Finally, when the oil ran over my backside, he'd fuck me. One way or the other.'

She looked up. Palmer was staring at her and appeared to have stopped breathing.

'So when you ask me what I felt and I say I felt sore, you can bloody well write that down. Along with all the other shit that's going to tell Alexander what he wants to know.'

'Look, Steph . . .'

She snorted contemptuously. '*Steph?* You make it sound as though we've known each other for years.'

'I'm only trying to be friendly.'

'Don't waste your time. Or mine.'

'There's no need to be so hostile.'

'Why are you asking me these questions? What do you think my answers are going to tell you?'

He averted his gaze. 'It's just a routine evaluation.'

Stephanie smiled and it was enough for both of them to understand the lie. 'Have you ever wondered what it feels like to kill somebody? I mean, as a psychologist – or whatever you are – I imagine you must have considered it. From a professional point of view.'

Palmer couldn't find anything to say.

'To look into someone's eyes – both of you fully aware of what's coming – and then to pull the trigger. Or to stick the blade in, to feel the hot blood on your fingers and around your wrist. Because I could tell you, if you like. I could describe these things in as much detail as you could take. But it wouldn't mean anything. Not by me telling you. My answers to your questions won't tell you anything about me. You're theory, I'm reality, and the difference between us is something you will never understand.'

Stephanie rose to her feet and began to circle the table, drawing closer to him.

'Look at you, all dressed up in your street-cred gear, trying to be someone I can relate to, not some-one remote. You read my file and picked this as a look, didn't you? Did you get your hair cut like that especially?'

There was an affirming silence. She rested against the edge of the table, her leg almost touching his. Now, she felt the icy calm that came with full control. Palmer was pale.

'You're in a conflict zone,' she whispered. 'You're hiding among a pile of dead bodies. You see conscript soldiers rape a young girl, then decapitate her. From start to finish, they're laughing, these bakers, teachers, farmers. Once seen, never forgotten, it's tattooed onto your memory. The only question that remains is this: how do you cope with it?'

His eyes were grey, she noticed. And unblinking.

'You're the psychologist. Do you know?'

He shook his head.

'Exactly. I don't know, either. You just do. Most of the time. Until there comes a time when you don't. And that time does come.' She turned her back on him. 'Don't take it personally – it's not your fault – but I won't answer any more of your pathetic questions. As for Alexander, tell him what you like. I don't care.'

5

You can make a home for yourself, you can make a life for yourself, but don't make anything for yourself that you can't walk away from in a second.

The man who'd taught her that was Iain Boyd, a reclusive figure cut from Sutherland granite. Boyd's past lay with the military. The details of that past were consigned to files that had been conveniently lost so that his career was now a matter of sinister silence. More than any other individual, he'd been responsible for turning Stephanie Patrick into Petra Reuter. He'd taught her how to survive in the harshest conditions, how to kill, how to feel nothing. Under his supervision, she had become stronger, faster and fitter than she'd ever imagined she could be. As teachers went, Boyd had been harsh, sometimes cruel. As curricula went, the lessons had been distasteful, sometimes brutal. As pupils went, Stephanie had never been less than exceptional.

She saw him through the carriage window as the ScotRail train slowed to a halt at Lairg Station. Big-boned but lean, with weather-beaten skin, he was leaning against a Land-Rover, arms crossed, a stiff wind raking thick blond hair. He wore old jeans, hiking boots and an olive T-shirt.

Stephanie was the only passenger to disembark. Boyd opened the Land-Rover door for her but made no attempt to help her with her rucksack. They pulled away from the station, passed through Lairg and travelled along the east flank of Loch Shin. Boyd drove fast, squeezing past other vehicles in the narrow passing spaces, occasionally allowing two wheels to chew the sodden verges. Stephanie clutched the door handle tightly and hoped he wouldn't notice.

The clouds raced them north, allowing occasional patches of brilliant sunlight. For a moment, there would be a shimmer of gold, purple, emerald green and rust, then the reversion to slate grey. The wind made the white grass a turbulent sea. They drove past the crumbling shells of stone houses left derelict since the early nineteenth century, past the boarded windows of houses more recently abandoned. The scars of progress. Intermittently, near the road's edge, they passed stacks of peat, cut in rectangles, piled high, awaiting collection and a slow burn in some local grate.

As they overtook a yellow lorry – the local mobile public library – Boyd said, 'Alexander tells me you've been living in the south of France.'

'Yes.'

'Under the surname Schneider.'

'That's right.'

'Your mother's maiden name.'

'Yes.'

He shook his head. 'That's very disappointing. You of all people, Stephanie.'

At the Laxford Bridge, they turned right, then right again, onto a rough track. It twisted and turned, compromising to the demands of the terrain. Over jagged ground, around vast boulders of granite sheathed in soggy moss, through pools of peaty water, across uneven bridges constructed from old railway sleepers.

She knew what lay ahead: bruises, strains, cold, exhaustion. Despite that, she felt at home. Or rather, she felt a connection. The further north she'd travelled, the clearer her mind had become. It was three days since Martin Palmer's failed assessment of her. She'd seen the resignation in Alexander's eyes; Boyd had been the only option. She was under no illusion about the regime but she was glad to be back.

The lodge was close to the loch, on a gentle grass incline, high enough to be safe from floodwater. Fifty yards away were three long cabins with new tarpaper roofs. Between them and the lodge, a large garage doubled as a workshop. Behind the lodge, there was a general outhouse and a second, smaller outhouse containing a diesel generator.

When she'd been here before it had been winter and she and Boyd had been alone, but during the summer months he ran corporate outward-bound courses, designed to foster teamwork among jaded office workers. Sometimes, the company client asked him to identify specific qualities among individuals in each group. Who's a natural leader but doesn't know it? Who thinks they're a leader but won't carry the others? Who's the subversive troublemaker?

The courses ran from May to the end of September. The men and women Boyd hired as help were all former colleagues from the armed services. During the winter, when the place was closed, Boyd remained open to friends. That category included special requests from the military. Or from climbers looking for tough physical conditioning. Or from Alexander.

Boyd brought the Land-Rover to a sharp halt outside the lodge.

'We've got a group in just now so you'll be staying with me. You might see them from time to time, but you're not to speak to them. Understood?'

'Yes.'

'Same goes for the staff. Not a word.'

'Whatever you say.'

His look was withering. 'That's exactly bloody right, Stephanie. Whatever I say.'

The first fortnight was a routine that didn't vary; the bedroom door banging open in the darkness, the cold dawn run, the medicinal heat of the shower, breakfast at a scrubbed wooden kitchen table. Boyd tended not to eat with Stephanie. Between breakfast and lunch, they sparred, self-defence or attack, mostly with hands, sometimes with blades. He reminded her how to transform a household implement into a weapon, how to kill with a credit card, how to incapacitate with a paper clip. They studied points of vulnerability: joints, arteries, eyes.

These sessions usually occurred in the garage, a space large enough to take three trucks. There were kayaks stacked on racks along two walls. At the far end, there was a wooden bench, a heavy vice, trays of oily tools. A punchbag was suspended from the ceiling. He began to instruct her on elements of Thai boxing. He had no interest in the sport itself but admired it for the flexibility and speed of its best practitioners.

Lunch tended to be meagre, a little vegetable soup, some bread, water. Too much food and Stephanie knew she'd throw up during the afternoon. Which most often happened anyway. Boyd didn't feel he'd worked her hard enough unless she was on the ground, retching.

They ran through coarse thigh-high grass that hid the treacherous ruts beneath, up and down scree slopes where even the surest footing failed constantly. Each tumble was marked by a new graze. They ran shin-deep through peat hags of liquid black earth. Stephanie remembered now what she had discovered then: nothing saps energy faster than a peat hag.

They ran in howling winds, through horizontal rain, under crisping summer suns. Even when cold, a northern Scottish sun tanned a skin as quickly and painfully as any other she'd experienced. Mist was the only exception, confining them to areas close to the lodge and loch. There were no patterns in the weather. It was not uncommon to experience all four seasons before lunch and another full year in the afternoon.

Knowing what to expect made it no less painful. The muscles she had allowed to soften burned in protest. Aches matured into cramps. Grazes and cuts were constantly aggravated and so never healed. Boyd kept her on the edge of exhaustion and she understood why; he wanted to provoke a reaction. Physical or emotional, either or both.

Four years before, Boyd had bullied her. That had been his task – to make her quit. The regime had been executed to a score of abuse. This time, it was different. Too much had passed between them the first time. From RSM and raw recruit, to mentor and understudy. Behind the granite façade, Boyd had been proud of her then. And she had felt some pride, too. In the end, he'd treated her with respect. There'd been equality. And with that, there had been something else. A subversive sexual undercurrent.

Neither had acknowledged it. Neither had wanted to.

Now, Boyd retained the power to intimidate but not indiscriminately. He'd tried to break her once and failed. They understood something of each other. They were not so different. The element of hostility upon which Boyd's training regime relied felt contrived. He knew that Stephanie would never do anything less than he ordered. She would always try to do more to show that her spirit had always been beyond his reach and, by proxy, beyond Alexander's.

In the evenings, Boyd allowed her to have a bath instead of a shower, to cleanse and soothe her collage of cuts and bruises. While she was soaking, he prepared supper. Some nights he ate with her, most nights he didn't. Afterwards, he read by the peat fire in the sitting room, or went to his small office, shutting the door on her. She was free to do as she pleased. That meant going to bed as early as possible because she knew that in the morning the routine would resume and that there weren't enough hours in the night for her to recuperate fully.

I'm sitting on a stone beside a cluster of mountain ash trees. Slender branches sag under the weight of dense clusters of brilliant red berries. According to Boyd, this is the sign of a harsh winter ahead. He might be right, but I predict some severe frost far sooner than that.

The weeks roll past as the tension between us grows daily. I know that I'm not helping matters because I react badly to his continual provocation. But that's the way I am. I use aggravation as a spur.

I can feel the metamorphosis. The body I had is reducing, hardening, changing shape. I preferred myself as I was – happy, healthy, feminine – but there is another part of me that celebrates the new condition. It toughens me mentally to see the physical change. It's difficult to rationalize. Perhaps it's the sense that Boyd is only making his task harder. The more I improve, the less his jibes matter. And the more distracted that seems to make him.

Within the parameters of our narrow existence, this should give me some pleasure. But it doesn't. I would like to ask what the matter is but I can't. Just as when he asks me about my time as Petra, I refuse to give him an answer. Not because I don't want him to know but because I don't want Alexander to know. Perhaps part of the reason for my discomfort lies there; I don't like to see a fiercely strong and independent man like Boyd acting as a mouthpiece for a snake like Alexander.

I'm watching from afar. He's by the cabins, flanked by three assistants, two men and a woman, all ex-Army. By the edge of the loch, the latest batch of guests have congregated around half a dozen kayaks. They've come from Slough. They work in telesales, peddling advertising space in magazines specializing in second-hand cars, DIY, computing, kitchens and bathrooms. I wait until Boyd steps forward to address the group before retreating to the lodge.

Inside, it's cool, dark and still. I hear the murmur of the Rayburn in the kitchen. Nothing else. I step into Boyd's office, the only room in his home from which I am expressly forbidden. It's a small cube with a single window onto the loch. A sturdy seasoned oak desk occupies much of the floor-space. Along one wall, there are four filing cabinets, all locked, which seems strange considering Boyd rarely bothers to lock his front door unless he's away for a matter of days.

I sift through the papers on the desk; a phone bill with no numbers I recognize, some correspondence from Sutherland Council, a receipt for a Caledonian MacBrayne ferry ticket to Islay, several letters from companies booked with Boyd over the summer. I ignore the computer, suspecting he'll know if I've tampered with it. Instead, I dial 1471 on the phone to see who his last caller was but they haven't allowed their number to be passed on.

Some of the shelves are occupied by books, mostly history, no fiction. There are two dozen CDs above a mini-system. They're all classical. Above the CDs, there are two rows of box files, each with headings down the spine. Most of them appear to be business accounts stretching back over a decade. On one shelf there are two small silver samovars. On the shelf beneath, there are framed photographs; Boyd in combat gear, hot scrub for a background, three other soldiers in the foreground, machine guns clutched as casually as friends; Boyd looking younger and with longer hair, Manhattan behind him – a snap from the top of the Empire State Building, I think; a head-and-shoulders portrait of a woman with light brown, shoulder-length hair, grey eyes, a petite nose and thin straight lips. I pick it up. Rachel.

There are other photographs of her, some with Boyd, some alone. In the ones that feature him, I see an entirely different man to the one I know. A man who used to smile, a man without emptiness for eyes. He looks warmly happy in every one. He hardly looks like Boyd.

All I'm aware of is the ticking of the carriage-clock on his desk.

I'm still holding Rachel. Something seeps out of the frame, through my fingertips and heads for my chest. Shame. Boyd has his reasons for banning me from this room and now I have my own. I watch him through the window. He's still talking. I wonder what it was that Rachel possessed to make Boyd fall in love with her. And then I wonder what kind of woman would fall in love with a man like Boyd.

*   *   *

Boyd had his back to the sink. Stephanie was leaning close to the Rayburn, letting its heat warm the backs of her thighs. Outside, a storm rampaged. Earlier, she'd watched the clouds gather. The rain had arrived as the light died in the west. Four hours later, the tempest was intensifying.

'When I heard you'd run after Malta, I wasn't surprised. I warned Alexander. I said you would, right from the start. I told him, if she gets a chance, she'll take it. But you were so good, he didn't believe me. He thought I'd trained you too well for that.'

'But you hadn't?'

'Depends on how you look at it. I take the view that I trained you well enough to think for yourself. Once you were out there, you weren't a programmed machine. You were versatile. Imaginative. Beyond containment.'

'Am I supposed to be flattered?'

'You're supposed to ask what went wrong.'

'Maybe nothing did.'

'You became Petra, didn't you? That was never supposed to happen. Once you'd vanished, you should have stayed vanished.'

'Nobody stays vanished. Not from them.'

'You could've.'

'They found me, didn't they?'

'Living under the surname Schneider,' Boyd said, making no effort to disguise his contempt.

Stephanie wasn't sure that had anything to do with it.

'If you'd been more careful, you could've made it work. You could've created a brand-new life for yourself. A *good* life.'

'I did. In the end.'

'It should have happened straight away. You had enough talent to do it. Once you were free, you could've done anything . . .'

'Like what? Settle down in Sydney or Reykjavik? Get a job, have children?'

'Why not?'

'I guess you don't know me as well as you think you do.'

'Maybe you didn't try hard enough.'

Goaded, Stephanie retorted, 'You mean, like you? Let's face it, we're not that far apart, you and I. Both of us are screwed up, neither of us able to live in the real world with real people, doing the nine-to-five.'

Boyd refused to rise to the bait. 'Mentally, you're in worse shape than when we first met. Then, you were just out of control. You were angry and aimless. Now? I don't know what it is but it's something more complex . . .'

His regret was wounding to her. Upset, she resorted to cheap sarcasm. 'A shrink as well as a soldier. You're a man of many talents.'

'And you used to be a woman of many talents.'

'If you see damaged goods, you should take a look at yourself. You made me.'

'I know. And I'm aware of that responsibility. Now more than ever.'

'It's a bit late in the day, isn't it?'

'Why did you become Petra after Malta?'

'That's none of your business.'

'You can't carry on like this forever.'

'Like what?'

'Avoiding the only issue that matters.'

'You mean, like you have? Look at you, living here in the middle of nowhere, trying to forget that Rachel's no longer alive.'

He contained himself but only just. After the silence, he said, 'I think we'd better call it a night.' He turned his back to her. 'Before one of us says something we'll regret.'

She lay on her side, curled into a ball, wide awake despite her exhaustion. Rain rattled the window. In the darkness, she could hear the curtains creeping on the draught. She felt the chill of loneliness. There was confusion in her mind, anger in her heart.

She rose from her bed, pulled on a large black sweatshirt, and tiptoed slowly down the passage. The floorboards were cold against the soles of her feet. Boyd's bedroom was over the kitchen. She opened the door. It creaked and she paused for a response. Nothing. Boyd was a man who heard whispers in his sleep; sure enough, when she put her head round the door, his bed was empty. She went downstairs and heard him in the kitchen. He was heaping coke into the Rayburn. She waited silently in the doorway. He sensed her before he saw her. He put the bucket down, stood up straight and turned around.

She said, 'I'm sorry.'

'Forget it.'

'The way I've behaved isn't the way I feel.'

'You're trained not to behave the way you feel.'

'I know. But I don't need to make any more enemies.'

She stepped forward and kissed him on the mouth. He neither embraced her, nor pulled away. When she broke the kiss and retreated, he said nothing.

'I've spent all my adult life not talking about the things I feel.'

'Stephanie . . .'

'Are you going to tell me this is a bad idea? Because if you are, don't bother. This isn't some reckless impulse. It's been in the back of my mind for the last four years. When we're running through the middle of nowhere, you shout at me but I can hear that your heart isn't in your voice. When you glare at me, your eyes give you away. Tell me it hasn't been on your mind, too.'

When he spoke, she knew his throat was dry. 'This *is* a bad idea.'

She pulled the black sweatshirt over her head and let it drop to the floor. It was warm in the kitchen, the heat welcome on her naked skin.

'Is this some kind of game, Stephanie?'

'It's no game.'

'What, then?'

'We're just two similar people in a situation. With nothing to lose.'

'Nothing to lose?'

'Do you know what I want more than anything?'

'What?'

'I want someone to see me as a woman. I want *you* to see me as a woman. I'm not a man masquerading as a woman. I'm not a robot, I'm not a killing machine. When Alexander looks at me, he sees a device. When I was Petra, the people I met looked at me and saw a threat. When I looked at them, all I ever saw was fear. That's not what I want.'

'Are you sure *this* is what you want?'

'I want someone to know me.'

'What about your friend in France?'

For a second, there was guilt. Then there was per-spective. 'Laurent was lovely. We had a good time but it was a casual arrangement. It could never be anything more than that because I could never show him who I really am. He didn't know me at all. But you could.'

A silence grew between them.

Boyd hadn't allowed his eyes to leave hers.

She said, 'For Christ's sake, look at me.'

He couldn't.

'I'm a twenty-seven-year-old woman. I'm standing naked in front of you. Do something.' She was amazed at how small her voice sounded. '*Please.*'

'It's not that simple. I . . . I . . . don't know what to think.'

It seemed a strange thing to say. It made him sound helpless.

'You're not supposed to think.'

'I'm not like you.'

'Which is one of the things that makes it easier for me to like you.'

'You don't like me.'

'You're wrong,' Stephanie insisted. 'I do.'

'If you saw me on a crowded street in a city, you wouldn't see me at all.'

'We're not in a city.'

'Put the sweatshirt back on, Stephanie.'

'Make love with me.'

'No.'

She felt the onset of panic. 'Then fuck me.'

He winced. 'No.'

'Then let me fuck you.'

'No.'

'You won't have to do anything.'

'Go to bed.'

'You're humiliating me.'

'You're humiliating yourself.'

Stephanie took a step forward. Boyd stood his ground by the Rayburn.

'I know you want me.'

'I don't want you.'

'Liar. I've seen the way you look at me. When we're running, when I'm stretching, when we're both drenched to the skin. I know what you're thinking. The same thing I'm thinking.'

'Stop it.'

She moved closer. 'Has there been anyone since Rachel?'

'That's enough.'

She was within touching distance. 'Has there?'

'I mean it.'

The Rayburn door was still open. She saw dark orange flicker across her stomach.

'You don't want me to go away. I know you don't.'

'Stephanie . . .'

She reached for his hand and pulled it close so that his fingertips brushed her pubic hair. 'If you want to, you can pretend I'm her.'

The light went out in his eyes.

He snapped his hand free of hers. Stephanie lurched backwards, caught her hip on the corner of the table, and stumbled. She clutched the sink. The moment fractured, her nakedness felt clumsy and cheap. Boyd gave her a look that was as full of hatred as any she'd ever seen.

'You've got sixty seconds to get dressed.'

*   *   *

They started along the track. By dark, it was treacherous. Then Boyd told her to veer right and they left behind the only relatively even surface for miles. It was a foul night; torrential rain, thunder, a piercing cold, flashes of sheet lightning. As the incline grew steeper, the grass began to cede to heather and rocks. They tripped and slid, jarring ankles and wrists, grazing shins, knees and palms. Only when she fell would Boyd allow himself words.

'Up! On your feet! *Get up!*'

She tumbled down a grassy slope to a rocky ledge fifteen feet below, landing on soaking granite, winding herself. Boyd scrambled to her side.

'Don't just fucking lie there! *Run!*'

She tried to get to her knees. Boyd bent down, grabbed her by the hair and started to drag her over stones. Despite herself, Stephanie yelped. When she clawed at his wrist, he kicked back with the heel of his boot, hitting her on the elbow. She cried out again.

'What are you squealing for? Isn't this what you wanted?'

On they went, Stephanie losing all sense of time and location. Somewhere amid the confusion, it began to occur to her that Boyd wasn't merely content to force her past the point of collapse; he wanted to force himself past it too.

They were climbing higher, the gradient growing steeper. They pressed along a ledge two feet wide, a slick wall of stone to the left, an incalculable drop into darkness to the right, loose scree beneath their feet. Scrawny trees sprouted from beneath slabs of black rock, spindly branches and twigs slashing at skin and cloth alike. Squinting fiercely through the rain, Stephanie slowed to try to make out the route ahead, only to feel the heavy prod of Boyd's fist in her back.

'Faster, not slower!'

When she fell, he made no attempt to catch her. She reached out blindly, her left arm clattering against a branch. She wrapped herself around it. Bark shaved skin off the crook of her arm. Her feet were airborne. Blinking furiously, she saw Boyd on the track, hands on hips, watching. She slowed her swing, steadied herself and climbed back to the ledge. On her hands and knees, she looked up at him. She expected an insult but he said nothing. He didn't have to. The message was in his stare; there's no safety-net out here.

They reached a plateau. Stephanie guessed it was the saddle between two peaks because suddenly the wind was stronger, the rain horizontal. With the incline gone, he forced her to go faster still. At the higher altitude there was no thick grass, just greasy tufts between slivers of sheered rock and sheets of smooth stone. Her T-shirt clung to her body like an extra skin.

Recklessly, they ran without direction, burning the last of the air in their lungs, the wind moaning in their ears. When she retched, she didn't stop. She just spat the last of her bile and saliva into the night. Sometimes she fell, sometimes he fell. She'd hear the grunt as he hit the ground and the crackle of loose stone beneath him. She never looked round. She carried on, forcing him to make up the lost ground. Will-power drove her on when her stamina began to fail.

Until she twisted her ankle.

It was a flat slice of land but her right foot skidded and then wedged itself between two rocks. She went over on it, felt the wrench in the joint, the searing heat up her calf and shin. The foot broke free as she fell.

She came to a stop close to the edge of a small pool of icy black water. She lay on her back, her spasmodic breathing beyond control. Boyd barked at her to get up. She did nothing and felt his boot in her ribs again. She rolled onto her side and then dragged herself to her feet. But when she placed the weight of her body on the right ankle, it folded. Boyd yelled at her once more.

'I can't!' she panted.

He grabbed the collar of the T-shirt, squeezing cold water from it. 'You *will*.'

'My ankle . . . it's sprained . . . twisted . . .'

'I don't care if it's broken! *Run!*'

Three times she tried, three times she fell, but Boyd was having none of it. As she lay on the ground, he stood over her and pressed the sole of his boot onto her right ankle. She squirmed but refused to cry out.

'The next time you fall down I'm going to stamp on this bone until it's fucking paste! You understand, you shilling *slut*?'

She staggered to her feet once more. The strike caught both of them by surprise. Stephanie wasn't fully aware of throwing it and Boyd had no time to avoid it. Her right hand cracked against the side of his face, loud enough to over-ride the cacophony of the storm, strong enough to put him down. But like a rubber ball, he was on his way up the moment he hit the ground. Stephanie never even raised her hands. He threw a punch, not a slap. It caught her on the right cheek, just below the eye. As she collapsed, stars erupted on the inside of her eyelids, the only spots of brightness in the night.

For a moment, there was nothing but rain and cold.

When Stephanie opened her eyes, Boyd had moved away. He was sitting on a mossy ledge, his head in his hands. She watched him, as still as stone, water dripping from him. Eventually, he looked up at her. Despite the darkness, she could see that the hatred was gone. In its place, there was sorrow.

6

It took two hours to return to the lodge. Boyd supported Stephanie so that she wouldn't have to put any weight onto her right ankle. At first, she was oblivious to the wind and rain but when she saw the faint shimmer of the loch and the vague outline of the cabins beyond, the cold cut in and the last of her strength evaporated.

Inside, he led her to the kitchen, sopping and shivering. He pulled a wooden chair from the table and turned it to face the Rayburn, making sure not to place it too close, before collecting dry clothes for her. He removed her wet T-shirt first – replacing it with a thick burgundy sweatshirt – followed by her tracksuit bottoms and trainers. After jeans, he pulled thick Alpine socks over her frozen feet. Finally, he wrapped a scarf around her throat. Then he put the kettle on one of the hotplates before disappearing to change his own sodden clothes.

Outside, the storm continued to rage.

Gradually, Stephanie drifted back. The thaw in her fingers and toes began to burn. They drank two mugs of sweet milky tea, Boyd telling her to sip not slurp. The clatter of wind on glass was curiously comforting now they were warm and dry. She was a child again.

Boyd waited until her body was able to generate its own heat before attending to her. He removed the scarf and pulled her chair a little closer to the Rayburn. He examined her right ankle, turning and pressing it. He strapped it with a bandage, wiped her grazes with antiseptic and rubbed arnica into the worst of her bruises. Neither of them spoke. Later, he fed her Nurofen, led her to her bed and told her to go to sleep.

It was mid-afternoon. She dressed slowly, easing her muscles through the stiffness. She pulled on the same pair of jeans, a thick roll-neck jersey, climbing socks and a pair of boots. Outside, the weather had cleared. The air was sharp, the sky a deep sapphire. She found Boyd servicing the diesel generator in one of the outbuildings, his sleeves rolled up to the elbows, his hands and forearms black with oil and dirt. There was a mark on the side of his face. She couldn't tell whether it was a bruise or just grime.

He laid a wrench on a strip of stained cloth. 'How's the foot?'

She shrugged. 'Okay.'

'And the rest of you?'

'Look, about what happened . . .'

'Don't say anything, Stephanie. It doesn't matter.'

'It does matter.'

'Well, it's in the past now. Better that we leave it there, don't you think?' When she didn't reply, he added: 'For both of us.'

'Can I ask you to do something for me?'

'What?'

'Cut my hair.'

Boyd frowned. 'I'm not much of a barber.'

'You won't need to be.'

*   *   *

The following morning brought frost, the start of a four-day cold snap. Stephanie awoke late and rose slowly. The wood-framed mirror above the chest of drawers was only large enough to reflect half her face. She had to crouch a little to see her dark hair. Cropped close to the scalp in ragged tufts, she thought it made her look vulnerable. Which was how she felt. And which she didn't mind.

Outside, the ground was glass beneath her boots. Above, the sky was almost purple in patches with a few wispy cirrus clouds. Boyd had gone on a run without her. She could see him on a ridge on the hill on the far side of the loch, a green-grey spot moving against a backdrop of wet rust.

She was waiting for him in the kitchen when he returned. He wasn't short of breath but the cold air and his heat had turned his cheeks red. Sweat lent his forehead a sheen.

He looked at the kitchen table. 'What's this?'

'What does it look like?'

'You don't have to make breakfast.'

'I know.'

'What I mean is, you don't have to make amends.'

'I know.'

Valeria Rauchman was a Russian-language teacher sent by Alexander during the last week of September. Snow-skinned with large, dark brown eyes, she had black hair with silver streaks that she wore in a bun at the nape of her neck. She looked as though she was in her mid-forties but Boyd later told Stephanie she was older. Squarely built, she was nevertheless elegant. Usually stern, she could never quite extinguish the sparkle in her eyes. For every obvious feature, Valeria Rauchman possessed a contradictory quality not far beneath the surface.

The first few days of tuition were intense since Stephanie was unable to exercise. 'Not as good as I'd expected,' Rauchman declared after the first lesson. 'But with a lot of time and effort, who knows?'

A week after Rauchman's arrival, the last commercial group of the season left. Stephanie watched them file onto two minibuses bound for Inverness. Boyd spent the next two days with his assistants, cleaning the cabins and closing them down for winter. On their last night, he spent the evening with them at the staff cabin. Stephanie and Rauchman remained at the lodge. After supper, Stephanie stood by the sitting-room window and looked out. Weak orange light spilled from the cabin's windows. It was a still night. Intermittently, they could hear faint peals of laughter.

Rauchman said, 'It's good that he's happy tonight.'

Stephanie looked across the room at her. 'How well do you know him?'

'I've known him for years. I knew Rachel, too.'

'What was she like?'

'Lovely. Quiet but strong. Stronger than him.'

Stephanie felt a pang of jealousy. 'How did you meet him?'

'That's not for me to say.'

'But you knew him before he came here?'

She nodded. 'We used to run into each other from time to time. Zagreb, Jakarta, Damascus.'

'What was he doing in those places?'

'The same thing I was doing. Working.'

'In a place like Damascus?'

'When I saw him in Damascus, he was on his way home from Kuwait.'

'The Gulf War?'

'After Iraq invaded Kuwait, he was sent in to gather intelligence. For the six months leading up to Desert Storm, he lived in Kuwait City itself. On his own, on the move, living in rubble, living off rodents, transmitting information about the Iraqis when he could. He stayed until the city was liberated.'

'And then you just happened to bump into him in Damascus?'

Rauchman smiled. 'Don't pretend to be so naïve, Stephanie. I know who you are. So you know how it is.'

'He doesn't talk about those things to me.'

'Of course not. He never talks about anything that's close to him. That's why he's never mentioned you.'

It was a week before Stephanie resumed training. A fortnight later, Rauchman was called to London for several days. Stephanie and Boyd embarked on a four-day trek. Boyd selected their clothes and prepared a small pack for each of them. He carried a compass, but when it was clear he made her navigate using a watch and the sun. She remembered the process: in the northern hemisphere, you hold the watch horizontally with the hour hand pointing at the sun. Bisecting the angle between the hour hand and the twelve, you arrive at a north–south line. From there, all directions are taken.

Her ankle healed, her stamina almost as developed as his, they travelled quickly, no matter what the terrain. Stephanie enjoyed the daily distance covered. By day-

light, they stuck mostly to high ground. In the late afternoon, they would find a river or burn and descend
towards it. Being the harsh landscape that it was, food
was scarce. They had nothing to bring down a stag, a
hind or a bird, so they fished for trout. In each pack
there was a tin containing fishing line, a selection of
hooks and some split lead weights. Stephanie proved to
be useless at fishing and caught just one trout in four
days, Boyd snagging the rest.

They carried groundsheets for night-time shelter.
They plundered saplings from forestry plantations and
draped the groundsheets over makeshift frames. Boyd
had allowed them the luxury of lightweight Gore-Tex
sleeping bags. By choosing places that offered some
natural cover, the groundsheets proved largely effective
against rain.

Each pack contained waterproof matches to light
small fires at night, the flames securely contained within
stone circles. They cooked gutted fish over glowing
embers. Boyd supplemented their diet with bars of
rolled-oat biscuits. When it was clear, he taught her
how to read the major constellations in the sky: the
Plough, Cassiopeia, Orion.

On the final morning, Stephanie awoke before Boyd.
It was still dark. She watched the creeping daylight in
the east and the rise of a plum-coloured sun. She heard
the distant roar of an old stag on the slope above. Later,
they spotted it, corralling its hinds along a ridge. They
tracked the animals, taking care to remain downwind
and out of sight. Boyd brought her close to them. They
crawled through a peat hag rank with the stag's musky
scent and then found a flat slab of rock that overlooked
the deer. When the animals moved on, Stephanie and

Boyd climbed to the peak, from where they saw the lodge, a speck dwarfed by a wall of granite.

They sat on a rocky lip, their legs dangling over a fifty-foot drop, and ate the remains of their rations. Stephanie glanced across at Boyd, who was chewing a rolled-oat biscuit. He was looking down at his filthy boots and at the air beneath them. He was smiling.

'What are you thinking about?'

He shook his head. 'I was just wondering what it must have been like for your parents. Having you as a child, that is.'

'And you find the idea of that funny?'

'I find the idea of it terrifying.'

'Thanks a lot.'

'Were either of them as strong-willed as you?'

'Both of them.'

'Christ.'

'So was my sister. And one of my brothers.'

'Must've been a lot of noise.'

Stephanie laughed out loud. There had been. All the time. 'But I was the worst.'

'You reckon?'

'I was a nightmare for my parents. Especially when I was a teenager. Too bright for my own good, too headstrong for anyone's good. I never wanted to be anything like them.'

'What teenager does?'

'True. I always tried to disappoint them. And I was pretty successful at it. I was the brightest in my school but I underachieved. I got caught smoking and drinking. I listened to the Clash and the Smiths and hung around with the kind of boys I knew they'd dislike.' Stephanie gazed at the drop, too. 'Is there anything in the world more self-centred and pointless than a teenager?'

'Of course not.'

'The strange thing is, now my parents are gone, I find I'm envious of them. If I ever got married, I'd want a marriage like theirs. With stand-up rows and unruly children.'

'And I thought the idea of you as a child was frightening.'

Stephanie turned to him. 'You can't see me as a wife? Or a mother?'

He opened his mouth, then checked himself. 'I was going to say "no" but the truth is, I really don't know.'

'I'd want a house like the one I grew up in. I'd want a childhood like the one I grew up in.'

'Don't tell me. You're just an old-fashioned girl at heart.'

She giggled, which was something she rarely did. 'I know. All that rebellion for all those years and then it turns out there's a part of me that's just dying to be a conformist.'

It was a wet Wednesday. The previous evening, Valeria Rauchman had returned from London. When Stephanie came downstairs, she and Boyd were talking in the kitchen. There was a large package on the table.

'Look what Valeria's brought us from London.'

'What is it?'

'George Salibi.'

The man with the disk. 'Any news on Marshall's killer? Or Koba?'

'Not yet.'

'What's the story with Salibi?'

'The disk is – or will be – in a safe in his penthouse in New York. This is the background material we'll need.'

They opened the parcel and spread its contents across the table. George Salibi, Lebanese billionaire banker, founder of First Intercontinental, aged sixty-four. A man with a penthouse on Central Park West, a house in London on Wilton Crescent, an enormous residence overlooking the sea at Villefranche-sur-Mer, a one-hundred-metre boat moored at the International Yacht Club at Antibes – named *Zara*, after his daughter – and a Gulfstream V to ferry him from one property to the next.

Salibi's wife was an Argentine called Sylvia, daughter of an army general who'd fled to Switzerland in 1975 with twenty million embezzled dollars. Ten years younger than Salibi, Sylvia remained a stunning woman: high cheekbones, large emerald eyes, Sophia Loren's mouth. She'd been twenty-seven when she married Salibi and it was not hard to see what the stout banker had fallen for. Her beauty was reflected in their children, Felix and Zara. Stephanie returned to a photograph of Sylvia at the time of her engagement. She'd been the same age as Stephanie was now. She'd had poise, sophistication, elegance. She looked entirely at ease with the glittering diamond choker that circled her slender throat. No rough edges, she looked everything that Stephanie wasn't.

'Salibi's a renowned paranoid,' Boyd said. 'He has security at all his properties whether he's there or not. Most of them are ex-Israeli Army, including his personal bodyguard, who's by his side twenty-four hours a day, three hundred and sixty-five days a year.'

'No holidays?'

'Not for more than three years.'

Boyd handed Stephanie a head-and-shoulders photograph: a stern expression, olive skin and chocolate eyes, black hair cut to stubble, powerful shoulder muscles.

'A woman?'

Boyd nodded. 'Ruth Steifel. Ex-Army, then ex-Mossad. Magenta House believe she may also have been seconded to Shabek on at least one occasion. Since she's worked for Salibi, she hasn't had a day off.'

'I wonder what Sylvia says about that.'

After lunch, they examined the architect's plans for the Central Park West penthouse. In a folder, there were photographs of the building from close and afar. There were three lists of observations and twelve pages of technical notes. It took Boyd and Stephanie an hour to go through the material for the first time.

'Initial thoughts?'

Stephanie was studying the vertical plans. 'Initial thoughts . . . if the disk is up for sale, perhaps it would be easier if Magenta House bought it.'

'I think it's going to be out of Alexander's price range. People like you are very expensive to run.'

'I had no idea I was such a luxury.'

'You're not. You're an unfortunate necessity.'

Stephanie returned her attention to the plans. 'I don't think I can get into the place from below so it's going to have to be from above.'

'I agree. But how?'

'Well, I can't go up the outside. I'd be seen.'

'And you can't go up the inside because it's secure.'

'And I can't drop onto the roof. Not realistically.'
Stephanie looked at the plans again. 'The lifts . . .'

'No. The main lift and the service lift both stop automatically on the floor beneath the penthouse. Every time the doors open, they're checked by the guards. You wouldn't even get to the right floor.'

'Not the actual lifts. The lift-shafts.'

It takes forty-five minutes to reach it. A large ledge of soaking black granite, sodden grass beneath it, grassy tufts and dead trees above it, and above them, a one-hundred-foot granite wall.

I look at Boyd. He grins mischievously. 'Not that. The ledge.'

Icy water falls from the ledge, a veil made of dozens of streams, some as heavy as a running tap, others needle-thin. The sound of the trickle, gurgle and rush is all we can hear.

'Look at it. Doesn't it remind you of something?'

I shrug. 'Not immediately.'

'Central Park West. The cornice around the top of the building.'

In my mind, I see the photographs again. Gothic, heavy, monstrous.

'The cornice above the penthouse is about the same size and angle as this piece of rock. You're going to have to come down over it.'

'I'll be suspended, though . . .'

'Yes. But you need to climb down over it, not drop.'

'Okay.'

'But before you make a descent here, I want you to try to climb up it.'

I look at the reverse angle. I've tackled far worse and Boyd knows it. My mother, who was Swiss, was a climber of some fame when she was young. She made it to the top of Everest at the second attempt and conquered most of Europe's greatest peaks, with the notable exception of the Eiger, which denied her twice. I've inherited her love of climbing and her lack of fear on rock.

I walk up to the face and place my palms against it. Hard, wet and freezing cold. Before I start, I make a map in my head of the route I'll take. Crevices for toes, slender finger-holds, chunks small enough to grab but large enough to take the whole weight of my body. It's join-the-dots. When I've seen exactly how I'll make it to the lip of the ledge, I start.

I'm ten feet off the ground when I fall. I'm reaching to my right, spread-eagled across the rock, leaning back at an angle of almost forty-five degrees. I grab a sharp but thick ledge and I'm beginning to transfer my weight when, without warning, the rock shears, coming away in my hand. There's no time to react. I'm already falling. I land on thick grass with a squelch.

As I struggle for breath, Boyd says, 'You okay?'

I try to say something but can't form a word. He leaves me to recover for a moment.

'I thought that might happen.'

To prove the point, he steps through the gossamer waterfall, grabs a secure-looking wedge of rock and yanks it. It snaps free of the face, leaving a light scar beneath.

'Bastard,' I gasp.

'It could happen again.'

I sit up. I'm soaked to the skin. 'What do you mean?'

'The plasterwork on the cornice. It's old and rotten. It's liable to come away in your hand.'

'You must be pretty pleased with yourself.'

'Very. Now let's try it from the top.'

Stephanie pulled the curtains. It was a breezy morning, the wind sending washboard ripples across the loch.

There was frost on the grass. She dressed quickly. The T-shirt she'd left to dry overnight was stiff and smelt of peat. She pulled a sweatshirt over the top. She collected her boots from the small drying room by the back door. They were warm.

Boyd was in the kitchen, drinking coffee, leaning against the sink. He wore an old pair of combat trousers and a chunky black V-neck over a white T-shirt.

'Aren't we going for a run?'

'Valeria's gone. She didn't want to wake you. She asked me to say goodbye to you.'

'When did she go?'

'Early this morning. I drove her into Lairg.'

'What's wrong?'

'Nothing.'

'Nothing?'

'Your preparation is over. At least, this part of it is.'

Stephanie wanted to say something, to protest. But she couldn't.

Boyd seemed to sense it. 'I got a call last night, after you'd gone to bed. Tomorrow morning, you're going home.'

'It's not home.'

Boyd poured coffee from the pot into an enamel mug and offered it to her. 'You can go for a run if you like, but I thought we might give it a miss this morning. You're in good enough shape.'

'But not so much fun to look at?'

He smiled. 'No, I'm afraid not. I miss the bouncy bits you arrived with.'

'You'll get over it.'

'Don't be too sure.' He refilled his own mug. 'I need to go to Durness. Do you want to come?'

She could taste the sea before she saw it. They drove slowly on roads where sheep were the major source of traffic. They entered Durness at midday, sweeping past the primary school before halting outside the Mace store, a small supermarket with a post office counter, where green fees could be paid for Durness Golf Club, mainland Britain's most northerly and windswept course. There was a BP filling station opposite the store, a small wooden hut beside the old pumps.

They bought groceries at Mace. There were half a dozen people inside the store. Boyd appeared to know them all. He fell into conversation with a couple at the till. A wiry man with copper hair shot a glance at Stephanie and then cracked a sly joke she couldn't hear. Laughter all round. A fat woman in a grubby black fleece asked Boyd how his season had been.

He caught Stephanie's eye. 'More challenging than usual, Mary. But more rewarding, too.'

There was more conversation, more laughter, Boyd at the centre of it, relaxed, social. To Stephanie, who was silent and watching, it was a minor revelation. Outside, he suggested a walk. They headed out towards Balnakeil, a mile away, past the Balnakeil Crafts Centre, where small shops were located in corroding concrete huts erected in the Forties to house German prisoners-of-war. Boyd parked the Land-Rover by the old house at Balnakeil, on the opposite side of the road to the walled churchyard. Stephanie said she wanted to look inside. He shrugged and said he'd wait for her by the gate onto the beach.

The tiny stone church had no roof. Its walls were coated in ivy. The graveyard was crowded. Most of the headstones were old, their engraving partly erased by decades of ferocious weather. Many commemorated men and women who were not buried in the cemetery: those who'd been lost at sea, or in colonial wars fighting for the expansion of the British Empire, or those who'd emigrated to Australia, India and South Africa, in search of a life less gruelling. Scattered among the old graves, there were a few more recent.

Including Rachel's.

It was in the far corner, by the stone wall. A small, unremarkable square headstone laid down the basic facts of her life. Dead at thirty-five. It made no mention of the cause but Stephanie knew that it had been breast-cancer. *Beloved wife of Iain.* The bottom half of the head-stone was blank, leaving enough space for another entry.

She looked across the cemetery. He was facing the sea.

She joined him at the gate and they walked onto the beach in the direction of Faraid Head, the farthest tip of the headland. The tide was coming in, but still low. The sand was hard, wind blowing a thin film of it across the rippled surface. They stepped over squelching beds of seaweed and scattered rubbish: a single shoe, part of a seat-belt, strips of slime-coated plastic. At the far end of the beach, a concrete track rose between dunes. In some places sand obscured it, but the direction was clear and they followed it. Between the dunes the wind died, in the open it was fierce.

As they crossed a cattle-grid, Stephanie said, 'There was a man in London before Malta. Frank White. I was in love with him. He was in love with me, I think. But it was a strange kind of love. I couldn't tell him anything truly personal. It was a love built on lies, except at the end. Then, I told him everything, and he accepted it. He'd known there was something about me right from the start.' She shook her head at the memory. 'After Malta, I disappeared. But I sent messages to him. I gave him the opportunity to follow me, to meet me. To vanish with me.'

'But he didn't?'

'No.'

'Any idea why not?'

'I guess he didn't love me as much as I thought he did. Or as much as I loved him.'

'Maybe he had too much to lose by following you.'

'Believe me, he didn't.'

'Have you tried to contact him again since you've been back in London?'

'No. It's been four years. He belongs to another part of my life. A part that . . . well, the idea of it's just too complicated.'

'I know what you mean.'

Stephanie doubted that. She took a deep breath. 'Anyway, when I realized there wasn't going to be a future with him, I didn't feel there was any future at all. I didn't disappear to escape from Magenta House. Not really. I disappeared to be with him.' Boyd had stopped walking so she stopped too. She smiled sadly. 'My first broken heart. I was twenty-three but I took it like a fifteen-year-old.'

'And became Petra because of it?'

'I didn't become anybody. I was already Petra.'

'I'm not with you.'

'I didn't choose to live Petra's life because my heart got broken. But I was confused and angry. If there's one thing I hate, it's self-pity, but when I look at the way I was then I don't see that I had much of a chance. Trained to perfection – to breaking point – I was bound to fracture sooner or later.'

'Probably,' Boyd conceded.

'In the end, all I did was *not* change. There was no real decision. Instead of Alexander, there was money, although it wasn't about the money. It was about the work. The day-to-day existence; rejecting contracts, accepting contracts, planning them, executing them, getting away with it. Attention to detail in all things.'

'What were you looking for?'

'Mechanical perfection. I wanted to be a machine. To feel nothing at all.'

'And did you succeed?'

'I think so. For a while . . .'

Beyond the cattle-grid, the road was tarmac with grass on either side, sheep roaming freely. In the distance, at the tip of the headland, Stephanie saw a small building, a look-out tower with black and yellow squares painted on the walls. An old Ministry of Defence facility, Boyd told her, with a concrete helicopter pad. Useful for air-sea rescue.

As they approached it, the incline grew steeper. Dozens of rabbits ran wild. Stephanie walked to the cliff's edge and peered at the two-hundred-foot vertical drop. She watched raucous waves hurling themselves onto the rocks below, cracking, foaming, receding. She felt the vertiginous pull, as familiar to her as the desire to succumb to momentary madness and to make the leap herself. She leaned further over and sensed Boyd tensing beside her.

'Why did you stop?' he asked.

She described Bilbao. 'I don't know why it happened.

It just did. In the first few weeks after it, I thought it was some kind of nervous breakdown. But now, when I look back at it, I think it was some kind of break-*through*. I think the nervous breakdown came before Bilbao. And after Malta.'

'And lasted for two and a half years?'

'Yes. I think my whole independent career as Petra was one long nervous breakdown. And that Bilbao – well, Arkan, to be specific – was the snapping point.'

Boyd was placing squares of peat onto the dying embers of the fire. He stood up and collected his glass from the mantelpiece. When he turned round, he found Stephanie at his side. She took the glass from his hand and returned it to the mantelpiece.

'Are you going to tell Alexander what I've told you today?'

'Not if you don't want me to.'

'He'll want to know.'

'He wants to know whether you're up to scratch.'

'And am I?'

'You're more vulnerable than you used to be.'

'That's not an answer. Am I up to scratch?'

'Yes. I'm afraid you are.'

She kissed him and tasted Pomerol. Boyd had produced a dusty bottle of Clos René at dinner. Stephanie had looked surprised and he'd said that he'd been saving it for a special occasion.

'You mean like finally getting rid of me?'

'No. Nothing like that.'

'What, then?'

'You work it out.'

She'd blushed instead.

Now, Boyd broke the kiss. But not by much. The only sound was the crackle of flame on peat.

Stephanie whispered, 'I want to make love with you.'

'No.'

'This isn't like before . . .'

'I know.'

He was still holding her. Stephanie looked him straight in the eye when she asked, 'Is it because of Rachel?'

'In a way, yes.'

Slowly, reluctantly, she began to move clear of him. 'Then I'm sorry. I don't want things to be awkward between us.'

'There's nothing to feel awkward about, Stephanie. I just don't want to get into that position.'

'What position?'

He turned away from her and collected his glass again. 'I was in love with Rachel. We both thought we had a long future ahead of us. But we didn't.' Stephanie watched him drain the last of his claret. 'The world you're about to go back to . . . we both know what the score is. I've already lost somebody I loved. I don't want to allow myself to get into the position where I might have to go through that a second time.'

7

He looks disappointed to see me. Maybe it's the black long-sleeved T-shirt I'm wearing. As I shrug off my donkey jacket, I catch him staring at it. Across the chest in gold letters it says: DON'T SEND A BOY TO DO A MAN'S JOB.

Alexander doesn't say anything. He doesn't have to. I know he disapproves, as surely as I know it's childish of me to wear it.

'We've been unable to identify Koba.'

'What a surprise. Who are the candidates?'

'Vladimir Vatukin, the man who succeeded Oleg Rogachev as boss of the Tsentralnaya crime syndicate, and Anatoli Medayev, who was Rogachev's right-hand man. Since Rogachev's murder in Paris, Medayev has drifted out of the picture.'

'Unlike Vatukin, who's benefited directly.'

'There's another man who might point us in the right direction, though. Konstantin Komarov. A Russian business-man. He's not a member of any gang in particular but he's affiliated to several. Or none, depending on your point of view. If the gangs are the cogs in the Russian criminal machine, he's the oil between them.'

'A lubricant? How tasteful.'

'Komarov travels a lot but he's based in New York.'

'Like George Salibi. Let me guess. You thought you'd save Magenta House an air-fare and get me to do two jobs for the price of one?'

'Komarov is a known associate of Koba's.'

'What does he do?'

'He's an investor. And a financial advisor.'

'A money-launderer . . .'

'Technically, he's clean.'

'A crook by proxy, then.'

'Not quite. He's done his fair share. But it's all in the past.'

'What's the deal?'

'You use Komarov to get to Koba.'

'How?'

'By masquerading as a buyer for Plutonium-239. Komarov won't want to know himself. But he'll see the chance to take a percentage by passing the business on to Koba.'

'And if that doesn't work?'

'Throughout the Russian criminal world, Komarov's reputation – and, by extension, his fortune – depends upon his integrity. If that reputation was undermined, he'd be in trouble. First things first, though. The approach to Komarov must look legitimate. If he suspects anything, it'll be a dead end. However, once he's vouched for you –'

'What if he won't?'

'You'll have to find a way to make sure he does.'

'How do we get to him?'

'There's someone here in London who can help. A Pole named Zbigniew Sladek. Rosie Chaudhuri will provide you with all the information you need.'

'Could Vatukin or Medayev have been responsible for Paris?'

'You're asking me?'

'Oh, for God's sake . . .'

As I get up, Alexander looks at my breasts again and, perhaps, at the slogan which runs across them. DON'T SEND A BOY TO DO A MAN'S JOB. I gather my tatty jacket from *the back of my chair. This gives him the opportunity to see what's written between my shoulder blades: SEND A WOMAN.*

'Is that your idea of a joke?'

I return his glare with interest. 'No,' I reply. 'You're my idea of a joke.'

Rosie Chaudhuri's eyes widened. 'God, what happened to your hair?'

'Don't ask.'

Magenta House, Basement Level Four, Room 2A, an octagonal room without windows. The halogen spots embedded in the ceiling were dimmed. All Stephanie could hear was the soft breath of air conditioning and the murmur of computer terminals. She sat down in the high-backed leather swivel chair next to Rosie. The three twenty-one inch terminals formed a curve in front of them. Rosie typed as she spoke. 'Sladek, Zbigniew, V. Birth date, 1963, September the fourth. Place of birth, Cracow, Poland.'

The three screens changed simultaneously. The one on the right subdivided into sixty-four squares, the monitor on the left drew down three script lists. On the central screen, there was a photograph of a young man with flat features, grey eyes with grey smudges beneath, and wispy light brown hair.

Rosie said, 'On the right screen, we have parcels of information. If you squint hard enough, you'll see that each has a heading. Just touch the one you want and it'll appear on the central monitor. On the left, you have reference tags to guide you to associated general information. It's pretty easy once you get the hang of it.'

Sladek ran the London branch of Almatinvest from a rented office in the Hyde Park Business Centre. The head office was based in Almaty, Kazakhstan. He lived alone in a first-floor, one-bedroom flat in Cadogan Square and drove a silver Mercedes Kompressor. Since his arrival in Britain two years before, his life had been a picture of propriety. Before that, however, he'd been a financial cowboy in the Wild East, pioneering new forms of banking in places where livestock was still the predominant currency. As a thirty-year-old, he'd run a small private bank named Vassex in Bishkek, Kyrgyzstan. Rosie went to one of the associated topics. A picture of snow-capped peaks formed on the central screen.

'This is the Tian Shan which straddles China and Kyrgyzstan. Kyrgyzstan is a tiny, mountainous country which, since the collapse of the Soviet Union in 1991, has become a sort of CIS version of Switzerland for those whose banking arrangements run to the unorthodox. Sladek spent four years in Bishkek before Vassex went into liquidation, along with three of its founders. The following year, he turned up in Moscow.'

She pressed another of the squares to her right. It was some film footage: a large room with a raised dais at one end and rows of chairs for an audience in front of it. Behind the dais, two large screens displayed rows of numbers beneath Cyrillic headings. Rosie pointed to a man in a double-breasted suit in the fourth row. 'That's Sladek.'

'What's this?'

'A Moscow currency auction, usually held in hotels – like this one – or in a conference hall, generally for between twenty and fifty people.'

Stephanie watched the silent movie. 'What are they doing?'

'They're bidding for dollars that the Central State Bank offers as lines of credit. They pay over the odds for the cash because they know they'll make a profit on the interest they'll charge when they lend the dollars to business ventures. It's a carve-up, naturally. Strictly invitation only.'

'How was Sladek involved?'

'This auction was back in 1997. He was buying on behalf of Ivan Timofeyev, a mobster-turned-banker. Timofeyev was *persona non grata* at these events but that didn't prevent him from sending his representatives. Or from being decapitated by Siberian bandits in Krasnoyarsk last October.'

'But these days, Sladek's clean, right?'

Rosie smiled. 'I wouldn't put it quite like that. But compared to some of the other companies he's worked for, Almatinvest is a picture of respectability.'

'Kyrgyzstan and Kazakhstan are neighbours, aren't they? Is there any connection with what he does now and what he did then?'

'It's true that Bishkek and Almaty are stranded together in the middle of nowhere. A lot of the money from Kazak and Azerbaijani oil fields has passed through institutions in Bishkek and a lot of Almatinvest's commercial partners and clients are in the oil industry. Then there's this . . .'

Another square, another image. A picture of Zbigniew Sladek shaking hands with Murtaza Rakhimov, president of Bashkortostan, one of the eighty-nine members of the Russian Federation. Rakhimov and his immediate family had come to regard oil-rich Bashkortostan as a private fiefdom; Ural, the president's son, ran one of Russia's largest oil companies. The file listed examples of their autocratic rule, of brutality, corruption, cronyism, media control, governmental fraud.

'Once you start to follow the leads,' Rosie said, 'you find yourself being dragged through Dagestan, Tatarstan, Chechnya, St Petersburg, the Baltic States and into western Europe. By the way, these are for you.'

She handed Stephanie a small plastic box. Stephanie removed the lid. Inside, there were embossed business cards: **Katherine March, Galileo Resources**. At the bottom of each card there was a phone number, a fax number and an e-mail address. But no physical address.

'When you go to see Sladek, this is who you'll be. In conversation, you're Kate, not Katherine. The identity isn't complete yet but the numbers and the e-mail address are established. We've removed Galileo Resources from the listed companies as a precaution. This should be enough to get you past Sladek but we'll give you a little leverage, just to make sure. We'll have the rest of the Kate March identity in place before you meet Komarov.'

Stephanie closed the Pole's file and touched the right-hand screen to open the first file on Konstantin Komarov.

'The Don from the Don,' said Rosie. 'That's the nickname the FBI gave him.'

'I thought he came from Moscow.'

'That's where he was born. But he's a Siberian.'

'Which still doesn't explain the Don connection.'

'The nickname comes from an incident in 1993 when an Uzbek moneylender was murdered in Voronezh. The

Uzbek had double-crossed Komarov in Moscow. That was about as close to a connection as anyone got. The suspicion was so slight it never graduated to a full allegation but the nickname stuck.'

Komarov had a long face, an aquiline nose and intense dark brown eyes. His black hair was flecked with small brushes of silver. He wore it short. His tanned features looked more European Russian than Siberian. She pressed another screen square. He was crossing a street in Paris, the traffic a blood clot along a cobbled artery. There was blossom on the trees. He wore a cream button-down shirt, a blue jacket, grey flannel trousers, black slip-ons. He had a lean build. Overall, his appearance was unexpected. Most of the Russian gangsters she'd seen were gross, the crassness of their taste expanding exponentially with their waists. Pasty-faced, moustached, guardians of the worst haircuts of the Seventies and Eighties, they were, almost without exception, the antithesis of taste.

She scrolled through his history. State orphanages, juvenile correctional institutions, the mainstream Soviet penal system, eventual release. Before moving to New York, he'd lived in Moscow for five years, where he still maintained business interests and an apartment. He'd dealt with all the criminal organizations that counted in the city: the Lubyertsy, the Dolgoprudniki, the Solntserskiye, the Balashikhinskiye. And Tsentralnaya.

Magenta House had obtained a copy of a file kept at Department Six of the MVD, the Russian Interior Ministry. In it, Komarov was accused of being an authority on Russian crime with a unique overview. It suggested that, apart from his legitimate business interests, he was also involved with money-laundering, gambling and prostitution. The report concluded that it was impossible to estimate his wealth because it was impossible to tie him to any of the companies that he was known to own. It seemed there was no one better at keeping his name off a legal document than Konstantin Komarov.

Stephanie looked at some of the other headings and picked one. The largest fraud that Komarov had been associated with had been perpetrated by the Tsentralnaya crime syndicate. It was well known that Russian criminal organizations targeted governments because they tended to be the largest generators of money. Moreover, they were usually very poor at monitoring it. Tsentralnaya had run a highly lucrative petroleum products fraud against the Czech government during the immediate aftermath of the Velvet Revolution. Relaxed laws had allowed foreigners to invest with confidence in the Czech Republic. No one took greater advantage of the new liberal atmosphere than Russia's most powerful criminal organizations.

Tsentralnaya led the way, although others were soon to follow. It hinged on one simple regulation: there was no duty on light fuel while diesel was heavily taxed. Tsentralnaya took measures to get round this. Sometimes they disguised the identity of rail-tankers bringing in diesel from Russian and CIS oil fields, so that they appeared to be carrying light fuel. Sometimes, they chemically adulterated the diesel to change its characteristics, reversing the process once the fuel was inside the Czech Republic. The scale of the fraud was enormous. At its height, a third of all the petrol in the country went untaxed. The profits made by Russian criminal gangs were vast and none of them made more than Tsentralnaya. A conservative FBI estimate suggested that the Czech government lost enough revenue to fund the construction of at least fifty hospitals.

Worse was to follow. Inevitably, such colossal profits attracted competition. Territorial squabbles erupted into violence. Prague became the backdrop for a Russian Mafiya turf war.

The MVD file accused Konstantin Komarov of being the man who conceived the scam on Tsentralnaya's behalf. Whether or not that was true, he'd certainly helped the organization to launder and invest some of the profits that were generated by it.

In the mid-Nineties, post-Soviet Russia had not been a democracy. It had been a kleptocracy, with Konstantin Komarov at the heart of it. A man who was as comfortable in Manhattan as he was in Moscow or Magadan. A chameleon. Just like Petra Reuter.

I get out of bed, put Garbage's first album into the machine and fast forward to the song I want: 'Stupid Girl'. The bass reverberates through me. I run a bath and then stretch. In the mirror, I see abdominal muscles moving beneath my skin, like liquid marble. My breasts are smaller and firmer, my thighs have hardened. Along my forearms, sinews ripple. My mouth is as ripe as ever but there's a hardness to my face, a coldness in my eyes. I look like Petra but I don't feel like her. Gradually, steam obscures me.

In the bath, I close my eyes and listen to the music. Laurent enters my mind. We're making love in my room at the farmhouse, a warm breeze coming through the open window. I can taste him and I can hear the sound our bodies make. Beneath the surface of the water, I press my hand between my thighs. My fingers are his fingers. I bite my lower lip until

*it hurts. At some point – I have no idea when – it's no longer
Laurent inside me. It's Boyd.*

*Wrapped in a towel, dripping water onto the sea-grass, I
traipse to the kitchen and switch on the kettle. The sheet of
paper is on the table, where I left it last night. I look at the
headings I made: eyes, hair, make-up, clothes, accessories.*

*I scoop coffee into the cafetière, pour the steaming water
through and leave it to stand.*

*I can't be bothered to change her eyes so they'll be dark
brown. My hair has grown since Boyd cut it with a pair of
kitchen scissors. It still looks a mess but it's not beyond salvage.
I think about colour for a few minutes but can't make up my
mind. And without a hair-style, I find it hard to think about
make-up. Normally, I don't wear any. In fact, I dislike it but
I have the feeling Kate would wear some. Clothes come easily.
I pick up the business card. Galileo Resources. It's not hard
to imagine the woman she'd be: tough, efficient and unafraid
of using her gender as a weapon, by letting it appear to be a
weakness. Accessories are harder to determine. Should she
wear glasses? Or a wedding ring? Should she carry an accent?
As a general rule, I don't use accessories unless it's absolutely
necessary. The problem is in knowing when that's likely
to be.*

Despite the rain, tourists clogged the pavement outside
Harrods. Stephanie crossed the road and stopped outside
a large wooden door. On the intercom, there were
twenty buzzers. She pressed the one marked Hyde Park
Business Centre. Inside, the lift was out of order so she
took the green linoleum stairs. Through a set of swing
doors, she found herself at a reception counter with no
one behind it. The Hyde Park Business Centre occupied
the first floor of the building. The space had been

cheaply partitioned to provide small offices off a maze of interconnecting corridors.

She walked past doors with plastic plaques on them: Vital Films, Go Latvia! Holidays, UK Root Crop Agency. She turned left at a junction and passed a chiropractor, a fertilizer distributor and a mail-order Tarot card company. Almatinvest was the last on the left; an eight-foot-by-six waiting room with three plastic chairs lined up against a flimsy partition wall. The anorexic receptionist looked bored. On the wall above her head was an aerial photograph of Almaty. Age had bleached most of the colour from the print.

'My name's Kate March. I have an appointment with Mr Sladek.'

Sladek's office was twice the size of the waiting room but no more luxurious. His suit looked expensive, though. Just like his home address, his car and the after-shave he was wearing; he was as out of place as she was. Rosie had told Stephanie that Almatinvest rented the office on a month-to-month basis, the rent paid in cash.

'And when I say cash, I mean cash. Used fifties and twenties.'

'In other words, the kind of place that can be abandoned in a moment.'

There were two phones on his desk. Next to them, Sladek had placed two mobiles. Stephanie wondered whether the fixed line phones were even connected.

She watched him take her in; five foot nine plus two-inch heels, a black suit from Joseph – the figure-hugging skirt falling to the knee, a black satin shirt unbuttoned at the throat, her dark hair freshly washed and cut, a touch of make-up, a little eye-liner, cherry lipstick, a man's Omega watch on her left wrist, a black calf-skin attaché case in her right hand.

'Coffee?'

'No.'

'Tea?'

'Nothing.'

They sat down and Sladek pretended to examine a notepad. 'So . . . what brings you to Almatinvest? How can we help?'

'I have a business proposition.'

He picked up her card. 'Galileo Resources. I don't believe I know the name. What line of business are you in?'

'The information business.'

'What kind of information?'

'The people kind. Or in this case, person. Singular.'

'Go on.'

'I'd like you to introduce me to Konstantin Komarov.'

The emotion that Sladek tried to conceal was fear, not surprise. 'I don't think I know . . .'

'Yes, you do.'

After a pause, a sniff and a clearance of the throat, Sladek regained his inscrutability, picked up a fountain pen and began to play with it. 'Even if I knew such a man, I can't think of a reason for me to introduce you to him.'

'What if it was in your interest? Hypothetically speaking, of course . . .'

'Hypothetically, how could that be?'

'You're a businessman, aren't you?'

He chewed on it for a minute. 'I'd need guarantees.' Stephanie maintained her silence, forcing him on. 'Give me a figure.'

'I'll do better than that. I'll give you a reason.'

Sladek's eyes narrowed to a squint. 'A reason?'

'You have a girlfriend who lives in West Kilburn. On Lothrop Street. Her name is Sally MacLeod and she comes from Sheffield.' Stephanie opened the attaché case and produced six photographs, which she tossed across the desk. 'You met her at Stringfellow's. She used to be a lap-dancer. Now you pay her not to be.'

Sladek put the topless shot to one side and flicked through the five beneath.

'You also have a cousin who lives in London. Jan Kaminski. The two of you are very close. When you were running Vassex out in Bishkek, he came to see you several times a year. The strange thing is, now that you're both living in the same city you don't see much of each other. When you do, you never meet in the same place twice. You never meet in areas in which either of you live or work. You use pay-phones to contact one another, never home phones or mobiles. Why is that?'

'You can't threaten me.'

Stephanie shackled him with a look. 'I'm not threatening you. Jan Kaminski has a wife. Mary, formerly Doyle, from Dublin. They married in July 1987. They live in a house on East Street in Walworth. They have two sons – Jerzy and Krzysztof – who attend Walworth Secondary on Trafalgar Street. The school is close to home and they walk there and back every day. They only have to cross two roads but that's okay. Do you know why?'

Sladek stared at her, mouth open, but silent.

'Because one is enough. That's all it takes. One of the boys steps off the kerb. The driver of a passing car

121

isn't paying attention. Or perhaps he's going too fast to stop. Who knows?'

C4 was in the Accounts Department of L.L. Herring. Of all the companies within the shell, the firm of numismatists was the oldest, the most legitimate, and Stephanie's favourite. The owner, Gerald Thornton, was as much of a relic as the rare and ancient coins in which he specialized. His office was a slice of history, a room of leather-bound reference books, paper turned yellow by the years, coins in display cases, tweed jackets and dust. He had two assistants who shared his fondness for silence.

The Accounts Department was behind Thornton's office. A cube with a single window onto Victoria Embankment Gardens, it was mostly in keeping with the rest of L.L. Herring; there were shelves of ledgers dating back to the firm's birth in 1789, every transaction filled out in spidery script. Surplus reference books were stocked along one wall in historical categories. But there were also three slim computer monitors arranged around two keyboards and a single chair.

Among Magenta House employees, C4 was known as the Memory Division. It created entire identities, conjuring up names, personal histories, employment and medical records. It dealt in family tragedies, failed marriages, conquered addictions, crippling weaknesses. Pasts were created for the ghosts of the future. The Memory Division was the womb from which Petra Reuter had emerged.

Stephanie found Rosie Chaudhuri there. Beside her, there was a black box-file, which she picked up. 'The rest of your holiday reading.'

'I can hardly wait.'

'Such sarcasm. When are you off?'

'Tomorrow morning.'

The previous evening, Sladek had phoned Galileo Resources. In a nondescript office somewhere in Magenta House, someone had masqueraded as a receptionist. *Galileo Resources. Good evening. How may I help?* Someone else had been Katherine March's secretary. *I'm afraid she's not in her office. Can I help, or can I get her to call you?* Sladek had left the number for his mobile. Stephanie already had it. She called him at ten. He'd spoken to Komarov, who was abroad on business. But he was due back in New York at the end of the week. Stephanie had phoned his secretary and had made an appointment.

Rosie said, 'Want to get a sandwich? I haven't eaten anything today.'

Stephanie wasn't sure. 'Okay.'

Lower Robert Street was a narrow road that twisted beneath part of Magenta House before disgorging itself onto Savoy Place. There was a door set into the curved wall. They used it as an exit and walked to the Strand.

They took a table at the back of a greasy spoon; steam on the windows, dirty magnolia walls, Abba on the radio – 'The Winner Takes It All' – foil ashtrays and red check tablecloths. Rosie ordered a tuna salad and a glass of water. Stephanie asked for a Coke.

Rosie slid a black-and-white photograph across the table. 'Boris Bergstein. Your contact in New York.'

He had a broad low brow, a thick nose, chunky lips, frog's eyes. His hair was cut to fuzz, a look reflected by the stubble along his heavy jaw-line. 'Christ, he's not much of a looker, is he?'

'He's no angel,' Rosie agreed. 'Not in any sense of the word.'

'A track record?'

'Naturally. A medium-sized fish in several small ponds. Based in Brighton Beach, he's got connections in South Florida. And in Moscow.'

'What's he into?'

'Anything that turns a profit. In his time, drugs, protection, prostitution – mostly in Russia, but also in Germany. At the moment, he's treading carefully. He'd like to become a US citizen but he's under investigation in connection with a failed property development in Miami.'

'I thought that was compulsory in Florida.'

The waitress brought their order. When she moved away, Rosie said, 'Do you mind if I ask you something . . . personal?'

Stephanie attempted a smile. 'You can ask.'

'Did he force you to come back? I mean, I never expected to see you again.'

'Nor did he.'

'What happened?'

'We made a deal. Once this job is over, he relinquishes his claim on me.'

'Do you believe he will?'

Stephanie sipped her Coke. 'To be perfectly honest, I don't know.'

'But you came back anyway.'

'The possibility was enough. I don't want to spend the rest of my life thinking about Magenta House. Even once I'd sorted myself out in the south of France, it was always there. This way, I can get rid of it for good.'

'What if he goes back on his word?'

Stephanie shrugged. 'I used to think about killing him all the time. But that was when I was Petra. I'm not like that any more. So I don't know.'

When they parted outside the café, Rosie kissed Stephanie on both cheeks. 'Good luck in New York.'

Two friends stealing a quick lunch in the middle of a busy day. That's what it would have looked like, Stephanie supposed. A scene repeated daily throughout the city. She didn't believe that Rosie had faked it. Yet to her, it felt utterly alien.

She caught the Bakerloo Line from Charing Cross to Baker Street. Her carriage was almost empty. She sat at one end, beside the door, and opened the box-file. The top item was a Visa card made out in the name of Miss K.E. March. She looked at the driving licence. K for Katherine, E for Elizabeth. Aged twenty-eight, she was just eleven months older than Stephanie. She found her parents, Alfred and Helen. Both had died from natural causes within the last five years. She checked for siblings, even though she knew what the answer would be. When she found it, it brought a wry smile to her lips. Brothers, none living. Sisters, none living. She was an only child.

The children of the Memory Division always were.

8

Stephanie caught the 6th Avenue Express from 57th Street to Brighton Beach, at the southern end of Brooklyn. The sun was razor sharp in a cloudless sky but the air was cold enough to freeze her breath. The steps down from the elevated station led onto Brighton Beach Avenue, still the heart of New York's Russian community. The road itself remained in perpetual shadow, beneath the overhead rails. Stores lined either side of the street, their signs in English and Cyrillic: laundromats, florists, jewellers, electronic retailers. Stephanie checked the address she'd scribbled onto a sheet of headed paper at the Sherry Netherland. The Surgut Pharmacy. She found it between Café Arbat and Vasily's Liquor Store.

Inside, it was dark. The air was sweet; there were incense sticks burning in a holder by the door. On the walls, there were sepia photographs of Siberian shamans: long black coats adorned with ribbons and tassels, shiny feathered head-dresses, gold rings and plates, flails. Boxes of wood and glass were laid out along racks beneath the photographs. They contained grasses, powders, dried leaves, roots. Each had a card with a list of the ailments it treated. At the back of the store, there was a varnished wooden counter.

'Is Boris Bergstein here?'

A desiccated man wearing a black cardigan beneath

an old grey jacket looked up at her from beneath the rim of his cap. She repeated the question in Russian. He parted the purple curtain behind him and coughed something unintelligible into the darkness.

When Bergstein appeared, he filled the doorway. Six-three, with broad shoulders and a barrel chest, he moved like a body-builder, rolling as he walked. His skin was pale pink and freckled. His three-day growth of beard had a ginger tinge to it but the stubble over his scalp was dark. He wore a burgundy leather coat over a thick black polo-neck and navy jeans. The polo-neck clung to him, drawing attention to stomach muscles that had softened to a slouch.

'Are you Boris Bergstein?'

'Who wants to know?'

'I'm a friend of Alan Kelly's.'

'That fucking prick.'

'We met last summer. At the Sputnik Cinema on Leninsky Prospekt. It was a double feature.'

Bergstein looked surprised, then annoyed. 'And the summer before?'

'At the dacha outside Domodedovo.'

'Okay, okay . . .'

'Who dreams up this rubbish?'

'Who do you think? Kelly. Who are you?'

'Kate March.'

'You with the FBI, too?'

Stephanie smiled but didn't reply.

Boris Bergstein was born in Odessa on the Black Sea in 1962. His father had worked in a factory making fur hats and rugs. He'd also been active in the flourishing black market, trading goods pilfered from work for fresh food, theatre tickets, clothes. In 1981, his parents decided to emigrate to Israel, which was an unwelcome shock for Bergstein, who liked Odessa and had never considered himself Jewish, despite his surname and the condemnatory stamp in his internal passport. In Israel, the family lived on a kibbutz, while Boris served three years in the Israeli Army. In 1985, he moved to West Berlin and entered the criminal food chain, joining a local Russian Jewish gang. He began as muscle for a loan shark. Later, he graduated to credit-card fraud. The gang had strong ties to Brighton Beach, the traditional first toehold in the United States. In 1988, Bergstein arrived in New York.

Now, he was an FBI informer under the control of Alan Kelly, a field operative who had transferred from a liaison with the IRS in Philadelphia to an undercover role in New York in 1999. Magenta House had provided Stephanie with the key contents of the Bergstein file, which included his codename – Sunflower – and the arrangement that he and Kelly had established before Kelly's departure for China in August.

Bergstein said, 'Let's get out of here.'

They stepped onto Brighton Beach Avenue. Around them, Stephanie heard Russian and Ukrainian. A train passed overhead, the clatter of steel on steel temporarily deafening. The ground trembled.

'Are you from New York?' Bergstein shouted.

'No.'

'Where, then?'

'Somewhere else.'

His grin revealed crooked yellow teeth. 'You people are all the same.'

'Do you like it here, Boris?'

'Sure. It feels like home.'

'What about Moscow?'

'What about it? I got a place there. In Krylatskoye. You know Krylatskoye?'

'No.'

Bergstein laughed coarsely. 'It's a fucking paradise. But it's not home.'

They headed down Brighton 2nd Street, past the playground at the junction of Brightwater Court. The playground was a stretch of concrete with climbing frames and swings for children. There were benches and tables for adults. Despite the autumnal chill, old men gathered in groups, playing dominoes, smoking, arguing.

'Kelly tells me you're in the furniture business.'

Bergstein shoved his hands in his pockets. 'With a couple of Ukrainian guys. We got a furniture store here in Brighton Beach, one in Bensonhurst and another in Bay Ridge. Also, I got a half-share in a garage in Borough Park.'

'Yet, like a new season, you turn up in Moscow four times a year.'

He shrugged. 'I have relatives . . .'

'Of course you do.'

They reached the boardwalk and turned left, past the Art Deco apartments that overlooked the Atlantic. A cutting wind skipped off the ocean. Bergstein took a cigarette from a pack of Kent, tore off the filter and cupped a giant hand around one end as he lit it.

'What do you know about Konstantin Komarov?'

He exhaled, the blue smoke vanishing instantly. 'I know he's rich. And that he has plenty of rich friends. I heard he's got a place on the Upper East Side, somewhere in the Sixties.'

'Does he ever come down here?'

'Sure.'

'What about his business interests?'

'Property, venture capital, import-export . . .'

'Import-export?'

'Uh-huh.'

'That covers just about anything, doesn't it?'

'He's got storage facilities over by the Bush Terminal Docks. You can see them from the Gowanus Expressway. You can almost jump through the window.'

'Anything else?'

'I heard he has a crew at Kennedy.'

'A crew at Kennedy?'

'You know. At the airport.'

'What kind of crew?'

'Well, not a fucking flight crew, that's for sure. Ground staff, customs, security, baggage-handlers . . . I don't know. Some kind of crew that makes sure nobody screws around with special deliveries.'

They stopped at Kalinka, a restaurant on the boardwalk. The large green neon sign over the entrance was broken. Bergstein hammered loudly on the locked door until the proprietor – a small man with octagonal glasses and worry for a face – let them in. Bergstein said they wanted tea and led Stephanie to a table by the tinted window that formed the entire boardwalk façade. There was a stage at one end of the dining room; a solitary microphone on a stand, speakers on either side, four coloured lamps suspended from a pole.

'What's Komarov like?'

'I don't know him.'

'From what you've heard.'

'These days, he pisses champagne and shits gold but

130

he used to be a vicious bastard. Probably still is underneath all those expensive clothes.'

'Any substance to the impression?'

Bergstein pulled a face; maybe, maybe not. 'How does a legend become a legend? It has to start somewhere.'

'Tell me.'

'When he was living in Moscow, he intervened in a dispute between two organizations. The Dolgoprudniki and Tsentralnaya. They were fighting over gambling concessions in Budapest. The disagreement got violent; there were some stabbings, a couple of shootings, plenty of beatings. Then a Dolgoprudniki deputy got blown to pieces by a car bomb in Budapest. The Hungarian police went crazy. Komarov intervened. Not for himself but for everyone. After a couple of days, an arrangement was reached and compensation agreed. Oleg Rogachev, who was head of Tsentralnaya then, agreed to pay two million US to Dolgoprudniki for casino protection rights. Komarov was asked to make the transfer in Budapest. Both sides trusted him. He picked a bag man he'd employed before, this guy from Tashkent. The thing is, he'd never asked him to deliver two million in used notes before. The rat took off. Disappeared into thin air.'

'With Tsentralnaya's money.'

'Yes. Leaving Komarov screwed. But he made the delivery anyway. It was too important so he used his *own* cash. Two million. That he just had lying around somewhere, like you do. You know, they say there are more one hundred dollar bills in Russia than there are in America. Anyway, Komarov made the payment and everyone was happy. He never even told Tsentralnaya or Dolgoprudniki about it. They only found out later. Meantime, he put a contract out on the courier. Half a million US. In Russia, you can get a man killed for a pack of Marlboro, so for that kind of money you'd think you could find anyone. But nothing happened. So Komarov went about his business, getting richer, and I guess the Uzbek thought he'd got away with it. But he hadn't. Three years later, he's on a business trip to Voronezh, just passing through . . .'

'The Don from the Don.'

'You know the story?'

'I just heard the name, not the details.'

'Okay. So this Uzbek, he's in Voronezh, just passing through, when he falls ill. He's got stomach pains. He goes to his hotel bar and has a couple of drinks to try to take his mind off it. Instead, he collapses. At the hospital, the doctor decides to open him up. It's a burst appendix or something. Anyhow, they cut it out, clean him up and sew him back together. Now he's got stitches across his gut so he needs to rest for a few days.

'According to the staff at the hospital, he was scared out of his mind. Tried to leave before he could stand. Didn't want to stay in Voronezh. Wanted to go home but wouldn't say where home was. As soon as he can walk, he discharges himself. It's evening. It's too late to leave the city so he's got to stay the night before catching an early train in the morning. He doesn't go back to the hotel where he collapsed. He picks a different place and spends the night there. In the morning, he decides to check out early. The lift comes up to the third floor. He steps in. Komarov is waiting for him. The doors close, the lift descends. Komarov gets out on the first floor. The lift then goes down to the lobby. The doors open and there's the Uzbek, dead on the floor, blood every-where. You know how Komarov killed him?'

'How?'

'A single punch. He was dead before he hit the ground.' Bergstein leaned across the table and lowered his voice, even though they were alone. 'Komarov hit him so hard that his fist went straight through the stitch-ing, straight through the abdominal cavity. He couldn't have killed him any quicker if he'd used a bullet.'

The tea arrived in a small tarnished samovar on a circular reed tray with two tall glasses suspended in brass holders. Bergstein filled the first glass and passed it to her.

'That's the thing about Komarov. He never forgets, he never forgives.'

'Like the FBI. Right?'

Bergstein looked as though she'd slapped him. 'What do you want?'

'George Salibi.'

'The banker . . .'

'He's coming into town tomorrow for three days. I want his schedule.'

For a while it seemed as though Bergstein wasn't sure. Then he nodded. 'Okay.'

'You can get it?'

'No problem.'

Stephanie smiled. 'Just what Kelly said to me.' She tasted her tea. It was strong and bitter. 'What happened to you down in Miami?'

The mere mention of the city seemed to deflate him. 'It was a property development near the Hialeah race-track. Some condos, some offices. I only had a small interest. Anyway, there were some broken contracts.

People didn't get paid, the police got called in, there were questions. Then it turned out some of the investors had tax problems with the IRS. That was the start of it. The next thing I know, the deal was dead and the FBI was at my door.'

'Just like that?'

'Just like that.'

On Broadway, there were street traders peddling jeans, trainers, jackets, sweatshirts. All the goods had a label, all of them were cheap. Counterfeit or stolen, nobody seemed to mind. Stephanie bought two pairs of Calvin Klein jeans, a pair of Reebok trainers and some underwear from a discount store. She also got a black rucksack and traded her leather jacket for a nasty, three-quarter length quilted coat with a Nike tick over the left breast. From a hardware store, she bought a large screwdriver, a hammer, a knife, a few nails, some black duct tape and two small combination padlocks. Finally, she went to a pharmacy for a few toiletries and a red nylon wash-bag.

Using Broadway as her centre, she trawled back and forth from the high Twenties, through the Thirties and into the Forties. She eventually settled on the Hotel Carter, on West 43rd Street, between Broadway and 8th Avenue. There was a small coffee shop beside the entrance. The lobby was on the first floor, up a dirty staircase. It was large and hideous with a psychedelic carpet made all the more effective by blue and red neon lighting. She'd wanted a place where the clientele weren't too particular about the quality of the accommodation and where the management wasn't too particular about the quality of the customers. The Hotel Carter looked like the right place.

She checked in under the name Jane Francis, a secondary, thumbnail identity provided by Magenta House. An Australian nurse from Melbourne, aged twenty-five, on a year-long sabbatical travelling around the world, if anyone cared to ask. No one did. She felt she could have written anything she liked on her room registration card. The ghost behind the desk gave her the key to a room on the sixth floor. Inside it, she bolted the door shut. For a while, she sat on the bed and did nothing. She listened to the muted sound of the street and to the rise and fall of footsteps along her corridor. The bed's mattress was lumpy, the springs shot, the headboard loose. She'd known hundreds of beds like it and the memories in which they featured turned her stomach.

The curtains had been closed when she entered. She went over to the window, parted them fractionally, and peeped through. Directly opposite, there was a twenty-four-hour garage, then the *New York Times* building. The blue garage doors were pulled shut. Above the exits, dotted along the length of the building, there were lights housed in opaque glass bowls with *Times* painted on them.

She checked the cupboard, the drawers, the space beneath the bed, the solidity of the walls. In the bathroom, she examined the toilet, the cistern, the panel around the edge of the bath. Back in the bedroom, she went to one corner of the room and peeled away part of the filthy carpet. There was no underlay beneath it, just floorboards.

She unpacked the clothes, zipped the tools into one of the rucksack's side pockets and fastened it with a padlock. In the bathroom, she distributed the toiletries

135

around the sink. In the bedroom, she messed up the bed. Then she left the Hotel Carter and returned to the Sherry Netherland on Fifth Avenue.

Once I've ordered room service, I turn on my laptop and draw down the files containing the plans of George Salibi's apartment on Central Park West. I can almost see the top of the building from my room, which overlooks Fifth Avenue, the Plaza and the south-eastern corner of Central Park. Then I call a number in the city that I haven't used for three years. It has nothing to do with Magenta House.

'Wu Lin?'

'Yeah.'

'The last time we met, your wrist was in plaster. You broke it in a car accident. We met on the Staten Island Ferry. I gave you five thousand dollars. Do you remember what you gave me?'

There's a long pause. Then: 'What you want?' I give him the list. 'When you want it?'

'As soon as possible.'

'Three days?'

'Try the day after tomorrow.'

'Too soon.'

'Try.'

His sigh is entirely predictable. 'I try . . .'

'How much?'

'Ten.'

'Fine. Give me the address.'

My food arrives. I sign for it and find that I've lost my appetite. Later, I strip down to my underwear and perform a series of exercises and stretches, taking some comfort from the pleasure of warm muscles. After half an hour, I have a bath and try to relax. Afterwards, I dress slowly. The TV is on, CNN regurgitating the same five-minute morsel of news between a slew of commercials and network self-promotion. Wherever Petra used to go, CNN stalked her. In hotel rooms, in airport lounges. I don't pay any attention to it. It's just aural wallpaper.

I've chosen a silk shirt that's such a deep, shimmering blue that under some lights it looks purple or black. I've also chosen a Max Mara charcoal trouser suit. It's beautifully cut, highly elegant, and I'm pleasantly surprised at how good I look in it. Which immediately makes me feel like a fraud. I don't do Max Mara or sophistication. Then again, who am I fooling? I am a fraud. I don't feel like Stephanie any more, I have no idea who Kate March really is and I know I'm not Petra Reuter.

A skyscraper of black steel and glass. The atrium was dominated by an enormous bronze horse rising from a square pond. Stephanie took the elevator. The doors parted at the twenty-ninth floor. She walked across polished granite to a curved reception desk carved from the same stone. Behind it, and behind a receptionist with hair that might also have been granite, capital gold letters formed a name: Gardyne Hill. An investment company established in 1971, it had endured twenty-seven years of mediocrity before sliding towards bankruptcy in 1998. That was when Mirsch, a Swiss investment firm, bought it, paying well over the value. At the time, Gardyne Hill had operated out of a crumbling block on 8th Avenue with a staff of seventy-one. Now, they occupied an entire floor of a prestigious building on East 52nd Street and had a staff of just nineteen. Not one of them had worked for Gardyne Hill before the Mirsch buy-out.

Stephanie was shown into an office and asked to wait. She declined coffee. When the door closed, she went over to the window. Ants scuttled up and down the congested sidewalk. She felt a lot further away than a mere twenty-nine floors.

Gardyne Hill could have had five times as many employees and there would still have been plenty of room on the twenty-ninth floor. On the surface, the simple economics made no sense. Beneath the surface, the truth was a complicated marriage that ensured Gardyne Hill paid no rent. The building was owned by a partnership between Saul Gulbenkian, the New York property magnate, George Salibi, founder of First Intercontinental, and Konstantin Komarov, owner of Mirsch, parent of Gardyne Hill. Gulbenkian had used First Intercontinental to finance the purchase from Cameron McGraw, the Canadian property developer and one of Gulbenkian's arch-rivals. It wasn't clear why or how Mirsch had become involved. That had been a matter for Gulbenkian, Salibi and Komarov.

On the walls of the office, there were a dozen paintings, all similar in style. To Stephanie's untrained eye, they might have been painted by the same artist. Oils on canvas, they were Russian rural scenes: icy forests, summer gardens, golden trees in autumn, harsh winter suns on fields of snow. She looked for a signature.

Behind her, a man said, 'Olga Svetlichnaya.'

Stephanie turned round. 'I'm sorry?'

The moment she saw him, she felt a kick of recognition in her chest. She thought she saw something similar in his expression. Curiously, she'd experienced no such feeling when she'd studied his file. She wondered who he was looking at. Kate March in her Max

138

Mara and make-up? Or the sullied creature beneath?

He was wearing a single-breasted suit – very dark blue – a cornflower blue shirt and a burgundy silk tie. He was less tanned than in the photographs she'd seen but his skin remained weather-beaten. She imagined a life at sea, not in air-conditioned offices and aircraft. He looked as lean in three dimensions as he had in two.

'The artist. That's her name. Olga Svetlichnaya.'

'Are they all by her?'

'Half of them. The other half are by Yuori Kugach. Her husband, as it happens.' He moved towards her. 'Poetic Realism. It's not everyone's taste – some people find it too bright, too simplistic – but for me, they have something I recognize.'

'Which is what?'

'Something you wouldn't understand. I'm Konstantin Komarov.'

They shook hands. His palm was dry and rough. When they sat down, he looked at her and then glanced at the framed photograph on his desk. She could only see the back of it.

There was some small talk, her part in it as bland and as automatic as required. Then Komarov moved on to Zbigniew Sladek and Almatinvest. 'He couldn't tell me much about Galileo Resources, Miss March. I had to find out for myself. It wasn't easy, believe me. It seems you work for a company with no office.'

'We're registered.'

He gave her the silence her answer merited and waited for a proper explanation. But what was there to say? Stephanie felt confused. There was something about him – and about her reaction to him – that

139

unnerved her. The initial reciprocity she'd thought she'd seen in him had gone. Now, he was inscrutable.

He produced a packet of Marlboro and offered her one. 'Do you mind if I smoke?'

She hadn't expected manners. She wasn't sure what she'd expected. But whatever it might have been, it hadn't been this. Somebody had got it wrong. She tried to picture the man in front of her surviving a decade in the Soviet prisons of the Siberian Far East. The image wouldn't stick.

'I spoke to Sladek and I have an idea of how I may be able to help you. He says you represent a group who have some money they'd like to invest – how shall I put it? – tax efficiently.'

'Yes.'

'Without having to answer too many questions about the money's origin.'

'Correct.'

'And I imagine they're anxious to protect their anonymity.'

'That's what I told Sladek, yes.'

'Are they represented in the US?'

'Yes.'

'And in Europe?'

'Yes.'

'Do they have a mixture of businesses?'

'A mixture?'

'Legitimate and non-legitimate.'

There were many options, he said, but his area of expertise was the offshore zones favoured by Russians. Switzerland was the primary choice, attracting almost fifty per cent of the business, although Cyprus was becoming increasingly popular.

'Visa-free entry, a reliable legal system, political stability and economic growth. Also, it's relatively close to Russia and has an established, expanding Russian population.'

Then there were the more exotic options. In 1999, Nauru and the Republic of Palau had accounted for almost forty per cent of funds transferred offshore. Even though that figure had declined to less than ten per cent, there were still advantages to be had. Nauru, a miniature sovereign state, was an eight-mile stretch of coral in the Pacific, not far from the equator. Until the 1980s, its main industry had been the mining of fossilized guano for fertilizers. That was when the local authorities turned Nauru into a zero-rated tax haven. In a run-down shack on the island there existed the Nauru Agency Corporation, with whom more than two hundred banks and companies from around the world had registered. Every day, tens of millions of dollars were laundered through such companies. The cost of registering with the NAC was less than ten thousand dollars a year. In 1999, more than seventy-five billion dollars passed through the island, the approximate equivalent of twelve million dollars per resident.

For a quarter of an hour, the information washed over her. She watched his mouth move but heard little of what he was saying. He had a small scar on his right cheek. His watch was a Breitling. She knew she was staring at him but she didn't care. In her mind, she returned to the hotel in Voronezh, the blood-splattered lift, the dead Uzbek on the floor. She couldn't see Komarov's bloody fist withdrawing from the pierced abdominal cavity.

He said, 'You can send a contaminated dollar to Nauru and get a pristine dollar back. Instead of seventy-five cents and some traceable residue.'

I feel sure I've met him before, yet I know with absolute certainty that I haven't. I know nothing about him but I know enough. He's not particularly good-looking yet I'm physically attracted to him in a way that I've never experienced before. The feeling is not in my heart. It's in my stomach. I'm listening to him so that I can memorize the sound of his voice, not what he's telling me. If, in a second from now, he asks me to kiss him, I will. If he said he wanted to make love to me, I'd let him.

I can't tell whether he feels anything similar or not. We're looking at each other – our eyes don't stray – but there's no way of knowing what's going on behind his. I feel ridiculous. All I really know about him is what I've read, which isn't good. There's no reason to feel like this. But I can't help it and that angers me. I don't do this sort of thing; I'm supposed to be beyond it. Was I not once the very definition of self-control?

I can't explain it but I feel sick with nerves. Then I remember why I'm here.

'The people I represent are looking to buy something.'

Komarov frowned. 'I thought that's what we were talking about. In a way . . .'

'They're looking to buy something through an associate of yours.'

'Who?'

'Koba.'

There was no visible reaction. 'What do they want to buy?'

'I'll tell Koba when I see him.'

'I don't know anyone called Koba.'

'Did you know someone called Oleg Rogachev?'

This time, Komarov stiffened.

Stephanie said, 'Of course you did. When he was murdered in Paris, there was a British intelligence officer with him. He was killed too. The assassin escaped and hasn't been caught. But the man behind the assassination has now been identified. Would you like to know who it is?'

Uncertainty bred agitation. 'I don't see what this has to do –'

'Would you like to know or not?'

Komarov tried to feign indifference with a nonchalant shrug. 'Okay. Who?'

'You.'

'Me?'

Stephanie nodded and hoped she looked like Petra. 'You hired someone to assassinate the head of Tsentralnaya.'

He looked a little relieved. 'You've been misinformed.'

Stephanie's heart wasn't in it. She knew his renewed confidence was misplaced. 'I'm sure that's what you genuinely think. I mean, why would you do such a thing? If it ever became common knowledge . . . well, at best, your reputation would be destroyed. At worst, Tsentralnaya would come after you.'

'Exactly.'

'The thing is, I have proof.'

'That's not possible.'

Her mouth was dry. She unzipped a leather document wallet and withdrew a single sheet of paper which

143

she passed across the desk. 'A photostat of a transfer of funds from one of your personal bank accounts to a private account in Andorra.'

'I don't recognize this. It's a forgery.'

'Actually, it isn't. It's real. So is the account in Andorra. It belongs to Sebastian Aumann, a second-rate hit man who was operating out of Brussels until August. That was when his Peugeot collided with a German articulated lorry on the A1 between Paris and Calais. But he left behind plenty of evidence to tie him to Rogachev's murder. And to you.'

She expected anger. Instead, she got puzzlement. 'This has nothing to do with me.'

Stephanie nodded. 'But that's no longer the point, is it? It doesn't matter who paid who. The assassin could even have been Koba himself. All that counts is what people believe. Perception is everything. Those who might be interested only need to be steered in the right direction.'

He slid the paper back to her.

'You're making a mistake.'

She looked directly into his eyes. 'I know.'

There was a charged silence.

Eventually, Komarov said, 'I've never met Koba. It was a mutual decision.'

'I don't believe that.'

'Think about it. We always use an intermediary.'

An arrangement not dissimilar to the one that she and Stern had used.

'Then put me in touch through the intermediary.'

'If that's what you want.'

Stephanie sensed a subtext.

'Is it what you want?' he asked.

144

Now, he was staring at her and she couldn't interpret it at all.

'Don't blackmail me. Others have tried. It never works.'

It didn't sound like a threat. It sounded more like a request. Or even a plea.

'What do you suggest, then?'

He ground out his cigarette in a china ashtray. 'Ask me.'

'I don't understand.'

'Ask me to do it for you as a favour.'

'Why?'

'Because then I can ask you for a favour in return.'

'What favour?'

'I don't know yet. But I'll think of something.'

It was a game she knew she shouldn't play. 'As a favour, then . . .'

'Good.'

'I'm staying at the Sherry Netherland. You can get me there.'

Komarov allowed himself a cold smile. 'I'll get you somewhere. You can be sure of it.'

9

Stephanie paused beneath the red awning of the Seven Joy Coffee Shop and pretended to understand the Chinese characters on the boards behind the glass. She glanced right, then left, and moved on. A truck had parked at the intersection of Mulberry Street and Broome Street. Two men were unloading carcasses of suckling pig and baby goat. In front of the Wang Hunan Restaurant, a trapdoor set into the sidewalk opened, black steel cracking against concrete. Bow-legged staff rose from a subterranean kitchen, shrouded in steam. The frosty air tasted of fried duck fat.

On the street, the Chinese congregated in groups, chattering, smoking, spitting. Stephanie passed a seafood market with fish laid out on beds of crushed ice, a beauty salon squeezed into a cupboard onto the street, an electrical goods retailer that also offered a fortune-telling service. She completed another circuit and headed down Mott Street.

A quarter of an hour later, she returned to the address on Mulberry Street, which was sandwiched between two stores, one selling kitchenware, the other selling VHS and DVD action movies from Hong Kong. At first, she missed it and had to step back; the slit between the buildings was barely shoulder-wide. The steps down to the basement were steep and poorly lit. At the bottom, there was an open door, a dark corridor ahead. Her senses sharpened, pupils expanding, nostrils keen to the scent of aniseed. There was a sign above the first door on the right: Chang Sun Travel Services Inc. The door was open, revealing a fat man, a desk, a telephone, crates in a corner, a haze of blue cigarette smoke. She moved on, passing a herbalist specializing in eczema and psoriasis, an optician, a meat-importer. The Wu Lin Dental Practice was the eighth room she came to.

There were six people – all Chinese – in a waiting room that only had space for one chair. When Stephanie appeared, the gossip stopped, all eyes turning to her. Then, curiosity satisfied, she was ignored and the chatter resumed. When the far door opened, a short, skinny woman emerged, a whining child in tow. Behind them stood a man in his fifties. Five eight tall, greasy silver hair, eyes lost in folds of spotted skin behind small, round glasses. He saw Stephanie, beckoned her to the front of the queue and ushered her into the room beyond. Nobody seemed to mind. He closed the door behind them.

The dentist's chair was blue leather, the holes on the armrests sealed with silver duct tape. The instruments on the rusted tray beside the chair looked old. On a square of medicated paper there was a bloody tooth.

Wu Lin said, 'You got the money?'

'I see my stuff before you see the money.'

'Not here.'

'Where is it?'

He shrugged. 'Close.'

'Then let's go and have a look.'

'First, I count the money.'

'You can count it but you can't keep it. Not until I've checked everything.'

Wu Lin considered this for several moments. 'Okay.'

Stephanie unzipped her jacket, pulled up her grey sweatshirt and unfastened the money-belt strapped to her waist. She opened it and handed over the notes, which were secured by an elastic band.

'Ten thousand, in used fifties, twenties and tens.'

Wu Lin began to count. He was wearing a white coat in need of a wash. Stephanie glanced at his assistant, who was sitting on a stool in the corner. A dull puffy face, a dumpy body, she looked young and bored. Stephanie stared at her until she averted her gaze.

When Wu Lin had finished, he said, 'Very difficult.'

'I'm sorry?'

'To get what you want. Too quick, not enough time.'

'I thought you'd already got everything.'

'Some of it. But very difficult. Cost more money.'

Stephanie took a step forward and held out her hand. 'We agreed a price.'

After a moment's indecision, Wu Lin returned the cash to her. 'Not enough. If you want it tomorrow, not enough.'

'What are you saying?'

'Fifteen.'

'Fifteen thousand?'

'Can't do it for less.'

The coldness descended. 'Cheating me is a mistake.'

Wu Lin seemed impervious to the threat. 'Not easy, what you want. Dangerous, expensive. Ten thousand, I lose. Fifteen, I break even . . . maybe.'

Stephanie knew that was a lie.

Wu Lin went over to the table next to the assistant,

scribbled something on a piece of paper and handed it to Stephanie. An address on Canal Street. 'Tomorrow afternoon. Four o'clock.'

When she returned to the Sherry Netherland, there was a message from Komarov. At six, she walked down to the St Regis at 5th Avenue and 55th. He was waiting for her in the King Cole bar. His clothes were different but the same: a beautiful double-breasted grey suit, a cream cotton shirt, oval gold cufflinks, a royal blue silk tie. Stephanie wore black trousers, a pair of DMs, a long-sleeved T-shirt – a burgundy body with orange sleeves – and a scruffy black jacket. She felt less than underdressed; she felt gauche. She wanted to apologize but said nothing.

Komarov was drinking a martini. He summoned a waiter. 'What would you like?'

At that moment, a triple shot of vodka.

'Champagne?' Komarov suggested.

Under the circumstances, she could think of nothing more ridiculous. 'Are we celebrating something?'

'I don't know. Are we?'

'Champagne would be fine. Thank you.'

When the waiter moved away, Komarov passed her a folded piece of paper. She opened it. The address was written in biro.

'Who am I looking for?'

'He'll be looking for you. His name is Mikhail Bukharin.'

'And he's Koba's intermediary?'

'He'll take you to the intermediary.'

'An intermediary between you and the intermediary? Isn't that a little paranoid?'

'Under the circumstances, no.'

'What circumstances?'

'I can't trust you.'

'You don't know that.'

'You blackmailed me. Remember?'

'I thought I asked you for a favour.'

He didn't reply.

'How will I recognize him?' she asked. Komarov described him. When he'd finished, she said, 'God, what happened to him?'

'A career with KGB Alpha. That's what happened to him.'

'KGB Alpha?'

'It was part of Spetsnaz, the Soviet Special Forces, but it was under KGB control, not military control. The elite of the elite. Back in 1979, Bukharin was part of the team that stormed the presidential palace in Kabul. That was the beginning of the Afghan War. Bukharin was the one who put the bullet into Prime Minister Amin.'

'And that's something to be proud of, is it?'

'He spent the whole war in Afghanistan and he's got the scars to prove it. All the time I was growing up, all the years I wasted in prison, I never met a man tougher than Bukharin.'

'When do I meet him?'

'Ten o'clock tomorrow morning. If no one comes by twenty past, leave. Then go back the next day, same time. If you have three no-shows, call me again.'

Stephanie's champagne arrived. She took a sip and looked around. A few beautiful people, rather more wealthy people, a mural by Maxfield Parrish, a sense of stillness, an absence of passing time. She turned back to Komarov, who was watching her.

She said, 'You could have left this information for me in your message.'

He said, 'Yes. I know.'

Stephanie entered the coffee shop on Union Square. It wasn't busy. A Roy Orbison song was playing; she recognized the voice but not the tune. She took a booth halfway down one wall and ordered some coffee. It was ten to ten.

The previous evening, she'd only spent half an hour with Konstantin Komarov, yet he'd lingered all night. Their conversation had been awkward and trivial; they'd talked but had said nothing. It was as though each was scared of asking the other a question for fear of the answer. At six-thirty, she'd walked back to the Sherry Netherland, her concentration shattered.

Now, after a night of fitful sleep, she wasn't sure why Komarov had bothered to meet her at all. She drank a second cup of coffee. At twenty past ten, a squat man entered, wearing a blue anorak, a wool cap with GIANTS across the brow, heavy boots and a pair of grey trousers. He scanned the room, ignored the waitress who tried to escort him to a table, and approached Stephanie.

The scars were just as Komarov had described them: the mesh around the left eye, the livid gash over the left cheek that ran down to the jaw-line, the shiny ruined skin in front of the ear. She looked at his left hand; two fingers missing.

He sat down opposite her. 'We wait.'

His English was heavily accented. The waitress poured him some coffee. They sat in silence. At quarter to eleven, Stephanie's phone rang. It was Boris Bergstein. He had the information she wanted. They arranged to meet. Just before eleven, Bukharin's mobile rang. The call consisted of a few gruff exchanges and lasted fifteen seconds.

They took a cab to West 54th Street and got out in front of a drab brick building of approximately twenty storeys. At street level, the entrances and windows had been boarded and padlocked. Once, there had been a large canopy over the main entrance; where it had met the building, there was now a pale brick scar. Stephanie looked up. Most of the windows had ancient air-conditioning units installed beneath them. The building tapered through the upper floors, creating some balconies halfway up, again at two-thirds, at three-quarters and at penthouse level. Bukharin led her to a tradesman's entrance. Beside it, an old sign remained: The Somerset.

He had a key for the padlock. When they were inside, he pulled the door shut, snuffing out the light and sound of the city. He produced a torch from his pocket and led the way through a series of narrow corridors. Eventually, they came to a large open space where slices of dusty daylight seeped through cracks in the boards over the windows. A single bulb hung from a heavy bronze hook that had once held a massive chandelier. The bulb was at the end of a long, orange rubber cable that fell to the floor and snaked away to a dark corner.

They were in a lobby. There were fluted columns rising from a black and white stone floor. The reception desk remained in place. Behind it, a mahogany grid of cubby-holes stood empty. In a cage towards the rear of the ground floor, there was a lift of polished wood and etched glass. The air was cold, still and damp. There was evidence of squatters: crushed cans, soiled newspaper, discarded syringes.

Bukharin headed for the broad staircase, which rose to the first floor before splitting left and right. They climbed to the fifth floor and headed down a long passage. All the doors were open. At this height, the windows were not boarded but they were dirty. The light they allowed was flat and grey. The furniture had gone from the rooms but the original wallpaper remained, black patches of damp coming through rotten plaster. The carpets had been stripped, leaving naked floorboards. Some fittings had been plundered, others had been abandoned. Wherever they were, Stephanie was aware of the soft patter of rats.

At the end of the passage, Bukharin waved her into a suite of interconnecting rooms. Tall ceilings, double doors, large fireplaces. The green flock wallpaper had a *fleur-de-lys* design, reminiscent, to Stephanie's mind, of a cheap curry house. When she turned round, Bukharin had backed up to the wall and had closed the door through which they'd just come. She was about to ask what he was doing when she saw the gun. A snub-nosed Colt revolver.

She flinched – she couldn't help it – and regretted it immediately.

Bukharin was too far away from her. Besides, for all her training in hand-to-hand combat, here was a man who was a master. A man who could probably take Boyd. A man for whom two missing fingers and the disadvantage of twenty years probably counted for nothing. The alternative was to run in the opposite direction. To retreat, to zigzag towards the far door. But Bukharin was ex-KGB Alpha, the best of Spetsnaz, a

153

former star of the Soviet Special Forces elite. Most likely, she'd be dead before she got halfway.

'Strip.'

She assumed she'd misheard. 'What?'

'Your clothes. Take them off.'

It was a large room and she was in the middle of it. There were no props, nothing to hide behind. No ready diversions. Bukharin rolled his wrist, drawing attention to the Colt.

She saw she had no alternative. She shrugged off her thick donkey jacket. Straight away, the chill nipped at her. Boots, socks, jeans, jersey, shirt. Bukharin watched, inscrutable. She stood in front of him dressed only in black underwear, goose-bumps for skin.

'Everything.'

It wasn't just her body that was cold. Her mind was frozen, too. She unfastened her bra and let it drop. She hooked a thumb through her knicker elastic and then stopped. *I can't do this.* But she did, and she took care not to let any expression cross her face.

When she was naked, Bukharin waved the gun at her again. 'The wall. Between the windows. Go.'

She turned and walked to the edge of the room, her ears alert for the sound of the click. The floorboards scratched the soles of her feet. When she looked back, he was moving towards her clothes. He picked up her bra and examined it. Stephanie's anxiety made way for perplexity. Then she saw him reach inside his pocket and pull out a device no large than a mobile phone. He ran it over the bra and then discarded the garment. Next, he picked up a sock. Relief surged through her. He was checking for bugs.

When Bukharin had finished, he retreated to the

wall and whistled. It echoed. To her left, there was movement in the darkness. A man emerged from the adjoining room. He stopped in the doorway, leaned against the frame and crossed his arms.

Something stirred within Stephanie. The face was vaguely familiar; long, thin, bony. She knew he was a Russian before he spoke; she'd seen his photograph at Magenta House.

He was smirking. 'You can get dressed.'

Medayev. That was it. Anatoli Medayev. The dirty hair was longer than in the photograph she'd seen. It was collar-length and short at the sides. The scraggy goatee beard was new but there was no longer any doubt in her mind. And with the recollection came shock. Medayev, one of the two candidates for Koba, here, in front of her, supposedly acting as a liaison for Koba. Magenta House had narrowed it down to a straight choice between Medayev and Vladimir Vatukin.

She still hadn't moved, to Medayev's evident surprise and pleasure. He said, 'If you don't want to put your clothes on, that's okay.'

Her senses gathered, she scampered towards the centre of the room.

Medayev lit a cigarette. 'I've heard people say that it's sexier to watch a woman dress than to watch her strip. Personally, I don't agree. Kostya tells me you want to meet Koba.'

Stephanie stepped into her jeans and began to fasten the buttons. 'That's right.'

'Why?'

'I'll tell him when I see him.'

'If you don't tell me, you won't see him at all. Anyway, I speak for Koba.'

If you are Koba, that would certainly be true, wouldn't it? One bullet into you and I'd step into a future free from the past.

'I represent a group . . .'

'People like you always do. What do they want?'

She chose to play it straight. 'Plutonium-239. Above ninety-three per cent purity.'

'How much?'

'Not less than eight kilos.'

He whistled. Another haunting echo. 'That's going to be very expensive.'

'Money's not a problem.'

He arched his eyebrows. 'You're not much of a negotiator, are you? Perhaps your clients would be better off if they met Koba face-to-face. Perhaps *I* should meet them face-to-face.'

'They use me for the same reason that Koba uses you. They're shy.'

'But Koba's not the one who needs something.'

'Koba's the one who stands to make tens of millions of dollars. Maybe . . .'

Medayev sucked on his cigarette for a few moments. 'Koba will need to know the identity of the end users. I mean, he doesn't want to find out that he's selling Plutonium-239 to a bunch of fucking Chechens, does he?'

'They're not Chechens.'

'Well, excuse me, *sweetie*, but I'm going to need more than your word on that.'

'When the time comes, you'll get it. For the moment, I don't even know whether Koba exists. Or whether he can deliver.'

*   *   *

Stephanie was late. Boris Bergstein wore a black leather coat, instead of the burgundy one he'd worn before, and a thick rust-coloured jersey. His faded Levi's were a full cut but his monstrous thighs made them look tight. Central Park was busy: joggers, dog-walkers, new mothers pushing babies, lunatics muttering to themselves. The trees were brilliant ruby, shimmering gold and emerald. Stephanie could smell the season as easily as she could see it. As a child, it had been her favourite, a time of cold afternoons, bonfires and glittering night skies. The season of decay, her mother had called it.

'Salibi arrives this afternoon. From Frankfurt.'

Stephanie knew that he'd been in Geneva the previous day, and in Beirut for the two days prior to that. It was assumed that the detour through Geneva had been to collect the disk.

'What's his itinerary?'

'He's busy tonight. Tomorrow, he's at the bank. Tomorrow night, he's out of town. I couldn't find out where but he has a place in Connecticut. He likes to spend time out there when he can. Sometimes he commutes, especially in the summer.'

'How far is it?'

'He has a helicopter. The day after tomorrow, he's not due back at First Intercontinental until midday.'

Providing Stephanie with the window of opportunity she needed, and that Magenta House had promised.

'What else?'

'At the end of the week, he leaves for Montreal, then Paris.'

'Fine.'

They walked for a while, then Bergstein said, 'Can I ask you something?'

'What?'

'How long's that bastard going to keep me on the hook?'

'Kelly?'

He nodded. 'At the start, he said a year. It's been almost three.'

'The answer is, I don't know.'

'But you work with him . . .'

'Well . . .'

'Will you speak to him?'

'Look, I really don't know him that well.'

'You know him well enough to be allowed to use me.'

Stephanie was tempted to confess the truth. Instead, she opted for a cheap lie. 'My superior arranged it.'

'I just want to put this behind me. I'm tired of it, you know?'

'Tired of what?'

Bergstein looked out across the park and shrugged helplessly. 'Everything.'

We're in a café on Amsterdam Avenue that prides itself on flouting the city's smoking regulations. I'm drinking hot chocolate, Bergstein's got a double espresso in front of him. He's pulling the white filter off a Kent cigarette. We've been here for almost an hour.

It's extraordinary how wrong a first impression can be. The moment I saw him in the Surgut Pharmacy, I knew exactly who Boris Bergstein was. A playground bully who had always relied upon his physique to get what he wanted. A man for whom criminality was a career choice. A man for whom money meant justification. A probable drunk, I could easily see him beating his girlfriend. But I was wrong. He's

158

not a saint but he's not what I thought he was, either. Even though he's tried to be.

'I was in fights all the time when I was growing up. When you're my size, you can't help it. People pick on you to prove how tough they are. At first, you just defend yourself, using whatever you can. Later, you strike first. It's still defence. It's just more efficient.'

I hear about his childhood in Odessa, then the move to Israel. *'It was a fucking nightmare. The Israelis treated us worse as Russians than the Ukrainians treated us as Jews.'* Life in West Berlin was better but the gravitational pull of crime proved impossible to resist. The only people he knew in the city were in gangs. *'At first, you tell yourself it's nothing. You do a favour, you run an errand. Slowly, you get sucked in.'* Bergstein's weakness made his graduation to full criminality inevitable. After the loan sharks and frauds, he drifted towards gambling, narcotics, then prostitution.

'They sent me to Moscow,' he tells me out of the corner of his mouth, as he lights the Kent. *'I ran a street rank on Voznesensky, just off Tverskaya. Me and this other guy. Arkoyam, a cruel bastard. In theory, it was easy work. The girls lined up along a wall. Even when it was fifteen below. We took calls from clients and dispatched them one by one. The classy ones we delivered and collected, the others went by public transport. They were all on the clock. The ones that were late back – or came back without the right money – well, they only did it once. We saw to that. At least, Arkoyam did . . .'*

A sickening chill runs through me. I close my eyes, then open them immediately because I don't like what I see in the darkness.

'Where did they come from?'

159

'All over. Moldova, Ukraine, Belarus, sometimes the Baltic States. Not too many from the south. Russians don't like to fuck blacks. As for foreigners, they only want to fuck Russians.'

'What happened?'

'In the end, I couldn't take it any more. The beatings . . . I mean, you should have seen some of these girls. Children, really. Skin-and-bone, hooked on junk and drink, thousands of kilometres from home.' He shook his head. 'Arkoyam didn't mind, though. He just loved the violence. He didn't feel alive unless he was kicking someone to pieces. Half my size, he was, a real psycho. Do you know how I could tell if a girl was a newcomer or a veteran?'

'How?'

'If she was hot off the bus, she'd be terrified of me. Once she'd been around a while, she'd be terrified of him.'

From Moscow to West Berlin to New York, Bergstein's criminal career was a litany of incompetence sprinkled with occasional, unexpected successes. The furniture stores were a recent venture, a bridge between two worlds, one honest, the other corrupt, the business itself on the cusp of both.

'I'm just looking for one score,' he tells me.

'Aren't we all?'

'A hundred thousand dollars, that's all I need.'

'What's that going to buy you?'

'There's this guy I know in Fort Lauderdale. He's setting up a boat-charter business. It's clean. For a hundred grand, I'm in.'

'What does Alan Kelly say about that?'

'He says I belong to the FBI for as long as the FBI want me.'

The same contractual bondage that Magenta House originally imposed upon me. He lets the rest of his professional life unfold. It's not hard to see why the FBI marked him as an

160

informer. He's incompetent but not an imbecile, he gives off the right aura but he's vulnerable. He looks the part and that's important. All his life, he's been out of his league, stumbling from one error of judgement to the next. He's just a big child with a big heart who never got the direction he needed. By the time we're ready to leave, we've crossed some invisible barrier. We're not friends, we don't trust each other, but we're no longer complete strangers.

As we rise from the table, Bergstein says, 'You want to see Salibi in the flesh?'

Chinatown. Stephanie examined the building from across the street, raising one hand to shield her eyes against a sun as sharp as a splinter. At ground level, she saw the New China Diamond Exchange, one of six brash jewellery stores along one block of Canal Street's north side. Above the exchange, there were four floors of brick. Air-conditioning units protruded from frosted windows obscured by painted Chinese characters. She crossed the street, slicing through two directions of slug-gish traffic.

Inside, Stephanie was directed to a staircase at the rear of the building and told to go to the top floor. She found Wu Lin in an office overlooking an alley. He was flanked and dwarfed by two sweating Chinese, one in Hilfiger, the other in Reebok. There were faded photo-graphic prints on the wall, promotional shots for a Chinese tour operator. Mountains, dramatic gorges, broad rivers, no cliché overlooked.

Both of Wu Lin's men were fat, she noted, and it was a small, tight space. One of them came forward to frisk her. Wu Lin remained behind his desk, smoking a cigarette. He'd swapped his white coat for a light grey suit and purple shirt. The top three buttons were unfastened, revealing a thick gold chain.

'You got the money?'

The Chinese who'd frisked her now stood behind her.

Stephanie said, 'Where's my stuff?'

Wu Lin bent down and lifted a black rucksack onto the table.

'I'll check it first. Then I'll give you the money.'

'Fifteen thousand?'

'Fifteen thousand.'

He waved his hand over the rucksack and took a step back. She opened it and spread the contents across the desk. First, the gun, a Glock P17, and a customized Steyr silencer. Stephanie dismantled the weapon. It was light – a mere 600gm without the magazine – due to the lightweight synthetic grip and frame unit. Fully loaded with a seventeen-round clip, the Glock still only weighed 860gm. She examined the unusual single trigger system with its auxiliary trigger set into the main blade. She'd asked for two full magazine clips. Wu Lin had taken the precaution of keeping the thirty-four rounds in a separate box.

She inspected the other items. Three Yugoslav compact CS gas grenades, three incendiary devices on timers synchronized by remote control, a Feissler bolt-gun with two barbed bolts, night-vision goggles, a breathing mask, a Korean radio microphone with a grip not dissimilar to the Glock's but with a twenty-five centimetre metal probe instead of a barrel, an Aiwa two-way radio linked to a Motorola mobile phone, a skeleton remote for the garage.

Stephanie didn't like the idea of letting Wu Lin cheat

her but recognized she had no option. Not for the sake of five thousand dollars. She replaced the items in the rucksack, closed it, and handed the money-belt to him. She waited for the frown.

He looked up at her. 'Only ten thousand here.'

Slowly, she reached into her jacket pocket and pulled out a roll of dollars, which she held in front of his face. 'This is the extra,' she said. 'Count it. And then count yourself lucky.' She dropped the notes onto the table in front of him. 'Cheating me is still a mistake.'

10

The apartment was in a block on Brighton 5th Street. Stephanie took the stairs to the third floor. Bergstein was waiting for her at the end of the corridor. He was dressed in black. His jaw was smooth, cheap after-shave flavouring the air.

It was a small two-bedroom place. The sitting room was dominated by a cabinet that housed a vast television, which was on – a rerun of *Dallas*, Sue Ellen's lips quivering absurdly – but without sound. There were five other people in the room, three women, two men. Stephanie knew that Bergstein was thirty-nine. None of the others looked younger than fifty. They were dressed for an occasion: stiff skirts, jackets, solid hair, make-up like icing on a cake, fake jewels around their throats. Bergstein introduced them – Max and Mia Ivanov, Yelena Jankovic, Pyotr Nedved – saving the oldest-looking woman until last.

'This is my mother. Maria Bergstein.'

She was small – no more than five foot two – with the skeletal fragility of a sparrow. Standing beside her brute son, the pair posed a genetic question.

Stephanie looked at her own clothes: khaki trousers, black boots, an orange shirt over a white vest and a mountaineering jacket by The North Face. 'I'm sorry, I didn't realize I was coming to . . . I would have dressed . . .'

Maria Bergstein turned to her son. 'You didn't tell her, Borya?'

She looked back at Stephanie and rolled her eyes. Pyotr Nedved touched her on the arm. 'Did he tell you who we're going to see?'

'No.'

Nedved's eyes lit up. 'Alla Pugacheva.'

Stephanie smiled. The name meant nothing to her.

There was a coach to take them to New Jersey. Every seat was occupied. Mia Ivanov said there were other coaches making the trip from Brighton Beach. Bergstein placed Stephanie next to his mother. As the coach turned onto Coney Island Avenue, she took hold of Stephanie's hand.

'You're not Russian and you're too young. That's two reasons why you can't understand. Borya thinks it's a big joke. But for those of us who are old enough – and who were there – it's important. We can't forget. We shouldn't forget. And Alla understands that. She suffered too but she made it, and we all watched and we were all with her. The thing about Alla is, she never forgot where she came from. She never forgot us and she never thought she was better than us. I tell you this, in the very darkest times, she was a light. And now that things are better, we can all look back together and remember how it was. For those of us who live here now, this is a way to remember Russia. We didn't just leave behind the bad things. We left behind *everything*.'

Maria Bergstein gave Stephanie the biography: the run-ins with authority, the husbands, the vodka and cigarettes, the lovers, the astonishing hair, the battles with fluctuating weight. And the music. As subtle as a punch to the solar plexus; sentimental traditional ballads, gypsy music, big show-tunes, anything. Alla Pugacheva, *the* pop star of the Soviet era, a cultural icon with album sales of more than two hundred million. Brash, brassy, but possessed of an undeniable voice. Starting as a teenager in the Sixties, through the Seventies and Eighties she survived and prospered, eventually outlasting the system with which she would forever be associated.

'To understand Alla, it's not enough to be Russian,' Maria sighed, as they hit the outskirts of Atlantic City. 'You have to have lived in the Soviet Union.'

Outside the Trump Taj Mahal, there were lines of coaches and stretch limousines. Glittering lights swamped the darkness. An enormous billboard had a painting of Alla: slender, red-haired, apparently in her thirties.

As they stepped off the coach, Stephanie tugged at Bergstein's jacket sleeve and hissed into his ear, 'What am I doing here?'

'What would you be doing if you weren't here? Sitting in your hotel playing with yourself?'

'If you think this is going to smooth out your problems with the FBI, you're wrong.'

Bergstein was cross. 'I had plenty of takers for your ticket. People who've always wanted to see Alla but who've never had the chance. I just thought . . .' He stopped himself and then made a dismissive gesture with his hand. 'Forget it.'

Inside the casino, the six-thousand-seat concert hall was packed. The majority of the audience had been cloned from those who'd gathered in the Brighton Beach apartment. All in their Sunday best. A mass of henna hair, a padded shoulders class reunion.

People were moving into the arena to find their seats. Bergstein touched Stephanie's arm and pointed. 'Over there. The enclosure. See him? Salibi . . .'

It took Stephanie a moment to identify him. She saw Ruth Steifel first: dark skin, short black hair, the bodyguard wore a blue dress that failed to conceal her muscles. Beside her, Salibi looked distinctly unimpressive. Balding, round, in a suit that was too large for him.

'In here, he's like you,' Bergstein said.

'What do you mean?'

'He's an intruder. We're not in Atlantic City any more. We're not even in the United States. We're in Russia.'

'So what's he doing here?'

'I don't think he's here for the music. Why don't you go and ask him?'

There were sixteen seats in Salibi's exclusive enclosure. Only four were occupied. 'Do you recognize the man with blond hair, or the redhead?'

Bergstein took his time. 'No.'

The lights went down and the audience roared its approval. When Alla Pugacheva took to the stage, dressed in black with a thin cream silk gown, beneath a tower of blonde curls, she looked twenty years older and thirty pounds heavier than she'd appeared on the billboard outside.

In the darkness, Stephanie became aware of late arrivals filling the seats in George Salibi's enclosure. By the time the show was over, it was almost full.

At the final encore, the audience rose to its feet, cheering, clapping. Alla waved, blew kisses and promised to return. Then she was gone. The house lights went up. There were smiles and tears. A mesh of moving bodies partly obscured Stephanie's view of the enclosure.

Bergstein said, 'The one with a face like a ferret. That's Vatukin. Vladimir Vatukin, the new boss of Tsentralnaya. And there . . . see the girl?'

There were several. 'Which one?'

'The beautiful one.'

Stephanie saw what Bergstein meant. For the first time, she understood the meaning of the phrase 'she moved like a colt'. She was tall with short dark red hair, parted on the left and swept to the right. The other girls – with their hard curves and Versace – looked cheap beside her. Although Stephanie was sure that 'cheap' was the one thing they weren't; four figures a night, she guessed.

'That's Natalya Markova. Vatukin's mistress. She used to belong to Rogachev.'

'Belong?'

'Belong. That's the way it works. When Rogachev was killed, Vatukin took over Tsentralnaya. And Natalya.'

'Is that significant?'

Bergstein laughed. 'You mean, were they screwing before Rogachev was killed?'

'Yes.'

'I doubt it. But it's possible.'

'If they weren't, then it's strange, don't you think?'

'Looking at her, not at all. I'd be tempted myself. What man wouldn't?'

'A smart man. The kind of man who'd see how such a thing might look.'

'Vatukin's better than a smart man. He's a hard man. He doesn't care how things look. He never did before, so why should he now? He's head of Tsentralnaya. Somebody doesn't like it? Screw them. What are they going to do about it?'

'What about her?'

'Look, he's an ugly bastard. He likes the look of Natalya, he sees her as a bonus that goes with his new position. As for her, she may be beautiful but she's not an idiot. She's practical. As tough as he is, in many ways. It makes sense, it keeps her in ice.'

Stephanie couldn't argue with the logic. She continued to stare into the enclosure. Natalya looked slightly familiar. Stephanie wondered if she'd ever been a model. She wouldn't have been the first one to end up on the arm of a criminal.

'Who's the man on Salibi's right?'

'Alexander Kosygin. Owner of Weiss-Randall, a pharmaceutical company.'

'A Russian?'

'Yes. But based here in New York.'

He was tall and slim. Stephanie guessed he was in his sixties. His grey hair was oiled back and cut short. His posture made him look haughty; ramrod erect, head held high, people viewed down the barrel of a long nose.

'What's his story?'

'He used to be in the Soviet Red Army. A lieutenant-general. Now, he looks like he was born on Wall Street. What an asshole. It's people like him who really screwed us all. For years, they kept us down. Then, when it was all over, they stole everything and disappeared into the night.'

'Weiss-Randall doesn't sound like a Russian company.'

'It's American. But Kosygin bought it for cash. Where do you reckon he got that from? Not from thirty years of Red Army pay, that's for sure.'

Stephanie froze. Everyone seemed to freeze; the people around her, the people in the enclosure. He was wearing a black single-breasted suit without a tie. Komarov. One of the late arrivals. Talking to another of the late arrivals. Anatoli Medayev. Or was it Koba? In any event, the last man to see her naked.

Bergstein was still talking but she couldn't hear a word he was saying. Komarov was pointing at Medayev, almost jabbing him in the chest. Vatukin said something. Natalya stood behind him, towering over him, silent, decorative. Kosygin said something to Komarov and then Medayev laughed. Salibi turned round and made a remark that everyone enjoyed and the tension dissipated.

Bergstein said, 'Come on. We don't want to miss the bus.'

Back at Brighton Beach, there was a party in Kalinka, the restaurant on the boardwalk where Stephanie and Bergstein had drunk tea. The green neon sign above the door had been mended. Inside, the tables were dressed: starched white cloth, glass, china, cutlery. There was a large buffet running the length of the far wall; sides of smoked salmon on silver salvers, tureens of soup, glass bowls filled with fish roe on beds of crushed ice, salads, plates of sausage and cold meat. Everyone at the restaurant had been at the show in Atlantic City. On stage, at one end of the dining room, beneath the hot glare of stage-lamps, there was an Alla Pugacheva double; taller, slimmer, with straight blonde hair, she sang to a backing track, running through the numbers from the

Trump Taj Mahal. Stephanie saw she wouldn't get anything out of Bergstein for the rest of the night. He was drinking to get drunk.

She left and caught a cab back to Manhattan. Her weary head against the window, she watched skyscraper lights sparkle in the night. It was quarter to midnight when she let herself into her room at the Sherry Netherland. She kicked the door shut with her heel and shrugged off her jacket.

'Don't tell me you've got all her albums.'

Startled, I jump. And because I'm tired, the shock makes me angry.

'What the hell are you doing here? Get out.'

Komarov is sitting in a chair by the window. The curtains are drawn. He's helped himself to a beer. He doesn't move.

'How did you get in here?'

An idiotic question to ask a man who's resourceful enough to launder a billion dollars.

'You don't look like an Alla fan to me.'

'Alla who?'

He smiles but he's not amused. 'I saw you.'

I haven't got the energy to resist. 'What can I tell you? I'm a fan of henna hair. I heard Atlantic City was the place to be tonight.'

He opens his hands. 'Well, that explains everything. I'll go, then.' But he doesn't. He stays sitting, staring at me, making me feel more awkward with every moment. 'You're wondering why I'm here. I'm wondering why you were there.'

I don't want to get sucked into this. 'I saw you arguing with Anatoli Medayev.'

'We were talking about you. He said he didn't trust you. He said he thought you were a fake.'

171

I feel myself tense. 'What did you say?'

'I said I didn't think you were. But I wasn't sure.' He takes a swig from the bottle. 'But that was before I saw you. You were on your way out. The big guy you were with – what's his name?'

I don't say anything.

'I think I've seen him before. A man that size is hard to forget.'

'I was following you.'

The bluntness of the statement catches him by surprise. 'Why?'

'The same reason you're here. I have a feeling about you but I'm not sure . . .'

The lie is automatic and, like all the best lies, it's laced with truth. Whatever he had planned, he's abandoning it. I can see it in his expression. We're silent for a full minute and it's the most comfortable I've felt since I entered the room.

Then he says, 'Are you hungry?'

I can't even think about food.

As they stepped out of the Sherry Netherland, a black Lexus pulled up in front of them. Komarov opened the rear door for her and they climbed in. He leaned forward and muttered something to the driver. They headed down Fifth Avenue. He told her he had to make some calls. Stephanie said she didn't mind and gazed out of the window, feigning disinterest. She picked up fragments and worked out where the calls were going. Zurich, Paris, Los Angeles. She looked at her watch. Five past midnight in Manhattan, five past six in the morning in Switzerland and France, five past nine in the evening in Los Angeles. He discussed rates of interest, bank transfers, investment portfolios. A busy schedule emerged: a forthcoming trip to Europe – Zurich, probably Paris, Valencia, possibly London, Berlin, St Petersburg and Stockholm – followed by a return to Manhattan via Montreal. Unless circumstances changed.

From Union Square, they took Broadway to Broome Street, then Mercer Street. Tomoko was a diminutive Japanese restaurant above an art gallery. The woman who greeted them recognized Komarov and spoke to him in Japanese. She led them to a private room. Komarov removed his shoes and sat down cross-legged on a silk cushion. Stephanie sat opposite him. She let him choose and he ordered a mixture of sushi and sashimi, some sake and two bottles of Kirin.

'Where did you learn to speak Japanese?'

'I don't speak that much,' he confessed. 'Take me out of a restaurant and you'd see.'

'That doesn't answer the question.'

'I've spent time in Nakhodka. There are some Japanese there. It's not too far.'

And you've spent time in prison on the island of Sakhalin, which is a lot closer. The La Perouse Strait separating Sakhalin and Hokkaido was less than fifty miles wide.

She asked him what exactly he did. He told her he was a financier. He was candid about Mirsch, based in Zurich, and the companies it controlled. Then he asked her about Galileo Resources and what she did, and she regurgitated the fiction that Magenta House had created for her. When he enquired about the people she represented, she said she was sure he could imagine them.

'You've probably done business with them.'

'Possibly. Tell me about having no office. It sounds like something I should consider.'

'Maybe you should.'

'Is there a reason?'

'I don't like to leave a trace.'

He digested this for a moment. 'Are you independent?'

'What do you think?'

'I mean, does your company really exist?'

'There are numbers you can call. You've got my card.'

'Which tells me nothing. Are you by yourself?'

Stephanie raised an eyebrow. 'Aren't we all?'

There was a silence that Komarov didn't feel compelled to break. Stephanie was glad. She'd always been good at silence.

'Are you legitimate?' she asked him.

She expected total evasion. Instead, he said, 'There's less reason for me to be illegal these days. Less reason and less desire.'

'It must be the latest fashion. Every Russian I meet is dying to go straight.'

'Look, Kate . . .' He hesitated. 'Can I call you Kate?'

I wish you'd call me Stephanie. 'Sure.'

'You and I . . . well, I won't pretend to be a virgin. The people I do business with – it goes beyond business. Even if I change, most of them won't. And if I *do* change, my relationship with them will always be the same.'

'So, they're Mafiya . . .'

He grimaced at her clumsy conclusion. 'I don't like that word.'

'They're criminals.'

'They're friends. Survivors. The bonds we have cannot be broken by outsiders.'

'Am I an outsider?'

'Of course you are. We both are.'

'You know what I mean.'

'Yes, you are.'

She was grateful he hadn't lied. He described a life she recognized; a life spent on the move, twenty-four-hour jet lag, a blur of cities, restaurants, offices, hotels. He was a twenty-first century nomad. The same creature she'd been at the end of the previous century.

11

I wake up at five thirty. It was after two when Komarov dropped me back, after three before I fell asleep. I've got a headache; too much sake and Kirin, not enough rest. We talked for two hours yet I feel I know less about him now than I did before. There is something between us but it's not trust. How could there be, given the circumstances of our meeting? It's dangerous for us to say what we want so why take the risk?

Coming to the hotel, taking me out to eat – neither was necessary. He chose to do both. But I can't tell what he wants from me. And I'm not sure what I want from him. If anything. Certainly, I feel a charge when I'm close to him. But that could be physical fast-food; a passing attraction that, once indulged, is forgotten. Whichever way I look at it, he's a bad idea. But I'm not fooling myself.

I try to go back to sleep and toss and turn for a while. Shortly before six, I get out of bed and pace. I admit to myself that I'm nervous. I wrap myself in a hotel dressing gown, ring room service and order coffee. I turn on my laptop and run through the plans for Central Park West again. Tonight, the penthouse should be empty. Magenta House believes that Salibi and Steifel will be out of town. Bergstein's schedule confirms that. If, however, there's a change and they're there, Ruth Steifel becomes significant.

I swore to myself in Bilbao that I would never kill anyone again. It never occurred to me that I would ever break that *promise. But if she's in the apartment tonight, I will. There's no alternative. In Scotland, Boyd and I ran through a variety of scenarios but the conclusion was always the same: if Steifel is there, she must be neutralized immediately. And given her expertise, the element of surprise is the only way to guarantee that.*

I examine her file. Born in Ashdod, Israel, on 30 June 1968, her father was a Mossad agent, who was shot dead by a Shi'ite sniper in Baalbek, Lebanon, in 1985. I imagine that influenced Ruth's career path. Her mother now lives with one of her uncles in an apartment in Tel Aviv. Ruth has two brothers. One's a doctor in Bethlehem, the other's a pilot for El Al. She's still part of a functioning family. Which is more than can be said for me. For her sake, and for the sake of the rest of her family, I hope that she and Salibi don't change their plans.

My coffee arrives as daylight creeps over the city. At eight, I curl into a ball on the sofa and watch the news on TV. My mind strays to Laurent. It's lunchtime in Salernes. I see him eating with hands covered in grease. He smokes a cigarette and flicks the butt into the road. I can smell him, a combination of sweat and oil that rubs off on me when we make love.

Sometime during the morning, I fall asleep. When I wake up, the TV is still on, I'm still in my dressing gown, I'm still on the sofa. At one, I order more room service. Lunch. This will be the last thing I eat until it's over. The tension is already tightening my stomach. In a few hours, I won't be able to keep anything down. I flick through the channels and watch a black-and-white Ronald Reagan movie. That occupies the early afternoon. Around four, I have a long, hot bath. As an attempt at relaxation, it fails completely. When I get dressed, I can't escape the fact that I'm not yet Petra.

I choose a purple knee-length skirt that I bought at Oxfam on Marylebone High Street, black tights, my Doc Martens and a long-sleeved T-shirt with a multi-coloured flying saucer on the back. SPACED OUT is written in silver across the front. Comfort clothes.

I leave the Sherry Netherland at six.

The Hotel Carter. Stephanie began to wipe each item clean. There were two coils of climbing rope, a belt, half a dozen hooks on a wire loop, a folding clamp, an electric screwdriver, a small Mag-Lite, a glass cutter, a compact suction cup, a pouch containing clear disks of strong adhesive plastic. She removed the hooks from each end of one of the coils of climbing rope and replaced them with the barbed steel bolts. Then she laid out on the bed the clothes she intended to wear later.

It was ten past eight in New York, ten past one in the morning in London. Alexander would be waiting for her at Magenta House. Standard operating procedure meant no verbal contact directly prior to an action. She attached her mobile phone to the laptop and sent a message instead.

NYC. Am I clear?

She closed her eyes and visualized the ground plan for the building. Then she gave it substance, raising it from two dimensions to three. In her mind, she traced every step, tried to predict every eventuality. When she'd completed the task, she drew up plans and photographs from her computer files and repeated her imagined route to see if there was anything she'd missed. At five to nine, a soft bell told her she had e-mail.

Clear. It's a gold Sony Mini-Disc. Tomorrow's first combination will be 437a9b0. Valid 0000 to 0600. Please acknowledge.

Four-three-seven-A-nine-B-zero.

Go. Final.

No more communication, no further use for the computer. She went over to the desk and collected the floppy disk. She inserted it into the laptop, accessed the only file on it and let the virus go to work.

Central Park West, one thirty-five in the morning. Stephanie made her way to the garage entrance. She aimed the remote at the sensor and the gate lifted. She dropped the remote into the manicured flowerbed that lined the entrance. Down the ramp to the two-floor subterranean garage, the cars hinting at the value of the apartments above: Bentley, Mercedes, Ferrari. The service elevator was by the fire exit. Entry to it was controlled by a swipe card but there was an access panel on the wall to the right. When Stephanie reached it, she shed her rucksack and overcoat, and removed her leather gloves. The gloves beneath were a skin of fine black rubber. She was wearing combat trousers, a silk polo-neck, a tight sleeveless jacket, all black. She pulled on a balaclava.

She took the electric screwdriver from a pocket on her left thigh, opened the access panel, bypassed the security and summoned the elevator. Inside, there was a slim ledge at waist height, which she used for a toe-hold. She unscrewed the hinged panel above, collecting the screws in her palm, and turned the metal bar which acted as a handle. The panel swung down into the cramped space. It was a struggle to squeeze the rucksack through the narrow gap. Once she had, she pressed the button, climbed up onto the roof, reached inside and pulled the panel up. Two shafts of light rose through the empty screw slots. She slipped both arms through the rucksack's shoulder straps and fastened the belt round her waist, tightening it so that it was secure to her back. Next, she opened the left chest pocket on her jacket – the tearing Velcro was loud in the dark shaft – and took out the Mag-Lite. She adjusted the head so that the torch would cast as wide a beam as possible but it was only when she got close to the top that she was able to pick out solid shapes. The elevator shuddered to a halt. She heard the bell and felt the clatter of parting doors. She knew the unexpected arrival would be investigated in seconds. She stepped off the elevator roof, placing her feet onto a horizontal steel girder, the Mag-Lite clamped between her teeth. She twisted the head until the light went out.

Male voices, the click of hard heels on the elevator floor, the sound of her heart. The total darkness. The guards retreated, the doors rattled shut. A jolt from above and the wheel began to grind. The elevator fell away into blackness.

Stephanie stayed still, her face pressed to the dust and grime of the wall. While the elevator was in motion, her greatest concern was that the running cables would snag the rucksack. When there was silence again, she switched the Mag-Lite back on, took it out of her mouth and leaned out into the elevator shaft so that she could examine the top of it. There was an access door to the roof – she'd seen it on the plans – but it wasn't visible from below.

It took five minutes to reach the top of the shaft. There was a small platform bordered by a rail. She stepped over the rail and tried the door. It was locked so she took the screwdriver to the hinges. Ninety seconds later, she was on the roof, crouching beneath a wooden water tower, scanning her surroundings. The city murmur was muted at this height. It was a cold night but her skin was clammy. The adrenaline was pumping but it was under control. Earlier, at the Carter, nerves had made her retch half a dozen times. That was when she'd remembered that the worst bit had always been the bit before. Later, the mind was preoccupied with procedure. Events gathered a momentum of their own. Time sped up and everything was concluded – one way or the other – before there was a moment for fear. At least, that was how it had been.

At the edge of the building, she worked out where she was, adjusted her position and climbed onto the stone ledge. She let the loose rope fall, turned round, took the bolt-gun and fired into the roof. The thump reverberated through the stone and up through her ankles. She attached herself to the rope, got onto her hands and knees and reversed her legs over the edge. She sought a toehold and felt paintwork flaking; like soaking granite shearing from a Scottish rock face.

She probed and tested until she was secure. Then she started her gradual descent over flourishes of stone and the gaping jaws of a ferocious gargoyle. Twice, she felt her hold begin to crumble and had to compensate instinctively. When she was close to the face of the building, she wedged her feet and locked them, allowing her to release one hand from the cornice and reach for the bolt-gun again, which was connected to her belt by a cord. The second bolt was attached to a karabiner. She fired the bolt into solid stone. Then she passed rope through the karabiner, so that she could descend close to the vertical plane of the building. It felt steady so she let go.

She stopped a little too high and made the necessary adjustment. She looked down at her shoes and at the abyss beneath, enjoying the pretence of floating. No vertigo, all she could feel was sharp elation. She reached for the stone window ledge with her toe, pushed herself back, and then swung towards it. As expected, the curtains were open. At this hour, the bedroom had never been an option. She pressed her face to the glass and confirmed the room; the study. The computer terminal was on the desk in the correct position.

She reached round for a side pocket on the rucksack and withdrew the circular plastic sheets. Perching on the window ledge – to allow her the use of both hands – she peeled the reverse sides off the clear adhesive sheets and pressed them against the glass, smoothing out the creases with the palm of her right hand. Some of them overlapped, compounding their strength. When she'd finished, the covered area was approximately half a metre square.

Next, she eased herself off the ledge, back into mid-air, where she waited for her movement to subside so that when she looked through the plastic-coated glass, she could picture an area of roughly two metres cubed in front of the computer screen. Stephanie unclipped the mobile from the belt round her waist.

The text message for Ruth Steifel's mobile had been prepared earlier. Stephanie knew that if Steifel was in the apartment, her phone would be within reach of her bed and that it would be on. She pressed the button and counted the seconds, imagining the sequence: Steifel waking up, fumbling for the phone in the darkness, pressing it to her ear, asking who it was, realizing that it was a text message, not a call. Rubbing her eyes, she would read the message which would inform her that there was a vital piece of e-mail that needed her immediate attention. She would be surprised, then confused, perhaps irritated. But she wouldn't ignore it. She was too professional for that.

Stephanie reattached the phone to her belt and freed the Glock. The silencer was already attached. She raised the weapon and waited for Ruth Steifel to enter the room. Nothing happened. After two minutes, she sent the message again. Still nothing. Had Steifel been there, she would have entered the study by now. She would have gone to the terminal, switched it on and accessed the download. As she did, she would have moved into the cube. Stephanie would have fired at least two shots, probably three. All the bullets would have passed through the plastic, ensuring that the window did not shatter, thereby reducing noise.

But there was no Steifel. Which meant the apartment was empty, as anticipated. There would be guards outside the front door – there always were, regardless of whether Salibi was present – but they would not hear her. Stephanie waited for another two minutes in mid-air before sending the message for the third time, just to be sure. Then she returned to the ledge. Once steady, she got out the compass glass cutter, its diamond point creating a perfect circle with an eight-inch diameter in the bottom right-hand corner of the window. She placed the suction cup inside the circle, fastened it and gave the handle a sharp jab. There was a neat crack and the cup was inside, glass intact. She played out the cord on the end of the handle, lowering it to the carpet. Then she slid her hand through the hole, released the brass catch and opened the window. Time for the night-vision goggles.

She shrugged off her rucksack and took out the clamp, which she attached to the frame of the window. She secured the harness and ropes, ready for her abseil exit. She placed the first incendiary device at the foot of heavy silk apricot curtains, the timer set for one hundred seconds. She tuned the Aiwa two-way radio and dialled Salibi's mobile number on the Motorola. No activity on that line. She tried other numbers. All quiet. She turned on the Korean radio microphone. From the doorway, she scanned the hall and the lobby beyond. She picked up male voices from outside the front door. Salibi never had less than two out there. Then there were those who'd checked the service elevator.

Stephanie headed for the master bedroom which overlooked Central Park. It was at the far end of the apartment. On the way, she passed the principal reception room, a vast space with a central partition, parquet flooring throughout, fluted columns, an enormous chandelier in either half. She placed the second incendiary device by the innermost wall. The hand-blocked Chinese wallpaper would take to the flame hungrily. She placed the last device so as to cut off the corridor between Salibi's bedroom and the marble entrance hall.

There was an antechamber to the bedroom. Stephanie put the rucksack on the carpet by a walk-in cupboard and checked the Glock. She opened the door. There was no movement and no sound.

From either of them.

Stephanie removed her night-vision goggles and felt for the switch on the wall. It took a moment to acclimatize to the sudden light and to the brightness of violent colour; there was blood everywhere.

Ruth Steifel was tied to a chair that lay on its side. Apart from the silver duct tape that covered her mouth, she was naked. Salibi lay on the bed, his hands tied behind his back. He, too, was naked. Both corpses had a bullet-hole at the centre of the forehead, both throats had been lacerated, both bodies had been beaten.

The muscles in Stephanie's legs seemed to liquefy. She'd seen worse but that didn't lessen the impact. She felt light-headed.

The fact that Steifel was tied to a chair suggested that the intruder had tortured her first, in an attempt to loosen Salibi's tongue. Stephanie assumed that had failed, leading to the direct approach on Salibi himself. She looked around the room until she saw the painting. An oil on canvas by Edward Hopper. It appeared the direct approach had failed, too.

There was blood splattered across the pearl silk curtains behind Steifel; droplets from an exit wound. Her underwear was on a white linen mat at one side of the bed, neatly folded, which seemed odd. Stephanie looked at the bed. Both sets of pillows retained the indentations left by heads. So, Steifel had been more than a mere bodyguard. It made a sort of sense – no days off in three years – yet it was hard to picture them together. But not impossible. She'd encountered far stranger arrangements.

The dizzy spell passed and Petra resumed control of Stephanie. She lifted the Hopper canvas from its hook and lowered it to the ground. The steel safe measured eighteen inches by eighteen. Beneath the handle, there was a keypad with letters and numbers, and a small digital display. She punched in the code that had only been valid for about two hours. Four-three-seven-A-nine-B-zero. There was a click. When she opened the safe, she stood to one side, as Boyd had instructed her; she couldn't discount the possibility of a booby trap.

Inside, there were several bulky manila envelopes, which she left alone. There were a dozen photographs clipped to several sheets of negatives. Stephanie saw a TV evangelist sprawled across a motel bed with two young Latino girls. There was a clear shot of a basketball player snorting coke off a glass table. Three photos featured oral sex; a French European Union Commissioner receiving from a blond boy half his age; two women Stephanie didn't recognize, one Asian, the other white; and, most disturbing of all, a famous spokesman for the National Rifle Association with an Alsatian dog. There were two diamond-encrusted Rolex watches, an emerald brooch, a necklace of diamonds and sapphires. There were six bricks of pristine one hundred dollar bills, bound by tape, each brick an inch thick. There was no disk.

She checked the contents again. Nothing. Salibi and Steifel weren't supposed to be there, but were. The disk was supposed to be in the safe, but wasn't.

She took the six dollar bricks from the safe, retreated to the antechamber, crouched beside the rucksack, unzipped the main compartment and placed the money inside. A perk of the job. That was how Petra would have regarded the cash.

Her behaviour had been instinctive. But not of Stephanie's instinct, and that distinction made her queasy. She took the money out of the rucksack and tossed it away.

She was halfway down the corridor when she heard footsteps. A soft tread on a hard surface, solid rubber on marble. She froze. The light was on in the entrance hall, a shadow passing across a distant wall, a breath of sound.

Now, Stephanie submitted to Petra completely.

She pressed herself against the corridor wall, eased the safety catch off the Glock and crept along the corridor to the doorway that opened onto the entrance hall. She saw two men and heard a third, away to her right, outside the partially open front door. She went down on one knee and opened the rucksack again. She took out the three small Yugoslav CS gas grenades, pulled on the breathing mask and night-vision goggles and reached for the remote control. She removed the safety-pin from the first canister and felt for the light switch. Her heart was rocking in her chest. She hit the remote timer for the three incendiaries, bypassing the one-hundred second delay. They detonated simultaneously and were brutally loud within the confines of the apartment. Three waves of percussive shock crashed into one another. Windows popped, showering glass. Stephanie extinguished the light in the hall and rolled the CS grenade towards the front door. It went off just as the door opened fully.

Spluttering, shouting, darkness and chaos. Everywhere. Men materialized from nowhere. Far more than anyone at Magenta House had anticipated. She tried to estimate. Eight? A dozen? In the confusion, it was impossible to tell. And how had they been alerted? Had the safe been wired after all? She saw three guards stumble along the corridor towards Salibi's study, cutting off her planned exit. Her heart sank. In a moment, they would find the open window, the suction cup with its disc of glass, the clamp and the abseil rope.

She struggled with the instinct to panic. She needed a clear head to think. There had to be an alternative exit; with the front door no longer an option, her two primary escape routes were both blocked.

Cries of alarm from the study, someone bursting out of the kitchen, heading back towards the entrance hall and now coming ... directly towards her. She fired twice and missed, the snap of the silencer still loud to her. The man threw himself to the floor, screamed something unintelligible – Hebrew, perhaps? – and then fired back. No silencer on the Uzi, the short burst that ripped along the corridor ceiling left ringing in her ears.

Thick smoke billowed from beneath the double doors into the reception room. Stephanie saw the man scramble to his knees. She rolled a second CS grenade towards him. It went off at his feet. He cried out, dropped his gun, staggered backwards, his face in his hands. She abandoned the rucksack and sprinted back towards Salibi's bedroom, fully aware of her diminishing options. She had already decided that there was no downward exit. She tore off her night-vision goggles. Even though it would be dark outside, she knew it would be easier with natural vision.

In the bedroom, she parted the bloodstained curtains behind Ruth Steifel and opened the window. The room acted like a lung, sucking in a deep gust of icy air. Stephanie pulled the pin on the last CS grenade, lobbed it towards the antechamber, tucked the Glock into the top of her sleeveless jacket and climbed out. Behind her, the grenade detonated.

On the narrow ledge, she rose slowly to standing and raised her hands above her head. Her fingertips felt the upper edge of the stone lintel. She put some weight on the grip. It felt secure. In her mind, she pictured the movement; one action, the entire body, one chance. She swung to the right and pulled her chin up to her hands. Her right foot found the hold; a smooth stone mould, part of the ornate frame of the penthouse window.

There was no time to think about the climb. She simply did it. Just as her mother would have. Some in the Swiss climbing community had considered Monica Schneider reckless. Stephanie's father had always maintained that she was merely fearless. At a reverse angle of forty-five degrees with no security against the drop, Stephanie scrambled over the cornice, compensating immediately for every disintegrating foothold or handgrip. Beneath and behind her, she heard a shout at the bedroom window followed by the crack of gunfire. Stone turned to dust by her ankle. As she rolled over the lip and onto the roof, the Glock dislodged itself and fell away into the darkness.

She heard the crump of another window blowing out on the far side of the building.

Everything that followed was reactive. The scamper across the roof to the top of the service elevator, the realization that the elevator was on the way *up*, the retreat back onto the roof, the search for the fire escape. She reached the top of it just as two of Salibi's bodyguards did. She elbowed the first of them in the face – he never saw her – and then spun round on the ball of her left foot to kick the other in the throat with her right heel. Both men tumbled backwards, cascading down the metal steps to the penthouse landing below. She started to descend towards them – to retrieve their weapons – when two more men appeared on the landing. They glanced up and fired. Stephanie flung herself back onto the roof and then sprinted in the opposite direction. She heard their boots; hard soles clattering metal.

The service elevator was the only option. Through the door, onto the dark platform. The cab was stationary somewhere below her. If she could reach the cable, she thought she could slide down to the roof. She heard the doors rattle shut, quickly snuffing out the thin strip of light she'd been able to see. She climbed over the rail, just as the wheel above her began to turn. The elevator began its descent and so did she; she jumped.

She was in free-fall for a second. Then she collided with the moving cable. Her left arm seemed to wrap itself around the cable while her body continued to twist. She stopped with a shudder. There was an explosion of pain in her left shoulder – she cried out – and then she fell again. The wrench tore glove and skin from her left palm.

She hit the elevator roof almost immediately. No second to spare, she grabbed the handle on the panel, twisted, and let it drop. Then she slid head-first into the square of light, falling to the floor below. Ignoring the fire in her shoulder, she pushed the panel back.

The gunfire came almost immediately. She pressed herself into the shallow awning offered by the metal doors. The bullets carved through the roof, showering her with debris. She glanced to her right, saw the floors falling away on the counter . . . twelve . . . eleven . . . ten . . .

She hit nine. The lift staggered to a halt. The doors opened. She stepped out. The gunfire stopped. Angry shouts echoed in the lift-shaft above her; either she was dead, or she was on foot and heading for the stairs. She tiptoed back into the elevator as the doors began to close. She held her breath, half-expecting a resumption of gunfire. The elevator lurched into life again.

For the rest of her descent, all she could hear was the shrill cry of a fire alarm growing fainter with each floor that she passed.

12

The rain was torrential. Fifth Avenue shimmered beneath a sky as brutally bruised as her shoulder. She'd stood by the same window a few hours earlier – around three thirty – after her return. From exactly the same position, she'd seen an orange smudge in the sky on the far side of Central Park. That smudge was now on television.

An excitable man with a solid wave of blond hair was reaching for superlatives. Behind him, the apartment block on Central Park West. The camera zoomed in on the penthouse. Thick black smoke billowed from two sides of the building. Flames raged while deep orange tongues curled upwards from blown windows and licked the cornice. The abandoned abseil rope flapped in the hot wind like a loose aerial cable. The camera pulled back again. Behind the reporter, Central Park West was gridlocked; fire trucks, police cars, ambulances, TV crews, onlookers. Blue stroboscopic light ricocheted off every surface. When the reporter's nasal whine was drowned by sirens, the editor cut to the studio, revealing an anchorwoman in a navy suit and a dry old man in a corduroy jacket. An expert in international terrorism. The anchorwoman asked him who the culprits might be. Stephanie glanced at the clock in the top left of the screen. 07.39. Where did one find an expert on international terrorism at twenty to eight in the morning? In the twenty-four hour society, anywhere.

Stephanie recognized one of the pictures of Sylvia Salibi: a glamorous shot of her stepping out of the Paris Ritz taken more than a decade ago. Next, some blurred footage of Zara on the deck of the yacht her father had named after her, and a still of Felix, the son, taken in Gstaad. George Salibi's body had only just been discovered but the networks looked as though they had been preparing for this moment for months.

Stephanie began to surf the channels, flicking from one bulletin to the next. First, the method. Most of the details were accurate. Second, the suspect. Or rather, suspects. There seemed to be an assumption that this was probably not the work of one man, but of several. And there was another assumption. That the assassins were men. Unless faced with evidence to the contrary, authorities tended to assume such work was perpetrated by men. As Petra, she had always found such entrenched prejudice a far more effective cover than any of the artificial identities she'd assumed. Third, the motive. Where to start?

In New York, in London, in the south of France, George Salibi had become a society figure, despite his reclusive nature. Two and a half billion dollars tended to buy respectability, regardless of how such a fortune was amassed. Perhaps only billionaire narco-terrorists were excluded from that category, although they certainly weren't excluded from the list of Salibi's acquaintances and business partners. For ten years, he had been a personal friend of José-Maria Moldovano, the notorious Colombian drugs baron. Moldovano was not typical of the breed. No street urchin, he came from a wealthy, aristocratic family and had completed his education at Yale. He knew how to hold a knife and fork and, for a snob like Salibi, this made him an altogether more suitable criminal to court.

An FBI investigation had yielded nothing concrete but suspicion had lingered among US authorities. Stephanie, on the other hand, knew that their relationship had strayed beyond the personal. She had seen photographs of Salibi at Moldovano's estate outside Cartagena. The shots were taken in April 1998 during a weekend when the two men had hatched plans for First Intercontinental to launder narco-dollars through Grand Cayman. She'd also heard a taped conversation recorded in a suite at the Alvear Palace Hotel in Buenos Aires. That had been in September of the same year. On the tape, the two men could be heard ironing out the finer details of the scheme. When Moldovano was murdered, Salibi grew anxious. His fear was fuelled by Carlos Arguello, the man who replaced Moldovano. Arguello was everything Moldovano was not; a butcher from the streets who'd scrambled to the top of the industry, slaughtering anyone who got in his way. Unlike Moldovano, Arguello liked to do his own bloody work. His preferred method of dispatch was the sledgehammer.

Salibi had tried to sever all ties to Cartagena but Arguello wouldn't let him. He'd insisted – in the way that only such men can – that the relationship between First Intercontinental and Moldovano should not alter in any way simply because Moldovano had been thoughtless enough to get himself murdered. And so it was. Business as usual, ever greater profits for both parties. But Salibi was not reassured; his rampant nervousness went unchecked. In recent weeks, there had been rumours that he was negotiating a deal with the financial authorities in New York and with the FBI.

Arguello was not the only suspect. Chinese and Russian crime syndicates were in the frame; they always were for crimes like this. Other candidates included criminal and terrorist associates from Salibi's days in the Middle East, when he'd been based in Beirut. More recently, the Mafia had developed a legitimate claim on him. First Intercontinental had been loosely associated with the Southern Star property fraud, a notorious case that had resulted in long jail sentences for fourteen *mafiosi*. Two First Intercontinental executives had testified against many of the chief defendants in return for immunity from prosecution and guarantees of witness protection. Both men were dead within three weeks of sentencing.

The truth was, nobody knew who was behind the murder of George Salibi and his bodyguard, Ruth Steifel. That included Stephanie. But she knew who'd take the credit. Petra Reuter.

After Central Park West, she'd returned to the Hotel Carter on foot, pulling off the balaclava as she hit the street. She'd left the equipment belt on the floor of the service elevator. Back at the Carter, she'd stripped and placed every single garment into the larger of the two rucksacks. She'd then added the smaller rucksack (crushed and rolled), the ruined laptop, the tools she'd bought and every single domestic item belonging to the Jane Francis identity. That left the clothes she'd worn from the Sherry Netherland to the Carter. She put them back on and left the room for the last time. Jane Francis had booked her room for a week. Stephanie wondered whether anyone would notice that she'd already gone.

On 8th Avenue, she'd caught a cab to the Brooklyn Bridge. From there, she'd walked past the Fulton Fish Market and beneath the elevated section of FDR Drive, until she'd found the perfect moment to heave the loaded rucksack into the East River. Near City Hall, she'd managed to hail a cab to take her back to the Sherry Netherland.

It was only once she was back in her hotel room that the adrenaline had begun to fade and the pain in her left shoulder had registered fully. As she'd watched the orange glow in the night sky – and listened to the chorus of distant sirens – she'd taken three Nurofen with two vodka miniatures. Later, she'd crawled into bed and fallen into a fitful sleep.

The clock on the TV showed 07.52. She swallowed three more Nurofen and ran a hot bath. Neither did much for the pain. As she dressed her skinned palm, the phone rang. It was Boris Bergstein.

The diner was on Lexington. Stephanie arrived first and slid into a booth by a window. A waitress poured her coffee. Over the bang and clatter of the kitchen, she caught fragments of conversation from other tables. *It was the Russians. Maybe it was the Israelis; the guy was Lebanese. Nah, that ain't right – his girlfriend was an Israeli. They found 'em tied up, you know, some kind of sex thing.* Then it drifted back to the usual topics; racism in the NYPD, office gossip, the Yankees, Hillary Clinton's hair.

Bergstein arrived half an hour late. He dusted raindrops from the shoulders of a brown knee-length raincoat. He was wearing a flecked grey polo-neck that made his skin seem paler than usual. He slid along the banquette opposite, beckoned the waitress and ordered breakfast. He looked in a good mood.

'So, what did you get up to last night?'

'None of your business.'

'What happened to your hand?'

'We weren't supposed to meet again. What do you want?'

He leaned across the table, dropping his voice to a conspiratorial murmur. 'When I saw the news, I couldn't believe it.'

'You *shouldn't* believe it. They were dead when I got there.'

'Bullshit.'

'I didn't kill them.'

'Then who did?'

'Search me.'

Bergstein shrugged. 'Whatever. Anyhow, what difference does it make?'

The waitress filled their cups.

'What do you want?' Stephanie asked.

'The chance to begin again.'

'Meaning?'

'A hundred grand and Alan Kelly off my back.'

'I can't help.'

'You could speak to Alan Kelly. Or your superior could.'

'I'm sympathetic – really, I am – but it's not going to happen.'

Bergstein's order arrived; a huge plate of French toast, a side order of crispy bacon, a tall glass of orange juice. The waitress refilled their coffee cups. Stephanie watched Bergstein attack his food; half of it disappeared in a blur of cutlery and mastication. Then he began to slow a little, but not to the extent of finishing a mouthful before speaking.

'The FBI have shafted me, Kate.'

'You're not the first. You won't be the last.'

'I don't want to put you in a bad position but if the TV networks discovered the FBI was involved last night, well . . .'

Stephanie's expression didn't change. 'Don't make a threat you can't carry through, Boris.'

'You think I wouldn't? For the chance to get rid of Kelly? For a hundred grand? It's my feeling somebody'll pay me that kind of money for the story.'

'And what story would that be?'

'Undercover FBI agent infiltrates –'

'What undercover FBI agent?'

'You.'

Even as he said it, the doubt set in. Stephanie let the silence do her work for her.

Eventually, he voiced the suspicion. 'You're not FBI?'

More silence.

'What are you?'

'I wonder what Alan Kelly is going to say when he gets back from China and discovers that you've been working for someone else. Someone you can't identify but someone connected to the killing of a man the FBI has been watching for five years.'

'Who the fuck are you?'

'I'm nobody you need worry about. By tonight, I'll be gone. The best thing you can do is forget I ever existed. That way, we both stay clean.'

The anger that had followed surprise now made way for uncertainty. 'What about Kelly?'

'Let's leave him out of this.'

After the doubt, the disappointment. 'Shit!'

'Finish your breakfast, Boris.'

But he'd lost his appetite. They drank coffee while he calmed down. Stephanie felt sorry for him but said nothing and didn't let it show. She felt sure Bergstein was no longer a risk. He'd been right about one thing, though: he wasn't cut out for the work. She hoped he'd find his money and escape.

He was staring into the rain, no focus in his eyes. 'What a night . . .'

'I've had better,' Stephanie agreed.

'I guess he'd say the same, if he could.'

'So would she.'

Bergstein frowned. 'Who?'

'Ruth Steifel.'

'I wasn't talking about Salibi.'

'Who were you talking about?'

'You remember the guy we saw at Atlantic City? Long, thin face, bad hair?'

She knew exactly. 'Anatoli Medayev?'

'Yeah, him.'

Stephanie felt herself tense. 'What about him?'

'You didn't hear? He's dead, too.'

She held back for a second. 'How?'

'Painfully. That's how. They found his body in the trunk of an old Chevy out at Palisades Interstate Park.'

'Where's that?'

'New Jersey. Bergen County.'

'What happened to him?'

'The fire department found him. They got a call from a passer-by. The car was burnt out. Medayev was in the

trunk wrapped in razor wire. Both his kneecaps had
been shot off.'

'Any idea who did it?'

He frowned again. 'You serious?'

'What do you think?'

'You mean, you don't know?'

She shook her head. 'Do you?'

'Sure. It was Tsentralnaya.'

'How can you tell?'

'The method. The razor wire, the car. The victim gets
put in the trunk while they're still alive. Then the car
gets torched. If they've got any strength left, they shred
themselves before they cook. Or get blown to pieces.
It's a signature killing.'

'Tsentralnaya's signature?'

He nodded. 'Some gangs go for car bombs, others
are into machetes, torchings, disembowelment. I mean,
they do the usual stuff, too. You know, knives, guns,
whatever. But when you want to send a message, you
need a signature.'

'Who knows about this?'

'You mean, apart from us?'

'Yes.'

'Just the NYPD, the FBI, half the population of
Brighton Beach and a hundred and fifty million
Russians.'

East 52nd Street, midday. His secretary was beautiful
and stony; matching scarlet lipstick and nails, every
dermatological blemish concealed. Her outfit – charcoal
jacket and skirt, black silk shirt – looked expensive. She
peered at Stephanie with undisguised contempt.

'You have an appointment?'

'Do I look as though I have an appointment?'

Last time, she'd worn Max Mara. This time, she was dressed in her scruffiest jeans, her SPACED OUT long-sleeved T-shirt and a jacket that was too big for her. The hair that had been cleaned, combed and parted was now a dirty riot. Stephanie marched past the desk. The secretary leapt up and scurried after her.

'You can't go in there!'

But she did. Komarov was slumped in the chair behind his desk. He shivered, clearly startled. Stephanie guessed he'd been asleep. He squinted at both women.

'I'm sorry, she just . . .'

'It's okay, Milla,' Komarov said. Stephanie glared at him. He yawned and rubbed his face. 'Could you leave us? Thank you.'

The door closed. Stephanie crossed the floor. She didn't sit down.

Komarov lit a cigarette and said, 'What happened to your hand?'

She picked a lie. 'It got burnt. What happened to Anatoli Medayev?'

'He got burnt, too.'

'Do you think that's funny?'

'Today, I don't find anything funny. What are you doing here?'

Where adrenaline had been the fuel, now there was anger. 'Take a guess.'

'You think I had something to do with it.'

'Very good. Go on.'

'Because Medayev was my connection to Koba.'

'I'm impressed. Don't stop now. You're on a roll.'

'I didn't kill him.'

'I know. It was Tsentralnaya.'

'I didn't arrange to have him killed, either. By Tsentralnaya or by anyone else. I knew Anatoli for more than twenty years. There's nothing more to say.'

'I saw you with Medayev at Atlantic City. Remember? You were arguing with him after the show. Vladimir Vatukin was right there, beside you. He's the head of Tsentralnaya, isn't he?'

Komarov looked wounded. He sucked on his cigarette and stared at her through a veil of smoke. Eventually, he said, 'Do you know Kimberley, over at the Royalton?'

'What are you talking about?'

'She works behind the bar. Half Japanese, half French, very beautiful. I dated her a few times but it didn't work out. She had a temper, we fought too much.'

'So?'

'So I don't kill people simply because I argue with them.'

'People are killed for less.'

He pointed a finger at her. 'I don't have to answer to you.'

'I don't imagine you answer to anyone.'

'Maybe you think I killed George Salibi, too.'

The name caught her like a slap. 'What?'

'You haven't seen the news?'

Stephanie shook her head.

'It's all over the TV.'

She was still trying to catch her breath. Komarov filled her in with the broadcast version of events on Central Park West.

Then he said, 'Salibi was also in Atlantic City. You remember the enclosure I was in? That belonged to

Salibi. I was a guest. So was Anatoli. And Alexander Kosygin. As far as I know, he's still alive but maybe I should call someone just to check that I didn't kill him too.'

Stephanie was so tired she felt sick and she knew it showed.

'Why did you come here, Kate?'

To confront him over Medayev. That was what she was going to say. But it wasn't true and she could see that Komarov would know it if she said it. She shouldn't have come at all. She'd been rash; she'd allowed herself to be directed by fatigue and anger. Boyd would have been furious. That thought, at least, brought a small, weary smile to her lips.

'I don't know . . .'

They walked north to East 65th Street. Komarov called ahead on his mobile and made a reservation. Ferrier was between Park and Madison. The restaurant was busy but he'd secured a table near the back. He ordered vodka on the rocks, she asked for Coke, then changed her mind.

'Vodka for me too.'

The alcohol was temporarily restorative. They ordered food and Komarov picked a wine without consulting the wine list. Stephanie watched him. Who among the other diners would guess – *could* guess – where Komarov had come from? He was entirely at home among the elegant people. How was that possible?

She held her tumbler in both hands, elbows on the table, and took another sip. 'Tell me about Alexander Kosygin.'

Komarov raised an eyebrow. 'Why are you inter-ested?'

'Because you brought up his name. But I've heard it before.'

'Are you working for Galileo Resources now?'

'No. Not now. I'm just curious.'

'He owns Weiss-Randall.'

'A pharmaceutical company, right?'

Komarov nodded. 'Based here in New York, with a plant upstate and one down in Baltimore. They have facilities abroad, too. Belgium, Switzerland, Sweden, Russia.'

'I understand he used to be in the Soviet Army.'

'A lot of men used to be in the Soviet Army.'

'But not you?'

'Apart from the prison system, I wasn't in the Soviet anything.'

'What do you mean?'

'My parents raised me to believe that the State had no authority over me. That it did not exist. I had no associations with it at all.'

Stephanie smiled. 'I can't picture you as an anarchist.'

'I wasn't an anarchist.'

'What, then?'

'You wouldn't understand.'

'Try me.'

He wrestled with the idea for several seconds. 'Do you know what *vorovskoi mir* is?'

'Thieves World.'

His eyes widened. 'You speak some Russian?'

'Enough to know how to translate *vorovskoi mir*.'

'But do you know what it is?'

'No.' He shrugged. She could see that was the end

of the matter. But she didn't want to relinquish the momentum. 'Kosygin was a lieutenant-general, wasn't he?'

'And a member of the Fifteenth Directorate.'

Stephanie took a guess. 'With direct access to Plutonium-239?'

'What?'

'I'm wondering if Kosygin had access to nuclear storage facilities.'

Komarov looked puzzled. 'Why would you think that?'

'I thought perhaps the Fifteenth Directorate was –'

'The Fifteenth Directorate was in charge of the Soviet Biological Warfare programme.' Stephanie looked perplexed, prompting Komarov to add: 'That's not a secret these days, Kate.'

Stephanie started with endives, walnuts and Roquefort. Komarov had lentil and beet salad with duck confit and a balsamic vinaigrette. They drank white burgundy. Afterwards, she ate pan-seared monkfish in a Chardonnay sauce. For Komarov, sautéed chicken with glazed pearl onions in a red wine sauce. Stephanie looked at the food on their plates and smiled.

'I remember my mother telling me about the first time she ever saw an avocado. She said it was like a fruit from outer space. The most exotic thing she'd ever seen or tasted.'

'I was thirty-five before I saw an avocado. Or drank wine that didn't come from Georgia.'

'When we complained, she said we were spoilt. We'd have to listen to how things were when she was young.'

'When you're young, you're never grateful enough for what you have. Even when you have nothing.'

'Did you have nothing?'

'I had a strong family who were part of a history that we took pride in. Wherever I was, whatever happened to me, I always knew where I'd come from. I knew who I was. So I had more than most of the people who had more than me. What about you?'

'I used to know who I was. When I was young. When they were alive.'

Komarov had been raising his glass to his lips. He stopped, just short. 'What happened to them?'

Stephanie faltered. Wrong parents. She couldn't remember the names of Kate March's parents, or whether they were even alive. Then she realized that she didn't care, that she was happy to have made the mistake.

Komarov took her silence for discomfort. 'How long are you staying in New York?'

'I'm leaving tonight. You?'

'Tomorrow night. Where are you going?'

'Where are *you* going?'

Komarov smiled. 'That *is* the problem we have, isn't it?'

'I'm sorry.'

'We have to make a decision, Kate. Can we trust each other at all?'

'I honestly don't know.'

'If we don't, what's the point?'

At last, confirmation. There were butterflies in her stomach. But what of the trust? It was too soon to resort to utter honesty so Stephanie resorted to what she knew best. 'I'm going to Frankfurt.'

She saw a weight lift from Komarov's shoulders. 'I'm going to Zurich.'

She remembered the midnight phone conversation he'd had in the Lexus. She'd worked out his itinerary. Switzerland first, unless circumstances changed. He was telling the truth. She was happy and disappointed simultaneously; she wanted to claw back her lie and make the same leap of faith that he'd made for her.

He kisses me and I'm seventeen again; I know it's wrong but it feels right. I'm as confused now as I have ever been. I'm a disagreement between Stephanie and Petra. I know that I'm here now because I won't be here tomorrow. It's a one-night stand – or rather, a one-afternoon stand – but it's been on my mind since the moment we met. When Petra was talking about Koba, I was thinking how hard it would be to keep my legs crossed if the right situation arose. This is that situation. As for justification, I know the answer before I ask the question.

Just once, I tell myself.

We are in his apartment on Fifth Avenue. We walked here from Ferrier. It took five minutes. He asked me whether I was married. The question shocked me. Not because it was from him but because I've never imagined myself married. I've tried. There have even been times when I wanted to be married – in theory, at least – but I was never convinced by the version of myself that I saw.

'No. I'm not married.'

'Have you been close?'

'No. Never been asked. What about you?'

'I used to be married,' he said, not looking at me.

'Divorced?'

He shook his head. 'She died.'

'I'm sorry.'

He shrugged off my apology. 'It was a car accident.'

It's a grand building; a marble lobby, two uniformed

porters, a lift of gleaming brass and mahogany to take us to the tenth floor. Komarov's two-bedroom apartment is small. I can tell that he had no input over the design. It's clinically luxurious. It could be a large suite in a smart hotel; parquet floors, Persian rugs, panelled walls in the drawing room overlooking the park, more oils on canvas by Olga Svetlichnaya and Yuori Kugach, a slim widescreen Sony TV concealed behind a rectangular mottled mirror built into the wall over the fireplace. The kitchen is brushed steel, shimmering chrome and slate, and looks as though it's never been used. All the trappings that come with money and I get the feeling that he doesn't really care about any of them. Apart from the paintings. They are the only personal touch. There isn't even a photograph of her. I don't know her name. He never told me and I never asked.

Now, in the bedroom, he takes my bandaged left hand and kisses the fingertips. I let him undress me. When he crouches to remove my shoes, I put my right hand on his shoulder for balance. The socks come off. My soles feel clammy against the wooden floor. When he pulls down my jeans, it's as though the denim carries a static charge. I feel his fingers slip between the elastic of my knickers and my skin.

I don't know what I'm doing here. I think of a slew of good reasons to be anywhere else. Then I think of all the other men I've had. A blur of faces, as seen through the window of a train speeding past a crowded platform. They could ruin this. But I won't let them.

I must be out of my mind.

The black cotton slips down over my thighs and calves. I'm holding my breath. Every sense seems heightened. Then he stands in front of me and takes hold of the hem of my SPACED OUT T-shirt. I raise my arms above my head and the pain of the movement makes me gasp. He stops.

'It's okay,' I tell him.

The shirt comes off and he sees that it isn't. Inexplicably, I feel ashamed of the bruises that have wrapped themselves around my left shoulder. He can't help but look at the collage of colour. And then at my dressed hand. And then at the one mark of injury that was there before. On my left shoulder, at the front and at the back, a ragged, circular scar.

'I had a car accident, too,' I whisper. 'When I was twenty-two. It was a piece of metal . . .'

I can't tell whether he believes me or not. He removes my black bra so that I'm naked. I've never felt so naked in all my life. I don't feel as though he's undressed me; I feel as though he's peeled me.

He kisses me again and then I start to undress him. My fingers find the buttons on his shirt. His eyes never stray from mine and soon I understand why. They emerge gradually at first; the flat light of a gloomy afternoon keeps them a secret for as long as possible. I tug the shirt off his right shoulder. His skin is blue and grey and green.

Tattoos. Everywhere.

I shouldn't be surprised. But I am. Until now, I've man-aged to overlook Konstantin's past. His demeanour, his dress sense, they've made it easy for me to forget. I've ignored the years lost languishing in prison but here are the badges of honour to remind me. I run my fingers over his stomach; there's no fat on him at all. To the eye and to the fingertip, it's green marble.

The shirt slides to the floor. Over both shoulders, around both biceps, across his chest and down his stomach, there are swirls of blue and grey. Seen with blurred vision, they could be the worst bruises in the world. Far worse than mine. Seen clearly, his skin is a map to his past. It's dermatological cartography.

I'm numb. I don't know what to think. I've never liked tattoos. But this goes beyond anything I've ever seen. It has nothing to do with the flippancy of fashion. What unnerves me is not the way they look. It's what they represent.

He's staring at me, waiting for a reaction. I kiss him on the mouth. I want him to take charge and he seems to read my mind. He lays me across the bed and lets his mouth roam. When he squeezes my shoulder, I cry out in pain.

'I'm sorry.'

'Don't stop.'

When he kisses my breasts, I see his shoulders in the gloom; green twisting serpents are moving over me, seducing me. They form a colourful union with my bruises.

Then his hands are on my legs, gently parting them. I stare at the ceiling and wait for his mouth. He waits, too, teasing me. It seems like an eternity. Then I feel his lips and tongue between my thighs. Somebody sighs. I suppose it's me.

13

She was exhausted but couldn't sleep. It was dark on the upper deck of the 747. Nearly all the other passengers were asleep, their seats fully reclined. Stephanie selected a movie but lost interest almost immediately. She opened the blind. It was a cloudless night, a full moon overhead, the stars like glittering dust. Moonlight reflected off the surface of the ocean thirty-seven thousand feet below. She saw the pin-prick lights of a giant tanker.

She pulled her blanket up to her chin and curled herself into a ball. Her body was a stew of aches, some beautiful, some ugly. She wasn't exactly sure how many times they'd made love; the afternoon had been a physical blur. They'd consumed the hours, eager not to waste a moment of the short time available to them. She had no doubt that the clock had added to the intensity. When Komarov had reminded her that she should go if she wanted to catch her flight – she was already late – he'd suggested she might like a quick shower. She'd said that was a waste of time and had used her mouth to prove it. Now, she was glad to be carrying him on her skin and inside her.

At his door, they'd kissed goodbye. She'd called him Konstantin. He'd said she should call him Kostya. She'd repeated the name twice, then kissed him for the last time.

It was too soon to know what to feel about it. Apart from sated and shattered. Her senses were splayed but she didn't care.

The movie was still flickering on the small screen in front of her. She looked at her watch and worked out roughly how far east of Newfoundland the aircraft was. Then she peered out of her window again. The black Atlantic looked majestic.

Tears were forming in her eyes.

Dr Brian Rutherford's private practice was located on George Street. Stephanie was sitting upright on an examination bench. Rutherford stood behind her, placed his right hand on her shoulder and then took her left biceps in his left hand. He pulled back slowly.

'Can you feel that?'

'Yes.'

He released the arm and circled the bench to face her. 'You can get dressed now.'

Stephanie had made two calls from Heathrow, one to Rutherford, the second to Magenta House. Then she'd headed for George Street. Rutherford had removed the dressing she'd applied to her left hand, disinfected it and applied a fresh dressing. Then he'd turned his attention to the shoulder.

For half an hour, he had gently turned and twisted her left arm, occasionally pressing his fingers into her flesh, seeking out the points of maximum discomfort. Stephanie saw him glance at the scar on her left shoulder; the circular, shiny disk of ruined skin that Komarov had kissed, and that was mirrored by a similar blemish on the back of the shoulder. Rutherford had been responsible for both. The front was an entry wound, the back an exit wound. For a bullet that had never existed. The scars were cosmetic. They were part of Petra's history, as surely as Komarov's tattoos were part of his. Stephanie didn't feel that they belonged to her. The explanation she gave to Komarov was the same one she gave to anyone who asked. A car crash lost in the mist of the past. When Laurent had said that it looked like a bullet wound, Stephanie had laughed at him.

'I wouldn't know. I've never seen a bullet wound.'

Rutherford watched her struggle into her shirt and looked unhappy. She followed him back into his office; oak panels for walls, shelves of medical journals, framed certificates, awards from pharmaceutical companies, photographs from conferences abroad and lunches at the BMA.

'What you have is a rotator-cuff injury. The shoulder is a ball and socket arrangement. There are three groups of muscles that hold the ball in the socket. They are known as the SIT muscles – *supraspinatus, infraspinatus* and *teres minor* – and it's across this group where you've sustained the most damage.'

'How serious is it?'

'It should be the most mobile joint in the body. But yours is quite restricted. And quite painful, judging by the look on your face. What you need is rest and physiotherapy.'

'I'll be sure to tell Alexander that when I see him.'

Rutherford smiled sympathetically. 'You should know that these injuries take time to heal. And that they recur with increasing ease.'

It was mid-afternoon when she reached Magenta House. Alexander was in his office, standing by the

213

window, smoking a Rothmans. His expression told her what to expect; he looked as though he was chewing a lemon.

'No Koba, no disk. Salibi, Steifel and Medayev all dead. Congratulations.'

'Don't mention it.'

'You find it funny that they died?'

'I find it pitiful. All of it.'

Alexander nodded and turned his face to the garden. 'How typical of you, Stephanie. I shouldn't be surprised, really. You've always been lowest common denominator.'

'You expect me to care about Koba? Or a disk?'

'What about people? Real people.'

'Real people? George Salibi, billionaire friend to terrorists and drug dealers? Steifel, Medayev?'

Komarov? Petra?

Alexander gave her his most patronizing stare and pointed out of the window. 'You think the people down there are real people? Worrying about mortgages and low-fat yoghurt? Gossiping about who's screwing who on *EastEnders*? Is that what you think? The real world has nothing to do with too much tax on petrol. Or football. Or DIY superstores on a Sunday afternoon. The real world is primitive and relentless. Strip away all the rubbish and that's all there is to it. The pond life out there – they're fodder. They don't know it and they don't care. As long as they've got satellite TV and the French to hate, they're happy.'

'You're out of your mind.'

'Not out of it. Just using it.'

'Was James Marshall a real person? Or Oleg Rogachev?'

'James Marshall died doing something he'd believed in all his life. He was a good man.'

'Or a careless alcoholic.'

'He was a better human being than you'll ever be.'

'I don't doubt it. But I never met him. To me, he's just a name. A statistic.'

Alexander looked outraged. 'Your youth keeps you callous.'

'No. *You* keep me callous.'

Two hours later, a black Mercedes pulled onto the Strand. Stephanie and Alexander sat in the back, partitioned from the driver by a raised glass screen.

'Anatoli Medayev wasn't dead when he was found.'

Stephanie hadn't heard that. 'Are you sure?'

'Astonishingly, he managed to talk. Got a paramedic to write down what he could. Seems he was keen to clean the slate before he died.'

Stephanie was exhausted and angry, after two hours of counterproductive debriefing when all she wanted was to go to sleep. The session was concluding in the back of the Mercedes because Alexander was late for another meeting.

'What did he say?'

'Not much, but enough. Koba is still talking to the end users who employed Hans Klepper to run Plutonium-239 through Heathrow.'

'So we can rule out Medayev as Koba, then.'

'Only if he was telling the truth.'

'If he was, that would leave Vladimir Vatukin as Koba.'

'Maybe.'

'Is there someone else?'

Alexander pulled a pained face. 'Medayev and Vatu-kin never got on. Medayev was too close to Rogachev for Vatukin's liking, and Vatukin was too much of an aggressive opportunist for Medayev's liking. If Vatukin *is* Koba, Medayev had a golden opportunity to finger him. But he didn't.'

They ground to a halt in traffic. Stephanie stared out of the window. It was raining hard. The homeless congregated in shop doorways for the night. Commuters and theatregoers marched past them, blind to the out-stretched palms, deaf to the requests for coins. Alex-ander's unreal people.

'The end users have changed their mind. They're no longer interested in acquiring nuclear material. They're now in the market for a biological weapon.'

Stephanie listened to Petra's assessment. 'Less cumbersome, less expensive. More versatile. It makes some sense.'

'There's going to be a trade.'

'When?'

'Medayev didn't say.'

'No clue as to the identity of the end users, or the target?'

'No.'

'Anything else?'

Alexander shook his head. 'He was dead before they reached the hospital.'

'So?'

'You need to find Koba and find out who the end users are. If you can't, you have to make sure that the trade never happens. Once the material is in their hands, it's gone.' Alexander lit a cigarette and opened

216

the window an inch. The sound of the city intruded. 'All we really know about Koba is that he's close to Tsentralnaya.'

'He couldn't be any closer if he's actually Vatukin.'

'That's something you'll have to find out. The thing is, you need a credible approach if you're going to penetrate Tsentralnaya where it matters.'

'I imagine you have something in mind.'

'Petra.'

They skirted Trafalgar Square and headed down the Mall.

Stephanie said, 'She's been quiet for a while.'

'We can change that.'

Of course. A Magenta House speciality.

'What about the disk?'

'In the light of Medayev's confession, the disk was worthless anyway. It was all nuclear-related. It's ancient history.'

Stephanie thought of Ruth Steifel's mother in Tel Aviv. She would probably never know how pointless her daughter's death had been but that didn't make Stephanie feel any better about it.

'Do you know where the disk is?'

Alexander was brushing ash off his jacket sleeve. 'No. What I do know is that Salibi was not going to sell it. He was planning to hand it over to the FBI as part of the deal he'd negotiated with them.'

'Let me guess. Immunity from prosecution?'

'Better than that. No further investigation by the financial authorities in New York.'

'Big money buys good lawyers.'

'The FBI don't know the threat is now biological, not nuclear. So they still consider the disk important.'

'And you don't see any reason to tell them, I suppose?'

'Information is currency, Stephanie. There's no point in tossing it away.'

'You people . . .'

They turned right, past St James's Palace, and travelled along St James's Street towards Piccadilly. Alexander finished his cigarette, ejected it into the wet evening, closed the window and asked, 'What's your opinion of Konstantin Komarov?'

The kick in her chest reverberated through the rest of her body.

'How do you mean?'

She thought she sounded breathless, guilty. She looked across the back seat. Alexander didn't seem to have noticed.

'He's done plenty of business with Tsentralnaya. He has a connection to Koba.'

'*Had.* Medayev was his connection to Koba. With Medayev dead, there's nothing to tie him to Koba. Or Tsentralnaya, for that matter, apart from the obvious business links.'

He considered this for some time. 'You're probably right. It was just an idea.'

They ground to a halt again at a set of lights on Piccadilly.

Stephanie said, 'If this is going to work, I'll need to be independent.'

'I'm sorry?'

'I'll honour the deal we made. The disk is gone but I'll deliver Koba. And James Marshall will be avenged. That was what we agreed. But I won't be tied to Magenta House.'

Alexander's snort was as contemptuous as it was dismissive. 'Ridiculous.'

'I'm not asking you. I'm telling you.'

'And I'm telling you . . .'

'Petra Reuter outgrew Magenta House.'

'What are you talking about?'

'The real Petra Reuter. The one I became, not the one you made.'

'It's been two years . . .'

'That makes no difference.'

He hesitated. 'You can have a degree of autonomy – I'll grant you that – but you'll – '

The last of Stephanie's fragile patience disintegrated. 'Degree of autonomy? Who do you think you are? I have an entire network out there. It's more complex than anything Magenta House ever created. It's a secret world and it belongs to me.'

'Stephanie – '

'If you don't like it, you can take Koba and stick him up your fucking arse. It'll be crowded up there but he'll be in good company.'

Alexander looked genuinely shocked.

Stephanie jabbed a finger at him. 'I'm not offering you a choice. I'm telling you how it's going to be. You want Petra? Fine. But I won't share her with you. I'll do it my way, you'll get what you want and we'll both be happy. So don't feel you can start threatening the rest of my family, or any old mechanic from Marseille. We're beyond that. Well and truly beyond it. I'll report to Rosie Chaudhuri if I need something. Or if I feel there's something you need to know. Apart from that, there'll be no contact between us. And when it's over, there'll be no contact ever again. Degree of autonomy!

You should try listening to yourself, you pompous bastard.'

They drove up South Audley Street and crossed Grosvenor Square in complete silence before Alexander pressed a button on his door handle. The glass partition lowered. He told the driver to pull to the kerb at the junction of Oxford Street and Duke Street. As the car slowed, he said to Stephanie, 'The need to legitimize Petra's return at such short notice – you understand that has to happen?'

'What are you suggesting?'

'Two jobs to raise the profile.'

'Christ . . .'

'In quick succession.'

She shook her head. 'I won't do it.'

'You won't have to. I'll send someone else. But you'll need to be close by. You'll have to show yourself a little to help spread the word.'

'How are you proposing to organize that?'

'Rosie will send you instructions.'

'But apart from that, I'm independent?'

'Yes.'

'Okay.'

Alexander said, 'You can get out now. From here on, you and I are heading in different directions.'

I close the front door to the flat and I'm alone. My mouth is still grossly arid; a hangover from the flight. I dump my bag on the bedroom floor but don't bother to unpack. For a while, I'm content to lie on the bed, not moving, not thinking, barely breathing. The only light comes from the lamps in the street. They throw dull rectangles onto the ceiling.

He's still in New York. It's mid-afternoon in Manhattan.

In a few hours, he'll be on his way to Zurich. If I was a journalist and he was a lawyer, I'd call him. But I'm not, so I won't. I think of him beneath me, above me, behind me, in front of me. Inside me. He's part of me, even if I never see him again.

Later, I cook spaghetti, adding a spoonful of pesto from an open jar in the fridge door. I eat in front of the TV, flicking from station to station, watching none of the rubbish on offer. I'm in bed by eleven.

I can't really say that when I wake up I'm Petra Reuter. But I do feel different. It's half past nine. The painkillers that Dr Rutherford gave me have allowed me ten hours of sleep. I run a bath and soak in it. The hot water rinses the last of Kostya from my body. He seems like a dream now. Distant, amorphous, as insubstantial as the steam which rises off the surface and colours my cheeks.

I'm independent again. I can't deny there's a thrill. Already, I'm starting to think like her. I'm making lists, trying to remember names, numbers, places. It's impossible to estimate how many will have changed.

After half an hour in the bath, I pull on some clothes, make a pot of coffee and switch on my new laptop. I browse through some of the websites he used. He always preferred sites with message boards that were refreshed every two or three days. World of Orixas, a site dedicated to the dispersed followers of the religion, is still up and running but I don't recognize any of the names on the message board. Moto-Europe has closed down. So has Parallel Universe, bizarre holiday specialists. An hour and eight sites later, I come to American Eagle Auction, an on-line auction house. I'm scrolling through their 'barter board' when I spot a name. Herman Jakobsen. I look at the message. He's selling a toy steam train, all

221

working parts, manufactured in 1911. There's a reference number: 0039968LR. Initials, every other number, initials. Wasn't that what it used to be? I compose an e-mail to HJ0398LR.

Hello, Oscar.

That's all I say and I send it to MSN and AOL.

Her first hour of physiotherapy complete, Stephanie stepped out of the Chelsea & Westminster into a persistent drizzle. The traffic on the Fulham Road was stationary due to three sets of roadworks in less than a mile. It was just after midday. She found a phone-box and dialled the number. It rang half a dozen times before a man answered. The sound of him made her smile. He'd always carried his age in the timbre of his voice.

She said, 'It's me.'

There was a long pause. She could hear him breathing. Then: '*You?*'

'Yes.'

'I never expected to hear from you again.'

'You're not the only one.'

'Where are you?'

'I'm close. Can I come over?'

At South Kensington Underground, she caught the District Line to Victoria. She walked down Wilton Place, turning right into Longmoore Street. Cyril Bradfield's house was towards the far end, near the junction with Guildhouse Street. A façade of brick, blackened by decades of dirt, window-frames crumbling from neglect. There were times when Cyril Bradfield looked as though he was crumbling from neglect, too: unkempt silver hair, sky-blue eyes in bloodshot whites, pale paper-dry skin. He was wearing grey flannel trousers stitched at the knee and an old Viyella shirt. The sleeves were rolled up to the elbow, the collar was frayed. The toes of his cheap tan slip-ons curled like dead fish tails.

He kept his house dark. The air tasted of sweet tobacco. Stephanie followed him up the stairs to the converted attic that he used as a studio. It was partitioned: a makeshift darkroom constructed from a large cupboard at one end, a small clear area for photography, two workbenches and a desk piled high with paperwork. Ikea shelves had been assembled to house solvents, paints, inks, different types of paper, plastics, boxes of stamps, three franking machines, four box-files full of credit cards. Stephanie had always been amazed by the amount of incriminating material Bradfield kept at home but he'd always possessed a remarkably sanguine approach to the art of forgery. And art was exactly what it was, as far as he was concerned.

There was a small fridge in one corner, a portable CD player on top, some classical piano playing. Stephanie didn't recognize it. Bradfield seemed to read her mind. 'Poulenc,' he said. She nodded dumbly. Bradfield saved her embarrassment: 'Tea?'

'Thanks.'

He switched on a paint-splattered kettle at the end of one of the workbenches. 'You don't take milk, do you?'

'No.'

'So . . .'

Stephanie felt like an errant pupil in front of a teacher. 'I need some stuff.'

'I thought you'd retired.'

'Apparently, I'm too young to retire.'

223

He still had his back to her. 'You're not in trouble, are you?'

She couldn't think of the correct answer immediately. He turned round, still waiting.

'I'm trying to put all my troubles behind me.'

'By coming to see me?'

'It's going to be my last job.'

'You sound like a heavyweight who doesn't know when to quit.'

'They usually have a choice, don't they?'

'So, you *are* in trouble.'

'I can take care of myself.'

He glanced at her left hand. 'Really?'

'Would you feel better if I told you I burnt it on the cooker?'

He smiled. 'What do you want?'

'I'm going to want several over the next few weeks.'

'Complete or partial?'

'Probably a mix, mostly complete. Today, just one.'

'What do you need?'

'A passport, a driving licence, two credit cards.'

'Nationality?'

'Preferably not British. French, Austrian, Swiss. Definitely not German.'

'Swiss, then?'

'Okay.'

'When do you need it by?'

'As soon as possible.'

Bradfield managed to look cross and concerned simultaneously. 'Most of the people I deal with . . . well, I don't care for them at all. But you're different.'

'I know what you're going to say . . .'

He cocked his head to one side. 'Yes, you probably

do. And I don't suppose you'd pay any attention to it anyway. Once your mind's made up, there's no changing it, is there?'

'Don't be cruel.'

He pulled down a white paper background from a roller. Stephanie stood in front of it. He pointed a Polaroid camera with four lenses at her. He tore the negative from the dispensing slot and checked his watch. Stephanie glanced at the papers on his desk. Several of them bore the insignia of the Inland Revenue.

'Having a laugh with HM's Inspector of Taxes, are we?'

Bradfield waved the negative through the air. 'I'm being investigated.'

Stephanie arced an eyebrow. 'Really?'

'Some officious little bean-counter marooned behind a desk, talking down his nose at me.'

'Is it serious?'

'Just routine. Apparently . . .'

The passport photographs were typically unflattering. Bradfield laid the quartered print on one of the benches and swung an Anglepoise lamp over it.

'You look a little washed out.'

'You really know how to make a girl feel special.'

'Your hair colour. Same as now?'

'Yes.'

'I remember the last time. Belgrade, I think it was. You used blue contacts for your eyes.'

'That's right.'

'How were they?'

'Uncomfortable.'

'What about this time?'

'Not for this one.'

'Ageing?'

'No. If I use it, I won't have time for alterations.'

'Ah, the Hail Mary . . .'

'Exactly.'

Bradfield took some more photographs, altering the light. He made her change for some of them; he kept a large chest of old clothes at one end of the studio. She gave him the details for the identity and they discussed the stamps she should have in the passport.

As he was making her a second cup of tea, Stephanie said, 'You remember Malta?'

'How could I forget?'

'And afterwards, when you went to see Frank White . . .'

'The man you were in love with. Of course.'

Bradfield had been her courier. He'd passed on her instructions to White. Had he followed them, White would have found her in Paris the following morning. A rented apartment in the *19iéme arrondissement*, just off the rue Armand Carrel. Reunited, they could have vanished forever. But he'd chosen to ignore her.

'Why do you think he didn't come after me?'

'I don't know.'

'You must have thought about it.'

'It was four years ago. I may have thought about it then. But not recently. And certainly not now.'

'I don't believe you.'

'I'm going senile. I forget things – '

'If you're going to lie to me, surely you can do better than that.'

'Leave it alone. It's history.'

'Perhaps he didn't love me.'

'I think he loved you.'

'Perhaps he didn't love me enough.'

'Perhaps he loved you too much.'

'Meaning?'

'Nothing.'

'Cyril . . .'

Bradfield looked agitated. 'Perhaps he was worried that if he followed you, he would be followed by . . . *them*. That he would lead them to you. Perhaps he thought it was more important for you to be free. Perhaps that's how much he loved you.'

Stephanie felt his ghost breeze through her. 'Is this what you think? Or is that the way it was?'

They stared at one another. It felt as though a lot of time was passing. Stephanie had no idea what was going on behind the pale winter sky of his eyes.

Eventually, he whispered, 'It was just an idea. That's all.'

It was another hour before Stephanie left. As she collected her overcoat from the bench, she said, 'Before I go, this business with the tax inspector. Are you sure it's okay?'

'Yes.'

'I feel as though I have a vested interest.'

'It'll be fine.'

'Are you positive?'

'Why?'

'I was just thinking . . . you know . . .'

'What?'

She met his gaze. 'If you wanted me to, I could take care of it for you.'

'How do you mean?'

'As a favour. From one friend to another.'

Bradfield frowned. 'I'm not sure I understand.'

'Come on, Cyril.'

'You mean . . . ?'

Her expression was set in stone. 'Don't look so worried. I'm good at what I do. The best. I'd make it seem like an accident. He steps off the pavement without looking. He trips and falls down the stairs. It could be a heart attack. Or a burglary that goes wrong.'

Bradfield's mouth opened but no sound emerged. Stephanie's eyes were lifeless. She let the silence gnaw at him.

'Cyril?'

'Yes.'

'Close your mouth. I was joking.'

Is that you, Petra? Give me a sign and then we can talk.

Stern. The information broker. Still at large in the ether.

She'd spent the morning visiting rental agencies, searching for short-term lets. The message had been waiting for her when she returned to Bulstrode Street, laden with groceries. She'd dumped the shopping on the kitchen table and unpacked her groceries while trying to think of something conclusive. Now, she sat down in front of the terminal with a mug of green tea.

Belgrade. No postcards since. Sorry. You still owe me $75,000 for Athens. How's that for a sign?

Five minutes later, his reply directed her to a private room.

What have you been doing, Petra? Not employing someone else, I hope. Infidelity's so cruel.

I was taking a well-earned break.

For two years?

Closer to three, now.

Is this a courtesy call or are you back in the market-place?

I'm buying, not selling. I want information, not work.

I'm not sure I believe you, Petra. I have the feeling you've been a naughty girl very recently.

Oscar, have I ever lied to you?

I don't know. Have you been to New York lately? The press reports talk about several suspects. I hear there was only one. A woman . . .

Stephanie wondered how Stern had heard that but knew she couldn't ask. I'm sure there are other people who provide the same service as you. They're probably cheaper, too.

In every sense, I should imagine. Have I touched a nerve? What do you want?

All you've got on a Russian criminal, alias Koba. I know there are plenty to choose from but this one is linked to the Tsentralnaya crime syndicate and was connected to a consignment of Plutonium-239 that was intercepted at Heathrow last year. The courier, a Dutch heroin trafficker named Hans Klepper, died. This incident is connected – somehow – to the murder of Oleg Rogachev in Paris in April.

Ah, Rogachev. Another good source of revenue for me this year.

Do you know who killed him? I'll pay for a name.

Petra, you'll pay for everything.

14

The following morning, Stephanie phoned Guderian Maier Bank in Zurich and asked to speak to Albert Eichner. She gave him her account number and answered the three clearance questions that he posed to her. Then she asked for a transfer to the dollar account belonging to the Sandolfino Shipping Corporation at Banco Alvaro Saracin in Mexico City. The amount, one million US dollars. That afternoon, she contacted Eduardo Ruiz at Alvaro Saracin and instructed him to transfer the money to Banque Henri Lauder in Zurich the following morning. The buildings of Guderian Maier and Henri Lauder were two hundred yards apart on the Bahnhofstrasse. The twenty-four hour transfer via Alvaro Saracin in Mexico City cost almost fifty thousand dollars, approximately twenty-five thousand per transaction. Under the circumstances, Stephanie considered that a fair price.

She rented a fully furnished one-bedroom flat in a block on Old Court Place, off Kensington High Street, signing for two months with an option for a third. The building had a high turnover, the agent told her, mostly foreign. The flat had the feel of a hundred hotels she'd stayed in: comfortable, stuffy, charmless. But not being associated with Magenta House made it more of a home than the place on Bulstrode Street.

Over three days, she made her preparations. She was

in regular contact with Stern, buying information from him, downloading it, printing it, and reading it repeatedly until she'd absorbed all of it. She taped sheets of paper to a drawing-room wall and began to write lists on each, cross-referencing them; names, ages, appearances, backgrounds. She trawled Oxfam for second-hand clothes and bought new garments from shops along Kensington High Street, using a debit card in the name of Helen Appleton, a customer at Lloyds TSB. She had Mastercard and Visa credit cards in the same name. On the third morning, she returned to Cyril Bradfield's house in Victoria to give him details for more identities. The ghosts were beginning to take shape.

She asked Stern to locate contacts she'd used in the past, some of whom he'd provided in the first place. Aldo Rivera was still in the stolen-car business. He'd moved from Turin to Lyon but his trade remained the same: prestige vehicles stolen in western Europe and shipped east to wherever the most money was. Bruno Kleist had been buying and selling information for thirty years. Unlike Stern, he was a physical presence. Stern had always maintained it was a miracle that nobody had murdered him. Three years ago, Kleist had operated from a bakery he'd bought in Prague. Now, he was the owner of an antiques shop in Vienna, specializing in lights. She remembered that Kleist had always been fond of antique lamps.

Stephen Brady, Walther Beck, Alan Paul and Preben Simonsen were all dead. The causes were, respectively, a bullet in Belfast, lung cancer in Dortmund, old age in Boston, a necklace of piano-wire in Copenhagen. Two others were in prison, one for murder, the other for fraud. Stern had failed to find Anne Mahrer.

Stephanie asked for information on other former associates.

On the second evening, Komarov left a message. It was short and blunt.

It's Kostya. I'm in Paris tonight. Call me.

She tried the number but his phone wasn't on. In the morning, among her other requests, she asked Stern for a profile on Komarov. The return was disappointing – there was little she didn't already know – except for one thing.

Komarov's deceased wife had been called Irina. No photograph was provided. The two had known each other since childhood. They'd grown up together and had married in 1994. They would have married sooner, it seemed, had Komarov not been incarcerated in Siberia. After his release, in 1992, he came to Moscow, where she was living, and their relationship resumed after ten years of hibernation. There were no children, Stephanie noted. She checked for details of the car accident that had killed her.

January 23, 1997. A car bomb explodes on Povarskaya Street, not far from the junction with New Arbat. The driver and his two passengers are killed. So are seven pedestrians. One of them is Irina Komarov. The blast is blamed on Chechen terrorists.

Komarov had described Irina's death as a car accident. Technically, one could say that it had been; she was just passing by when the device detonated. But the way he'd said it had been intended to mislead.

I'm sitting in a café on Queensway. The radio is playing a song by Texas: 'Say What You Want'. *I'm at a table by the window, watching litter blow down the street, drinking my* second cup of coffee. I'm thinking about Eric Roy when my mobile rings.

'It's me.'

Two tiny words and my heart is in my mouth. The next instant, I'm disgusted with myself. Have I forgotten who I am? I'm not some gauche sixteen-year-old.

Not sixteen, anyway.

'Where are you?' I ask.

'At the airport. I just got off a flight from Paris.'

'Which airport?'

'Frankfurt.'

What I feel is contradictory. Elation and deflation. 'I'm not in Frankfurt.'

All I can hear is the airport Tannoy relaying a message. In German.

'Where are you?'

'London,' I reply, before my brain has a chance to vet my mouth.

'London . . .'

'Why are you in Frankfurt?'

'I have a meeting. It was scheduled to take place in Mannheim. I asked them to change the location. I was hoping . . . you know . . .'

I can't help it. I get the same bittersweet feeling. 'I'm sorry, Kostya . . .'

'It was going to be a surprise but I guess I should have called you first.'

'It's still a surprise.'

He laughs. There's another announcement in the background. 'I'm going to Moscow tomorrow, Kate. Then back to New York.'

I want to tell him that I want to see him again. As soon as possible. Instead, I find myself saying, 'I see.' My tone

233

couldn't be more neutral or disinterested. Sometimes, I really
can't believe myself. He asks what I've been doing. I give him
hazy answers, which may or may not be sensible. I don't
know because I'm too wrapped up in a sense of disappoint-
ment, which is ridiculous. Five minutes ago, I had no idea
that he was hoping to see me. I should feel smug and warm.

'I have to go,' he says.

Another opportunity presents itself for me to give him a
sign. But I can't. I don't know what it is that stops me. The
words congeal in my throat, choking me.

And then he's gone.

The following day, half past midday. Stephanie sat
cross-legged on the sitting-room floor with a bowl of
vegetable soup and a sandwich bought from a bakery
on Kensington Church Street. The TV was on but silent.
Around her, scattered in an arc across the carpet were
printed pages of A4 and handwritten notes on scraps of
paper. The laptop was beside her. She scrolled through
the details of the homes that Vladimir Vatukin had
acquired: in Moscow, a house in Setun and an apartment across the road in the exclusive Golden Keys complex, a grand apartment in Rome, a chalet in Zermatt
and a villa in Cyprus. His ex-wife and three children
lived in a house on the Lake Geneva shoreline and had
an apartment in Knightsbridge, London. Vatukin also
maintained a modest apartment in Novosibirsk, his
birthplace. And one of Tsentralnaya's birthplaces, too.

Stephanie accessed the Tsentralnaya files and sub-
selected Vatukin. Four photographs appeared on the
screen: Moscow – 23 July, leaving White Square, a club
on New Arbat; Hamburg – 27 July, on his way into
Terminal Four at Fuhlsbüttel Airport; Almaty – 19

August, stepping out of the Hotel Otrar on Gogolya Street; Yekaterinburg – 4 September, walking along Voznesensky Prospekt. All taken since he'd assumed control of Tsentralnaya following Oleg Rogachev's murder.

Stephanie examined the photograph taken in Almaty on 19 August. Vatukin was next to Anatoli Medayev. Medayev had been a trusted confidant of Rogachev but was supposed to have been frozen out of Tsentralnaya after Paris. Yet here he was, a few months later, walking shoulder to shoulder with his mentor's successor.

Stephanie came across Natalya Markova, Vladimir Vatukin's mistress. In the photograph, her hair was long and blonde, not short and dark red, and the man at her side was Oleg Rogachev, not Vatukin. The date told the story. It was eighteen months old. Before Vatukin, then. Rogachev and Natalya were climbing into a black Mercedes outside the Metropol in Moscow. Stephanie programmed a close-up for Natalya's face. Hers was an unusual beauty: a little too angular, perhaps, for the bland perfection required of the ideal model. High Slav cheekbones, a strong chin, almond-shaped eyes. In the photo, Natalya was exactly what she was supposed to be. A luxurious made-to-measure accessory. Like a beautifully tailored overcoat, she made Rogachev look good.

When she'd finished her soup, she took the bowl to the kitchen, returned with a cup of instant coffee and turned her attention to the information package Stern had sent her mid-morning.

The Tsentralnaya crime syndicate was based in Moscow but its origins lay further east in Yekaterinburg, in the Urals, and in the western Siberian city of

Novosibirsk. The senior figures within the organization, including Vladimir Vatukin, had all been raised according to the rules and traditions of *vorovskoi mir*, Thieves World, a closed criminal society whose origins dated back to the peasant banditry of the seventeenth century.

With hindsight, the activities of the bandits were as political as they were criminal, a protest against the brutal rule of the Tsars. Robbers who attacked government officials were celebrated. A culture of silence grew up around perpetrators. The bandits organized themselves into groups where each man was equal and where profits were divided. In other words, they based themselves loosely upon a Communist ideal that, officially, wouldn't be born for another two hundred years.

In the Soviet Union, there was no organized crime. That was the official Party line. The truth was rather different. One of the most crucial tenets of *vorovskoi mir* was its refusal to acknowledge the State, be it Tsarist or Communist. This wasn't mere rejection, this was a deliberate failure to recognize that the State even existed. To pay taxes or to serve in the army was regarded as complicity with authority and was, therefore, a crime against *vorovskoi mir*. There was no middle way and there was no age limit. Such blatant defiance resulted in the wholesale imprisonment of this criminal class during the Soviet era but it did not signify the end of their world. Far from it.

The underworld bosses simply ran their empires from behind bars. From the Ural mountains to the Kolyma region of eastern Siberia, along the entire length of the Trans-Siberian railway, hundreds of labour camps were established, linked by a necklace of steel track. From the blasted wilderness, *vorovskoi mir* flourished, running the black market created by central government's inability to provide for the people; they traded in alcohol, jewels, spare parts for cars, food, timber, petroleum, anything for which there was a demand. So efficient was this underworld – and so inefficient the authoritarian world above – it was inevitable that there would be collusion between the two. Corruption bloomed, those in the loop prospered and, up to a point, the arrangement worked.

With the collapse of the Soviet Union in 1991, however, a vast vacuum was created. When the gates of the prisons opened, the blinking *vory* stepped back into a world that looked very different from the one they'd left behind. The rigid authoritarian structure was gone. There was nothing to replace it. The chaotic free-for-all that followed gave birth to a new breed of criminal. Not raised to respect the ways of *vorovskoi mir*, the new criminal took what he could, eliminating anyone in his way without a thought for the consequences. Because, more often than not, there were no consequences.

Traditionally, the *vory* had not been motivated by materialism. Theirs was a brotherhood where fraternity was valued more highly than possessions. The new criminal had no such morality. He was in it for what he could get. And if he could get what you had too, even better. To make matters worse, the most efficient practitioners of this new criminality tended to be Uzbeks, Azeris, Chechens. Regarded as filthy southerners from the Caucasus, their poisonous presence soon began to be felt in St Petersburg and Moscow.

The leaders of *vorovskoi mir* were presented with an awkward choice: to stay true to the principles that had served them so well since the early seventeenth century or to confront the new threat directly. From within Khabarovsk Central Penitentiary, Oleg Rogachev, then head of Tsentralnaya, had overseen his organization's expansion from Yekaterinburg and Novosibirsk to Moscow. He was not about to allow 'a bunch of dog-fucking monkeys from the south' to jeopardize Tsentralnaya's evolution. Even before his 1992 release, he was orchestrating retaliation from his frozen cell five thousand miles to the east. Attempts to muscle in on Tsentralnaya business were brutally countered. Released, Rogachev moved to Moscow and intensified his campaign of violence against 'others', and, in particular, 'southern others'. During the first Chechen War, Tsentralnaya supplied Russian troops with vodka and extra food parcels. These were paid for by Rogachev himself, a gesture that would have been unthinkable to the traditional *vory*. But that was the point. Rogachev was neither one thing nor the other.

This change, he was fond of saying, was nothing less than Darwinian. Tutored in the ways and history of *vorovskoi mir*, Rogachev, like many others – including Konstantin Komarov – had adapted to ensure the survival of the species. And having adapted, he'd continued the Darwinian theme by then doing his best to eliminate the greatest threat to the species: namely, all his business rivals. Viewed in such a context, his own violent end had been entirely predictable, although the timing of it remained less clear cut.

The buzzer went at five past seven. Rosie Chaudhuri was wearing a navy overcoat and a purple silk scarf. Stephanie said, 'I'm sorry to drag you over here. I didn't want to come in.'

'That's okay. I was on my way home, anyway.'

'Where to?'

'I have a flat on the Seven Sisters Road.'

'This is hardly "on the way home" then, is it? Can I get you something to drink?'

'No. I'm fine.'

'Seriously. It's the least I can do. There's a bottle of wine in the fridge.'

'All right.'

Rosie shed her overcoat and scarf while Stephanie headed for the kitchen. She returned with a bottle of Sauvignon Blanc and two glasses. They went into the sitting room and she watched Rosie take in the organized chaos: charts, lists, sketches, road maps, photographs. They sat on the sofa and Stephanie ran through the contact procedures she'd prepared. It took twenty minutes. Rosie absorbed everything. The information was written down but Stephanie could see that was unnecessary.

As she refilled their glasses, Rosie said, 'You know, Stephanie, I still find it hard to believe you went independent.'

'I still find it hard to believe you work for Alexander.'

Rosie looked embarrassed.

'Let's face it, we both know why I worked for him. And in a world of twisted logic, that made some kind of sense. But you? I just don't get it.'

Stephanie knew she was staring but didn't care. Flawless skin, full lips, eyes almost as dark as her own, and with thick, long, black hair. Slim but not thin, elegant when she moved, always well dressed, articulate, intelligent, the idea of Rosie working for Alexander seemed criminally wasteful. Stephanie felt a pinch of envy but a greater measure of puzzlement.

Rosie shrugged lamely. 'Somebody has to do what we do.'

'And that's enough for you?'

'Well, it's not the *only* thing in my life, you know. I have friends, a family. I go out, I take holidays. Just like everyone else.'

Stephanie rolled her wineglass between her hands. 'And the people in your life – your family, the friends you go on holiday with – what do you tell them when they ask about what you do?'

'Probably the same thing as you tell the people in your life. Whatever works.'

'Poulenc?'

He looks at me and smiles sweetly. 'You've got a functioning memory but no ear. It's Bach. Goldberg Variations, played by Glenn Gould.'

The three identities are laid out on the workbench. Irish, French, German. Passports, vaccination cards for some, driving licences, credit cards (not yet activated). I've already picked up the Swiss identity. The final passport – Kelly Reynolds, an American – is not yet ready. I hand over the padded envelope with the money in it. Bradfield's sense of discretion won't allow him to count the cash until after I've gone. We don't have to worry about trust. Unlike Kostya and I.

The Irish and German passports are relatively new. The others are older and Bradfield has taken care to age them; the corners are dog-eared, there are puncture points in some of the pages made by fictional staples that once fastened visas. Some of the stamps are bold, others are almost illegibly faint. The signature on the French passport is slightly smudged. The ink has faded with the passing of imaginary years.

'They're beautiful.'

He blushes. 'Thank you.'

I kiss him on the cheek, which fuels his shyness. However, just as I'm about to scoop all the documents into my navy knapsack, I notice the name on the Irish passport. I check it twice, to make sure.

'I'm sorry, Cyril. I didn't spot that. This one's no good.'

He looks mortified and I feel bad that I've upset him. 'What is it?'

I hand the passport over. 'The name.'

He looks at it, frowns deeply and shakes his head. 'What's wrong with it?'

'You are joking, aren't you?'

'No. What is it?'

Either he's a master of deadpan, or he genuinely doesn't know. 'You don't get out much, do you, Cyril?'

'Sorry?'

'When was the last time you went to the cinema?'

It takes him ten seconds to make a guess. 'Sometime in the Eighties, I should think. Maybe a bit earlier.'

'Do you watch much TV?'

He looks apologetic. 'I prefer to read.'

'But not Hello! *magazine, I don't suppose.' He shakes his head. Impulse swamps me. This time, I kiss him on both cheeks and then hug him. 'You're gorgeous.'*

'Stephanie, please . . .'

'Julia Roberts is a film star, Cyril. She makes ten million dollars a picture. She's about the most famous female face on the planet. The last thing I need is a name that makes every airline or hotel check-in clerk look at me twice.'

Groningen, Wednesday afternoon. Stephanie drank a cup of coffee at a café on the Grote Markt. It was raining. The large square was almost empty. She gazed at the Martinikerk, in the northern corner. The top of its tower was almost lost in the low cloud that had loomed over northern Holland all day.

It was five to four. She left coins beside her cup and ventured outside. It took ten minutes to walk to the address on Brugstraat. There was a bell beneath an old Agfa film sign but the door was ajar, so she didn't bother ringing. The air smelt of mould. A narrow staircase took her to the first floor. The office was a single room. The sign on the frosted window said Northern Line Containers. Beneath it, a name: Frans Leyden. On the wall to her left, an old poster of a cargo ship, on the wall to the right, a calendar and peeling mauve paint over cracked plaster. A crooked man sat at a computer terminal, shrouded in cigarette smoke, his back to her. He raised a hand and said something in Dutch that she didn't understand.

In English, she asked, 'Are you Frans Leyden?'

'Who wants to know?'

'Somebody who believes that Frans Leyden's real name is Eric Roy.'

The spine tensed, the hand froze. Very slowly, he turned round. She watched recognition wash over him, followed by fear. Roy's pale skin turned grey, matching his unkempt hair, which had been mousy brown the last time she'd seen him. He was wearing glasses. She wondered whether the lenses were clear. He'd never worn them in the past and he might have felt in need of a prop to change his appearance. The dramatic loss of weight made him look gaunt and old. Perhaps he was ill, she thought. Or perhaps his nerves were shot. He'd always been the anxious type.

'Hello, Eric.'

'Christ. You.'

'Yes, Eric. Me.'

'I heard you were dead.'

'Maybe I am. You look as though you've seen a ghost.'

'What do you want?'

'What I always want from you. Information.'

'I'm not in that business any more.'

'That's a shame. You really should have stuck to arms dealing. You knew what you were doing with that. But hardcore child pornography on the Internet? I'm disappointed in you, Eric. Although not surprised.'

'I'm not doing that any more, either.'

'No, I guess not. I imagine that's why you left Amsterdam and came to Groningen. And I suppose that's why you changed your name and set up this vast multinational in this palatial office of yours. Northern Line Containers? Where *are* your containers, exactly? Dotted all over the great ports of the world? Or stacked up against a wall in your imagination? And what are you transporting these days?' She watched his face and followed the lead he inadvertently gave her. 'Or could it be that you don't have any containers? Maybe you've

243

decided to go back to doing what you do best.' He flinched. 'Maybe you're *back* in the arms business.'

'What do you want to know?'

'Well, well. I'm one step ahead of my source. That makes a nice change. It'll make a nice profit, too, when I let him know.'

Roy was on the verge of panic. He extinguished his cigarette and fumbled for a fresh one. Stephanie closed the office door and stepped closer. Roy squirmed in his chair but made no attempt to get up. Had she wanted to kill him, he would have offered no resistance. There were some who were like that. When the moment came, they froze, apparently resigned to their fate. Like sheep.

'Weapons, Eric. They've always been your speciality. Not pictures of gang-rape.'

He swallowed, then nodded. 'I can get you anything.'

'Hardware?'

'Hardware, software. Menswear . . .' His attempt at the joke and the giggle that followed were equally pathetic. 'Anything.'

'Nuclear?'

He sagged a little. 'Christ . . . I don't know. Maybe . . .'

'BW?'

'No fucking way.'

'Don't lie to me. You said you could get me anything.'

'Biological is different . . .'

'Istanbul, January 1999. Weaponized anthrax. You were the broker. The vendors were Russians, the end users were anti-Taliban Afghan militants. The deal fell through.'

For a moment, he looked as though he might cry. 'It was the only time. BW's not my thing. Same with

244

chemical or nuclear. I hate that shit. I'm hardware and software. You want an Apache or a MiG, let's talk.'

'But you managed it.'

He was shaking his head. 'Look, it wasn't my deal . . .'

'I'm not looking to buy, Eric.'

'No?'

'No. But somebody else is. And I need to find out who. As soon as possible.'

He recovered a little composure. 'I guess I could ask around.'

'You'll do better than that, Eric. I'm serious. I want names. And if I don't get them, the nice folk of Groningen are going to get a name from me. Yours. I don't know what they think about Frans Leyden but I'm pretty sure they won't be too happy with Eric Roy. Not when they learn he's wanted in Amsterdam for running pre-teen pornographic websites.'

'Bitch!'

'Don't bother, Eric. Flattery will get you nowhere.'

When Stephanie stepped onto Brugstraat, it was still raining. In the Northern Line Containers office, Eric Roy was kneeling on the floor, cupping his broken nose with both hands, blood leaking through his fingers.

Zurich, Thursday, one thirty in the afternoon. They were at a table set in an alcove at the rear of the Brasserie Rudolf, a small restaurant just off the Bahnhofstrasse, a short walk from Guderian Maier. The dining room was dark, warm, discreet; a small tasselled lamp on each of the nine tables, net curtains over the windows, a log fire crackling in an iron grate.

Albert Eichner was eating *Geschnetzeltes Kalbsfleisch*, thin slices of veal in a cream sauce. Stephanie had grilled chicken breast and salad. They were drinking Puligny Montrachet.

The previous afternoon, in Groningen, she had looked a grubby twenty-five, dressed in khaki combat trousers, Caterpillar boots, a tatty V-neck jersey and old denim jacket. Her hair had been a gelled mess. Now, she could have been a sophisticated thirty-five, with her hair parted and slicked back, with her black Joseph suit and the cashmere overcoat hanging on a peg by the door.

When Eichner talked about his wife, three children and seven grandchildren, he was the embodiment of contentment. It wasn't a life Stephanie would have wanted but it was all he had ever aspired to; a large house outside Zurich and a villa in Tuscany, a comfortable job in an elegant office on the Bahnhofstrasse – he'd inherited the job from his father-in-law – and the respect of his peers. Yet when Stephanie had first met him, three and a half years earlier, he'd been a man on the verge of suicide.

He'd described it as a moment of madness. A business trip in North America, too many cities, too little sleep, a temporary absence of sense. He'd never been able to rationalize it. He'd been in New York when it happened. A late night drink at the bar in the Westbury, where he was staying. Tired and a long way from home, it had been one drink too many, really. He fell into conversation with a woman: Italian, dark-skinned, long dark red hair, a real beauty.

At that point, Stephanie had imagined she could see where the confession was heading. But she was wrong.

Eichner and the woman drank some champagne and

then went up to his bedroom. They kissed and shed their clothes. Eichner remembered feeling quite drunk. The next thing he remembered was waking up alone and being violently ill. No ordinary hangover, his whole system felt poisoned. His body ached all over, there were bruises on his neck and arms, flecks of blood on the crumpled white sheets. There was a hole in his memory and no sign of the woman. He checked his wallet, which was on the table. No money was missing. He sorted through his papers. They were complete. Then he returned to bed, where he remained for two days.

A week later, he was back in Zurich. Four days after that, a hand-delivered envelope appeared on his desk at Guderian Maier. Inside, photographs, forty-eight of them, in colour. And no negatives. There was no Italian beauty, either. Instead, Eichner was presented with snapshots of himself and a young, muscular, dark-skinned man with gold nipple-rings. Flicking through them, the bruises and aches began to make sense.

'I thought I was going to have a heart attack,' he'd confided to Stephanie. 'Right there in the office. I think the only thing that prevented it was the thought that the photos would be found beside me. News of an affair with a woman – a beautiful Italian woman, for instance – would be a scandal in a world like mine. But not necessarily a terminal scandal. However, this was something entirely different . . .'

The woman phoned and demanded to see him. When they met, she laid down the conditions for the negatives: money to be bled from certain Guderian Maier accounts and information to be supplied for a selection of account holders. Impossible, Eichner told

247

her. She told him to consider the consequences and gave him a week to decide. Stephanie met Eichner five days later in Copenhagen.

She'd been Petra then. And being the predator she was, she'd seen an opportunity.

'I don't have much time,' Eichner had told her.

He'd been ghostly pale, trembling constantly. It had occurred to her that he might die of natural causes before the deadline. She'd asked what he'd do if she turned him down. He'd stiffened his spine and met her gaze with as much dignity as he could muster. 'All I can do to protect my family and my bank from the shame of my disgrace.'

That wasn't the reason she'd taken the job. It wasn't the money, either. It was his refusal to accede to the woman's demands that had persuaded her.

'I'll do it on one condition.'

'Name it.'

'You become my banker.'

Too terrified to deny her anything, he'd nodded.

Petra had smiled when she said, 'Consider them dead.'

And within a week, they were.

The name of Petra Reuter had never been mentioned. In Copenhagen, she was just a woman who might be able to help. Later, she became who she was in the south of France – Stephanie Schneider. Stephanie was sure it must have crossed Eichner's mind that she and Petra were one and the same. When her name appeared in the papers, money soon appeared in Stephanie Schneider's numbered account and he could be under no illusion about her line of work. One day, she'd always promised herself, she would ask him.

'So, Stephanie, enough of my news. What brings you to Zurich?'

'I need a favour, Albert.'

He patted her hand fondly. 'For you . . . anything.'

'I need to hear the kind of whispers that don't reach my ears.'

'Go on.'

'It might involve a breach of your code of confidentiality.'

He nodded. 'Shall we order some coffee? A little cognac, perhaps?'

'Sure.'

He summoned the waiter, placed the order, and bought himself the time he needed. When they were alone again, he said, 'You are the one exception who proves the rule. Before you, there were none.'

Vienna, Friday. It was a beautifully crisp morning, a stiff breeze blowing down Dorotheergasse. Kleist didn't open until ten. Stephanie checked her watch. It was five past. The sign over the door was gold German Gothic script on black wood. It had been distressed to give it age but Stephanie knew that the shop had been open less than three years.

Inside, she found herself in a brilliant forest of brightness. Dozens of lights hung from the ceiling, all at different heights. Light was refracted through the cut glass of two dozen chandeliers. There were lamps of all sizes with every type of base: porcelain, brass, copper, wood, ceramic, glass, Perspex. Columns, curling stems and chubby cherubs, they sat in clusters on the floor, they swamped coffee tables, desks, mantelpieces, chests of drawers. Stephanie wondered how many bulbs were illuminating the room. Three hundred, four hundred?

'I've often wondered whether I would ever see you again. Almost always, I've concluded that I wouldn't. You're still the most beautiful menace I've ever seen.'

She turned to the source of the sound. He was sitting absolutely motionless in a high-backed leather armchair beneath a halo of candlelight.

'I see you haven't lost your silver tongue.'

'I heard you were dead.'

'That's becoming a contagious assumption.'

'It's a natural assumption. Not many of your type live to retire. You make too many enemies. When we stop hearing about you, we assume the hunter has become the hunted.'

Bruno Kleist rose stiffly from his chair. The wispy remains of his hair were now entirely white. Thick-lensed glasses hung from a red ribbon round his neck. He wore a navy cotton shirt, a heavy bottle-green cardigan and a pair of worn corduroy trousers. He looked like everybody's favourite grandfather. And not at all like a veteran of the Stasi, the dreaded former East German secret police.

Following the collapse of the Berlin Wall, the Stasi was disbanded. Many of its operatives transferred their allegiance to the SVR, formerly the First Chief Directorate of the KGB, with responsibility for Russia's spies abroad. Bruno Kleist chose not to. He opted to become independent. Before fleeing East Germany, he took care to excoriate himself from Stasi records and to plunder as many top secret files as he could. These provided the basis for his new business. Like Stern, Kleist became an information broker. Unlike Stern, he preferred direct contact with buyers and sellers alike.

Stephanie made a show of admiring her surroundings. 'So, after all those years hiding in the shadows, you've decided to come into the light.'

'You're not the first to make that joke.'

They went into the back of the shop where there was a diminutive kitchenette. Stephanie stood in the doorway because there wasn't room for two inside. Over a spluttering gas ring, Kleist prepared hot chocolate for them, adding a vanilla pod to each mug.

'What are you looking for?'

'Anonymous end users. They're in the market for a biological weapon. The vendor is a Russian, alias Koba.'

Kleist handed her a mug. 'Have you spoken to Eric Roy?'

'I saw him the day before yesterday.'

'What did he say?'

'Not much.'

Kleist raised a bushy white eyebrow.

Stephanie shook her head. 'He's still breathing. Through a sore nose.'

'Do you know about Istanbul?'

'I know he brokered a deal that fell through.'

'The purchasers were Afghans. They couldn't raise the money. They were going to fund the deal with opium. But they started to argue with each other like Afghans always do.'

'And so it collapsed.'

'It was called off.'

'By Roy?'

'Roy wasn't the broker. He was just a front.'

'Who was behind him?'

'Salman Rifat.'

The name sent a shudder through Stephanie. A man who'd enjoyed being behind Petra. Many times. 'Roy never mentioned that.'

'I would imagine that Rifat was nervous about dealing with temperamental Afghans, so he paid Roy to act on his behalf. And Roy, being Roy, looked no further than the money.'

'That sounds plausible.'

'If I were you, I'd find Salman Rifat.'

They talked for a further half hour. They exchanged contact procedures. Kleist wanted nothing in return for the information. He was clean, he told her. Had been for eighteen months. A shop full of antique lights was enough. After twenty years with the Stasi and a further nine as an independent, all he wanted now was a quiet life. And where better for that than Vienna?

When she left, he escorted her to the door. 'I'm happy you came,' he told her. 'And I'm happy that the rumours were wrong. I may be out of the business but that doesn't mean I can't reminisce. To talk like this, over a cup of hot chocolate, I can almost convince myself that it was worth it.'

'But it wasn't?'

He smiled. 'Of course it wasn't. It was a waste of time, a waste of resources, a waste of lives. You don't need me to tell you that.'

She stepped onto Dorotheergasse. A hundred yards later, her mobile rang.

'Where are you?'

She stopped walking. 'Vienna.'

'Will you be there tonight?'

'I could be. Where are you?'

* * *

The first time, I can't pretend we're making love. It's just sex. Hunger, perspiration, rawness. It's lust first, emotion later. When we've come, we lie on the bed in a knot of warm limbs and say nothing. The second time is slower, deeper, sweeter.

Pigeons dart past our window against a darkening sky. We're on the third floor of the Pension Elisabeth. Our room is in the eaves of the roof; a varnished wood floor, a couple of worn rugs, a creaking brass bed, lithographs of the Hofburg on the wall. In the cramped bathroom, there's a deep free-standing bath with green stains around the plughole. The enamel basin has yellowed with age.

Kostya lights a Marlboro. I'm running my fingers over his damp skin. At the centre of his chest, there's a church floating on clouds. A Russian Orthodox cross rises from a central onion dome. Angels circle overhead.

'Do they mean something?'

'Each spire is a conviction.' *He has four. He points to a tattoo on his right bicep.* 'This is the White Guard crest. The White Guard fought against the Red Army during the Revolution. It signifies seniority within a gang.'

'Were you with a gang?'

'No. But I was close to many people in many gangs. It's a mark of respect.'

'Do all of them mean something?'

'Not all, but most. Tattoos are the language of prison. Spiders are drug addicts, cats are thieves, skulls are killers. A skull on an epaulette means the victim was significant: a high-ranking member of another gang, a public figure. Barbed wire on the forehead means a life sentence. Some tattoos are given as punishments. Sex offenders get a dagger through the neck or shoulder.'

'How are they done?'

'Needles, old razor blades, sharpened knives. The colours

come from soot, ink, shampoo.' Kostya takes a long draw from his cigarette. 'Even urine.'

'Didn't you ever get infected?'

'I was lucky. Others weren't. Some of them died.'

I continue to trace them with my fingertips. 'It's weird. Even though I can see them on you, I don't really believe that you have them. They look as though they belong to somebody else.'

'They do belong to somebody else. They belong to the man I used to be.'

'You were a criminal then. You're a criminal now.'

He doesn't take offence. 'I wasn't a criminal then. I was just a man trying to stay alive.'

'And now?'

He thinks about it, then shakes his head. 'I don't know what I am.'

'But you know who you are, don't you?'

The tone in my voice makes him turn to me. 'Meaning?'

'Your background, vorovskoi mir. Whatever you are, wherever you are, you always know who you are.'

He smiles but there's caution in it. 'What about you? Do you know who you are?'

'Not any more. I think I've forgotten.'

'Personally, I think you're a woman of secrets.'

'You could be right.'

'Since New York, I've been trying to discover who you are. It hasn't been easy.'

Something flutters in my chest. 'And what have you found out?'

He rolls a hand back and forth. 'A little of this, a little of that.'

'Tell me.'

He looks into my eyes. 'I know the assassin who killed

George Salibi and Ruth Steifel in New York was probably a woman.'

A sucker punch and I've walked straight into it. I try to be inscrutable but fail.

Kostya carries on. 'I know Salibi's bodyguards chased the killer across the roof of the building. The assassin jumped into the elevator shaft. The bodyguards heard a cry. A woman's cry. She must have suffered some kind of injury. But she still managed to escape. By a process of elimination, that narrows the range of possible injuries.'

'You're guessing.'

He puts his hand on my injured left shoulder and squeezes softly. 'That doesn't make me wrong.' Then he takes my left hand, which is healing but still badly marked. 'Does it?'

I'm trying to imagine what he's thinking. He assumed I was in New York to reach Koba. He knew I met Anatoli Medayev at the Somerset. And now he can place me at Central Park West.

'The phone number and fax number for Galileo Resources in London are no longer working.'

True. Magenta House closed them down once I was back from New York.

'Kate March is a mystery.' He glances at my clothes, which are scattered across the bedroom floor. 'I think if I looked through your things, I'd find out you were someone else. Who does your passport say you are? Or your credit cards?'

I can't tell what he feels. Is he angry, anxious, oblivious?

He touches the cosmetic scar on the front of my left shoulder. 'You said you got this in a car crash. To me, it looks like a bullet wound. Entry here, exit at the back.'

All I can muster is: 'I'm sure you'd know.'

'I do know.'

'Well, like you said, I'm a woman of secrets.'

'Is Mechelen a secret?'

I freeze. There's no point in lying now.

'From New York to Moscow,' he says, 'there are too many names to go with too many theories about what happened on Central Park West. But of the serious candidates, there are only a few. And of those, fewer still are women. But there is one. An assassin. A terrorist. She's not been around for a while but her record speaks for itself. She has the talent, no question. The problem is, nobody knows where she is or what she really looks like. There is one thing, though. One distinguishing mark. A few years ago, she was part of a gang in Belgium. There was a shoot-out with police in the town of Mechelen. She was wounded but managed to escape. Her injury? A bullet through the left shoulder.'

I'd say something if I could but I can't. For Kostya, my silence is enough.

'Your name is Petra Reuter.'

Now, I'm more naked than I want to be. I sit up and pull a blanket around myself. Kostya doesn't move. When I do find something to say, it sounds angry, irrelevant and petty. 'So, you thought you'd fuck me a couple of times before bringing this up . . .'

'And if I'd said nothing? How many times would you have fucked me before bringing it up?'

They found a cheap Italian place; faded photographs of Sicily on the walls, red check tablecloths, candles in green glass bowls on each table, Neapolitan love songs oozing from hidden speakers. They ate pizza and drank Chianti. Komarov wore the suit he'd arrived in, but no tie. It was a Brioni. Stephanie had seen the label while they were dressing. Most men wore suits like pyjamas. Crumpled and ill-fitting, they were an insult, not a compliment. Lean and with an upright posture, Komarov wore them beautifully. The man on the other side of the table was not the same man who'd shared a bed with her all afternoon. He was a businessman; cultured, rich, confident. Not a tattooed ex-convict. It seemed absurd that a few clothes could make such a difference. But there it was.

'Does it matter?' Stephanie asked.

It was the question she had been wanting to ask for an hour. For once, she'd found herself uneasy in the silent spaces. Now, she could bear it no longer.

'I can still be Kate March, if you want me to be. That's the beauty of Petra.'

'That's crazy.'

'Of course.'

'I don't want you to be Kate March.'

'But you don't want me to be Petra Reuter, either? You seem . . . reluctant.'

Komarov drained his glass and refilled it. 'When I realized it might be you, I kept telling myself, that's not possible. Now that I know for sure . . .'

Stephanie felt something close to panic. 'What?'

'The more I learnt about you – about what you've done – the harder it was to accept that you and she are the same person. It didn't seem to fit. It still doesn't.'

She wanted to say that Salibi and Steifel had been dead when she found them but knew that Komarov wouldn't believe her. She was there, they were murdered. Now, because of the chaos that had followed, it was assumed that the assassin had been female, hardening the case against her. Had she been in Komarov's position, she wouldn't have believed herself.

'What about Medayev? Did Tsentralnaya have him killed?'

'Apparently.'

'You think it could have been someone else?'

'Anatoli lived in dark corners. I knew him as well as anyone but I didn't know him at all. It looked like Tsentralnaya but it wouldn't surprise me if it turned out to be someone else.'

'What about Salibi?'

'What about him?'

'You were in business with him.'

'He's not the first of my business partners to be killed.' The way he said it was so matter-of-fact. No emotion, no surprise. 'In Moscow, being murdered is an occupational hazard for any rich businessman. If there's a dispute, that's the solution. In New York, you use a lawyer. In Moscow, you use an Uzi. It's quicker, cleaner and cheaper.'

'You don't have any feelings about Salibi?'

'We weren't friends. Money was all that kept us together. And that's not a good reason.'

'I'm not sure you're telling the truth.'

'Maybe you'd prefer a sentimental answer?'

'Never.'

He smiled but it was chilly. 'I didn't think so.'

'What about me? Who I am, what I do – does it matter to you?'

'Not unless I'm a professional assignment.'

'I don't have sex with professional assignments.'

A waitress cleared their plates. They ordered two espressos. Komarov asked for a glass of Calvados, then lit another Marlboro.

'How could it matter to me, Petra? Am I one to judge?'

'I can't tell and I don't care.'

'Take it from me, I'm the last person who could object. Perhaps I should be asking you the same question.'

'You'd get the same answer.'

'Exactly. We can't pretend we're other people. Not with each other.'

If only that were true.

'I needed to hear you say it.'

'Do you really want to be judged against a standard that doesn't apply to us?'

'Is that what you think it is?'

Komarov nodded. 'Their rules are different to our rules. Their morality is different to our morality. To compare the two . . . you might as well compare a car with a banana.'

They were in Vienna for two days, making love, eating, drinking, drifting from one tourist attraction to the next. She rearranged her schedule for Komarov, breaking the most fundamental of the laws that Boyd had taught her: *never let any element of any single thing become personal.* At night, warmly drunk, they would try to stay awake for as long as possible. The best part of each day was waking. Finding him there beside her. Kissing him, memorizing the feel of him, the smell of him. The aroma of coffee mingling with his first cigarette of the day, a trace of aftershave, the taste of the bitter air outside. She was sure she would forget none of it.

When she told him that she knew how Irina had died, he seemed strangely ambivalent. When he asked how old she was, Stephanie said thirty-three because she'd forgotten Petra's age. Komarov told her he was forty-four and asked if she minded that he was so much older. She thought he looked like a little boy when he said it. She kissed him, told him not to be stupid and wondered if he'd feel better or worse if he'd known she was twenty-seven.

When he talked about business, it was impossible to connect him to his incarcerated past; now, it was wheat prices, a pharmaceutical joint venture with American and Finnish partners in Russia, a Latvian forestry project, an Estonian ferry company, a telecommunications joint venture with Swedish and German partners in western Siberia, the renovation of former State-owned factories in Novosibirsk and Yekaterinburg, property management in Manhattan, banking, hotels, airlines, oil, nickel, gold, gas, coal, diamonds.

'Is there anything that Mirsch isn't interested in?'

'Anything that's going to lose it money.'

She learnt that he liked Italian food best of all, loved Japanese, Thai and Indian but had never really enjoyed Chinese. He said he drank more than his expensive Manhattan doctor recommended but less than almost every Russian he knew; red wine through choice, vodka when the situation demanded it. She found out that he'd never owned a car.

'I'm never in one place long enough for it to make sense. Anyway, wherever I am, there are always people who will lend me a vehicle if I need it.'

'Always?'

'Always.'

He was a keen reader, when time allowed, but never chose fiction. When he watched films, he forgot them instantly. A nervous flyer, he'd learnt to sleep on aircraft because they were the one place where he couldn't be disturbed. He wasn't interested in possessions for the same reason he had no car but he was happy to spend money on good clothes because he wore them most of the time. His suits were all by Brioni or Canali, his formal shoes were all from Church's.

'These days, I spend ninety per cent of my time in a suit. When I was young, I would have considered that a form of heresy. And an impossibility.'

Which was about as close as either of them got to talking about the past. As soon as their conversation veered towards it, caution cut in. Both sensed it, neither mentioned it, not wanting to risk the fragile beauty of their time together.

The last morning came too quickly. Exhausted, Stephanie resented the hours lost to sleep. They made love in silence, they packed in silence. They drank coffee in the small dining room downstairs. There was a dread in her stomach that killed the appetite that had been so raucous. They checked out of the Pension Elisabeth and walked through the drizzle. Komarov said they had to be a secret. For purely professional reasons. She knew he was right but it hurt to agree. It seemed so corrupting.

They were standing by the airport bus at the Süd-bahnhof. The plump asthmatic driver said it was time to leave and climbed aboard. Stephanie stood on the bottom step and turned back to kiss Komarov for the last time.

'When will I see you again?'

'Soon.'

'*Where* will I see you again?'

'Somewhere.'

16

The complete resurrection of Petra Reuter took six weeks. If there were those who doubted that she had been responsible for the carnage of Central Park West, by the end of the first week in December there were few who doubted that she was back in business.

You should hear some of the gossip, Petra, Stern had said, via laptop, as she sped between Lyon and Paris on a TGV.

I'm already paying you a fortune, Oscar.

I offer this to you for free.

You're going soft in your old age. Go on, then.

Reasons for Petra's three years of silence: serious injury; unplanned pregnancy; retirement to the South Pacific; imprisonment in Indonesia, Colombia, Turkey or China – take your pick; a failed marriage, or a happy marriage; recruitment to the BND!

Stephanie had laughed out loud. When her co-passengers had turned to look at her, she'd covered her mouth with both hands. She'd typed her reply, still grinning.

Petra working for the BND or Petra as the next Pope? Which of the two is the least likely, I wonder.

For a month, she traversed Europe. Cheap hotels and hostels, cold train stations, airless airport terminals, overnight bus rides that left her reeking of old cigarettes and body odour. In Bremen, she caught food poisoning and spent thirty-six hours hunched over a toilet with a leaking cistern. In mid-November, she contracted a bout of influenza. For a week (through Maribor, Ljubljana, Split and three days in Bologna), she felt like an addict trying to kick a habit: virulently feverish, nauseous, shot through with aches and cramps, her mind scattered. London was always a pit stop; a change of clothes, a load of washing, a decent night's sleep, a new identity. She ate out or bought ready-to-eat food because there was no point in buying anything to put in the fridge. Long-term became twenty-four hours.

She communicated through Rosie Chaudhuri, as agreed, and, during the third week, when she was still in Germany, she received from her an address, a date and a set of brief instructions that took her to Paris. Two days later, at the specified time, she entered a crumbling apartment block in Montmartre. In a dark hall that smelt of drains and disinfectant, she found a package in the cubby-hole belonging to the apartment on the second floor. Janine Elway, c/o Yvette Blanco. Inside, photographs, addresses in Toulouse and Marseille, road maps with streets highlighted in fluorescent yellow. There was also a seventy-two hour timetable to follow. She took the trains and buses on the list. She ate at the appointed cafés at the appointed hours, she walked the routes, rang the numbers, spoke the words. She stayed at the selected hotels under the names chosen for her by Magenta House. Marseille was the last stop.

When it was over, she returned to Paris for her first reunion with Komarov, who flew in from New York. He'd booked a suite at the Crillon on place de la Concorde. Tired and fed up, Stephanie was less than gracious. She said it was conspicuous and stupid to stay at such a hotel. He agreed and kissed her.

'Kostya, I thought we had to be secret.'

'We do. Which is why we can't step outside these rooms until I leave.'

He was smiling and she couldn't be angry with him. 'When's that?'

'The day after tomorrow.'

The following morning, *Le Figaro* carried the story. Marat Manov, human-trafficker, shot in the back of the head as he stepped out of his apartment in Marseille. Stephanie recognized the address: the last place she'd visited, less than six hours before the shooting. Manov, a Russian from Nizhniy Novgorod, had been living in Marseille under an alias: Roman Casales. He'd been wanted in France for more than a year, accused of running a gang that smuggled illegal immigrants from eastern Europe and former Yugoslavia into western Europe. The majority arrived through ports along Italy's Adriatic coast – Lecce, Bari and Pescara – before moving on to France, Britain and Germany. Many of the women were forced into the sex industry to pay for their passage. Manov's gang ran prostitutes in Paris, Marseille, Toulouse, Lyon and Bordeaux.

The local authorities in Marseille said they suspected Manov's killer was a woman. One of his illegal immigrants, perhaps. There was a certain smugness in the suggestion. Further details were vague but Stephanie noted that the police in Toulouse were making enquiries of their own.

Komarov saw the story later. Stephanie was in the bath, half-asleep, when he appeared through the steam. She noticed the paper in his hand, folded to the correct page. He held it in front of her.

'Your work?'

'Don't ask.'

After Paris, Komarov returned to New York. Stephanie flew to Amsterdam and took the train to Groningen. She intercepted Eric Roy, who blanched when he saw her on Brugstraat, standing by the front door. As before, he made no attempt to resist her. He didn't even try to flee. Stephanie took him by the arm, escorted him upstairs and closed the door so that they were alone in the Northern Line Containers office.

'I hate to have to preach to the perverted, Eric, but you should have been more forthcoming when I was last here. Then I wouldn't have had to come back.'

'What do you want?'

Stephanie felt Petra's steel core. Gradually, as the days elongated into weeks, the old feelings had returned. Now, looking at Eric Roy, all she could muster was contempt. 'Istanbul. The deal that fell through. Why didn't you mention Salman Rifat?'

'I . . . I don't know.'

'Really? Let me guess. You didn't mention him because you're more afraid of him than you are of me.'

'No.'

She spent ten minutes with Roy. He answered all her questions. The more honest he was, the more she despised him. She'd seen the kind of pornography he'd traded and she knew the kind of man he was. He saw himself as a victim, not a co-conspirator. He couldn't see that trading images of sexual abuse made him a party to each act depicted. *It's only a picture.* That would be his defence, his justification. And his greatest weakness.

Stephanie stood up to go. 'I see the swelling's gone down. Is it still painful?'

The cartilage had been straightened, the bruising had almost faded, but the three stitches had left a ragged scar over the bridge of his nose. Roy couldn't bring himself to answer her. She leaned towards him and pressed the tip of her forefinger onto the shiny new skin.

'The next time you're deciding who to be afraid of, choose me.'

Later, she regretted breaking his nose again. Not because she felt any sympathy for Roy but because it had been unnecessary and, far worse, uncontrolled. In her prime, Petra wouldn't have bothered. The threat would have been enough.

Stephanie spent her birthday alone in Germany. She woke up in Dresden and went to sleep in Hannover. It was a miserable hotel; broken heating, damp down one wall, a family of Albanian immigrants on the other side of it. They argued most of the night. Somebody cried a lot. Stephanie could hear the fear in their raised voices. She was glad when the rain came and diluted the sound of them. In the morning, she woke with red bites up and down her arms and legs. Bedbugs.

She spent Petra's birthday with Komarov at the Atlantic Hotel in Hamburg.

'Come back to New York with me, Petra.'

'I can't.'

'I thought you could do whatever you liked.'

'That doesn't mean I don't have commitments.'

'To?'

'Come on . . .'

'A client?'

She took offence at his tone. 'Yes. A client.'

'Cancel. Change your schedule. Do something.'

'Why me? Why not you?'

'Because it's not so easy for me.'

'Not so easy? Why not? One call –'

'You're independent. I have a greater responsibility.'

Stephanie's laughter was hollow. 'Sure. The Don from the Don.'

'What do you mean by that?'

'Would you say this relationship was a partnership of equals?'

'It's not something I waste my time thinking about.'

'Well, waste a little now.'

'No.'

'Why not?'

'Because I'm not some self-obsessed sub-American who's always worried about what they feel.'

'Do you feel anything at all?'

'That's a cheap question.'

'Do you?'

'What do you think?'

'Well, you look as though you're enjoying yourself when you're fucking me. Apart from that, it's hard to tell. Who knows? Maybe you fake it. Maybe you feel nothing at all.'

He took a step towards her and stopped. He looked furious, then shocked.

'What's wrong, Kostya? Afraid to slap me?'

Silence.

'That *is* what you were going to do, wasn't it? Be a proper man, a proper Russian. Keep your lippy woman in her place with a black eye and a split lip.'

He met her stony stare fully.

'Because that's what it's about, isn't it? Gender. Control.'

Komarov looked genuinely mystified. 'Why are you being like this?'

'Why is it that we meet where *you* want to meet, and only when *your* schedule allows it?'

'Because that is the only way I can see you. The alternative would be not to see you at all. That would be worse.'

'Jesus Christ, that's not good enough! I won't be part of a relationship like that. Who do you think I am? Some bimbo with a gun who skips across Europe to lie spread-eagled on some hotel bed whenever it's convenient for you. What kind of relationship is that?'

He shook his head. 'I don't know but I can tell you one thing.'

'What?'

'It's nothing like our relationship. This situation we're in – this *affair* – isn't like anything I've ever known. Or even heard of. It's different. Because we're not like other people, we don't live by their rules, we don't accept their standards. So how can our relationship be judged next to theirs? None of the criteria apply. We have to make this up as we go along.'

'Fuck you.'

Stephanie turned for the door.

Komarov said, 'Before you go, you should know something about me, Petra. I've never hit a woman. I've never come close. Not even in the last sixty seconds.'

It's been raining all morning. I walk down Belgrave Place and turn into Eaton Square. It feels strange to have been in London for more than a single night. Sooner or later, though, Petra was bound to bring me back here. I press the brass button and look up at the brace of cameras over the door.

The lobby has two large antique mirrors, an Italian marble table, a smooth granite floor. I take the lift. In the upper lobby, outside the penthouse, I'm frisked by two olive-skinned men in tight dark brown designer suits. Rent-a-monkey. Long on brawn, short on brains, they're the kind who can't wear Versace without a Beretta. As they touch me up, I drip rain onto their clothes, which ruins their fun.

The flat is an excrescence; a corridor of chocolate walls and carpet leading to a drawing room with three black leather sofas, zebra-stripe cushions, large gold lamps on chrome coffee tables with smoked glass, a white carpet, crimson walls and ceiling. There's a huge lacquered cabinet to my left, housing four TV screens, VHS, DVD, satellite and an integrated sound system. To an outsider, this might be a joke. To me, it's a sign. I don't need to know the individual; I know the breed.

He's sitting in an armchair by the sliding windows that lead onto the balcony. Loose-fitting black slacks, Gucci slip-ons and a blue silk shirt, open at the throat, sleeves rolled up to the elbow, revealing muscular forearms the colour of gravy. His hair used to be stubble. Now, his scalp is smooth and shiny. His goatee beard is neatly trimmed. The watch is a gold Rolex. He wears a thick gold bracelet around the other wrist and a gold chain around the neck. Nothing but the most expensive for this one. Which is something I detest.

I, by contrast, have tried to look as shabby as possible. It hasn't been difficult. Light grey second-hand sweatpants, dirty Converse sneakers, a faded U2 T-shirt beneath a black V-neck with a hole in one elbow. And my old raincoat, of course, which is continuing to drip onto the white carpet. I could have caught a taxi but I chose the rain instead. Strands of dark *hair are plastered across my forehead. My nose is red and I'm cold.*

He's smoking a small cheroot. 'No umbrella, Petra?'

Salman Rifat. Turkish arms dealer. A man who'll smother you with charm before cutting you to pieces with a machete. Frankly, it's a surprise to see him here. When Stern tracked him down, I questioned it. Rifat in London? Unlikely, I replied. He used to come here a lot but the more successful he's become, the less safe it is for him to travel to countries like Britain, France and Germany. Stern sold me his mobile number and told me to call him personally.

'How long's it been, Petra?'

Not long enough. I've suppressed the dread but I haven't got rid of it. When Bruno Kleist suggested I find Rifat, I ignored his advice. I told myself I'd find another way. But I didn't. And my return visit to Groningen to see Eric Roy only con- firmed what I should have accepted from Kleist.

'Classy place you've got here, Salman.'

'I'm borrowing it from a friend.'

'What are you doing in London? Selling faulty guns to the Irish?'

Rifat's snort is contemptuous. 'I don't deal with amateurs any more. Or psychopaths.'

'What about anti-Taliban militants? Not the most stable group I can think of.'

'Personally, I consider being anti-Taliban as proof of a balanced mind. What about you, Petra? I hear stories . . .'

'You should know better.'

'I tried to find you. For two years, nothing. Then, suddenly, you're everywhere.'

'These days, I can afford to pick and choose. Like you.'

Rifat rises from his chair. I'd forgotten how large he is. Six foot seven, it says in his file. But it's not just his height.

He's immensely broad. His shoulders and neck are solid rolls of muscle, like old gnarled oak. His waist is so slim, it looks almost feminine. Rifat's been body-building for twenty years. He spends several hours a day doing weights, no matter where he is. I remember the hard flesh, the corrugated veins, the curious odour his steroid-rich skin emitted. The memory of it turns my stomach.

He opens the sliding glass door. We step onto the balcony, which is covered by a canopy. It's not his apartment, so he's worried about the wiring; he'll only speak freely in the open. It's cold, our breath freezing around us, but Rifat doesn't mind. He leans on the stone, peers into Eaton Square Gardens and puffs on his cheroot.

'What do you want?'

'Information. I'm willing to pay good money.'

I give him the list. We talk about Koba, terrorist groups, biological weapons and the identity of Rogachev and Marshall's assassin. He doesn't give me answers, he just refines my areas of interest. We're out there for ten minutes, the sound of the rain drumming on the canopy adding to our privacy.

When we go back inside, I say, 'Can you help?'

He nods. 'I can give you some of it now, the rest in forty-eight hours.'

The two monkeys in brown are where we left them.

'How much?'

'How much have you got?'

'Just tell me the amount and where you want it. I can have it arranged in an hour.'

Having flicked the last one onto the street below, he picks another cheroot out of a silver case. 'I don't need money, Petra. I've got too much already. I couldn't tell you how much that is. Not even with a margin of error of – let's say – five million dollars.'

'What do you want?'

'How did you find me?'

'An old contact.'

'Who?'

I could never sacrifice Bruno Kleist. But Eric Roy . . . that wouldn't be so bad.

'If I give you the name and where that name can be found, would we have a deal?'

He stares at me for half a minute. Then, without a word, he leaves the room. When he reappears, he's carrying a small bulbous blue bottle with a cork in the top. My blood turns cold. I know what's in the bottle. Olive oil from the estate he owns in Greece.

'You haven't forgotten, have you?'

God knows, I've tried.

He takes the cork out of the bottle. 'This is the deal.'

I look at him and then at the pair by the door. 'Those days are over, Salman. Think of something else.'

'Don't worry, Petra. I'm not an idiot. There may be three of us but we know who you are and what you can do.' He lights the new cheroot. 'I don't want to pressure you. I want you to choose to do this. Just like you used to.'

'You don't believe it was like that, do you?'

'In those days, you always looked a billion dollars for me. Today, you dress up as a tramp. Why is that? To discourage me?'

'I won't do it.'

'Let's be honest. You're here as a last resort, Petra. And this is the only thing I want from you.' A wolfish grin spreads across his face. 'You don't have anything else to bargain with.'

I shake my head and mutter, 'Not for the first time, you've overestimated yourself.'

*　　*　　*

272

Lev Golta was shot twice in the back of the head as he climbed into his rusting Volkswagen Passat outside the apartment block in which he'd been living for five months, close to Tempelhof Airport in Berlin. The killing took place just before six on a Monday morning. It was still dark, there were no witnesses. Stephanie had left Berlin the previous evening, shortly after seven. She'd been at Golta's apartment during Sunday afternoon to deliver a thick envelope that she had received earlier in the day. She'd removed the envelope from the DHL packaging but had not opened it. She'd taken the lift to the seventh floor, where she'd pressed the envelope through the narrow letter box in his door. On her way down, she'd passed two women on the stairs. They were the only people she saw.

It wasn't until Tuesday that she read of Golta's murder. She was between Nürnberg and Munich. It had been raining heavily and she'd been driving for five hours. She pulled into a service station for petrol and coffee. She spent half an hour reading a copy of the *Süddeutscher Zeitung*. It was a short report; Lev Golta, a Russian criminal wanted in Britain, had been shot dead in Berlin the previous morning. There were few details but the paper offered a brief profile. In the mid-Nineties, Golta had become notorious in Moscow as a ruthless gunman. His name became synonymous with wanton brutality; he'd disembowelled three of his victims and had tortured a fourth with a blowtorch. Video tapes were sent to the relatives of each victim. It was only a matter of time before Golta became the subject of a contract himself.

When it happened, he fled Moscow, headed west and changed careers. In London, he rented a flat in

Streatham and imported the latest machines from Russia to allow him to manufacture copies of American Express, MasterCard, Diners and Visa cards, which he sold for up to £400 each. He also used the cards to purchase goods – most often designer clothes, or electronic equipment – which he then sold for cash on the black market. When the police broke the ring, they arrested two of Golta's associates who named him as the man behind the scam. But it was too late. Golta had fled again. This time, to Berlin.

Stephanie didn't know why Magenta House had chosen him to be Petra's second victim. She'd just followed her instructions, as she had with Marat Manov. Alexander had said there would be two killings to legitimize her return to public life, so she now considered herself clear.

After her failure with Salman Rifat, she'd returned to continental Europe. She spent time with Komarov in Antwerp and Zermatt. After the tension of Hamburg, Antwerp was a relief. The bitterness had gone and the three days they spent together were passionate and intense. He'd acted as though the row had never happened.

'We don't have time to let it linger, Petra.'

Of course not. How could they, when their relationship was based on a few hours hastily stolen at a moment's notice? So she was happy to agree. By the end of Zermatt, there began to be familiarity in their intimacy. Previously, Stephanie had only achieved familiarity with a few men. It was usually accompanied by complacency and followed by boredom. She preferred to reserve intimacy for strangers, finding it easier to reveal more of herself to someone she knew she'd never see again. It was a truth she'd chosen not to confront. She had no interest in learning what it said about her. But with Komarov, things were different. Familiarity brought warmth, contentment, security. And she found herself wanting more of all three.

After Zermatt, Stephanie drove her rented Peugeot to Zurich to see Albert Eichner, who, as instructed, had left an e-mail for her at one of her AOL accounts. She arrived late in the afternoon and checked into the Hotel Leonhard on the Limmatquai. She went out to eat at eight thirty. When she returned, shortly before ten, there was another e-mail waiting for her. From Rosie Chaudhuri.

They met in a café just off the Münstergasse at eleven the following morning. Stephanie arrived first and secured a table in a corner at the back. The place was quiet, just half a dozen customers, a couple of them smoking, one whispering into a mobile. There were signed photos of downhill racers on the wooden walls and a set of antique wooden skis over the fireplace.

When Rosie entered, Stephanie didn't recognize her immediately. Her hair was shorter, not even collar-length, and she looked a lot leaner. There was a bruise on her right cheek and a bandage round her right hand. Stephanie's expression asked the question.

'Karate,' Rosie said.

'Karate?'

'I've joined a class. Three nights a week. There's a club up on the Seven Sisters Road, not far from my place.'

'What happened?'

She smiled but looked embarrassed. 'I wasn't paying

attention. I took a blow to the face, fell over and sprained my wrist.'

'Why karate?'

'Why not? I was bored with just going to the gym, getting fit. I wanted something a little more . . . a little more . . . well, *you* know.'

Stephanie wanted to say that she didn't but just nodded instead. Rosie sat down and unzipped the black leather bag she'd been carrying. A waitress with a bleach blonde crop and three rings through her left nostril appeared at the table for their order. Hot chocolate for Rosie, coffee for Stephanie.

Rosie produced a portable DVD player from the bag with a set of earphones. 'We couldn't send you this. That's why we had to meet.'

The disk was already in the machine. Rosie pressed play, then pause. The frozen footage was black-and-white: a small room with a single table bolted to one wall, one chair on one side, two on the other, three men in the room.

'A gift, courtesy of the Hungarian police. The one sitting down is a Russian. Strogvin, the manager at White Square in Budapest. Tsentralnaya runs a chain of White Square clubs. They're part casino, part restaurant, part nightclub, part strip joint. They've got four in Russia plus Prague, Bucharest, Budapest, Sofia, Athens, Berlin.'

Strogvin had a potbelly and long dark hair gathered in a ponytail. He wore a dark bomber jacket, a pale T-shirt, dark tracksuit bottoms. He was smoking a roll-up.

'There was a shooting outside the club so they dragged Strogvin in for questioning. He's not exactly a novice in the interview room; every time there's a Russian murder, Strogvin and his sort are given a grilling. It's a ritual. Everyone's on first-name terms. This is a recording of Strogvin's second interview. We're about ninety minutes in.'

Stephanie put on the headphones and Rosie hit the pause button again. The still began to move. The interview was conducted in Russian. At first, the questions centred on the petroleum smuggler who'd been shot outside White Square. He'd been with two girls who worked at the club.

'Were they prostitutes?' one of the officers asked.

'No way. I wouldn't allow that.'

'Do any of your girls sleep with the customers?'

'Not in White Square. We don't provide beds,' Strogvin joked. His voice was strangely feminine. 'Just drinks and a good time. What they do outside – in their own time – that's their business.'

'Business?'

He shrugged. 'If that's what they want. I don't know.'

The officer changed the sphere of questioning. 'Tell us about Anatoli Medayev.'

'He's dead. He was killed in New York.'

'Do you know why?'

Strogvin shrugged.

'There won't be a deal if your mouth stays shut.'

'Medayev was close to Rogachev . . .'

'Another dead man.'

'Exactly.'

'There was a connection between the deaths?'

Strogvin nodded. 'Koba.'

'Koba killed them?'

'Maybe.'

'Come on . . .'

'Look, there was a rumour. That's all.'

'What rumour?'

Strogvin avoided the gazes of both men.

'*What rumour?*'

'I heard that Koba's involved with terrorists.'

'What kind of terrorists? Chechens?'

'I don't know.'

'How's he involved?'

'He's gonna sell them . . . something.'

'Something nuclear?'

Strogvin shook his head, then nodded. 'Maybe. Something serious. He was going to do it last year but it went wrong. It got cancelled. Now, there's a new plan. Something in January.'

'How did Rogachev and Medayev fit into this?'

'What I heard was, they were involved with the first operation. The one that got cancelled. They travelled with Koba so they must have known about it. But the rumour is, they were against the sale.'

'Why?'

'Too dangerous. They didn't think the money was worth it. They didn't think *any* money was worth it. But Koba . . . well . . . once his mind is made up . . .'

'Where did they travel to?'

'Paris, first. Then Berlin. I think they were also in Amsterdam and Frankfurt. Then back to Paris.'

'When?'

'Earlier this year, end of January, early February.'

Rosie spoke over the top of the interview. 'There's more to go on than this. Reported sightings, hotel bills, airline bookings, credit card receipts – all in names he's known to have used. Not just in the places Strogvin mentions, but also Munich, Budapest, London and Baku.'

'Who told you?' asked one of the officers.

'No.'

'No name, no deal.'

Strogvin turned sharply in his chair. 'Then you can eat your deal! I'm not giving you *that* name.'

The shorter of the two officers asked, 'Who is Koba?'

'He comes from Moscow. He's got serious connections in America. And in Europe. Anywhere you can bribe an official or a policeman.'

'Here in Budapest?'

'I don't think so.'

'Why not?'

'The cops don't take bribes here. Not so much. I've heard they do in England. And in Germany. In America, they always do.'

'Koba's a big, fat man, right?'

Strogvin frowned. 'No. He's sort of medium build –'

'So you *have* met him?'

'Someone described him to me. They said he was slim and hard-looking.'

'Just like my mother,' sneered the shorter officer.

The interview ended. The image died and was replaced by a still photograph of a burnt-out Skoda in a ploughed field. There was a blurred village in the distant background.

'Where's this?' Stephanie asked.

'About twenty miles outside Budapest, less than forty-eight hours after the interview.'

'Let me guess. Strogvin was found in the boot wrapped in razor wire.'

Rosie frowned. 'You knew about this?'

'I know about the signature. It's Tsentralnaya. It's the way Medayev was killed in New York.'

Rosie turned off the DVD player. 'You heard him, Stephanie. Something in January. That's what he said. That's what he *knew*. And he was murdered for it.'

So, at the end of the first week in December, they met again in Paris. Stephanie booked a room at the Hotel Castex in Marais. Quiet, old-fashioned, family-run, it felt like a better place for them than the Crillon. Komarov said she looked exhausted and she didn't deny it. He seemed tired, too. The first night, they slept heavily. It was after ten when Stephanie opened her eyes the next morning. Outside, a steel sky, slanting rain. Later, they walked to the Picasso Museum.

When Stephanie asked him what he thought of Picasso, he said, 'Not ideal. But okay.'

'Not ideal?'

'I've rinsed thirty-five million dollars through Picasso canvases. In a perfect world, though, you want an artist who's less famous but whose paintings still command high prices.'

'Christ, Kostya. Why don't you say that a bit louder so that everyone can hear?'

For lunch, they bought sandwiches from a Jewish delicatessen on rue des Rosiers. In the afternoon, they went to the cinema. It was a Bertrand Tavernier retrospective. They watched *L627*. Afterwards, they returned to their hotel, made love, slept a little, shared a bath and then a drink. For dinner, they walked to a nearby bistro. It was hot inside, the air flavoured by the kitchen, condensation on the windows, candles flickering in clay holders on scrubbed wooden tables. Komarov chose rabbit, Stephanie ate fish stew. They drank a brutal bottle of red burgundy. And then ordered a second.

'What is it?' he asked. 'You look like you want to say something.'

Stephanie refused to look him in the eye. 'Nothing.'

'Petra . . .'

She took a deep breath and let it out slowly. 'I have to ask you something. I wish I didn't but I'm in a situation and . . . and I don't want to let anything come between us.'

'Like what?'

'I need you to introduce me to Vladimir Vatukin.' There was no visible reaction. 'As soon as possible,' she added.

More than anything, she felt disgust. For once, Stephanie was in tune with Petra; the request sounded cheap, which, to judge by his expression, was also how Komarov regarded it.

'How long have you been waiting to ask me?'

A fair question but one that she didn't want to answer. She shrugged instead.

'A couple of hours? A couple of days? Longer?'

'Forget it.'

'Since we were in Zurich? Or even Hamburg? What about the last time we were in Paris?'

'It doesn't matter?'

'It *does* matter, Petra.'

'I'm sorry, Kostya. I should never have asked.'

'But you did.'

'Can't we just forget it?'

'Not now.'

'Why not?'

'Because what you're asking me to do could change everything.'

'Then don't.'

'I've known you for a few weeks but I've known Vladimir for twenty years. If the world was black and white, the choice would be simple. But the world is grey.'

'Why? Are you sleeping with him too?'

Komarov smiled, then narrowed his eyes. 'The first time I went to Yekaterinburg, it was known as Sverdlovsk. I was nineteen and I travelled from Moscow with Vasily, a cousin of mine. At twenty-three, he was already a veteran of the Soviet black market. On our third day there, we had a meeting with a group of local racketeers. About one in the morning, Militia raided the depot where we were. We ran for it. Vasily got away but three Militia officers caught up with me on Lenin Street, right in front of the statue of Yakov Sverdlov. They gave me a real beating, until Vladimir stepped in. Believe me, in those days, nobody attacked members of the Militia. Absolutely *nobody*. But that's Vladimir for you. Never a nobody.'

'He knew you?'

'No. We'd never seen each other before the meeting. But he wasn't about to let Militia hand out a kicking to anyone. Especially not some idiotic teenager. The risk meant nothing to him. That was the start of it. Later, when we were both serving sentences at Khabarovsk Central Penitentiary, we looked out for each other. When he got into a fight with this huge Siberian bandit – Batov – he got stabbed three times with a spoon that had been sharpened into a blade. I nursed him back to health. He would have died without me. About a month later, while he was still getting better, he took me aside and said, "Kostya, I want you to do me a favour. I want you to make that prick Batov know what it feels like to be stabbed by a fucking spoon!" So I did. Because that's the way we were. And that's the way we are.'

'I thought you and he weren't that close.'

'We're not friends, if that's what you mean.'

'Sounds like you are.'

'I didn't take care of Batov because I liked Vladimir. I took care of him because it was good for business.'

'What business?'

'The survival business. With us, it's always been business. All that's changed is the nature of the business. In the Siberian Far East, we survived the authorities and the competition. Vladimir wasn't the only one. I had the same relationship with Oleg Rogachev and many others. As a group, we survived together, then got rich together. What we have is a common history. A bond. An understanding that is forged in steel.'

'So, what are you saying?'

'I'm saying you shouldn't assume that sleeping with me puts you in front of them. Not when it comes to trust.'

'You don't trust me?'

'I didn't say that.'

'Christ . . .'

'Don't get emotional, Petra. Think about it. We know what we feel about each other but what do we actually know? If I do what you want, I'm taking a huge risk. I'd like to pretend that it doesn't matter because it's you. But I can't. That's not the way it works in the real world. I need to be sure.'

Stephanie felt the heat of humiliation colour her

283

cheeks. When she apologized, she thought she sounded feeble.

'You're not the only one who doesn't want anything to come between us, Petra.'

'Then forget it. I'll find another way.'

He reached across the table and took her hand. 'You're not listening to me. I'm not saying I won't do it. I'm saying that if I do . . . well, it won't be a game.'

'I never thought it was.'

17

Russia appears without warning. *The Lufthansa aircraft drops out of dense cloud and suddenly there's land beneath me but no colour; it's all pewter and coldness. I'm flying over a jigsaw of lakes, rivers, birch forests, small farm holdings. Three days have elapsed since I was in Paris with Kostya. Three days since I swore that I would never put anyone ahead of him. Three days since he said he'd do it anyway. The wheels clatter the runway and I'm on the ground.*

At Sheremetyevo 2, I hand Claudia Baumann's passport to the immigration official. Claudia is a thirty-one-year-old freelance journalist. The official doesn't give the document a second glance. Why should he? It's a beautiful forgery, just like the Swiss passport sewn into the lining of the leather jacket I'm wearing.

I take a taxi into Moscow, check in at the Kempinski Baltschug, unpack and change into something more appropriate: jeans, boots, a thick jersey, a padded coat. I open the lining of the leather jacket and take out the documents that Cyril Bradfield has created for me. Her name is Irene Marceau. I put her in a plastic pouch with two rolls of cash, dollars and rubles. I turn on my laptop and retrieve the address that Stern sent to Audrey Smith at MSN. I picked up the keys from the Braun-Stahl agency in Munich yesterday. When I've memorized the address, I delete the message. It takes quarter of an hour to walk to the Metro station on the far side of Red Square.

Bibirevo is a microdistrict in the north of the city, just inside the outer ring road. It's no vision of beauty; a clutch of crumbling high-rise apartment blocks situated around a few open spaces. At the edge of the microdistrict, at street level, there are shops, a pharmacy, two bars, a TV repair shop and a medical clinic. All are in a similarly dilapidated condition to the blocks that rise above them.

I pass through the open spaces between buildings; patches of ground with a threadbare carpet of grass, a bench, a playground, a few trees without leaves. Gathered beside the entrance to one of the blocks, three skinheads in grubby tracksuits share a cigarette. They don't look old enough to be teenagers. One of them shouts something at me and the laughter that follows is lecherous.

There's a lift inside the entrance hall. The out-of-order sign looks as though it's been there a long time. I take the stairs to the sixth floor and find my front door along the end of a dark, narrow corridor; three of the four bulbs have failed. Inside, I'm immediately struck by the stuffy warmth. This apartment, like all the others, has central heating. So central, in fact, that it's not even optional. There are no thermostatic controls.

The owner works in the Siberian gas fields and only returns to Moscow for one month a year. For the other eleven, he rents it out. To foreigners, if possible, because they pay more. Although nobody pays much to stay in Bibirevo. If anyone examines the terms of this rental, they'll discover that the money is paid by Volgen, a photographic agency in Munich. Not one of my names is connected to the property. This apartment is an insurance policy. A refuge of last resort. Just like the Swiss identity I've brought to it.

One bedroom, one living room, a small bathroom, a tiny kitchen opening onto a slender balcony. The walls are thin. In the living room, I can hear the television next door quite clearly. I stand at the window and look across the city to the south. More concrete boxes set against a dark smudge. I catch myself thinking of Entrecasteaux, a chilled glass of wine, a warm dusk. With Kostya, not Laurent.

I examine the apartment thoroughly for hiding places but there's nothing secure. Later, I go down to the supermarket, Bibirevo-84. There's a stall selling books; hardbacks with gaudy covers. At the centre of the paved floor there's a medical dispensary: a glass cube with a woman inside, half-asleep. Two more women are buying salted herring from the fish counter. At the meat counter, there's an entire piglet's carcass lying among sausages. It's pale beige. I buy a few household items. As I'm returning to my block, I pass a row of green sheds. Garages, padlocked against thieves and vandals. At the end of the row, there are two more ramshackle wooden buildings. One of them houses pigeons. I peer into it in vain; there's not enough light to see what I want. But an idea is planted. In the darkness, the birds coo softly.

I go up to the apartment, collect the documents – and a spoon from the kitchen – then return to the pigeon hut. There's a padlock over the bolt, a basic model. I use a pick I bought in Geneva three years ago on Stern's recommendation. Superficially, it looks like a modern car key – black plastic body with a straight metal slide – but the button on the side of the body activates the main mechanism, a laser that reads the slot and adjusts the key, which is not solid. It's actually one hundred and fifty independent slices of tissue-thin metal on a central mechanical rod.

The pigeons ignore me and murmur among themselves. There's a drain at the rear of the hut. The grille isn't fastened. It doesn't look as though anyone has ever bothered to clean it. I yank it four times before it comes loose, splintering the crust of pigeon shit that's formed around the edge. I tie a black nylon cord around one of the filthy struts. At the end

of the cord, I attach the sealed plastic pouch, which I then
lower into the drain. I ease the grille back into place and
sweep some dirt over it. Outside, I secure the padlock and hide
the pick in a patch of ground at the rear. I brush aside some
weeds and scoop a shallow dip in the hard earth with the
spoon. I press the key into the ground and scatter loose earth
over the top so that it's thinly covered. With the weeds back
in place, the tiny mound is invisible.

Stephanie kicked the door shut, pressed him against it, then pressed her mouth against his. 'God, I've missed you.'

'Petra, we haven't got time.'

'I don't care.'

Her tongue on his tongue, she began to unbutton him. He resisted for a second, then pulled her close. They staggered into the room and onto the bed. He shoved her skirt above her waist and yanked her knickers down over her thighs.

'Kiss me,' she panted. When Komarov brought his face close to hers, she added: 'Lower.'

Afterwards, he said, 'When we leave this room, we hardly know each other.'

Stephanie was wriggling back into her knickers. 'What? No footsy under the table at the restaurant?'

'No footsy, no looks, nothing. We act cautiously. Like we're not quite sure about each other. Like there's no reason to care. And afterwards, you come back here and I go home.'

'Do I look all right? Or does it show?'

'You look fine.'

He was standing by the window. She said, 'You haven't looked at me. How can you tell?'

He turned his head and gave her half a smile. 'You look great. You look too good to be with me. Which means nobody will suspect a thing.'

In the bathroom, Stephanie checked herself, tidied her hair and tried to smooth the creases out of her skirt. When she moved, she was aware of the stickiness at the tops of her thighs and the damp heat between them. And she was glad of it; she would keep him inside her all night.

Outside, there was a black Shogun with dark windows. Komarov drove them across the Moskvoretsky Bridge, swung past the gargantuan Hotel Rossiya and headed up Lubyansky Prospekt. He lit a cigarette and dialled a number on the vehicle's phone.

'Let's see where we're going.'

'You don't know?'

'Vatukin doesn't book restaurants until just before he arrives. Security.'

'And if they're fully booked, somebody will happily give up their table?'

'Or unhappily. Either way . . .'

'Whose vehicle is this?'

'Paul Karsten. A German. He owns two gold mines in Siberia. They pay for a lot of vehicles. The last time I heard, nine. That's just here in Moscow. But without me, he'd still be walking to work in an office in Dresden.'

Café Pushkin's opulence was spread over three floors. Stephanie and Komarov were led upstairs to the first floor. There were oval mirrors set in elaborate mouldings along cream walls, candle-bulbs in elegant holders, frescoes on the ceiling, parquet floor underfoot and a large antique globe that reminded Stephanie of the one that Alexander kept in his office. The dining room was partitioned by aged wooden bookcases filled with ancient leather-bound books.

'Do you like all this old-world sophistication?' Komarov asked.

'It's . . . unexpected.'

'It's fake. This place only opened a couple of years ago. It cost a lot of money to make it feel so old.'

Vladimir Vatukin wore a black suit, black slip-ons, a dark blue shirt and no tie. He was no taller than Stephanie and as lean as Komarov, which made both of them rarities among their peers. Natalya Markova, Vatukin's mistress, was wearing heels. Without them, she would have been an inch taller than Vatukin. A clinging black dress revealed a spectacular figure; slender yet athletic, elegantly powerful. Too powerful, perhaps, for the anorexic tastes of the West, but Stephanie understood the attraction for a man like Vatukin. Natalya's physique was not so different from her own.

Komarov introduced her. Vatukin's small sharp eyes, set closely together, never blinked and never left her. His smile was ice. So was his grip. He insisted that she sat on his left. Natalya sat to his right. He introduced his bodyguards as his lawyers. Stephanie smothered the withering response that sprang to mind. There was a business associate whom Komarov appeared to know – Arkady – and there were three girls, a blonde, a brunette and a redhead. They were completely different but exactly the same: three versions of beauty, equally appealing; three different designer outfits, similarly expensive; three backgrounds, a common role.

The girls were smoking Davidoff Slims. When it was time to order, they chose the most expensive main course on the menu. The food arrived in waves. Blinis and caviar, smoked sturgeon, herrings and potatoes, a selection of salads – Caesar, *Officiel*, Vinaigrette, marbled beef, lamb and *sterlets* – baby sturgeon found only in the upper reaches of the Volga. They drank champagne, cranberry vodka and Pétrus at two thousand seven hundred dollars a bottle. Stephanie didn't drink much. Nor did Natalya, but Arkady and two of the girls were already drunk. The third girl, the blonde, and Vatukin's bodyguards were sipping Coke. Komarov and Vatukin drank like seasoned veterans, letting it take off the edge, but nothing more.

It was an hour before Vatukin turned to her and said, softly, 'I knew who you were, of course. But I never thought I'd meet you. It didn't seem like our paths would cross.'

It was hard to hear him over the din of the table, even though they were next to one another. Stephanie recognized Natalya's stare. It felt as surgical as Petra's finest.

'In my line of work, you never know whose path you're going to cross.'

Vatukin had a mean, weasel's face that didn't lend itself to humour, but he smiled. 'How true. I hear that it pays to stay off your path. Especially recently. I guess somebody should have warned Marat Manov and Lev Golta.'

Stephanie offered no visible reaction.

'Is what I've heard correct?'

'I don't tend to discuss my work with people I don't know.'

A flicker of annoyance was gone almost as soon as it appeared. 'Golta was a piece of shit who had it coming.

They say his father wanted him to become a butcher. Which, in his own way, is exactly what he became. I met him a few times before he left Moscow. A disgusting creature, even by our standards. The world is better off without him.'

'I didn't do it for humanitarian reasons.'

Vatukin laughed. 'Then let us say that your bank account is better off without him.'

'True.'

'And without Manov.'

'Also true.'

'I liked Marat a lot.'

The mischievous humour was gone. In its place, slate eyes full of hard intent, focused entirely upon her. Stephanie went dead herself. She took a sip of Pétrus. *As casual as you like . . .*

'Whether you liked him or not, it seems somebody else didn't. Which is unfortunate for you. And for Manov, of course. But what can I say? It's what I do.'

Vatukin's eyes continued to bore into her but the longer it went on, the less it affected her. He seemed more distracted by the silence that had descended over the table than she was.

She put her glass down. 'Do you want me to feel something for someone I never met?'

'I want you to know that *I* felt something for him.'

'Fine. But don't expect me to get all misty about it. From what I know, he wasn't a monster, he wasn't a saint. The point is, to me, he was just a shift at the factory.'

Now, it was her eyes drilling through to the core, not his. He didn't seem insulted. Stephanie thought he actually seemed reassured. Gradually, the murmur of conversation resumed. Vatukin drained a glass of cranberry vodka which was replaced immediately by an overattentive waiter. He lit a Marlboro and blew three smoke rings.

'Kostya tells me that we can do business together.'

She nodded. 'I hope so, yes.'

'What kind?'

'I'm acting on behalf of a client. We're looking for a weapon. Chemical or biological.'

'Which?'

'If possible, biological.'

'Who's your client?'

'No.'

'No client, no deal.'

'I understand that. And they understand that, too. But they don't want their identity revealed *until* there's a deal. That's to say, if you and I don't come to an arrangement, they'd prefer it if you'd never known about them in the first place. If it goes ahead, you get the identity, so you'll still have the power of sanction.'

'What exactly do they want?'

'They don't know. Which is why I'm here.'

'You know about biological weapons?'

'No, but I know about my clients. What they need is something easy to handle. To be frank, I wouldn't trust half of them with a hand grenade.'

'They sound like blacks. What are they? Uzbeks? Azeris?'

'They're not from any part of the old Soviet Union.'

'That still leaves a lot of baboons to choose from.'

'Well, you know what they say: it's a jungle out there.'

Vatukin sniggered and rolled an inch of ash into his ashtray. 'BW's not easy.'

'I know. And I've explained that to them.'

'If we came to an agreement, when would they want it?'

'Soon.'

'How soon?'

'How soon is now?'

'It can't be rushed. Different people are involved. They have to be persuaded . . . you know how it is.'

'Of course. You're providing a service. We get what we pay for.'

'Just so. And what you're proposing isn't going to be cheap. You want it fast-track? For fully functional delivery, in terms of US dollars, we're talking . . . eight figures.'

'Seven.'

'Low eight.'

'Seven.'

'High seven.'

'Maybe. As long as it's reasonable, they'll pay. Money's not the issue.'

Vatukin tried to match her insouciance but she saw the flutter.

It was one thirty by the time they reached New Arbat. From the sidewalk, a steel spike rose twenty feet to a point. On top of the point, there was a large, revolving cube of silver mosaic. Above the club's gaudy neon entrance, there were spotlights, which were aimed at the cube. As it turned, it threw out spears of brilliant white light. Glittering beams cut through the icy drizzle.

White Square.

Security carved a channel through those queuing to get in and Vatukin's party were ushered through it. Inside, a long corridor connected the entrance lobby to the rest of the club. Running its length, there were rectangles of reinforced glass set into the walls and floor. Behind the glass, water, rocks, swaying weeds. And piranhas.

Komarov had told her about the piranhas over dinner one night in Paris. He'd said they were famous in Moscow. They'd had a bit to drink so she'd assumed he was joking. Or at the very least, exaggerating. If anything, he'd been modest. She stopped halfway and was surrounded by hundreds of them. They darted beneath her feet and past her face. Bone, sinew, skin, no flesh; supermodel fish. Komarov had said Oleg Rogachev was reputed to have fed more than one adversary to them.

Inside, muscular men in black suits formed a protective ring around them as they moved through the club. Vatukin's procession was royal; the more fawning compliments he received, the more contemptuous he looked. Stephanie recognized the hardness in the eyes, the arrogance. For a slight man, he radiated extraordinary physical presence. Natalya trailed behind him, a beautiful shimmering shadow.

They settled in a VIP area on the balcony, overlooking the rest of the club. There was a private bar, staffed by a beautiful Eurasian girl in a short black skirt and gold Versace T-shirt. The brunette and the redhead were competing for Arkady's attention. All three were drunk. They collapsed onto a burgundy leather sofa, giggling. He kissed one, then the other, and then drained one of the glasses of vintage Krug that had been lined up on the table.

Vatukin said to Stephanie, 'You want to see the club?'

'Sure. Why not?'

She caught Komarov's eye. The blonde was by his side. He couldn't have looked more neutral if he'd tried. She felt a stab of jealousy, then anger. Natalya's expression was a contradiction; she was smiling for Vatukin, but her stare, which was directed at Stephanie, had all the cosy warmth of a bad night in Grozny. When Vatukin went to speak to one of his bodyguards, Natalya hissed, 'Don't even think about it.'

'Think about what?'

Natalya checked to make sure Vatukin wasn't looking. 'I don't give a fuck who you are. He belongs to me.'

'I'm not interested in him. It's purely business.'

Her smile was as sarcastic as her tone. 'It's always purely business.'

'Who said love was dead?'

'I'm warning you. Leave him alone.'

There were six bars, a restaurant, a casino, a dance floor and a strip joint. There were also eighteen private rooms. No expense spared, no vulgarity overlooked, White Square was a monument to post-Soviet hedonistic excess. Vatukin took her to a suite of offices at the rear of the cavernous building. In Soviet times, it had been a cinema with two thousand seats, serving up a diet of State-produced drivel. In the security office, there were monitors banked along one wall. Vatukin allowed her glimpses into a selection of the private rooms. In one, four grotesquely fat men were being entertained by six strippers. They were surrounded by bottles of beer, vodka and wine.

'Kazaks,' Vatukin spat. 'They come once a month, this lot. Based in Almaty, they run weapons in and out of China through Kazakhstan, Kyrgyzstan and Tajikistan.'

'Do the Chinese authorities know?'

'They should do. They're in partnership. These maggots have an office in Beijing. They don't pay rent. The government leases it to them for free.'

In another private room, four young girls were doing lines of coke off a silver tray watched by two handsome young men in silk suits. In a third room, three women sat huddled on one of the sofas, smoking, talking, looking bored. The four men they were with were all unconscious; there were empty bottles everywhere.

Vatukin grinned. 'Like the rest of us, they're making up for lost time.'

He took her to the strip joint in the basement. They stood in the doorway. She could feel it was a test so she showed him nothing. Men sat in clusters around small tables. Thudding music cut through the room, the bass rumbling. It was hot and humid. Skin shone. She could smell sweat through the sour cigarette smoke that curled upwards through cones of dim light. Glassy-eyed girls moved among the men, lap-dancing for rubles, dollars, deutschmarks.

Vatukin lit a Marlboro. 'Kostya tells me you're staying at the Baltschug.'

'Yes.'

'If you want, I can arrange a man for you.'

Despite everything in her memory, the offer shocked

her. Not so much for the content, but for the casual way in which it was offered. She tried to be offhand when she turned him down.

'No.'

'I can have him sent to your room. Like a sandwich.'

'Not tonight.'

'Another time, then?'

'I don't think so.'

'If you don't see one here that you like, there are others. The best-looking, any colour, any . . . *size*. Any number . . .'

'Like I said, I don't think so.'

'How about a woman? Perhaps you'd like that better.'

Stephanie excused herself. In a washroom where every surface was marble, she went to the toilet, then checked her appearance in the mirror. Full, fleshy lips, pale skin, fathomless dark eyes. She ran a hand through her thick hair. *Not too bad, all things considered.* But she still felt like the oldest twenty-seven-year-old in the world.

She headed back to the VIP area. It was his size that caught her eye. The height, the breadth. She stopped and looked. There was a crowd between them. He was staring directly at her; he'd seen her before she'd seen him. The thick lips, the big lumpy nose, the bulbous frog's eyes. Ultra-violet light illuminated his pale, freckled skin.

Boris Bergstein.

Stephanie had no idea how many seconds elapsed. Neither of them looked away. Not until Petra took over and she started to move towards him. Even from a distance, she saw his panic. He began to retreat. She pressed through the bodies between them, ignoring barked rebukes and hissed insults. She saw his head bobbing above the crowd. She was closing in. But he was too far ahead. He disappeared through a doorway into a horseshoe-shaped passage. When she reached it, there was no sign of him.

It was four fifteen when they pulled away from White Square.

'I know it's late but there's something I need to do. Do you mind?'

Stephanie shrugged, too tired to care. Quarter of an hour later, Komarov turned off the Mira Prospekt and headed north-west along Murmansky Prospekt, which ran parallel to the rail tracks running out of Leningrad Station towards St Petersburg. Then he turned right into a mostly residential area. Brick apartment blocks, dilapidated cars at the kerb. They parked on Kalibrov-skaya Street next to the wall of the Prokatdetal Factory. A chimney belched smoke that drifted down the road. Stephanie climbed out of the Shogun and saw the ruined Ostankino TV tower in the distance, its astonish-ing size picked out by lights. Her energy fading, the cold was an immediate assault. She turned up the collar of her overcoat. The factory was humming.

'Watch where you walk,' he said.

They crossed the street, headed along a path between two sets of corrugated iron garages flanked by poplar, birch and lime trees, and came to a five-storey apart-ment block. There were two entrances but Komarov led her down the side of the building. The feeble light of the street lamp was soon redundant. Stephanie slowed until her eyes had adjusted to the darkness. Just as they had, there was a hint of brightness ahead. Komarov was opening a heavy metal door.

A narrow staircase took them down to the building's basement. They entered a large room with dimmed lamps on the wall. Komarov turned to her and put a finger to his lips. In the low light, Stephanie was able to make out two rows of camp beds, one along each wall. Dull mounds covered in dark blankets, every bed appeared to be occupied. The room was warm and smelt vaguely necrotic. It caught her at the back of the throat. She followed Komarov through the door on the far side. The second room was small and cool. There were boxes stacked against the walls. The third room was warm again.

'Kostya!'

She was short and fat with large glasses and a pudding-bowl haircut. She wore dark green dungarees over a thick grey sweatshirt. Stephanie guessed she was in her fifties. She had a zigzag scar across a dimpled chin.

'How is it tonight, Ludmilla?'

'Not too busy.'

'Who's here?'

'Max, Alexei, Valeria.'

'They're in the back?'

She nodded. 'Do you want something to eat?'

He looked at Stephanie, who shook her head.

'Tea?'

'Yes,' Komarov said. 'Always.'

In another room, there was a makeshift kitchen: three Primus stoves beneath a crude air vent, a wooden sink that had been illegally connected to the block's water supply and a table stacked with bowls, spoons and pans.

'What is this place?' Stephanie asked.

'It's a refuge.'

'For?'

'The homeless. Who else?'

'What are *we* doing here?'

'I have some business to attend to.'

'Here?'

'I have business everywhere, Petra.'

She unbuttoned her coat. 'You're lying. But that's okay. If I knew everything about you, I'd get bored of you.'

The tea was strong and bitter. He left her alone in the room for fifteen minutes. She thought about Natalya – *he belongs to me . . . leave him alone* – and Vatukin. Beneath Natalya's obvious aggression, there had been desperation. Vatukin was a second chance in a world where most girls never got a first. When Komarov reappeared, he offered no explanation for his absence.

They headed south through the city.

'When I was young, Moscow was dark at night. Even when I came back from the east, it was nothing like this. Not many lights, almost no billboards, very few cars. It's completely changed in the last ten years.'

'For the better?'

Komarov smiled but took a while to answer. 'If you live in Manhattan, on the Upper East Side, sure.'

'And if you don't?'

'There used to be a structure and it screwed the people. Today, there's no structure but the people are still being screwed.'

'By people like you?'

He lit a cigarette. 'How was it with Vladimir?'

'He's going to get back to me.'

301

'Did you tell him you were looking for Koba?'

Stephanie stiffened. 'No.'

'But you are, aren't you?'

To lie, to tell the truth, or a version of the truth? Stephanie couldn't decide.

'Why do you want him?' Komarov asked.

'Don't make me lie to you.'

It was after five when she entered her hotel room. Alone.

18

The market existed in the shadow of the colossal Izmailovo Hotel complex. The taxi dropped her outside the gates, close to a small compound patrolled by three tethered bears. Inside, there were dozens of small stalls arranged in straight lines, creating narrow alleys. It was raining. The ground beneath her feet was sticky. Pools of icy water collected in the plastic sheets that traders had erected over their stalls. A young girl in traditional gypsy costume was playing a violin, the fingers of her bowing hand hidden up her sleeve to shield them from the gnawing cold. Stephanie smelt burning charcoal and cooked meat. An elderly woman blocked her path and tried to sell her hats of mink and polar fox. When Stephanie said no, the woman spat into the mud by her boots.

She came to the part of the market dominated by military paraphernalia. It took her quarter of an hour to find the stall that Stern had described. At the back, on wire coat hangers, hung a selection of blue-grey military overcoats. Some had seen service, others looked brand new. There was a box full of fur hats, each with a red enamel star. On the table at the front of the stall there were revolvers, daggers, medals, compasses, binoculars, badges. There were six German helmets from the Second World War. Frayed by rust, two of them had ragged bullet-holes. The man behind the table was short with dark, creased skin. He wore a dirty white

Fila anorak. Stephanie picked up an old telescopic sight and turned it over in her hands.

'Helped kill Germans at Stalingrad, that did. A genuine piece of history from the Siberian 284th Rifle Division.'

'Is Rudi here?'

He looked surprised, then cautious. 'He's at the hospital.'

'Is it serious?'

'His wife's giving birth again. Their fifth.'

'That bad?'

The exchange complete, his suspicion seemed conquered. 'What do you want?'

'Something that works.'

'When?'

'Now.'

'You think I keep stuff here?'

'How soon can you get it?'

'Depending on what it is, twenty minutes. No more than an hour.'

'What have you got?'

'A couple of Nagants –'

'Do I look like an antiques collector?'

He glanced left, then right. 'How about an MR73, or a Glock 21? The Glock's nice. I've seen it myself. Seventy percent polymer, takes fifteen rounds with one up the pipe. Got a phosphorescent sight. Or I've got some Czech-made CZ75s. If you're looking for something bigger, how about an Ingram 7.65mm submachine gun?'

'How about a SIG-Sauer P226 and a silencer?'

Eleven thirty. Stephanie got off the 733 minibus close to the By The Hill restaurant, on the opposite side of

Moscow to Izmailovo. The weather had deteriorated; the rain was almost snow. Krylatskoye Hills-35 was a drab seventeen-storey apartment block set among dozens of identical buildings. There were two beetroot-faced women gossiping inside the entrance. Stephanie dialled a land-line number on her mobile with frozen fingers.

A man answered. 'Yes?'

'Is Galina there?'

'Who?'

'Galina.'

'Wrong number.'

He was home, at least. The women stepped out into the cold. Stephanie took the lift to the fifteenth floor. It reeked of urine. The doors parted to reveal a narrow corridor that ran the breadth of the block. There was no one around. She walked past his door, checked the corridor was still empty, then took the SIG out of her coat pocket and attached the silencer. She hit redial on her mobile.

'Yes?'

'You've got a problem.'

'Who is this?'

'They're on their way. You've got two minutes. Three, if you're lucky.'

She moved into place. When he yanked open the door, the SIG was already pointing at his head; she knew his height. He shuddered to a halt, eyes drawn to the centre of the silencer.

'Hello, Boris.'

Bergstein's jaw slackened. 'Shit!'

'Give me an excuse and I'll do it.'

'Fuck!'

'Move back slowly. No sudden movements.'

Stephanie closed the front door and made him move through the apartment at gunpoint. The kitchen was cramped and revolting: crusty plates and cutlery in the sink, empty bottles, cigarette butts stubbed out on plastic carton lids, sour milk fouling the air, cockroaches scurrying over a grey loaf of bread. The bathroom smelt of shit. The bath itself was full of Diesel jeans wrapped in cellophane. Stephanie supposed they were fake. The living room was piled high with boxed electrical goods: CD, VHS and DVD players, laptops, TVs, personal stereos. All the brand names. There was barely any free floor space for the small sofa, which was covered in a shiny olive material, a small TV, a phone and a pink plastic plate that served as an over-used ashtray.

'I like what you've done with the place, Boris. It's very . . . *you*.'

'How did you find me?'

'The first time we met in Brighton Beach, you told me you had a place in Krylatskoye.'

He frowned. 'But I don't own it . . .'

Stephanie gave him her most enigmatic smile. 'I know.'

Or rather, Stern had known. For the appropriate fee.

'Move over to the window, Boris. Then get on your knees. I want your back to me.'

'What are you doing here?'

'Just the question I was going to ask you. Now do it.'

Slowly, he sank to the carpet. 'You're here because of last night?'

'What do you think?'

'It was a coincidence.'

'The people I know who believe in coincidence wind up dead.'

'When I'm here, I always go to White Square. It's where the best girls are.'

'You're not winning me over with your charm, Boris. What are you doing in Moscow?'

'I come here four times a year. You know that.'

'Why now?'

'Business.'

'What business?'

He shook his head. 'Please . . .'

'What business?'

'I can't . . .'

Stephanie fired. The silencer sounded loud within the confines of the room. A piece of wall exploded in front of Bergstein, just beneath the windowsill, showering him with plaster. He lurched, then toppled onto his side and made no attempt to get up. Stephanie prodded him with the toe of her boot.

'Back on your knees, face the wall.'

He began to shake.

'Don't make me say it again. *Up!*'

Slowly, he rose to kneeling.

'What did you see last night?'

'Nothing.'

'What did you see?'

'I swear it. Nothing.' His voice was high-pitched and faltering. 'When you looked at me, that was the first time I saw you.'

'Tell me about your business, Boris.'

'Please . . .'

'I'm not going to ask again. I'm just going to put one

307

in your spine. You'll die, but not too quickly. And it's going to hurt like hell. Five, four, three, two . . .'

'In my pocket.'

'One . . .'

'It's in my fucking coat pocket!'

Stephanie stepped forward and pressed the tip of the silencer against the nape of his neck. 'Be careful, Boris. If I see anything resembling a weapon . . .'

'I promise you.'

'Come on, then. Let's have it.'

Very slowly, he dipped his left hand into his left jacket pocket and withdrew a small tin. It looked like a tobacco tin but there were no markings on the outside. Stephanie took it and stepped back. She flipped off the lid. There was a thin layer of cotton wool on top. Beneath, fifteen to twenty small squares of paper, neatly folded.

'Another drug dealer. Just what the world needs.'

Bergstein was shaking his head. 'What are you talking about? It's not drugs.'

Stephanie unfolded the top square of paper. 'Well, well . . .'

Three brilliant-cut diamonds.

'If you take those, I'm dead,' Bergstein whined.

'I can imagine.'

'And if you shoot me – or if I disappear – then my mother's dead.'

That stung. Stephanie was glad he was still facing the wall.

'Who are you working for?'

'Nobody you know.'

'You have no idea who I know. Get up.'

He did so in stages, the muscles in his legs now

beyond control. As his bladder had been; when he turned round, there was a dark stain over the crotch of his trousers. He couldn't bring himself to meet her gaze.

'You're out of your league, Boris.'

'I know.'

From the fifteenth floor, Stephanie could have seen all of Moscow on a clear day. Looking at the chemical haze over the city, she wondered when that had last occurred. The apartment's height may have had the advantage of a view but it had the disadvantage of being completely exposed to the rapier winds from the Urals. Stephanie could feel the draught around the window-frame and could hear the wind moaning in the fabric of the building.

From the bathroom, the splash of running water and the squeak of a turning tap. A couple of minutes later, Bergstein returned to the living room, having swapped his grey trousers for a brown pair.

'Good colour choice,' Stephanie said. 'Just in case you decide to crap yourself.'

'Funny girl,' he scowled.

'Don't worry. Your secret's safe with me.'

'You want something to drink?'

'I don't drink with cockroaches.' He looked offended. Stephanie said, 'I've seen your kitchen, Boris.'

He opened a box that was intended for an Aiwa sound system and pulled out a clear bottle of dark spirit. 'That's why I keep it in here.' He extracted the cork and offered her the bottle.

'What is it?'

'Armenian brandy.'

'It's a little early for me.'

'For me, too. But then it's not every morning I get some woman sticking a gun in my face.'

Several sharp swigs and a cigarette later, his nerves began to calm.

'Diamonds, Boris? Do you know what you're doing?'

'Taking them to New York. That's what I'm doing.'

'If I were a betting woman, I'd put money on you not declaring those to customs at JFK.'

Bergstein scratched his nose and shrugged. 'That's why they're paying me twenty-five grand.'

'To go towards your boat-charter business down in Fort Lauderdale?'

'Maybe.'

Stephanie separated the silencer from the SIG. 'Any idea how you're going to do it?'

'Sure.'

He was lying. 'Come on, Boris . . .'

'Not yet. But I got some options.'

'Tell me.'

'No way.'

Stephanie smiled. 'If I'd wanted to, I could have shot you in the head, put them in my pocket and just walked out of here.'

'So why didn't you?'

'Because I'm not a thief. And because I don't shoot dumb, defenceless animals.'

He told her. Three schemes, all equally hopeless.

'Christ, Boris. What good's twenty-five grand going to be when you're serving fifteen years?'

'You got a better idea?'

'No.'

'Well, then . . . I'll take a chance.'

'You don't have a chance.'

Bergstein pressed his cigarette onto the crowded pink plastic plate and immediately lit up another. Stephanie found herself thinking of Maria Bergstein, of her inexplicable fondness for Alla Pugacheva, of her small apartment in Brighton Beach.

'Boris, I'm going to make you an offer. And I want you to listen to it. I can probably get you a secure route into the States for those stones.'

He looked suspicious. 'How much do you want?'

'I don't want money. I want you to do something for me.'

'What?'

'I want you to make your delivery, collect your twenty-five grand and then walk away. You haven't got a bloody clue. You said so yourself in New York. People take one look at you and think you must be some kind of hard case.' Stephanie glanced at his crotch. 'They don't see what I've just seen. I don't know who you're working for but I can guess what kind of people they are. The kind who saw you coming from a mile. If you don't get away from them, they'll land you in it. Maybe not today, maybe not tomorrow, but sometime. Or else they'll kill you.'

Bergstein looked genuinely perplexed. 'Why are you doing this?'

'Because – against every decent instinct within me – I quite like you. And I liked your mother. I'd hate to think of her standing over your grave for no good reason at all.'

'Shit! I'm late!'

They'd been talking for ten minutes. Bergstein

reached for the phone and began to punch numbers. 'I'm supposed to go see my uncle at his house. I promised him.' Then he paused and looked at Stephanie. 'Is it all right?'

She shrugged.

'We're done? You're not going to shoot me when I walk out the door?'

'Not today.'

He pressed two more numbers, then paused again. 'You want to come?'

'No.'

'You'll like him. Everybody likes him.'

'Boris . . .'

'Under the circumstances, this is the least I can do for you. He knew George Salibi.'

Her curiosity was pricked. 'Really?'

Bergstein drove a battered Audi saloon that was fifteen years old. Stephanie asked if he was sure that it would get them there. He said it had never let him down before. They were on the outer ring road when her mobile rang. It was Komarov.

'Where are you?' he asked.

'In a car.'

'Can you talk?'

'Kind of.'

'I want to show you something. What are you doing tonight?'

'Sounds good already. I'm not doing anything.'

Komarov gave her a set of detailed instructions and then repeated them. 'You've got that?'

'I'll be there.'

From the ring road, they took a country lane past Scolkovo and across open fields. There were no road signs. A while later, they turned onto a narrow, twisting dirt track lined by silver birch, which led to a clearing by a small lake. Long ago, the wooden house at the water's edge had been painted turquoise. Despite years of hostile weather, the window frames were still bright green. A smoking metal chimney protruded from the roof.

Josef Bergstein came out to meet them, flanked by two Alsatians. He wasn't much taller or heavier than his sister. They might almost have been twins. He greeted Boris with an enthusiastic hug and then shook hands with Stephanie. Formal but polite, he gave her a small bow.

Inside, an iron brazier kept the kitchen and living area warm and dry. On the floors, there were cheap Samarkand carpets and reindeer-skin rugs. There was a large sofa, two leather armchairs, two desks, an old bookcase, framed ink drawings on the walls. It was cosy and felt like a real home.

They ate soup and black bread – prepared by Josef, an act that Boris found amusing; he said it reminded him of his mother – and they drank tea. Josef Bergstein told Stephanie that he'd had the opportunity to emigrate to Israel when the rest of the family had gone but that it had never occurred to him to leave. He told her how Boris had pleaded to be left behind with him but how his sister, Maria, had been adamant that her son should emigrate too.

'I think she was worried that he might turn out like me. Anyway, what chance did I have? Maria was always headstrong. But not always right. She swore there would be a better life for them in Israel and what happened? They left. When I think about what a mess

Russia is in these days, you know what I do? I think of Israel and I feel better.'

'Weren't you tempted to go to New York when they moved to the States?'

He began to roll himself a cigarette. 'I've been to New York four times. I never saw anything that made me want to live there.'

'Four times?'

'I've been to Chicago, too. And Boston. I used to travel abroad five or six times a year.' He licked the cigarette paper and then sealed it. 'On business.'

'And what is your business?'

'What did Boris tell you?'

'He didn't really. He just said that you knew George Salibi.'

Josef raised an eyebrow. 'You knew him too?'

Stephanie glanced at Boris. 'Not really. I only met him once. He wasn't very communicative.'

'I'm surprised.'

'Why?'

'If you don't mind me saying so, you would have been his type. Dark-haired, athletic, strong-willed . . .'

Stephanie pictured Ruth Steifel. 'You think I'm strong-willed?'

His smile was thin and tight. 'Call it instinct. Anyway, I read about his death in the papers. It was on TV. Did you see the obituaries? Brezhnev, Andropov, Gorbachev – he knew them all, in the old days. Yeltsin, too, when he was a party official in Siberia and still capable of coherent thought.'

Boris left the sitting room. Stephanie said, 'How did you come to know Salibi?'

'It was a banking matter.'

'You're a banker?'

'Not exactly.'

He told her how they'd first met in Cyprus in the early Seventies. He'd been on official government business. Salibi had been keen to forge relationships with the Kremlin. Bergstein had been part of a clandestine entourage dispatched from Moscow to listen to Salibi's overtures.

'In the years that followed, I came across him from time to time. Beirut, Athens, Berlin. Several times in the United States. I liked him. He was nervous with strangers but generous and warm to his friends.'

Stephanie felt herself tense. 'You were a friend of his?'

Josef Bergstein laughed. 'No, no, no. I was more of an observer, that's all. I just saw how he was with other people.'

Stephanie tried to sound casual when she said, 'The time I met him, he was with another Russian. Konstantin Komarov. Ever heard of him?'

He nodded. 'Lives in New York, I think. The FBI have a name for him . . .'

'The Don from the Don.'

'That's it.'

'What do you know about him?'

Josef Bergstein narrowed his eyes. 'They say he murdered an Uzbek in a hotel in Voronezh with a single punch.'

It was getting dark as they headed back towards Moscow. One of Boris Bergstein's headlamps was broken but it wasn't slowing him down.

'Your uncle never did say what his job was.'

'He doesn't work so much now.'

'And in the past?'

'In the days when it existed, he was with the KGB.'

'Doing what?'

'He was a paymaster. He controlled funds used to finance agents abroad.'

'Really?'

Bergstein nodded. 'It took him all over the world.'

The taxi cruised along the banks of the Yauza River north of Lefortovo and dropped her on Semyonovskaya Street. It was snowing, fat flakes fluttering across the windscreen. Stephanie followed the directions that Komarov had given her.

At one time, the Metallurgist sports complex had belonged to the Hammer & Sickle factory as a recreational facility for its workers. Now, it was open to the public. Although not at ten to midnight – the complex closed at nine – which was why there was security by the main gate. Stephanie skirted the perimeter fence. Komarov had promised that the pedestrian side entrance would be unlocked. Inside the complex, she kept off the main path, crossed two football pitches in darkness, and approached the rear of the two-storey red and white brick building at the centre.

She peered round the corner. Lined up in front of the entrance were limousines and four-wheel-drive vehicles. Bodyguards and drivers stamped their feet against the cold, smoked cigarettes and passed round a bottle.

Stephanie retreated into the darkness, scrambled onto the creaking metal canopy over the winch-house at the side of the building and reached for the first-floor window above it. It wasn't locked. As she climbed inside, she heard the muted echo of raucous applause. It was cold, a stiff draught blowing along the passage. She felt her way in the blackness. Ahead, she saw spots of brightness. Lamps on a balcony, three on either side of the building, all pointing down. *Stand behind the middle lamp on the near side.*

The first thing to strike her was the heat rising up from the ground below. The second thing was the smell. Tobacco, perfume, body odour and something she recognized but couldn't quite identify.

She looked down. The lifting apparatus and the free weights had been cleared away. At the centre of the gymnasium, there was a boxing ring inside a cage. There were two men in the ring. One was huge and slow, the other sinewy and quick. The six balcony lamps were focused on the ring. As Stephanie's eyes adjusted to the light, she saw blood. It coated the men and the ring's canvas floor. When the big man tossed a right hook, his left foot skidded, leaving a light scar in the crimson underfoot. The crowd jeered. The sinewy fighter threw a flurry of punches. One of them caught his opponent on the jaw, spraying an arc of blood and sweat through the air. That was when Stephanie noticed that neither man was wearing boxing gloves.

There was a small group packed tightly around the ring. They were mostly male. Puce faces dripping with perspiration, shouting, waving their fists at the fighters. Of the rest of the audience, Stephanie guessed a third were female. Set further back, there were tables and chairs, and a temporary bar along one wall with staff serving drinks.

Now, she identified the smell she'd recognized. Blood. In the humid heat of the hall, the air was thick

317

with the taste of it. As Petra, she'd witnessed far worse but she didn't think she'd ever seen anything quite so gratuitous. It was the Coliseum; the gladiators and the baying mob. She cast her gaze over them. It didn't take long to find him. Komarov was sitting at a table with Vatukin, Natalya, half a dozen other men and two women. Just as he'd said he would be.

The larger fighter rallied, catching his opponent with a thunderous blow to the lower abdomen. Stephanie heard the wheeze over the cheers. It was like a balloon deflating. The smaller man crumpled but managed to scamper across the slick canvas to avoid a clumsy kick to the head.

Stephanie couldn't see Komarov's face but Vatukin seemed utterly absorbed. Natalya, by contrast, looked emotionally frozen.

When I was younger, I knew many potential Natalyas. They came from Crewe, Cardiff, Aberdeen. I saw one or two who made it the way Natalya's made it, but I saw many more who fell by the wayside. Refugees from the underclass who had one thing going for them: their looks. Lacking formal education, they relied on common sense, determination and male weakness. They were boxers battering their way out of the ghetto. They were in it for the money as ruthlessly as a venture capitalist but I never thought of them as mercenaries or gold-diggers. I always thought of them as people who made their own luck, be it good or bad. They swallowed their pride and gambled on themselves.

Although I know nothing about her, I feel sure I know Natalya. The daughter of a signalman at the rail depot, or a career soldier who never rose as high as he should have. The daughter of a woman who tolerated a violent drunk as a

*husband. A woman of unceasing stoicism, just like her mother
and grandmother before her. I see Natalya in a provincial
city, grey and cold and backward, growing up among similar
children until the onset of puberty begins to mark her out,
her blooming beauty as striking as a physical deformity. I
see hungry eyes following her, I feel her self-consciousness
mounting. And then there comes a moment where she crosses
over. I hope it's an ignorantly tender affair. In my own experience, it's more likely to be brutal and uncaring. After that
... well, she hardens as she suffers. And, eventually, she
comes to the realization that her looks are not only a tradable
commodity but the only thing that will allow her to escape
the bleak inevitability of her future should she stay. So maybe
she steals some money. Or sleeps with the fat bank official
who lives on the floor below. However she does it, she gathers
enough to get her to Moscow. Metropolitan Moscow. The bright
lights, the key to a future that isn't mired in the past.*

*But it's a fragile future. And if it shatters, then what? A
return to oblivion?*

The crowd bellowed. The skinny fighter was so busy
raining punches onto his opponent, he never saw the
clubbing left hook. Now, he lay sprawled on his back,
covered in his own blood and the blood of all the fighters
who'd already been and gone. The crowd urged him
back to his feet. He hauled himself to a crouch. The
thug grabbed him by his soaking hair and kneed him
in the face. There was an eruption where his nose
should have been. Stephanie shut her eyes but could
still hear thudding blows over roared approval.

And then it was over and the crashing din subsided to
conversation. The audience began collecting and paying
out on their bets. People drifted between tables. The

lifeless fighter – it was impossible to tell whether he was dead or merely unconscious – was carried from the cage on a makeshift stretcher. Nobody seemed to care enough to watch. Stephanie looked back at Vatukin's table. Komarov was gone. A minute later, there was a murmur behind her.

'Did you have any problems?'

Stephanie turned round. He was little more than a shadow. 'What the hell is this?'

'Entertainment for those who like it raw and who've got the money to pay for it.'

'What are you doing down there?'

'Showing clients a good time.'

'The strangers at your table – who are they?'

'Americans. Two of them are property developers. One's a hotelier. The other three are investment bankers.' He moved closer so that she could see his eyes. He said, 'They'd sooner watch this than have sex. They say it's more exciting. They say they can have the most beautiful women in the world any time they want in Manhattan. But this . . . this is something *real*. That's the word they keep using.'

'They should get out more.'

'I agree. But that's how jaded they are.'

'And what are you doing with them, Kostya?'

'The same thing you're doing with Vladimir. Business.'

'You mean you're helping them to spend some dollars in the "everything must go" sale?'

'Everything must go?'

'Former state assets sold dirt cheap? Isn't that the game?'

'You're five years out of date, Petra. Maybe ten.

320

They're not here to discuss investments in Moscow. They're here to discuss investments in New York. And the currency in question is not the dollar, it's the ruble.'

It seemed appropriate to be standing in the dark. 'And what am I here for?'

Komarov moved closer, put one hand on her hip and pointed to a table near the boxing ring. 'You see the dark-skinned one with the gold earring?'

'Yes.'

'That's Sergiyev from Bashkortostan. He deals in petroleum products. He has strong connections with Tsentralnaya. You see the fat one on the table behind? The one with the tall redhead to his right? That's Barsov. A Muscovite. Second-in-command with the Lyubertsy. The skinhead at three o'clock is also local. Felix. A member of Solntserskiye. On the other side of the ring, there's a small man with big glasses and a walking stick.'

'I see him.'

'That's Ullman. He's from Odessa. And the last one is . . . where's he gone? There he is. Red hair, huge bastard. His back's turned to us. That's Antonov. Dolgoprudniki.'

'Is there a point to all this?'

'They've got two things in common.'

'Apart from being sick enough to consider this spectacle entertainment?'

'One: you people would class all of them as criminals . . .'

'I would never have guessed.'

'Two: they're all Koba.'

Inside the cage, a man was mopping the bloody canvas before the next bout. He wasn't making it any cleaner.

'*All* Koba?'

'At one time or another, they've all used the name. These people use several names at once. Dozens in a lifetime.'

'You brought me here to tell me this?'

'To *show* you this. To make the point. To make you understand it.'

'What point?'

'You're wasting your time. You won't find the Koba you're looking for unless he wants to be found. The real Koba is a legend. A myth.'

Just like Petra Reuter.

'What about Vatukin? Has he ever been Koba?'

Komarov said nothing.

'What about you, Kostya? Have *you* ever been Koba?'

'No.'

Stephanie wasn't sure whether she felt relief, uncertainty or outright disbelief.

19

It's five thirty in the morning. I'm standing by the window in Kostya's living room, looking down onto Kutuzovsky Prospekt. I'm amazed at how quiet it is. All I'm wearing is a jersey but I'm warm, even though snow is falling just a few inches away from me. So much for caution. We've thrown that to the wind by spending the night together, but coming here was much more than a foolish impulse. It was a declaration of intent. This is not just a nomadic affair. It runs deeper than that and neither of us has to say it to know that it's true.

His apartment is smaller than his place in Manhattan and far less comfortable. One bedroom, a diminutive kitchen, a bathroom and this living room. The carpet is dark green and looks thirty years old. So does the floral wallpaper. The print has faded in patches. There's a cheap coffee table, an uncomfortable sofa that needs upholstering, a small Samsung TV. A single bulb hangs from the ceiling, housed in a cream shade speckled with brown burns. There's a standard lamp beside the armchair in the corner.

The place is spartan and unloved. It says nothing about him. Then again, nor does his apartment on the Upper East Side. Just as Old Court Place says nothing about me. Most homes reflect something of those who live in them. The places Kostya and I occupy are like the clothes we wear; a veneer designed to hide the truth about us.

Half the bookshelves contain books, the other half are

empty. Except for one shelf, which has four framed photo-graphs. Two are of the same woman; big-boned, strong looking with a round face and a mass of thick dark curls. In one, she's lying on a rug in a field. There are trees in the middle distance. She's laughing. In the other, she's sitting at a table. She glances over her shoulder at the camera. She looks more serious. Both prints are old. The third snapshot is of a man. It's Kostya's father; the similarity is striking. He's in a dingy room, a grey net curtain over a square window diffusing the light. Dark thinning hair, a creased face smiling. The smile itself is pure Kostya – the same crooked shape – but there's nothing in his father's eyes. He's not really smiling at all.

The last photograph also features a woman. The shot is more modern. So is she. Good cheekbones, dark hair, pale skin, a generous mouth and dark eyes. She looks a little familiar. I pretend it might be his sister because I don't want her to be anything else. But I can see she's in love with the photographer and I'm assuming that's him. She's blowing a kiss into the lens and she . . .

The realization sends a shudder through me. The person she reminds me of is me. Not quite as tall as I am, more generously proportioned, better looking overall, there is never-theless definitely something we share.

His presence makes me jump. He's standing in the door-way, watching me. There's a towel wrapped round his waist. I feel ashamed and confused in equal measure. He doesn't display any emotion at all.

'Is this Irina?'

'Yes.'

'I'm sorry. I shouldn't have . . .'

He doesn't tell me that it's okay. That it doesn't matter. He just stands and stares. I put the photograph back on the shelf.

'Couldn't sleep?'

'I slept beautifully,' I tell him. Which happens to be true. 'Just not for too long.'

'Coffee?'

'We look a little similar, don't you think?'

Kostya doesn't say anything.

'I'm sorry. But I need to know. Am I some kind of substitute?'

'Nobody could be her substitute.'

It was after seven when Stephanie returned to the Baltschug. Komarov had said they might meet later. She'd asked why they might not. He'd said it depended. On what? Meetings, calls, the usual things. She'd asked why he was still so secretive with her and he'd been evasive.

'For the same reason you're secretive with me, Petra. It's safer.'

Back in her hotel room, she ordered coffee from room service, took a shower, contacted Stern, outlined her requests and asked for a price.

This doesn't sound like you, Petra. Diversification? Diamonds?

I'll try anything once.

At five to nine, Vatukin called, asking her to meet him at eleven. The casinos of New Arbat looked cheerless by daylight; no neon, a bruised sky overhead. Inside, White Square smelt stale. Under full house lights, the place looked tacky. Even the piranhas looked sick. An old woman was sweeping shattered glass with a broom. Vatukin was waiting for her in an administrative office on the first floor. He looked as though he'd been up all night. Pale skin, bloodshot eyes, stubble on his jaw. They drank coffee and he smoked. There could be a deal, he said. But the technical side needed to be addressed first and the man with that responsibility was not in Moscow.

'When will he be?'

'It's impossible to say. But not soon. Maybe not at all.'

Vatukin suggested a compromise. London, three days before Christmas. It worked for them, could it work for her? Stephanie hoped the kick in her chest hadn't manifested itself anywhere else. She said London would be fine.

'You know, a woman of your talent could find a lot of work in Moscow.'

Stephanie smiled coldly. 'I find a lot of work everywhere.'

'Well-paid work.'

'That's the only type I do.'

Red tail-lights pierced the gunmetal gloom. It began to snow again. Komarov was in a Mercedes, three cars ahead of the battered Audi that she'd borrowed from Bergstein. She'd met him in the bar at the Metropol at lunchtime. She'd handed over an envelope with instructions inside.

'It's up to you now, Boris.'

He'd scooped the envelope into his coat pocket. 'And you still don't want anything?'

'Nothing except your word. And your car for the afternoon.'

She'd known where Komarov was having lunch: Tamerlan, a Mongolian restaurant on Prechistenka Street. When he stepped out of the restaurant shortly before two, he was in conversation with one of the American businessmen who had been at the bare-knuckle boxing. Stephanie had been parked across the street, waiting.

Now, Komarov was heading north-east, in the direction of Izmailovo, close to the market from where Stephanie had bought the SIG. He turned onto 16th Park Street, which was too quiet to allow the Audi to follow. Stephanie pulled to the kerb just shy of the junction. She watched the blue Mercedes creep through the snow. A hundred yards later, the vehicle turned left again and parked immediately beside a metal fence. Komarov got out, went through the nearby gate and vanished behind a screen of black trees.

Stephanie stepped into the cold. She checked the SIG, fastened her jacket to the throat and walked up 16th Park Street. Snow squeaked beneath her boots. Freezing air scalded her cheeks. The city was almost silent.

The black iron fence surrounded a small compound with a drab three-storey building at its centre. The compound was overlooked by tall apartment blocks. They were joined to one another by a network of interconnecting paths that was hidden beneath the snow but outlined by birch trees. Wet branches sagged under the weight of the recent fall.

Stephanie reached the gate. On the other side, there was a rusted metal sign: Children's Aid Home No. 23. She looked around but saw no sign of life. She passed a children's slide with icicles drooping from the steps. Beside it, there were two swings hanging from an A-frame. Only one of them had a seat. At ground level, each window had a black wrought-iron grille. Stephanie reached through the frozen spokes and rubbed dirt from a small patch of glass. A bleak room; grey gloss paint on the walls, a hard floor, three tables with benches on either side. She followed Komarov's footprints in the snow. They led her round the corner to a door. Protective metal plates had been bolted to it. She turned the handle and pushed.

Inside, an empty corridor, no overhead lights, cream walls, a bare concrete floor, a rectangle of brightness at the far end. A distant background murmur echoed off the hard surfaces. She could smell disinfectant. Instinctively, her fingertips found the grip of the SIG but she resisted the temptation to draw the weapon. It was cold inside; she could still see her breath. She moved along the corridor and passed an office. The door was ajar; a single desk, a swivel chair sprouting stuffing from the armrests, a paper chart on the wall with a list of forty or fifty names. There was a portable radio on top of a filing cabinet playing Muscovite pop. On the desk, steam rose from a glass of tea beneath the drooping head of an Anglepoise lamp.

The brightness at the end of the corridor was a large room. A classroom, perhaps, or an assembly room. There were five towers of stacked plastic chairs along one wall, an old television on a telescopic stand in one corner, a wooden coat-stand in another, two trestle tables to the left, no children. On the walls, there were old posters: children running down a hill, a young girl laughing, a leaping dolphin, a field of wheat rolling like an ocean beneath a sparkling summer sun. There were large square windows at the far end of the room looking onto a playground. Komarov was standing in front of one of them, in partial silhouette, his back to her.

He didn't turn round. 'Found what you're looking for?'

She didn't move or think. She just felt angry; always her first reaction to shame.

'You don't know what you've done by coming here.'

When he did turn round, she wouldn't look him in the eye.

'I thought I could trust you.'

'You can,' she whispered.

'What are you doing here?'

She held open her hands. 'Following you.'

They were still at opposing ends of the room. 'Why?'

'To find out where you go. Who you see.'

'Why?'

She couldn't bring herself to say it.

'*Why*, Petra? Am I a target?'

'No!' She saw that her denial was too quick, too insistent. Too desperate. 'You're not a target. I promise you. I wouldn't. I *couldn't*.'

'Why, then?'

She said, 'Because you wouldn't tell me. And I wanted to know. I *needed* to know.'

But it was a lie. Komarov was right. It was a matter of trust. Or rather, lack of it. Despite all her desire to do so, she couldn't bring herself to trust him completely. She had to see for herself. Now, that made her feel dirty and cheap.

A stranger appeared in the doorway on the far side of the room. He was Stephanie's height but thinner. Dark-skinned, dark silver hair, the collar of his check shirt was too large for such a scrawny throat. Over the shirt, a crudely-knitted brown V-neck jersey and a charcoal grey jacket that was too big for him.

Komarov shook his head – more through sadness than anger – and said, 'This is Mohammed Saev. He runs the place.'

And then he was gone. Stephanie wanted to say something – to apologize, to ask for forgiveness – but she needed the right moment.

Saev led her through the rest of the ground floor; a dining hall, an ill-equipped kitchen, a medical station with no supplies. The children were in class. Stephanie and Saev watched them through the windows in the classroom's swing doors. Pale and malnourished, they were all shaven-headed.

'Lice,' Saev said. 'A razor and some disinfectant . . . it was the cheapest way.'

Upstairs, there were dormitories; long, cold, naked rooms with bunks running along each wall. Damp mattresses, grey, gossamer-thin sheets, blankets with more holes than material. There were cheap wooden cupboards between each bunk. Most were missing doors, half of them had no shelves. In the communal bathroom, Stephanie saw that four of the six basins had been disconnected. A shower dripped. She smelt rotten plaster. Ice had turned the windows opaque.

Saev suggested coffee. They took the back stairs to the ground floor.

'This place . . .'

'It's a State-run children's home. Built thirty years ago.'

'What's his connection?'

Saev turned to her, surprised. 'He owns it.'

'I though you said it was State-run.'

'It was. And you can see what that means.'

They entered the kitchen. Saev put a kettle over a

330

ring of gas. Stephanie looked through the window. Komarov's blue Mercedes was gone. She pretended not to care. 'So, this place – did he buy it?'

Saev smiled, revealing a mouth missing a third of its teeth. Those that remained were brown. 'They almost paid him to take it. Just like the others.'

'What others?'

'This is the sixth. The third in Moscow.'

'Kostya owns six children's homes?'

'Yes.'

'All like this one?'

Saev looked indignant. 'Of course not. I mean, at first, maybe. But not later. Not after the improvements. We haven't had time to start on this place yet. But we will, soon. Then there'll be better clothes, better food, more warmth, better medical care. A TV that works, maybe. Some soap to go with the hot water . . .'

'How long's he owned this place?'

'Less than a month.'

'I'm missing something. I don't understand.'

'You didn't know?'

'No.'

Saev smiled again. 'That's good.'

'Why?'

'Because that's how it has to be.'

He tore open two sachets of coffee powder and mixed them with boiling water. He handed Stephanie one of the buttercup mugs.

'Were you here before?' she asked.

He shook his head. 'I only arrived in Moscow a year ago.'

'Where are you from?'

'Grozny. I'm a Chechen. But I haven't been home

in four years. Before Moscow, I was in Yerevan, then Kazan.'

'Why did you come here?'

'To look for work.'

'And this is where you ended up?'

'I ended up in the gutter. Like every other Chechen who comes to this city. The people here think of us as dogs. In fact, they think less of us than that. We are the worms inside a dog's intestine. They have an idea about us that does not allow them to see us as real people. It does not allow them to see me as a doctor.'

'*Are* you a doctor?'

He nodded. 'Fully trained. But could I get a job here? Or even in Kazan? Not a chance. Most Muscovites would sooner suffer than be treated by a Chechen.'

'So what did you do?'

'I drank. To take away the frustration. And the cold. And the beatings. There's a hole in my memory now. It's six months in size. Before it, I was homeless, drinking anything I could, sleeping around Leningradsky and Kazansky stations. After it, I was in this refuge near Murmansky Prospekt.'

'Ludmilla?'

The mention of her name lit a candle in Saev. 'Yes.'

'I was there. Kostya took me. Is that something to do with him too?'

Saev nodded. 'It's all part of it.'

'Part of what?'

'You should ask him. It's not for me to say.'

Stephanie took a sip from her mug. The taste bore no resemblance to coffee but the warmth was welcome. 'Go on.'

'There were others there like me. At first, it was just

somewhere to sleep, somewhere warm and safe. There was food there, too. And company. Soon, I found I didn't want to leave when morning came. I started to spend all day there. Just talking, taking the rubbish out, doing small things. Then Ludmilla asked if I wanted to help the medical assistant. That was how I came to be involved. During his last visit to Moscow, Konstantin told me about this place. He brought me here. We had a look around and he asked me if I could run it, if he managed to buy it. To be honest, I wasn't sure. But he said he'd find the money and the staff, so what could I say?'

'I had no idea about any of this.'

'Nobody does.'

'A man of secrets.'

'That's true. But he's much more than that. Did you know that his wife was killed?'

'Irina? Yes, I did. A car bomb.'

'Did you know that it was planted by Chechen terrorists? More than any other Russian I've met, he had a reason to hate us – to hate me – but he doesn't. He's not like most of them. It's his greatest quality. And his greatest weakness.'

Aragvi, on Tverskaya Square, had three dining rooms. One looked like a German beer cellar. Another looked like an indoor swimming pool: walls of white marble tiles to a height of ten feet. Above the tiles, the upper walls and hemispherical ceiling were painted with scenes from Georgian fairy tales. The style was basic, the content heroic; men grappling with tigers, knights on horseback, maidens and meadows for decoration. The third dining room was far smaller than the other two: a clutch of tables, wooden panels for walls. Komarov was waiting for her at a table by a pair of shutters set into one of the walls. There were only two other diners. In the farthest corner, a middle-aged man sat opposite a girl half his age and size. They were leaning towards one another, holding hands, whispering.

Komarov was wearing a dark grey Canali suit. His white shirt was open at the neck. He looked tired. On the table, there was a bottle of mineral water, a glass ashtray and an ice bucket with a bottle of Georgian champagne in it.

'I wasn't sure you'd come.'

'I wasn't sure you really wanted me to.'

There had been a message for her when she returned to the Baltschug. *We need to talk. Meet me at Aragvi, at eight.* They sat down.

'This was Stalin's favourite place. And Beria's.' Komarov opened the shutters to reveal a small wooden balcony that protruded from the wall of the main dining room, allowing them to look down onto the tables below. 'In this room, they could have all the privacy they wanted and still spy on everyone else. A great comfort for the great paranoids.'

'I wasn't spying on you, Kostya.'

'Yes, you were. On the ceiling in there, you can see Georgian myths in glorious colour.'

'Very clever. Koba . . .'

'I thought it was appropriate.'

She rose from her chair. 'If you're going to behave like a jerk all night, I'll leave now.'

'Sit down.'

'Fuck off.'

'Sit.'

Her mind stormed out of the room. But her body sat. Komarov poured her a glass of champagne. She poured herself a glass of mineral water. It was warm and tasted slightly salty.

'I thought we were supposed to be a secret in Moscow.'

'Those two in the corner are okay. No one else will be coming into this room.'

'You know what I mean.'

When he nodded, he looked defeated. 'I'm tired, Petra. Tired of all this.' He leaned back in his chair and held open his hands. 'If it's a risk . . . it's a risk. So what? I've been taking risks since I was a child.'

'And the children out at Izmailovo – are they a risk, too?'

Instead of an answer, he lit a cigarette.

'Saev told me you have six children's homes. He told me about the refuge off Murmansky Prospekt. Why are they secret?'

'Because they're vulnerable. And more important than that, they're a sign of vulnerability.'

'How?'

'The easiest way to put pressure on me would be to put pressure on them.'

'So why did you get involved?'

He frowned at her. '*Get* involved? I've always been involved.'

'I'm not with you.'

She saw the debate going on behind the eyes and she was patient.

'When my mother disappeared, and when my father was sentenced to twelve years at Norilsk, I was sent to a State orphanage. It was nothing like Izmailovo. That's a modern place by comparison. My first orphanage was built in the middle of the nineteenth century. Nothing had changed. I was eight years old. Seven of us arrived on the same day. It was late at night – it was bitterly cold, I remember, twenty-five below, snow everywhere – and we slept crushed into two beds. The following morning, those of us whose parents had been sent to prison were separated from the true orphans. There were three of us. They took us into a large hall where we were addressed by the head of the orphanage. He told us our parents were enemies of the State and that we were there to be re-educated. We were given a form to sign. It said that we agreed to renounce our mothers and fathers and that the Motherland was now our only parent. Of the three of us, I was the only one who could read.'

'Did you sign the form?'

'No. To have signed it would have been an admission that the State existed.'

'For God's sake, you were eight.'

'I was old enough to know. My parents had made sure of that. We all knew. It was another form of indoctrination, I suppose. But I believed it, even then.'

'And now?'

'Still now, yes.'

A sleepy waiter rolled over to their table. Komarov ordered for both of them. Stephanie looked at the other couple. At first glance, she'd assumed he was a rich, older man with a young, attractive girl, who was probably charging by the hour. Now, she wasn't so sure. The body language was wrong; he looked demoralized and she appeared to be trying to console him. The waiter receded.

'Did the other children sign the form?'

'Yes.'

'What happened to them?'

'They joined the general population in the orphanage.'

'And you?'

'I was transferred to a children's asylum in the south of the city, near the Moskvich factory.'

'An asylum?'

Komarov drank some champagne. 'I wouldn't sign the form so I was mentally ill. That was the logic of the time. The doctors told us nonconformity was a sickness and that we would be given treatments to cure us. They gave me lumbar punctures. They said they needed to drain fluid from my spine to remedy the illness in my head. There were other treatments, too. Injections, tablets. At one point, I had a headache that was so violent I couldn't move. It lasted for six months.'

'Were all the children in the asylum like you?'

'About fifty per cent were. The other half really were mentally ill. Of the half that weren't, I would say two thirds became mentally ill over time.'

'But not you.'

'I was lucky.'

'Doesn't sound like it.'

'No? Well, I was. In the end. And I had my revenge, in a way.'

'How?'

'I bought the asylum in ninety-five at a government property auction. Then I destroyed it. Burnt it to the ground. I lost half a million dollars but it made me feel better.' He smiled but it was unconvincing. 'There's no trace of it left now. All you can see on the site is a half-built Korean engineering plant. They ran out of money in ninety-nine. It's been derelict since then. Personally, I like that.'

Stephanie drank some of the champagne that she'd so pointedly ignored. It was heavier and sweeter than any champagne she'd tasted before.

'So now you buy children's homes to cure your past?'

'It's not quite like that, Petra.'

'Convince me.'

'This country goes from one crisis to the next. Look at something like the sinking of the *Kursk*. That was a tragedy. It was also good TV: all the weeping mothers gathered in Murmansk, Putin showing his true colours, that old KGB mentality. We read about one environmental catastrophe after another and we blame the Soviet past. But the biggest tragedy in Russia today is ongoing. It's the collapse of the future. Children without homes, without education, without medical care, without parents. And children who would be better off without the parents they have. I'm a businessman, Petra. An investor. And I'm investing in the future. That's all.'

'I don't buy that for a moment.'

'It's not a line. It's the truth.'

'It might be part of the truth.'

'You have no idea.'

The waiter brought the first of their food: *satsivi*, cold chicken with garlic and walnuts, *kharcho*, a thick soup served with rice, *khachpuri*, cheese bread, and a plate of red and green beans. He opened a bottle of Georgian red and left it to breathe at the end of the table.

'How long were you in the asylum?'

'Four years.'

'Then what?'

He shrugged and smiled. 'A life in business. Or crime, depending on your point of view. Now, when I look back – I was still only a child then – I think of myself as a capitalist waiting to happen.'

'I don't think of you as a capitalist at all.'

'Perhaps not in the Western sense.'

'In what sense, then?'

'You wouldn't understand.'

'Don't patronize me, Kostya.'

'I mean it. It's like when the Soviet Union collapsed. The Americans and the western Europeans thought they were going to come here and make a fortune. They spent millions because they expected to make billions. And a few did. But who controls the real money in Russia today? Russians. Not Americans or Germans. Which is the way it should be. But they're wondering where it all went. They thought it would be different here. But I can tell you that as a man who operates in the East and the West, the practice is essentially the same. Business, politics, crime; the Holy Trinity. We're new to the game – so perhaps our methods seem crude at times – but we're quick learners. But the real difference between us is a matter of perception. For us, it's not so black and white. Business and crime are merely different points on a spectrum.'

'Believe me, I understand different points on a spectrum.'

'Maybe *you* do. But you also understand what I'm saying . . .'

'I know that some kinds of certainty leave you vulnerable to reality.'

Komarov raised his glass to her. 'Exactly.'

'So how did you end up in prison?'

Another smile. 'It was easy. And inevitable. I was involved with the black market from the age of fourteen. Running cigarettes, stealing fresh vegetables, manufacturing vodka, enforcing protection. I was always in trouble. Most of the time, you just paid the police to look the other way. But sometimes that didn't work.'

'You make it sound so casual.'

'It wasn't. There just wasn't an alternative.'

'Because everything else was collusion?'

'Yes.'

Komarov, the new *vor*. Not the same as his *vorovskoi mir* predecessors, not the same as the recently rich Russian criminal fraternity. Instead, a pioneer for a new breed of criminal. Or businessman. *Depending on your point of view . . .*

The waiter removed the first course and brought the second: *chakhokhbili*, a chicken and vegetable stew. Komarov poured her some wine. It was heavily aromatic and tasted faintly Spanish.

'What happened to your parents?'

'My mother died in prison a few days after I last saw her. They said it was a heart attack. It probably wasn't. I didn't find out she was dead for two years.'

'And your father? You said he got twelve years.'

'Twelve years in the nickel mines at Norilsk. In reality, a life sentence.'

'He died?'

'Actually, no. He was a statistical oddity. He survived. Not just twelve years, either. In the end, he was in prison for nineteen.'

'Is he still alive?'

'Yes.'

'Here in Moscow?'

Komarov shook his head. 'In Norilsk. When they let him out, he stayed.'

'Why? I mean, I've never been to Norilsk but . . .'

Komarov painted the picture for her. A town marooned in an ice-blasted wilderness two thousand miles north-east of Moscow. Temperatures down to minus fifty Celsius in winter. A grid of grey streets carving up concrete towers and factories. Roads competing with rail, the cars as sluggish and rusty as the trains. At the town's perimeter, a forest of industrial chimneys belching noxious fumes into a lead sky. Ten months of winter every year. Started in 1937, Norilsk was a town built by a slave nation. By the time Komarov's father arrived, there were nickel mines, cement plants, brick factories, copper plants. It was a town that could only have been born of forced labour; no civilians would have tried it or survived it. Komarov's father had described it as a town 'built on bones'.

'For many years, I had no idea that he'd survived. I was in prison myself. Kolyma Central 3, Sakhalin, Khabarovsk Central Penitentiary. It was only after my release that I learned that he'd made it. It took me years to find out that he was still there; like you, I'd assumed he'd moved away. Returned to Moscow maybe. But no . . .'

'So you went to see him?'

'In February ninety-seven. He was living in a one-room apartment in the same building as the man who was his chief prison guard for seven years. You should see the shit-hole he calls home. But after nineteen years in the mines, anything is luxury. Anyway, I flew up to Norilsk. I spent a week with him. It was the strangest seven days of my life. Nothing in the prisons, or in the asylum, or in the orphanages came close to that week. We were complete strangers. When we talked about my mother, we talked about her as though she was a casual mutual acquaintance. We couldn't say anything to each other. Ninety per cent of the time we spent together, we spent in silence. But I could feel the words. Like I can with you. He felt guilty.'

'Why?'

'For raising me into a life that was destined to be harder than it had to be. He always said being born Russian was as much of a curse as a blessing. But he felt pride, too. After everything, he still had his integrity. The State tried to break him and the State lost. And then died. And *vorovskoi mir* survived.'

'And you?'

'Mixed feelings, I think. He can't understand the way things are now, the way I am. For him, progress stopped the day he boarded the train for Norilsk. The last snapshot is the way it was and the way it will be as long as he lives. I tried to persuade him to come back to Moscow. I bought an apartment for him – a smart place in the same building as mine, three times the size with a woman to look after him – but he didn't want to know.'

'Why not?'

'Because Moscow was no longer home.'

'But Norilsk is?'

Komarov had finished eating. He lit another cigarette. 'The thing he kept saying to me was this: "I hate this town. I love this town." Just like that. One sentence, then the next. When he refused to come back here, I asked if there was somewhere else he wanted to go. No, he told me, there was nowhere. I said there

342

had to be *somewhere*. And he looked at me and said, "Where can I go now? When they let you out, they give you a release form. It shows that you are free. But you're not. Norilsk is a life sentence. When I left the prison, I had nowhere to go. So I stayed. And the way I live now is the way I lived then. It's just a little warmer and there's more food. But it's still day-to-day with no past and no future. I hate this town. I love this town. It's been my whole life and that's why I'll die here." And do you know something, Petra? He's right.'

'Why?'

'Because modern Russia isn't necessarily a better Russia. Today, all the industries he helped to build have been privatized. They're closing down the factories. Wages don't get paid and for the first time since the first train stopped at the end of the line in the middle of nowhere, there's unemployment in Norilsk. All the people who died up there, all the injustice and suffering – was it for nothing?'

'What do you think?'

'I think it was. That's why he can't allow himself to consider an alternative. He's not a prisoner of a town, Petra. He's a prisoner of a mind-set. Just like you are. Just like I am.'

They ate more food, drank more wine, the couple in the corner grew more melancholy. Komarov asked Stephanie about her past and she gave him Petra. Born in Hamburg in 1968, her father, Karl Reuter, was a police officer who had transferred to Hamburg from Stuttgart. He was forty-five when Petra, his only child, was born. His wife, Rosa, was twenty years his junior. Karl Reuter had been a World War Two veteran; as a teenage conscript, he'd served with the 371st Infantry Division at Stalingrad under the command of Lieutenant-General Stempel. Komarov asked whether her father had ever talked about it and Stephanie found the lies flowed as easily as the wine. Yes, she said, ignoring the twist in her gut, her father had talked about the cold, the hunger, the rats, the disease, the fear and the extraordinary pride he'd felt at being part of Paulus' doomed Sixth Army. Both her parents were now dead. Then she gave him the details of Petra's metamorphosis: angry left-wing student raging at the complacency of the consumerist late Eighties and early Nineties; the evolution from campus radical to underground anarchist; the surge from anarchist to terrorist; the backlash.

'What backlash?' Komarov asked.

'From terrorist to mercenary. Trading ideals for money.'

'Why?'

For a long time, she couldn't think of an explanation. Eventually, she said, 'Because I came to the conclusion that it made no difference. Left-wing, right-wing . . . as you would say, they were just different points on a spectrum. There was no black and white, nothing to believe in.'

'You could have walked away.'

'It's what I do, Kostya. You might as well ask a doctor to give up medicine.'

Two musicians entered the dining room. One played the accordion, the other played the doudouk. They serenaded the couple in the corner. The girl with the red hair began to sing. Her voice was frail. The man smiled, his eyes glossy with tears. She sang in Georgian, then Armenian. One song after another. The room was still.

Stephanie felt suspended in a single moment. As it elongated, she knew she would always return to it. Komarov took her hand as the doudouk carried her through five centuries of Central Asia.

'What are we going to do, Kostya?'

'I don't know. But you have to promise me one thing.'

'Anything.'

'After all we've said tonight – after what you saw today – don't make the mistake of thinking of me as a good man. I'm not.'

20

Aeroflot to Frankfurt, British Airways to London, it was ten forty-five when her flight touched down at Heathrow, five past midnight by the time she reached Old Court Place. The flat was cold and damp. She adjusted the thermostat. There was nothing in the fridge except a pack of butter, a jar of olives and half a bottle of sparkling mineral water. With no sparkle.

Stephanie couldn't be bothered to unpack, or even brush her teeth. She stripped, crawled beneath the duvet and curled into a ball. It still took her an hour to fall asleep. She dreamed that Komarov was making love to Natalya and that she was watching, resigned to it. When she woke, just after eight, she couldn't rinse away the dream's bitter aftertaste.

In Moscow, there had been snow. In London, there was rain. She ran a bath and stuck a CD into the machine; *New York* by Lou Reed. She sorted through the pile of mail. Most of it was junk, some of it was for the flat's previous occupant, none of it was for any version of her. Later, she took some clothes to the Modern Express Dry Cleaners on Holland Street before having breakfast on Kensington Church Street; croissants and coffee with a large glass of orange juice. Afterwards, she brought groceries from Safeway and spent the rest of the morning cleaning the flat. Sometimes, she found a little domesticity strangely cathartic. It grounded her, allowing her to pretend she was normal. She didn't mind that it was a charade. She scrubbed the bath, ran a vacuum cleaner over the floors, wiped the kitchen down and opened some windows to circulate the air. She'd always liked the sound of falling rain.

After a lunch of minestrone and warm bread, she phoned New York. Komarov was at his apartment on Fifth Avenue. It was a beautiful morning, he told her. Clear and frosty. His flight from Moscow had been delayed. It had been quarter to midnight when the aircraft finally landed.

Stephanie said, 'You were in my dream last night.'

'What was I doing?'

'Making love to me.'

Vladimir Vatukin and Natalya Markova arrived in London on the evening of 20 December. They were accompanied by the two bodyguards who'd masqueraded as lawyers at Café Pushkin. There were two dark green Bentleys to transport the group from Heathrow to the Lanesborough on Hyde Park Corner.

The following morning, Stephanie got up at six. Twenty minutes of stretches, a warm shower, a light breakfast. She left the flat at seven, dressed for walking and rain. She reached Hyde Park Corner at twenty-five past seven. At the bus stop, commuters came and went but she always appeared to be waiting for the next bus. Vatukin left the hotel at eight fifteen, unaccompanied. The bodyguards stayed with Natalya.

There was an entrance to the Underground in front of the hotel, which he used. She took the entrance next to the bus stop and caught sight of him by the ticket machine. She melted into the rush-hour. He took the

Piccadilly Line to King's Cross. She nearly lost him on the concourse, which was congested with passengers disgorged from the northern trains, scurrying commuters and a group of potbellied Newcastle United supporters who were drinking cans of Stella Artois. It was five to nine.

She followed him at a discreet distance. He crossed the Euston Road, walked down Judd Street as far as Tavistock Place, where he turned left. The building he entered had been residential once; four floors of brick blackened by two centuries of pollution. Stephanie waited several minutes, then passed by the entrance. There were five names on the brass plaque over the intercom, all companies. She walked on and then wrote them into the notebook she'd brought with her. Vatukin emerged twenty-five minutes later.

By ten fifteen, they were at the Russian Orthodox Cathedral in Ennismore Gardens. Vatukin was inside for less than five minutes. At eleven, Stephanie found herself on a street of terraced houses in Kennington. When Vatukin appeared at five past, he was carrying a plastic bag with a bulky parcel inside. At Kennington Underground, he took the Northern Line to Moorgate, from where he walked to Finsbury Circus. At quarter to one, Vatukin returned to Moorgate, no longer carrying the plastic bag. He caught the Northern Line to King's Cross and the Victoria Line to Green Park. Just before one thirty, he entered Diverso, an Italian restaurant on Piccadilly, where Natalya and the two minders were already at a table.

The afternoon was a retail orgy; Asprey's, Cartier, Hermes, Prada, Armani. They spent an hour in Graff being fawned over. Stephanie spent the same hour on

New Bond Street being rained on. Watching, waiting. Gaudy Christmas decorations sparkled in the rain. When they emerged, Natalya looked smug. Vatukin looked bemused. In Moscow, the bodyguards carried weapons. In London, they carried shopping bags. At four thirty, the group went to Fortnum's for tea. Afterwards, Stephanie followed them back to the Lanesborough, where they remained until seven thirty, which was when the Bentleys returned to ferry them to the Dorchester. Five minutes after they'd arrived, a black Mercedes pulled up outside the hotel, a small Russian flag fluttering from the front of the vehicle. Playing the tourist, Stephanie photographed the front of the hotel with a digital camera, making sure she caught their faces. Ten minutes later, she entered the Dorchester to verify that they were with Vatukin. It was five past eight.

At eight twenty-eight, I kick my front door shut with the heel of my boot. I'm cold, tired and wet. I shrug off my overcoat and go into the kitchen. I pour myself a glass of wine, traipse to the bathroom, turn on the taps and wriggle out of the damp trousers that have stuck to me like a second skin, and which prompt me to think of Boris Bergstein in his apartment in Krylatskoye. By nine, I'm in the kitchen, warm and dry, and almost human. Goldfrapp's Felt Mountain is playing, I'm on my second glass of wine, the water is coming to the boil, my fingers are sticky with garlic. I chop plum tomatoes and add them to the pan with a splash of wine and some fresh basil.

The laptop is on the kitchen table next to the notebook, which has swollen with moisture. I download the photos from the digital camera, type out a list of requests, bundle them together and send them to Stern. I choose spaghetti over penne or tagliatelle.

I'm halfway through eating when I get my first response. It's the house in Kennington.

The property belongs to Forrester Whiley, an investment company with an office on the Strand. They have a property portfolio, mostly residential, middle-to-lower market. There are three apartments in the property.

I ask for details on the people living there and then finish eating. Another glass of wine and I'm reaching that perfect state: slightly fuzzy, all the rough edges smoothed away. Back to an old favourite: Version 2.0 *by Garbage. I pick the song I want – 'You Look So Fine' – and think of Kostya. It's twenty to ten in London, twenty to five in Manhattan. I picture him in his office at Gardyne Hill, on the twenty-ninth floor, overlooking East 52nd Street. Milla, his frosty secretary, outside, the Olga Svetlichnaya and Yuori Kugach canvases on the walls inside. When Stern returns, he says that the ground-floor flat in Kennington is rented by a German named Jurgen Foegel.*

Is that significant?

It's not his real name. He's actually Leonid Kichenko, a Ukrainian. He ran prostitutes for Tsentralnaya in Moscow for five years. He's wanted for the 1999 murders of a Croat and a Slovene. Both girls were under his control. Both were stabbed to death with a broken bottle. By the way, I have more information on Forrester Whiley. Do you want it?

Yes.

Forrester Whiley is wholly-owned by a company called Arcadian, an off-the-shelf outfit registered in Jersey. It owns a variety of businesses throughout Europe and the former Soviet Union. The range includes travel agencies, restaurants, limousine services, dry-cleaning businesses and a chain of nightclubs.

A chain of nightclubs?

The White Square chain. Mostly based in eastern European cities, including Russia. Interestingly, the Arcadian purchase price was one US dollar.

One?

One.

Who was the vendor?

A Swiss firm. Mirsch.

Kostya.

Mirsch is Kostya's in a way that Gardyne Hill is not. Mirsch is the real Komarov. With Switzerland as a home, it is invisible, hiding behind other companies in the same way that Kostya hides behind a Brioni suit or a Fifth Avenue view.

Stern and I communicate until after midnight, questions and answers racing through space. It's like looking through static on a TV screen; it takes time for the picture to emerge. The building on Tavistock Place is owned by another company in the Arcadian stable. And the five names on the brass plaque all have roots that return to the same source. I follow the threads of the web: legal firms, investment firms, property development and property management, accountancy, hotels. All in London, all controlled directly, or indirectly, from Jersey, established by a corporate ghost in Switzerland and – I have little doubt – answerable to a man in Moscow.

Politicians and journalists pontificate on the threat posed by the Russian Mafiya but they can't agree on the likely impact of such criminal cartels. They squabble about the measures that should be taken to prevent these organizations from establishing themselves in Britain. But the truth is on the screen in front of me. It's too late. Tsentralnaya is already here.

Stern has identified the people in the two digital images I took outside the Dorchester. One of them is an official at the Russian Embassy, the other is a Russian entrepreneur.

Come on, Oscar. Russian entrepreneur? Could you be any more amorphous?

He's in the cell-phone industry. He's an arbitrageur of electronic minutes.

I apologize. I underestimated you. Arbitrageur of electronic minutes. That has to be the most amorphous job description I've ever heard.

His former job description is a little more down-to-earth. He used to work for the KGB. Electronic surveillance. Which makes a kind of sense, don't you think?

The mention of the KGB prompts another enquiry from me. It takes twenty minutes for Stern to come back with an answer.

Josef Bergstein is a former KGB employee. He joined in 1969 and remained with the organization's First Chief Directorate until the KGB was partitioned. He then worked for SVR until 1998.

I know he ran funds that financed agents abroad. Do you have any extra information on that?

You've been misled.

Sorry?

Josef Bergstein was a Level One KGB assassin.

Five to eleven, Piccadilly Circus. A fat Father Christmas was standing beside Eros singing 'Jingle Bells'. Tourists and shoppers clogged the Circus and all the arteries leading off it. The air tasted of cheap pizza, greasy cheeseburgers and roasted chestnuts. Christmas-tree lights competed with advertising neon and lost.

Stephanie had called Vatukin at nine. He'd said the meeting would be at eleven and to call back at ten for the location; the same caution he'd shown in arranging to meet at Café Pushkin in Moscow.

The entrance was next to a souvenir shop on Shaftesbury Avenue. Plastic Union Jacks, saucy postcards, British Bulldog mugs, ceramic busts of Winston Churchill flicking his victory 'V' sign. The usual overpriced crap. A couple of giggling Japanese girls were trying on a plastic policeman's helmet. When the lock released, Stephanie went up to the second floor. Samson Entertainment occupied three rooms at the rear of the building. Vatukin was waiting for her at the top of the stairs, dressed in an expensive-looking leather bomber jacket. Stephanie was sure that Natalya had bought it for him. Or rather, that she'd persuaded Vatukin to buy it for himself. It didn't suit him; it was too flashy.

'I apologize for this place. I didn't want the three of us to meet in public.'

He led her into a cramped office. On the walls, posters of 'models' in skimpy bikinis, their skins tanned and oiled. They were draped across car bonnets or straddled gleaming motorcycles. Each poster had Samson Entertainment stencilled across the top in red.

'This is Alexander Kosygin. Alexander, Petra.'

They shook hands. Stephanie guessed he was six three. He was thin, not lean, with short grey hair, combed back over the scalp. Pale blue eyes full of miserly suspicion were set in bloodshot whites. He wore an ill-fitting single-breasted black suit. There was a sand-coloured overcoat draped over the chair beside him. Stephanie remembered him: once a lieutenant-general in the Soviet Red Army, now the head of Weiss-Randall, a pharmaceutical company based in the United States but with facilities in Belgium, Switzerland, Sweden and Russia. The Trump Taj Mahal in Atlantic City. That was where she had seen him. In George Salibi's private enclosure with Vatukin. And Komarov.

Vatukin lit a Marlboro. 'Alexander needs to ask you some questions before we can proceed.'

In the past, Kosygin had been a member of the Fifteenth Directorate, which had controlled the Soviet Biological Warfare programme. If one assumed he'd used his past to furnish his future – given the nature of Weiss-Randall's business, that was not an unreasonable premise – it was easy to imagine that he still had connections in Russia with those who'd assumed control of the Biological Warfare programme after the Fifteenth Directorate's dissolution.

'I need to know what your clients intend to do with the weapon. That way, we can make sure they receive the appropriate device and agent. Firstly, is it intended for a closed urban situation, or something more open?'

Stephanie keyed into the scenario she'd invented. 'Rural, low population density, flat open land, small villages.'

'Are they looking for a number?'

'A number?'

'Of casualties.'

'They never specified one.'

Kosygin began to talk about rates of mortality and infectivity. There were some strains of weaponized anthrax, he told her, that were now close to perfect. Perfect being a one hundred per cent mortality rate, which seemed a perverse use of the word. He discussed incubation, symptoms, risks, delivery systems, relative costs.

'Weaponized smallpox could be a possibility. Have

you ever seen what natural smallpox does to a child's face? Some of the engineered strains are worse. If it's important to have pictures on TV, or in newspapers, this could be a consideration.'

It was so casual. Like choosing a new kitchen. Units over the sink, or just shelves? A virus that erupts within twelve hours of infection, or one that lurks for a week? What kind of cooker, gas or electric? A secondary infection capability, or just your standard primary infection?

Stephanie tried to play the game. She could hear traffic on Shaftesbury Avenue, a helicopter passing overhead, the dull thud of a sound system from next door. The real world was carrying on around them. Or was that just Alexander's pretend world? Perhaps he'd been right. Perhaps *this* was the real world; birth, the bit in between, death.

They spoke for two hours. When it was over, Kosygin turned to Vatukin and nodded.

'Looks like we can work something out,' Vatukin said.

'When?'

'Natalya and I are going back to Russia tomorrow morning. Every year, I have a New Year's Eve party at my dacha outside Moscow. Come to it. We can talk there. Then we'll make the final arrangements when our heads are clear.'

Stephanie looked at Kosygin, who said, 'We won't meet again. Vladimir will be in charge of everything from now on.' He smiled sickly. 'But I'll be reading the newspapers.'

Komarov flew in to London that evening and called her from Heathrow. She gave him the address. An hour later, they were kissing at her flat on Old Court Place. She said, 'I missed you the moment I left you.'

'I missed you too.'

She showed him around. He asked if the flat was hers. No, she said, it was just a rental. A temporary place. He asked whether she had a permanent place. Not now. She had, at one time, and she wanted to again, but, for the moment, she was a drifter.

She cooked for him. It was the first time and it felt good not having to eat in a hotel, or at a restaurant. Chicken breasts stuffed with mushrooms, with new potatoes and French beans. They drank white burgundy, then red. After they'd eaten, they lay on the sofa, drinking the last of the wine, not talking much.

Before sliding into sleep, Stephanie set the alarm for six thirty. They stepped onto the street at seven fifteen. It was chilly and quiet. They loaded their bags into the boot of the car that she'd hired the previous day, then headed north, arriving early in the afternoon.

The Percy Arms Inn was just north of the Kielder Forest, on the border between Northumberland and Scotland. Alan Smiley, the owner, said he wasn't quite sure which side of the border they were. It depended on who was asking. At the other end of Kielder Water was Falstone, the village where Stephanie had grown up. And where she was buried.

Five years had elapsed since she'd stood on a windswept roadside, Alexander next to her, and watched her brother follow her coffin into the cemetery. Magenta House had killed her in a car crash. At the time, it had seemed vaguely surreal. It had been a while before the full impact registered: she would never see Christopher again. Or Jane, her sister-in-law, or James and Polly,

356

her nephew and niece. Since then, Philip had been born. Jane had been pregnant with him on that blustery afternoon.

Christopher was all that remained of her immediate family. With her death, Stephanie had left him truly alone. She'd never ceased to feel guilty about that because she could have made the other decision. But she'd had her reasons and she hadn't looked beyond them.

Now, she was back, for the first time in five years. When she'd thought about where she and Komarov should spend Christmas, this had been the only place she'd considered. Her childhood Christmases had been magical. The wild countryside and the inclement weather had played their part as surely as the stockings, the presents, the church service and the lunch. Each year, her parents had given them the Christmas that all children crave. Each year since their deaths, her Christmases had been universally bleak.

She wouldn't see Christopher, of course. But he would be close enough. The land would bind them together. She would know what they were doing. She would see the tree at the foot of the stairs in the hall, feel the heat of the fire in the sitting room, taste the fruit cake that was always overcooked and a little dry. Somehow, she would communicate all these sensations to Komarov without saying a word.

There was a part of her that wanted Alexander to know where she was. She wanted to see the panic followed by the fury. There was another part of her that was terrified he might somehow find out and ruin everything.

When they checked in, Stephanie did so as Claudia

Baumann, Komarov as Ivan Andreyev. Alan Smiley's expression suggested he was going to say that it made a change from Mr and Mrs Smith. He took them up to their room.

'We've got six,' he said, 'but there's only one other couple here at the moment. I reserved the best view for you.'

Rugged land fell away then rose into hills. They could see folds of rough grass sprinkled with sheep, stone walls, a meandering river, trees crippled crooked by the wind. Once they were alone, Komarov came up behind her and wrapped his arms around her. He kissed her on the neck.

'Amazing, Petra. How did you know about this place?'

'I've been here before.'

On Christmas Day, they drove to Housesteads, the Roman fort on Hadrian's Wall. The National Trust office and museum were closed. The site was deserted. They parked in the car park and walked the half mile to the stone remains of the fort. White clouds rolled over a sapphire sky, the hard easterly wind bringing tears to Stephanie's eyes. The tip of her nose turned red. They walked along the top of the wall towards the west, then paused at a point over a two-hundred-foot escarpment. Below, marshy white grass and roaming sheep. Ahead, more rough land, a small house by a lake, a forest, then the snow-capped Cheviots in the distance.

Stephanie said, 'There was a time when this was the edge of the world. You can feel it, can't you?'

'Petra?'

'Yes.'

'I love you.'

He was standing behind her. She was glad he couldn't see her.

He said, 'Everything has changed.'

There was a lump in her throat. She struggled to keep the quiver out of her voice. 'Why?'

'Because there's no room for love in my life. It's not possible to live like I do and to love someone. Not if it's going to work.'

'What are you saying?'

'I'm just telling you what I know.'

She wanted to tell him what she knew; that she loved him too. But she couldn't. Those words – they wouldn't sound right coming from her. Not at that moment.

'What can we do, Kostya?'

He put his hands on her shoulders. 'We could disappear.'

The twenty-seventh. The curtains were open. Spits of rain hit the window. In bed, Stephanie was draped across Komarov. She ran her fingers over his chest, over his throat, back over his collarbone, feeling for the familiar landmarks: two small scars over a rib on the left, a cluster of moles at the base of the throat, a patch of dry skin on the shoulder. She wanted to absorb every detail. Nothing was too minor.

They'd spent Boxing Day touring the area. They'd had lunch at a pub in Hawick, where Stephanie had made Komarov try a pint of Guinness. He thought it was disgusting. In the evening, the bar at the Percy Arms had been busy, a clutch of locals stretching last orders to midnight, the men drinking bitter, the women on spirits and wine. There had been a couple of pipe-smokers among them. Stephanie could smell it on Komarov's skin and on her pillow. In the bar, he'd entertained a captive and inebriated audience with tales of growing up in Russia, some true, some not. Stephanie had been content to fade into the background, just to sit and listen. In the past, that would have disgusted her and she was forced to admit that there was still a part of her that felt uneasy about it.

Now, she could hear Smiley and his wife moving around downstairs.

'When you said we could disappear, what did you mean?'

He stroked her hair. 'New identities are not a problem for us, are they? We have money. You could teach me all the precautions that we'd need to take. Then we'd just vanish. We could go anywhere.'

'When would we go?'

'Now.'

She looked up at him. 'Are you serious?'

'Completely.'

'You would leave your whole world behind?'

'For you? Yes.'

'Right now?'

'Today. Within an hour.'

At that moment, she felt a scorching love for him. But the feeling was soured by a greater reality. She said she couldn't do it. Not now. Nothing could have pleased her more than to abandon her obligation to Alexander but, somewhere out there, faceless people had made a deal that was nearing fruition. In her mind, she saw the possible consequences of it: piles of dead children, their skins grotesquely blistered, people gasping for air as poisonous fluids seeped into their lungs, gradually drowning them. The suave and casual voice of Kosygin, the biological butcher, echoed in her memory.

'I have to see this contract through, Kostya.'

'Why?'

'I don't want to tell you.'

He looked annoyed but contained it. She was grateful and hoped he could see it.

'And after that?'

'After that, I'll be free.'

'When will that be?'

Not long. Wasn't that the truth? Her skin prickled. Time was running out. Koba, or no Koba, somebody was preparing for the transfer to a group with no identity. Which meant no target, no motive, no chance of prevention.

'I'm not sure. But soon. Days, not weeks. I'm going back to Moscow on New Year's Eve.'

'To Vatukin?'

'Yes. Will you be there?'

'If I haven't run away with you, yes.'

She felt crushed. She couldn't delay the inevitable any longer. It was time to let Petra take control. Time to do whatever needed to be done. But not before she'd spent her last few hours with Komarov. As Stephanie.

They ate breakfast, then checked out. They drove to the coast and walked along the beach beneath Bamburgh Castle. Seahouses, Dunstanburgh Castle, Lindisfarne, the Farne Islands – all prominent features on the landscape of her childhood. To walk with Komarov along the same beaches where she'd played with her two brothers and her sister felt right. It didn't matter to Stephanie that he had no idea.

They strolled side by side, his arm round her

shoulder. A fierce wind whipped sand around their ankles. The sea was black and angry, the crests of waves disintegrating into clouds of spray. In the distance, a small speck of a tanker rolled in and out of view. They passed a woman trying to teach a boxer puppy to walk to heel. The dog paid no attention to her at all and sprinted round and round in ever-tighter circles. Growing up, there had been boxers at home in Falstone. Two or three, usually, naughty, soppy and raucous. Whenever she saw one now, it warmed her heart, then stabbed her there with the dagger of loss.

The way Komarov was looking at her made her stop walking. 'What is it?'

He shrugged. 'Here we are on this beach, walking along it like any man and woman might. And I'm thinking, who are you, really? The woman I know, or the woman I know you are? In my time, I've seen things – *survived* things – that would stop your blood but when I look at you, I still can't imagine what it's like to do what you do.'

'Our worlds are not that different, Kostya.'

'Mine is easier. It's not so solitary. Or so . . . cold.'

She wanted to argue the point but couldn't.

'How do you do it? How do you survive?'

'I honestly don't know.'

'I couldn't do it. I'd lose my mind.'

That struck a chord. She saw something in Petra that she didn't see in herself. 'The most important thing is to lose your imagination.'

'What do you mean?'

'If you do what I do, you *have* to, if you want to last. If you don't lose your imagination, you *will* lose your mind. For instance, you're in a strange city – in a subway, say – and you see a peculiar expression on a face in the crowd. You have to tell yourself that it means nothing. That you're not being watched. But you also know that it's possible you *are* being watched. That night, you're asleep in your hotel. You hear a creak. You could easily convince yourself there's someone outside your door when, in fact, it's just the tired fabric of an old building. The skill is in knowing the difference and in losing your imagination. Those that can't, burn out. They grow paranoid, which makes them unstable. And vulnerable. And when that happens, you might as well be dead.'

21

When she put the phone down, she was trembling. She'd asked him how long it would take to get the information together. An hour, he'd said. *An hour.* Nothing at all, really. She suspected he already had it. They'd agreed to meet at midday. She felt sick. She glanced at the clock-radio on the bedside table. Ten thirty-five, eleven thirty-five in Zurich, where Komarov was. Twenty-four hours ago, they'd been approaching Bamburgh. She'd driven. They hadn't spoken much; they hadn't needed to.

He was right. It couldn't go on. Not like this.

She hadn't slept. Not because she missed Komarov but because of what lay ahead. She'd tossed and turned. So had her stomach, the tension crunching her muscles so that now they ached. Three and four had been the darkest hours of the night. She'd wanted to cry, to jump out of the window, to go to the airport, to fly to him and vanish. Shortly after five, she'd surrendered the struggle and got up. There was no point in fighting it. All one could do was prepare for it. So she'd tried to concentrate, to focus on becoming Petra. She'd pictured herself in Groningen, breaking Eric Roy's nose – twice. She could still do it. Ask Bruno Kleist. He knew quality when he saw it.

Now, however, she found herself struggling with a resurgent sense of panic. *Force your breathing to slow. It's impossible to panic once your breathing is under control.* This was something she knew to be true. She had a bath to help her relax and began to close down the mind. Just as Boyd had taught her, five years ago. Visualization, breathing. *See the change and the change will happen.*

A tight, knee-length black skirt, a pair of heels, a purple silk blouse. She applied some eye-liner, a little make-up and a generous sweep of scarlet lipstick. In the mirror, Stephanie saw a woman ten years older than she was.

London was quiet. She'd always enjoyed the period between Christmas and New Year. The city felt empty and civilized. She hailed a cab, gave the address and sank into the seat. At the other end, she wasn't really aware of paying the driver, or pressing the button, or taking the lift. The doors parted; the lobby, the chocolate corridor, the crimson walls of the drawing room, the white carpet, the canopied balcony, chrome and smoked glass.

Salman Rifat said, 'I knew you'd come back.'

Stephanie said nothing.

'I gave everyone the rest of the day off. I thought it would be better. Drink?'

'Vodka. And I wouldn't take anything for granted, if I were you. You're going to have to convince me that you've got something worth coming back for.'

'Of course.'

'What have you got?'

'What have *you* got?'

Show him nothing. Not even when you're naked.

Stephanie unbuttoned her shirt and let him catch a glimpse of the black bra beneath. 'I want to know what we're talking about. Otherwise, we do it the other way.'

Rifat's eyes widened.

She said, 'You know I would, if I felt I had to.'

He nodded. 'I can give you the end users, the type of weapon and the city where the trade will take place.'

'What about the date?'

'Yes.'

Stephanie looked around the room and saw it on a circular silver tray. The small blue bottle of olive oil. Rifat looked nervous. But not as nervous as she felt.

The choice. Bilbao and the promise. Break that and what was she worth? But what of Komarov? Then again, the alternative was worse, surely. She wasn't going to get what she wanted by breaking Rifat's nose, the way she had with Eric Roy. Rifat was a different creature altogether.

He took her silence to be compliance and said, 'Take off your skirt.'

Rifat fell back onto the sofa, panting. His grotesquely muscular physique was shiny with sweat, veins rising from the skin. He offered her a shower – *another* shower, in fact; he'd made her take two during the course of the afternoon – but Stephanie declined. She just wanted to leave. Her entire body was quivering. Rifat reached for the tumbler of Chivas he'd set at the foot of the sofa and watched her stand up. When she bent down to pick up her knickers, he told her to leave them where they were. He said he was keeping her underwear as a memento. Stephanie saw what he was trying to do and bit her tongue. She pulled on her shirt. Her damp skin stuck to it. She could smell him on her; corrupted and necrotic. She remained on automatic, which was what had carried her through the crawling hours. She'd given

him nothing. It was possible that her defiance had pro-
longed the ordeal but Stephanie didn't care. He could
do what he liked to her but she wasn't going to whimper
or cry out for him.

As she zipped up her skirt, he tried once more. 'You
know, we should do this again.'

'Then next time you touch me, I'm going to kill
you.'

'That's the thing I love about you. You're not just a
great fuck. You're a hard bitch, too.' He lit a cheroot. 'I
swear, there's nobody like you in the world.'

'There are far too many people like *you* in the world.'

'Come on, Petra. You made a decision. You chose to
do it. Like I said you would.'

It was six thirty when Stephanie left the building
and turned right on Eaton Square. She felt completely
numb but knew that it wouldn't last. *Couldn't* last. Six
hours . . .

She called Rosie Chaudhuri.

*I slam the front door shut, go to the kitchen and open a bottle
of rough red wine. I fill a tumbler and drain it; I want to
burn away the taste of him. Then I refill the glass and take
it to the bathroom, where I spend half an hour beneath a
scalding shower. I soap and scrub and rinse. My skin turns
bright pink. Except where the bruises have started to show.
After the shower, I wrap myself in a large towel. I fetch a
black bin-liner from the kitchen and put everything I wore
into it, including my overcoat and shoes. I don't want to keep
anything. I add make-up, eye-liner and lipstick. Then I dump
the bin-liner outside the front door. I can't even bear to have
it in the flat with me.*

This is proof, if proof were needed, that I'm not really

Petra Reuter. During her post-Magenta House independence, Petra had sex with men when the situation required it. She would have done what I did this afternoon and then had a cup of tea. Do it, deal with it, move on. It wouldn't have worried her because she wouldn't have allowed it to. That was the whole point of her; to function perfectly, to feel nothing, to eliminate the flawed human element so as to become a beautiful machine.

In those days, Salman Rifat was one of those men. As Petra, I let him do what he wanted and I gave him what he wanted; I moaned with pleasure or I cried in pain. It depended on the situation. Both were part of my arsenal. They were what made Petra so good; lying, stealing, fucking, killing. She did them all equally well.

The turmoil I feel now should be a good thing. It shows I'm not her. It shows I'm human. Last night, I tried to rationalize what I knew I'd do today. I told myself it would be Petra having sex with Rifat, not me. I told myself that it would be a price worth paying if it helped set me free. I tried to console myself with the fact that I wouldn't be doing anything I hadn't done before. I thought I could force myself not to let it scar me. I tried to convince myself that I wouldn't be betraying Kostya because it wouldn't mean anything emotionally. How naïve. She may be a sublime liar but I'm the one person Petra can't deceive.

The next morning – 29 December – Rosie arrived at Old Court Place at five to eight. Stephanie yanked on a pair of jeans and a pink T-shirt while Rosie came up.

'God, you look awful. Are you all right?'

Too much wine, too much guilt – too much physical discomfort – and not enough sleep. She said, 'I picked up some kind of bug in Moscow. Coffee?'

In the kitchen, Rosie said, 'He didn't know the name of this group?'

Stephanie shook her head. 'It's not a group. They're just a few individuals. He didn't know how many. Half a dozen, he guessed, maybe less. Extreme Serb nationalists, highly motivated, money no problem. Former hardline supporters of Milosevic.'

'When does the trade take place?'

'On January the ninth in New York. Eleven days from now. But he didn't know where in the city, so it hardly helps. The target could be anywhere, any time after the ninth. Until we find out exactly who these Serbs are, we have no way of knowing. If the trade takes place, the weapon will be lost. What have you got for me?'

She handed over a blue file. 'I had some people throw this together overnight. It's a bit rushed and a bit slim but it's all you'll have time for because you've got a meeting at eleven.'

'With?'

'Yevgeny Vlasko. This is his address and phone number. He lives under an alias. Klocek.'

'Never heard of him.'

'He's the best there is. He used to be deputy director of the biological warfare division of Biopreparat, the Soviet State pharmaceutical and chemical concern. You'll find all the background information you need in the file.'

'And the weapon . . . Marburg U-13?'

'You don't want to know.'

When Rosie had gone, Stephanie opened the file. Yevgeny Vlasko had been a student at Moscow State University. The son of a doctor, he trained in medicine and graduated top of his year before entering the Tomsk Medical Institute to study epidemiology and infectious diseases. Three years later, in 1977, he was transferred to the Council of Ministers of the Soviet Union and sent to work at the Institute of Applied Microbiology at Obolensk in the Moscow region. Between 1982 and 1986, he was based at the Progress and Scientific Base at Stepnogorsk, Kazakhstan, where he helped develop production lines for bioweaponized anthrax, plague, tularaemia and glanders.

During his spell at Stepnogorsk, he led an investigation into the military possibilities of Marburg, one of the haemorrhagic fever viruses. In 1986, he was transferred to Yoshkar-Ola to oversee the design and construction of specialist equipment used in biological warfare research and testing. In 1987, he took charge of Vector – full title: the Institute of Molecular Biology – at Koltsovo, in the Novosibirsk region of Siberia. This reunited him with the research he'd initiated into haemorrhagic fever viruses at Stepnogorsk.

Considered the leading bioweaponeer of his generation, Vlasko rose to become deputy director of Biopreparat and one of the non-military members of the Fifteenth Directorate, the controlling body for the Soviet biological warfare programme. In 1992, without warning, Vlasko defected. Britain was his objective and he chose a Biopreparat-sanctioned trip to Paris as the right moment to make the move. There were photographs of him. Stephanie saw him as a university student – skinny, earnest-looking, dark-haired – and through the years that followed. Still skinny, still earnest-looking, but blond.

*   *   *

370

Yevgeny Vlasko lived in a Victorian terraced house on Geraldine Road in Wandsworth. There were net curtains over the ground-floor window, weeds sprouting through the cracked brick path, green paint flaking off the front door. When he opened it, Stephanie was shocked by his physical condition. Vlasko was in his late fifties but looked much older. What was left of his hair was dark silver. His skin was parchment dry and discoloured in patches. The backs of his hands were covered in large liver-spots.

He led her through to a small kitchen at the back of the ground floor. It was dark and narrow. The units looked thirty years old; they certainly preceded Vlasko's arrival in Britain. The cork effect on the floor tiles had worn away to reveal patches of naked vinyl.

'Can I offer you tea?'

'Thank you, yes.'

'I prefer it the Russian way.'

'So do I.'

He put a battered kettle on a blue circle of gas.

'You've studied me, I suppose. Some file somewhere . . .'

'Yes.'

'I can imagine the impression you might have of me. The man least likely to be voted humanitarian of the year.'

A platitude formed in her mouth but she swallowed it. 'Given my own history, I try to avoid judging others. Can I ask you about something that wasn't in the file?'

'You can ask.'

'Why did you leave Russia in ninety-two?'

He took a packet of Benson & Hedges from the pocket of his chunky grey cardigan. His hands trembled; he had difficulty with the lighter, only finding a flame at the sixth attempt.

'I left because of the truth. Whatever I may have become, I was the son of a doctor and I have always been a doctor at heart. As a young man, I took the oath that every Soviet physician took, and I took it in good faith.'

'Are you telling me you spent fifteen years developing biological weapons without realizing what you were doing?'

'I'm telling you that in the Soviet Union, through the Seventies and Eighties, there was a world of difference between what someone said and what they meant. I was told that I would be helping to develop curative drugs and vaccines to combat the biological weapons manufactured in the West. I believed that. And I believed that we needed to match the West to deter them from ever using such weapons. We *all* believed that. The grey area came later, when it became clear that I was to be used to create those weapons.'

He spilled tea into and around two glasses set in tarnished brass holders. He offered her jam to stir into hers. She watched his gnarled fingers clutch the spoon.

'In the early days, we felt an immense pride in our work. I can't deny it. The thrill of the science outweighed all issues of morality. We were young, we were pioneers, we were revered, even by those who were uncertain of our existence. They never knew us but they knew *of* us. Within the parameters of life in the Soviet Union, we wanted for nothing. I'm not talking about money, of course. In those days, money mattered less. I'm talking about honour. About approval. Our budgets were vast, our influence immense. We worked like dogs but never complained. Despite all that, I began to have doubts. Even before I knew the truth. Perhaps it was a delayed sense of maturity, perhaps it was a growing disenchantment with authority. It could have been the cumulative effect of working myself too hard for too long.'

'What happened?'

He stared out of the French windows that opened onto the tiny garden. Stephanie imagined it was walled but couldn't tell. It was completely overrun with bushes and weeds. She doubted he had ever tried to maintain it.

'Biopreparat was more than a military machine. It was also responsible for civilian medicine. That was how the military programme was concealed; the budget was hidden in civilian medical costs. This sleight of hand not only hid the truth, it allowed Party leaders to boast of the enormous expenditure the State lavished on its people. On the ground, though, the reality was different. I remember the first time I went to Grozny in eighty-seven. At the hospital, they were sterilizing needles with steam because they couldn't get any new needles, and they couldn't replace the broken sterilizing unit. The following year, when I returned there, they were reconstituting needles.'

'Reconstituting?'

'Sharpening them because the tips had become blunt through repeated use.' He shook his head at the memory. 'That's just one example of how people suffered so that the state could finance our programmes. I could give you dozens of others.'

'And that was what did it for you?'

'No. The truth was what did it for me.'

He led her into the living room. The wallpaper was dark green. The filthy net curtains she'd seen from outside choked off almost all the natural light. There were two armchairs in need of upholstery, a three-bar electric fire in the fireplace. The lampshades were dark plum and gold. It was a room of infinite gloom and stillness.

When Stephanie sat down, it hurt. She shifted awkwardly in her search for a less painful position. Instinctively, she thought of how Rifat had inflicted it – the brutal grip, his grunted aggression – and the memory made her shudder.

Vlasko continued, unaware. 'At that time, I was deputy director of Biopreparat. I sat on the Fifteenth Directorate. In October 1990, the Soviet Union came to an agreement with the USA and Britain, permitting supervised visits to selected sites suspected of being involved with biological warfare. When the British and the Americans visited us, we took them to the places they'd asked to see – including Obolensk and Vector at Koltsovo – but we kept them away from all the sensitive areas at those sites. To be honest, we were pleased with the way it went. Our reciprocal visit to the USA was scheduled for December 1991. We submitted a list of facilities we wanted to see. They included the United States Army Medical Research Institute of Infectious Diseases at Fort Detrick, Maryland, the Dugway Proving Ground near Salt Lake City, the Salk Center in Swiftwater, Pennsylvania and the Pine Bluff Arsenal in Arkansas.

'When we signed up to the 1972 Biological and Toxin Weapons Convention, we did so as readily as the United States because there was no provision within the convention for inspection of sites. Consequently, we assumed they would break the terms of the convention. In fact, one could say that our entire programme was predicated on that assumption. And the reason we made the assumption is because we were convinced they would make the same assumption about us. The fact is, America did continue its research into biological warfare but it restricted itself to a defensive capability. There was no offensive programme at all. The December 1991 visit confirmed what some of us had begun to suspect. That we'd been living a lie.'

'Did you say so when you got back to Russia?'

'Yes.'

'How was that received?'

'We were told that we must have made a mistake. We were instructed to look harder. Later, we were ordered to produce some evidence of America's *offensive* biological warfare programme, no matter what it took. When we insisted that we couldn't, we were ordered to say nothing. Biopreparat was in crisis. It needed a credible threat in order to justify its massive expenditure. The generals were scared; they feared losing their jobs, their income, their prestige. That was when I knew that I had to leave. If I stayed, the truth would be buried. At first, I shrugged my shoulders and pretended to look the other way, in order to retain the trust of my superiors. Which I achieved. That was why they felt there was no risk when they sent me to Paris in 1992.'

Vlasko took his glass of tea in both hands and raised it to his lips.

'Do you feel bitter?'

'Not as much as I used to. But sometimes, yes. I gave them everything. My trust, my intellect, the best years of my life. My health. I have the most extensive range of allergies you can imagine. I can't eat pork or poultry or eggs. I can't touch anything involving dairy products: butter, milk, cheese. I'm allergic to citrus and to wheat. Three times a day, I have to rub ointment into my skin because it no longer has any natural lubricants. I swallow five anti-allergy pills four times a day. The vaccinations I took mean I have no natural resistance to illness. I catch a dozen colds a year and have to wear these specially tinted lenses in my glasses so that my pupils receive no UVA light.'

'All that through your work?'

He nodded. 'For ten years, I was blond.'

'I noticed that in some of the photographs.'

'Do you know why?'

'No.'

'In the restricted areas, they used to spray hydrogen peroxide into the air as a disinfectant. The memory of the smell of it – and the taste of it – still makes me feel nauseous. For a decade, it not only coloured my hair, it entered my body every time I breathed. All in all, it's a miracle that I can still breathe at all.'

'If you don't mind me saying so, I'm surprised you choose to smoke.'

'Pah! Let me tell you something. When I was told that I was leaving the Tomsk Medical Institute to go to Obolensk and Stepnogorsk, do you know how my colleagues congratulated me?'

'How?'

'Warmly and sincerely. They shook my hand, they hugged me, they kissed me on both cheeks. And then they told me that I would be dead in two years. That was the reputation the division had. But I didn't care. None of us cared. We saw such assignments not only as an opportunity but as a patriotic honour. I never believed I would live to this age. And after all that I've put my body through, I don't think a few cigarettes – or even a lot of cigarettes – are going to make much difference. I've already outstayed my welcome.

'In November 1986, while I was at Yoshkar-Ola, I was asked to come up with a design for a new form of delivery vehicle. Something small. Something that would not be part of a warhead attached to a missile. The mechanism was intended for close-contact delivery. I submitted several blueprints. In August 1987, I was transferred to Vector at Koltsovo and I heard nothing more about the designs I'd put forward. Then there was M-8389.'

'What's that?'

'The post-box number for the Central Asian Branch of Applied Biochemistry at Almaty. The most secret sites were always referred to by their post-box number. As for the full name, this place was nowhere near Almaty. It was hundreds of kilometres away. From anywhere. It appeared on no map and until the advent of satellite photography the West had no idea of its existence. It wasn't alone in that; there were dozens of such places scattered across the barren wastelands of the Soviet Union.'

'What happened?'

'In 1990 there was an outbreak of Marburg Variant U-13. This was a particularly lethal form of Marburg, engineered from Variant U, which itself had been created following another accident at Koltsovo in eighty-eight. In that instance, the infected man – Nikolai Ustinov – had some of his ruined blood removed *post mortem* in order to help create a new strain. U for Ustinov, hence Variant U. U-13 was an improved, deadlier version of it. Ustinov died because the Marburg passed into his system through the tip of a needle that accidentally pierced his protective clothing. U-13 was engineered so that it could be contracted through the air. We use the phrase ''by aerosol''.

'I wasn't in charge of M-8389 when the accident occurred but I was deputy director of Biopreparat; M-8389 fell into my overall sphere of responsibility. I flew out to Kazakhstan to oversee the final stages and the aftermath. Three cleaners had contracted the virus in an area where it should never have been located. An investigation was launched but it proved inconclusive.'

'Did the cleaners die?'

'Yes. And in a far more startling way than we'd ever encountered before. Their decline was much quicker than natural Marburg. Within hours, the filoviruses were decimating their cells, bursting them. They vomited. Their black diarrhoea was uncontrollable. They bled from the nose, ears, anus, genitals. Even from the nipples. Their organs liquefied inside them and they sloughed their guts in front of us. That's what Marburg U-13 does. In the end, they were crying tears of blood . . .'

Rattled by the recollection, Vlasko paused to light another cigarette.

'Until the incident at M-8389, I'd had no idea that U-13 was so far developed. Two months later, I made my report to the Fifteenth Directorate in Moscow. Building 112, which housed the secure zone in which the accident had occurred, had to be sealed permanently. We never discovered how the U-13 had penetrated the airlock where the infection took place.

'When I presented my report, I said we had reached a stage where we could no longer be sure of quite how virulent U-13 had become. For an aerosol weapon, that is totally unacceptable. In short, I told them that U-13 should be destroyed and that we should not attempt to deliver Marburg by aerosol. There was a furious argument. Major-General Kalinin, my boss, threatened to fire me. I told him I'd be delighted if he did. I said this was a matter that went beyond the boundaries of a career. I told all of them that U-13 had the potential to be as much of a threat to us as to any of our enemies. Eventually, the Directorate agreed with me.'

'And the programme was closed down?'

'Under my supervision, yes.'

'And the U-13?'

'Destroyed.'

'All of it?'

'As far as I know.'

'Could some have survived?'

'Either that, or the technology itself was not destroyed. Science moves quickly and it's almost impossible to un-invent something.'

'Did every member of the Fifteenth Directorate know about U-13?'

'As far as I can remember.'

'Was there some kind of governing protocol during its existence?'

'Of course.'

'Under whose control?'

'The three most powerful figures within the Fifteenth Directorate at that time.'

'And who were they?'

'Colonel Alexander Modilianov, Major-General Ivan

Oskoi – both deceased, by the way – and Lieutenant-General Alexander Kosygin.'

Kosygin. Of course.

'One final thing. Marburg U-13 . . . what if it comes to the worst?'

'It depends on where the device is used and whether there are secondary infections. In a city, from a high vantage point, in a wind, you're talking about thousands of deaths. Perhaps tens of thousands, maybe more; in the way I've just described. But that's just for primary infection. If those who are infected begin to infect others – secondary infection – it's impossible to say where it will end. All one can say with any clarity is that it will be a completely new kind of horror.'

'And the device?'

'By the time I finished working on the delivery system, you could transport the agent in a secure container the size of a large briefcase. But that was over ten years ago. Today . . . who knows?'

'In my position, what would you do?'

While Vlasko considered this, Stephanie could hear his wheezing chest. Eventually, he said, 'There is one man who might help you. Sergei Roskov. He was my deputy at Biopreparat. He succeeded me after I defected. If you find him, you can trust him.'

'Where is he now?'

'Somewhere in Moscow. In fact, I've heard he's in hiding.'

'Why?'

'I don't know.'

'How can I find him?'

Vlasko shuffled over to a chest of drawers and produced a silver and leather cigarette case that he pressed into Stephanie's hand. 'Find Valentina Rudenko first. She's an old friend. If anybody knows where Roskov is, she will. Many years ago, she gave me this cigarette case as a present. Before I left for Paris, I told her I was going to defect. I didn't tell anyone else. We agreed that if she ever saw this again, she would know that it came from me. Find her and ask her. If she doesn't know where Roskov is, the chances are, he's already dead.'

22

It was minus fifteen in Moscow on 30 December, a blizzard blowing. Her flight was delayed and it was after eight by the time she reached Kutuzovzky Prospekt. She paid off the taxi and hesitated in front of the arch. *He's going to know. He'll see it in my eyes, smell it on my skin.* He met her at the lift and kissed her. Inside his apartment, he poured her some wine. *Any moment now . . .*

'How've you been?'

Stephanie told him the truth. 'I was lonely. Before I met you, when I was alone, I was never lonely. How was Switzerland?'

'Pretty. And empty.'

When he undressed her, she thought her bruises would betray her. In truth, they'd never been that pronounced. Now, they were virtually undetectable. But she felt them anyway. The first time they made love, she was tense and ashamed. Afterwards, she drank heavily to rinse away the guilt. The second time, she almost managed to pretend that it had never happened.

They ate slices of Milano and Napoli salami, some Italian cheese and Scottish oat biscuits, all bought at a delicatessen in Zurich. They lay on the sitting-room floor on a mattress of discarded clothing, wrapped in two sheets. Stephanie hoped they would never move again. Komarov was smoking. They'd been silent for ages when he asked what she was thinking.

'I was thinking about all the time you spent in prison. How long it was. The waste of it. The conditions. I was wondering how you survived it.'

His answer was almost dismissive. 'I survived it the way most of us survived it. By accepting it.'

Stephanie propped herself up on an elbow so that she could see him. 'You *accepted* it?'

'Not the sentences, or the authority that issued them, but the duration. The sooner you accept the reality, the sooner it passes. Once you're inside, you can't fight it. The ones that do suffer. For every day that goes by, they pay a toll of two. You can see it in them, the deterioration.'

'But *how* do you accept it?'

'By not caring. You shut yourself down. You don't think of the past or the future, you don't think of the things that you miss. You try not to think at all. You have to live in a single moment and feel nothing. Mentally, you force yourself to go numb.'

'And physically?'

Komarov smiled. 'In Siberia, you don't have to force that.'

Stephanie pinched him. 'You know what I mean.'

He stroked her hair. 'Physically, you're either strong or weak. Lucky or unlucky. That's all. There's nothing you can do. Except wait.'

It was dark when the phone went. Komarov answered at the second ring. A few inaudible exchanges, then he was out of the bed, dressing. Still groggy with sleep, Stephanie asked what was wrong. Nothing, he told her. He had to go and meet someone. It was just business.

'What time is it?'

'Twenty past five.'

'Business at twenty past five?'

'It's twenty past nine in New York.'

'You're going to New York?'

He leaned over the bed and kissed her. 'No. I'll see you later.'

But he didn't. He called at midday. There were complications. He couldn't talk over the phone. He'd call her when he could but he didn't think he'd be able to make it to Vatukin's New Year party. Stephanie said she didn't want to go, in that case.

'You have to. If I pull out, then you pull out, how's that going to look?'

'I don't care.'

'Nor do I. But you see what I mean, don't you?'

The Rublevo-Uspenskoye Highway, a potholed single carriageway twisting through the pine and birch beyond the outer ring road. It was still snowing, the headlights carving tunnels in the darkness, fat flakes flickering across the windscreen. Sagging branches arched over the road, brilliant against the latticed darkness beyond. Stephanie sat in the back of the Mercedes that Vatukin had sent for her. The latest model, bulletproof body, dark windows, TV. The driver was not the latest model; fat, in a leather jacket too tight for gut and gun, a succession of cigarettes between his cracked lips.

They passed Barvikha and Zhukovka, villages that were gone before one realized they'd arrived, before making a left turn down an unmarked, snow-covered track. A hundred metres off the road, there was a barrier and a gatehouse, manned by two armed guards. After a little banter, the barrier was raised. The Mercedes crept through the silent forest. It was a kilometre before the dacha emerged; floodlit within a walled compound, an architectural grotesque. It was not a copy of the house Vatukin had so admired during a brief stay in the Norwegian port of Bergen. It *was* the house. He'd liked it so much, he'd bought it, dismantled it, transported it back to Russia and had it reconstructed. But it wasn't big enough. His solution? To build another next to it. Siamese buildings, just like Magenta House. But it still wasn't large enough so he'd added two floors to each side. Now, it was impossible to see what had originally attracted him.

Komarov had sounded contemptuous when he'd described it to her the previous evening: two saunas, every en-suite bathroom complete with a jacuzzi, a private cinema, a games room large enough for a Russian billiards table and a pool table, an indoor swimming pool surrounded by fake classical statues.

'There used to be a proper dacha there. Smaller but traditional. He tore it down to make way for . . . well, you'll see.'

'You disapprove?'

He'd shrugged. 'What's the point? In a generation, everybody will have forgotten.'

'Forgotten?'

'Where we came from. Why we did what we did.'

Beyond a second barrier, there were two dozen limousines parked outside the dacha, all filthy. Inside, a warren of rooms, a cacophony of competing sounds. The staff wore black and gold, the waitresses in miniskirts. Stephanie guessed there were more women than men but knew immediately that she was a rarity; a female guest. The other women were girlfriends or entertainment. Not many looked like wives. Young, brash, beautiful, they swarmed around the men regardless of how unappealing their appearance or behaviour. There were some who definitely looked out of place. Men who wore moustaches, scars and Hugo Boss. Men who'd adapted to the harshest prisons imaginable but who hadn't yet adapted to wearing a suit.

In one reception room, there was a large buffet: caviar, silver platters of meat, salads, sides of smoked salmon and sturgeon, cheeses, tureens of soups, all manner of breads. In another reception room, one of Russia's favourite TV comics was spinning his own brand of lewd humour, to the delight of those gathered around him. That was where Vatukin found her. Dressed in black, looking lean and sober, he took her to one side, asked if she was enjoying herself, whether there was anything he could do for her. He only mentioned Komarov once – *it's a pity he can't make it, but that's the way it is, I guess* – and then suggested they meet on the morning of the second.

'That will allow us time to think clearly.'

But she could see that he was already thinking clearly, that he had no intention of getting drunk. He introduced her to some of his guests. An official from Mayor Luzhkov's office, a journalist with a crumbling British accent – Stephanie thought he might be Canadian – a Swedish surgeon, two executives from Gazprom, a property speculator from Manhattan, directors of Bashkreditbank, Bank Severnaya Kazna, Dalkombank and Bank Austria Creditanstalt.

At midnight, there were fireworks, a gorgeous extravagance that lit up the night. Everybody spilled outside, alcohol insulating them from the sub-zero cold for a while. Gasps of wonder, applause, more drink, laughter. Smoke drifted across from the detonation platform, which was hidden behind a screen of trees. Stephanie smelt cordite beneath cigars. When the display was over, there were cheers and toasts. The drunk began to sing. By one, there were naked bodies in the swimming pool.

Stephanie was passing through a room at the back of the dacha. There were three large wide-screen televisions playing simultaneously. Set into a wall, one above the other, all the screens were active but silent; Juventus versus Barcelona on the top, a dubbed Chuck Norris film in the middle, hardcore Dutch porn on the bottom. There were a dozen people in the room, draped over sofas and stuffed into armchairs, some watching, some talking, one passed out.

'Not quite Bambi Park, is it?'

She turned round. His presence was so unexpected that his name deserted his face.

'But I somehow feel that this is more Marko's style. Especially the bottom screen.'

Claesen. Marcel Claesen. The Belgian intermediary. January 2000, Pozarevac, in the run-up to Arkan's assassination. The same waxy skin, the same greasy hair falling over the left eye. Bambi Park, their rendezvous, was an amusement park built by Slobodan Milosevic's son, Marko.

'The Russians love Chuck Norris,' Claesen said. 'And he loves the Russians. These days, he's everywhere in Moscow. Like HIV.'

Serb terrorists on the loose and Claesen turns up in Moscow.

'Still busy in the Balkans?' Stephanie asked.

'From time to time. You?'

'Not since then. How come you're here?'

He grinned. 'You show me yours and I'll show you mine.'

'Tempting, but no thanks.'

The last time she'd seen him, they'd been driving back from Pozarevac to Belgrade. Claesen had made a clumsy pass at her. She'd told him to grow up. Told him she was out of his league. He hadn't had the nerve to dispute it.

'Neat job at the Inter-Continental.'

'Your information made it easier. He *was* wearing a bulletproof vest.'

'After Belgrade, you dropped out of the news.'

'I thought I'd take a break.'

'But when you decided to go back to work, you gravitated towards Moscow . . .'

She smiled sourly. 'Just like you.'

'I owe you an apology.'

Natalya's not wearing any lipstick. Every other woman is. Her pale, buttery skin looks flawless. The way she's dressed casts the others into the shade but I'm not sure any of them would understand why. There's not a designer label on her. She forgoes the obligatory miniskirt, preferring, instead, something tight and knee-length. In its own way, it shows as much, but it suggests far more. She wears a formal black silk shirt. She's undone one more button than propriety would deem decent, revealing a glimpse of cleavage. There's a delicate platinum choker encircling her throat, a small Russian Orthodox cross hanging from it. The other women make me feel old, she makes me feel dowdy.

'An apology?'

'For being rude to you at White Square. I didn't know who you were.'

'How could you?'

When she smiles, there's gratitude in it. 'In my position, it's not always easy to give the benefit of the doubt. There are many other girls who would like to be in my place.'

'I can imagine.'

'They will seize any opportunity – and do anything at all – to make it happen.'

We find somewhere more tranquil to talk. A small study. The wooden walls were retained from the original dacha, she tells me. From them hang a series of black-and-white photographs in graphite frames; pricey erotica by Helmut Newton. They would blend in with any other room I've seen but, in here, they look faintly crass.

'These are Vladimir's idea of art. They were expensive. If they'd been cheap, he would have considered them pointless pornography.'

'What about you?' I wonder. 'What do you think they are?'

'I think they're boring.'

We talk for a while and then she catches me with a blunt question. What does it feel like to kill someone? It comes straight out of the blue.

I play for time. 'Why don't you ask him? I'm sure he'd know.'

'I mean . . . as a woman?'

Without hesitation, I tell her the truth. 'In that situation, I'm not a woman. If I was . . . well, in the first place, I don't think I could do it. And even if I could, I don't think I'd cope with the emotional consequences of it. It's like sex. Men can have us and feel nothing. But we're not the same.'

'But you do kill.'

'I step outside myself. For as long as I need to be, I'm someone else. Divorcing myself from the act is how I live with it.'

She nods and looks away. 'I know what you mean.'

I'll bet she does. Same feeling, different context. I decide it's safe for me to probe a little. 'Where are you from, Natalya?'

'Omsk. You know Omsk?'

'No.'

'Between Yekaterinburg and Novosibirsk, just north of the border with Kazakhstan.'

'A long way from here . . .'

'A long way from anywhere.'

'Why did you come to Moscow?'

'Because there was nothing for me in Omsk. Nothing I wanted, no future. I thought if I could get to Moscow, I could get anywhere. Europe, America. When I arrived, I had no money but there was a girl I knew from Omsk already living here. She got me a job at Rasputin. Do you know it? It's a restaurant. I was a waitress there. We worked topless.' When I raise my eyebrows, she shrugs; you know how it is. 'Japanese businessmen found it amusing to spray champagne over our breasts and lick it off. That's the kind of place it was. Later, I got a job at White Square, which was where I met Oleg Rogachev. I didn't know who he was. But he knew who I was. Or rather, what I was.'

'And that was it?'

'When I found out about him, yes. That was it.'

'True love.'

She smiles, instead of snapping. 'Sometimes, love is a luxury you can't afford. Oleg was my passport to a new life. We both knew it. Most girls never get the chance he offered me.'

'What was he like?'

Her answer is painful to hear but laced with truth. 'Better

than I had any right to expect.' She catches my eye. 'Better than Vladimir.'

I nod and hope it conveys sympathy. 'I heard about what happened in Paris.'

She shrugs. 'I wasn't so naïve – I knew the world Oleg lived in, the people he mixed with – but I never thought it would happen to him.'

'You never do. It's like a car crash. It always happens to someone else until it happens to you.'

'When he was killed, I was desolate. Not because everything was taken away from me but because I really felt something for Oleg.'

'But not everything was taken away, was it?'

'Not everything. But everything good. Vladimir took over Tsentralnaya, then me.'

'You could have said no, maybe?'

'I'm tougher than I look. A survivor. And I wasn't going back to Omsk. Not even in a box. Most girls don't get one chance. I got two. I didn't have to be asked twice.' There's a passion burning in her eyes now. 'Besides, I felt nothing. I did what I had to do and I did it in my sleep. Being a more typical man than Oleg, Vladimir couldn't tell.' She allows herself an unconvincing smile. 'And still can't.'

'That's good.'

'And easy.'

'Even better.'

'What about you? Do you have someone?'

I'm tempted to say no but then change my mind. 'Yes.'

'And how is that?'

'It's . . . a surprise.'

'Why?'

'Generally, I have to lie to the men I get close to.'

Natalya laughs. 'And that's a surprise?'

'You know what I mean.'

She nods. 'But with him, you're honest?'

'Yes,' I reply, hoping the cheapness I feel isn't audible. Then I make an unplanned confession. 'I never expected to find the right person and not to have to lie to him. And I don't believe love can be built on lies. That's why I always thought I'd be alone.'

Natalya is staring at me with an intensity that simultaneously warms me and unnerves me. She takes my hand and squeezes it. Her grip is strong. As for the look in her eyes . . .

'It's strange,' she says. 'We're so different but we're the same.'

She's right. I feel it too. But in my head, there's an image that won't go away. It's me. I'm shooting Vatukin, robbing her of her second chance, casting her back into the wilderness.

New Year's Day, a slate-grey sky, intemittent snow flurries, ten below zero and no word from Komarov. She'd left messages for him. They'd remained unanswered. She'd been to his apartment. No one there. So she'd conjured up reasons to try to dampen her anxiety, but they weren't good enough.

The taxi wheezed through the rusty sludge along Leningradsky Prospekt, past the Dinamo Sports Complex, before turning right, then left. The driver pulled up at the junction of Red Army Street and Academician Ilyushin Street. Number 21 was a ten-storey block. Yevgeny Vlasko had given Stephanie the address but it had been Stern who'd provided the number for the keypad lock on the battered metal front door. Inside, she took the stairs to the fifth floor, found the apartment and knocked.

'Who is it?'

'A friend of Yevgeny Vlasko's.'

There was a long pause. 'Yevgeny's not around any more.'

'I know. He's in London. I saw him just a few days ago.'

Silence.

'He gave me a present to give to you.'

'What kind of present?'

'A cigarette case.'

There was another protracted silence before Stephanie heard the scrape and scratch of chains and locks. Valentina Rudenko was a bony woman with a stoop. She wore a garish yellow shawl round her shoulders. Stephanie handed her the cigarette case. She took it with arthritic fingers, examined it, then beckoned her in.

The apartment was dark; in a cramped living room, heavy sapphire curtains were half-drawn. The green walls had black patches of damp. There was a cheap carriage-clock on top of the television. It chimed feebly. There was a plastic icon nailed to one wall, a lousy acrylic painting of St Basil's on another.

'So, how is Yevgeny? I haven't heard from him for so long, I thought he might be dead. He was always ill, you know.'

'I get the impression he's living on defiance.'

Rudenko smiled. 'That would be Yevgeny. If only Ivan had shown as much fight.' Her smile faded and she looked across at a series of framed photographs on a circular table covered by a lace cloth. 'Mind you, when you smoke as ferociously as he did . . .'

She went into the kitchen and returned a couple of

minutes later with two glasses of tea. They talked about Sergei Roskov.

'It's true. Ivan and I were close to Sergei and Katarina. After Yevgeny defected, Sergei took his place as deputy director at Biopreparat. He had mixed feelings about the appointment. And about Yevgeny, if we're being honest. He shared Yevgeny's doubts but disapproved of his defection. That was the difference between them, though. Sergei was quieter, he hated confrontation, whereas Yevgeny was always outspoken. Personally, I think it was because he knew he was brilliant. He liked to use his genius to intimidate high-ranking officials.'

'Did Roskov continue their work at Biopreparat?'

She shrugged. 'I wouldn't know. All I can tell you is that eventually he lost his job. It wasn't his fault. It was a situation we were all in. Rampant inflation, everybody in a panic. Biopreparat was short of money. Cuts were made in every area. Sergei was unlucky.'

'How did he take it?'

'Badly, like so many others. Before the crisis, he and Katarina had wanted for nothing. Suddenly, they had no income. Inflation turned their savings into thin air. The thing that hurt most, though, was the loss of status. The perks, the privileges. They took away the prestige and that was what brought on the depression.'

'Vlasko thought there might have been offers from abroad.'

'There were, Katarina told me. From South Korea, from Iran. He was asked to attend the Biotechnology Trade Fair in Tehran. But he refused. There was also an offer from Cuba. Can you imagine that?' Rudenko raised her eyebrows. 'After all those years in Kazakhstan? More money in a year than he'd earned in twenty.'

'So he turned the offers down?'

'First and foremost, Sergei is a patriot. A *Russian* patriot.'

'What happened?'

She shrugged, as if to say, *the usual thing.* 'Katarina was less idealistic. She was always the practical one. She tried to persuade him to take one of the offers. They argued. It led to more drinking, to fighting. You know how it is . . .'

Rudenko lapsed into silence, inviting Stephanie to fill the empty spaces.

'Katarina was good-looking, not just practical. In the end, she resorted to that. She found herself another man. A fat Ukrainian who got lucky.'

'Lucky?'

'An army bureaucrat, here in Moscow. An administrator, a pencil-pusher. When the Central Committee of the Party decided to abandon its monopoly on political power and property, he did what so many others did. He transferred the equipment under the department's control to private ownership. *His* private ownership. And then sold it off. Jeeps, lorries, cars, even tanks. He had buyers coming in from the Asian republics, from the Caucasus, from the Middle East. In a year, there was nothing left and he had a fortune. When Katarina met him, he was nervous and looking to leave Russia. He liked the look of her and she didn't take much persuading.'

'Where did they go?'

'Cyprus. He bought two hotels in Limassol. Now, they live in a big villa with servants. I hear he's even fatter than he was before. When they get bored, they go shopping in Paris and Milan.'

'And Roskov?'

'Let's just say, it didn't do much for his drinking. But then his luck changed. A former colleague at Biopreparat offered him a job at a private pharmaceutical company. Siberian Star. A man of his expertise would obviously be a benefit to –'

'Who was this friend?'

'He never said.'

'When was this?'

She paused for a moment. 'Ninety-six, I think. Or maybe ninety-seven.'

'And this worked out?'

'For a while. The pay was okay. Not a fortune but enough to get him back on his feet. He rented an apartment in this building, three floors below ours. He seemed much like his old self as long as nobody mentioned Katarina. But earlier last year, his demeanour changed. He became depressed and started drinking again. He was anxious all the time. When I asked him what was wrong, he would tell me it was nothing. I never pushed him because with Sergei . . . well, if you knew him, you'd know there was no point.'

'This depression was related to . . . what? His work? The past? Katarina?'

'I don't know. He looked awful, though. Dishevelled, tired . . .'

'When did he disappear?'

'Autumn. I can't remember the date exactly.'

'Do you know where he went?'

'He said it was safer for me not to know.'

'Has he contacted you since he disappeared?'

'He calls sometimes. Not often. Always from a pay-phone. He asks if anybody has been to his apartment. Or if anyone has called here and asked questions about him.'

'And has anyone?'

'Not recently. Just after he vanished, the police came round, once or twice. They asked the obvious questions, then lost interest. Since then, nothing.'

'But he still calls?'

'Occasionally. Once, he asked me to go into his place – I have a key – and to pack a bag for him. I took it to Kievsky Station and left it by one of the ticket booths.'

'Did you see him?'

'No.'

Stephanie took a sip of tea. 'I need to speak to him. Face to face.'

'I don't think so . . .'

'Can you ask him?'

'He calls me. I don't call him.'

'Is there any way you can get a message to him?'

Valentina Rudenko looked into her tea.

Back to her hotel, no messages, no phone calls. She tried his numbers. Nothing. To distract herself, she turned to Stern. By late afternoon, she had the information. Siberian Star had originally been one of Biopreparat's civilian facilities. Started in 1989, finished in 1991, it had been a state-of-the-art plant producing medicines for the domestic market. In 1993, it had been sold to a Swedish pharmaceutical firm, Knutson. New production lines were installed to produce a different range of drugs for the western European market. A precious

State asset sold at a discount for private use. Cheap local labour increased profit margins.

Stephanie asked Stern about Knutson and the answers were sadly predictable. The company was owned by Weiss-Randall. The plant outside Moscow had been renamed Siberian Star in 1999 but Weiss-Randall had owned Knutson since 1995.

How circular. As one of the most senior figures on the Fifteenth Directorate, Lieutenant-General Alexander Kosygin had, for many years, been Sergei Roskov's ultimate superior. As head of Weiss-Randall, he had continued in that role when Roskov agreed to join Siberian Star. In both cases, it seemed, Roskov had joined the venture in the belief he was helping his people. In both cases, it had turned out not to be true.

She wanted Komarov to wake her. A gentle kiss on the eyelids, his warm body sliding next to hers beneath the duvet. Instead, it was anxiety that woke her. She looked at her watch. Seven fifteen on the second of January. Nine days until the trade in New York, two days since she'd last seen him, and not much less since she'd last heard from him. He could be anywhere. When the phone did finally ring, she found she was scared to answer it, and then disappointed. It wasn't Komarov. It was Vatukin.

'Are you ready to meet?'

'Yes.'

'I'm going to send a car.'

It arrived at nine fifteen. Another Mercedes. The traffic moved like a glacier. Stephanie expected to head into central Moscow but the driver ventured west. Half an hour later, they were just inside the city limits, on a cratered road between decaying factories and pockets of crumbling housing. The Mercedes turned into a large industrial yard. There was a rusting sign above the entrance: The Board of Mechanization Automarket. A depot that used to deal in spare parts for road maintenance vehicles, the driver explained.

There was a guardhouse by the gate. Outside, chained dogs barked. They drove past a line of decrepit turquoise trucks with large yellow cranes on their backs. Beyond them, half a dozen coaches, most without windows, three without wheels. Beyond the coaches, a four-storey office block attached to a vast factory shed with ageing chimneys protruding from the roof, all gently smoking, red lights winking at the top. Filthy Volgas, Ladas and Volkswagens were parked outside the office block. The driver drove past them and into the shed. He parked beside a Range Rover. There were seven other vehicles.

Stephanie got out. It was freezing inside the factory. She looked up. There were gantries the length of the roof and across it. Huge steel tracks ran down the centre of the building, like some vast metal spine, supporting heavy-duty winches. Chunky hooks hung from chains blackened by dirt and grease.

Ahead, shrouded in gloom, she saw a cluster of bodies. The shed's echo smudged the sound of their conversation. As she moved nearer, she tried to count them. They formed a rough circle of a dozen. Or maybe fifteen. It was only when she was close enough to see their faces that she saw the extra body beyond.

His hands had been tied behind his back with thick cord, which had been slung over a steel hook and then hauled upwards. His feet were several inches clear of the floor. The cord had eaten into his wrists; there was blood all over them, a dark pool on the ground beneath him. She wondered whether his shoulders had dislocated yet. His face was so badly bruised, she couldn't tell who it was. Not immediately. Gradually, however, an identity emerged from the injuries.

Oh God, no. Not him. Please not him . . .

Boris Bergstein looked unconscious, his head lolling to one side. Vladimir Vatukin was standing close to Bergstein, warm in a thick overcoat and fur hat. He was smoking a cigarette. There were two thugs wielding lengths of rubber hose, another clutching a piece of metal pipe and a stunted man with one ear holding a bloody monkey-wrench.

Petra didn't allow Stephanie a visible reaction. But there was an internal one: a blend of shock, revulsion, pity. And relief. It wasn't Komarov.

Vatukin said, 'As you can see, we have a problem.'

He grabbed Bergstein by the hair and snapped his head back, exposing him to the feeble overhead light. Stephanie's stomach turned. His right eye was simply a slit in a puffy ball of purple and blue. His lips – meaty at any time – were grotesquely swollen. He was breathing heavily through his open mouth. She saw bloody fragments of broken teeth. His nose had been smeared to the left.

'Recognize this beauty?'

Be Petra. And so she was. The lies flowed smoothly, almost effortlessly.

'I met him in New York.'

'Where?'

'A restaurant in Brighton Beach.'

'Name?'

'Kalinka. It's on the boardwalk.'

'When was the last time you saw him?'

'The last time I was there.'

'When was that?'

'In the summer.'

'Why were you there?'

'None of your business.'

Her feisty response took Vatukin by surprise. He raised an eyebrow. 'You know what he says? He says your name is Kate March. He says he saw you here in Moscow, just before Christmas. Around the time we met.'

'You hit people often enough, they'll say anything.'

'He says he saw you in White Square, the night we went there.'

'Maybe he did. But I never saw him.'

'We've been to his apartment. A dump in Krylats-koye. He's got two pictures of you there, information on a laptop –'

'Let me guess,' she interrupted. 'He wanted a hundred thousand dollars from you.'

Vatukin hesitated. 'A hundred thousand dollars?'

'That's what he wanted from me.'

'In New York?'

She nodded. 'He's a hustler. He thought he knew something about me. But he was wrong.' Stephanie took a chance. 'He thought I was from the FBI, working for, or with, a man named Alan Kelly. Any of this sound familiar?'

The silence that followed suggested it did. Her eyes had adjusted to the murkiness, allowing her to pick out shapes from the darkness beyond. There was a rusted

Passat behind Vatukin. On the concrete floor beside the boot, she saw a large coil of razor wire and a can of petrol.

Vatukin glanced at Bergstein, then at her. 'From me, he wanted two hundred and fifty thousand.'

'So much for sexual equality.'

'You know what else he says?'

'What?'

'He says you helped him smuggle diamonds to New York.'

'For God's sake, what am I doing here?'

'He says the two of you became friendly. That you actually grew to like him.'

'If he'd told you that he was Peter the Great in another life, would you have believed that?'

Vatukin smiled but it was a façade. He reached into his overcoat pocket and produced a Beretta. Stephanie wondered how long Bergstein's suffering had lasted. Whatever he'd had to say, he would have said it between the first and second blows. He wasn't the type to hold out. Vatukin pressed the gun into her hand.

'Why don't you do it?'

23

Boris Bergstein was dead and her deal was in the gutter. Sitting in the back of the Mercedes, she knew she was lucky to be alive. But she didn't feel lucky. She felt ruined.

Without blinking, she'd taken the gun – just as Petra would have – and had fired. Not just once, but until the clip was empty. Five, as it happened, the spent cases clattering onto concrete. She'd felt the surprise in the silence that followed. It came from all the men except Vatukin, who'd just stared at her with his flint eyes. When she'd handed the gun back, he'd said there would be no deal and she'd known better than to protest or plead. He'd said his driver would return her to her hotel and that he hoped she enjoyed the rest of her time in Moscow. He'd even wished her well for the future. As civilized as you like, but in his stare, there'd been murder.

Now, there was the protective cocoon of shock. She recognized the symptoms: the fuzzy warmth, the sense of detachment, the strange air of unreality. The in-built coping mechanisms. Fine while they lasted. The trouble was, they never did.

Through the arch, through the snow. The cars that hadn't moved recently were just smooth white mounds, a row of hillocks in the courtyard. She punched the number on the keypad with a finger that had started to go numb the moment it left her jacket pocket.

'Yes?'

Her heart stuttered. 'Kostya?'

Then nothing. But it *had* been his voice, she was sure of it. She pressed the number again. No answer. And again. Still no answer.

She'd known that she'd go mad marooned in her hotel room. It hadn't mattered to her where she went. Anywhere was better than nowhere. And Komarov's apartment had seemed slightly better than anywhere, even though there'd been no answer when she phoned.

Now, she kept prodding the number into the keypad. Had she imagined his voice? It didn't seem so absurd. Not today. More than a dozen times she tried, perhaps as many as twenty . . .

Clunk.

The lock released. She spoke his name into the intercom. No reply. She took the lift and crept down the hall to his front door, which was ajar.

'Kostya?'

She entered, closing the door behind her. He was in his living room, crumpled in an armchair beneath the window. The air was blue with cigarette smoke. There were bottles on the table and on the floor. Also on the floor, cigarette butts, books, broken glass. The TV lay on its side, the flex ripped free of the plug. Stephanie saw the photograph of Irina that she'd held; the frame snapped, the print torn in half.

Komarov looked terrible, as pale as a ghost, unshaven, the rims of his eyes dark red with grey smudges beneath them. A third of a cigarette remained clamped between the fingers of his right hand, smoke spiralling upwards, adding to the haze.

'Kostya?'

'How did it go with Vladimir?'

'Kostya, what's happened to you?'

'*Tell me.*' When she wouldn't, he said, 'Bergstein . . . who is he?' He took a drag from the cigarette, shadows forming beneath his cheekbones. 'Or should I say, *was* he?'

'Just some guy . . .'

Komarov coughed a sarcastic laugh. 'Just some guy?'

'Where have you been?'

'Maybe that's the question I should be asking you.'

'What do you mean?'

'You remember the call, the day before yesterday?'

'Of course.'

'It was Vladimir. He said there was a problem. We met and he talked about Bergstein. Then about you. How sure was I about you, the lethal Petra Reuter? You see, Vladimir's the cautious kind when it comes to trust; he'd sooner slit a throat than misplace it.'

Komarov extinguished one cigarette, then lit another. Stephanie didn't sit down or take off her coat.

'He needed all the reassurance he could get. My word – my *lie*, as it happens – wasn't enough. His initial instinct was to kill you. That's always his initial instinct. One hundred per cent caution, one hundred per cent certainty. But you're different. To be honest, I think he's slightly in awe of you, or slightly in love. One or the other. So the word went out, calls were made, favours banked, rewards offered. Yesterday afternoon, Vladimir asked me to contact an associate of ours who was alleged to have done business with you in the past. I agreed

405

and, as it turns out, this man's word was good enough to save your life, even if it couldn't save your deal. You should be grateful to him. But vouching for you wasn't the only thing he told me about you. I wonder if you know who I'm talking about.'

She knew. And there was no Petra to rescue her now. 'Kostya . . .'

'Or is he . . . *just some guy*?'

She felt beyond coherence. First Bergstein, now this.

'Vladimir told me that he thought you two had done some business about two or three years ago. When I asked, it turned out to be closer to four years ago.'

He gave her the opportunity to say something but she couldn't.

'But also more recently. I didn't get it at first but he explained it to me. In detail. How it was, then and now. How you turned up just before Christmas, how nothing happened, how you turned up again a few days ago. It was just like old times, he said. Maybe even better. And all this time, I was in conference with a group of accountants in Zurich –'

'I had to,' she blurted.

'Why?'

'I just had to. There was no pleasure in it. *Ever*.' She could hear the desperation rising in her own voice. 'I swear it, Kostya, it meant nothing to me. Not once. It was disgusting. It was . . . it was just . . . just . . .'

She couldn't bring herself to say it.

'What?'

She shook her head.

'*What?*'

'It doesn't matter.'

'Business? Is that what you were going to say?'

She looked at her feet and sniffed. A teardrop splattered on the toecap of her boot.

'Please, Kostya . . .'

She thought she could smell the alcohol seeping from his pores.

'He told me about the olive oil, Petra. About what you did for him. Can you imagine what that's like? To have to listen to that?'

She noticed a picture on the floor. A seventeenth- or eighteenth-century lithograph of a small town. The glass was broken; there were dark flecks over some jagged fragments and on the frame. She glanced at his hands. The knuckles of the left were lacerated, the blood now black and dry.

'You know what he said to me before I put the phone down? He said, "If you ever get the chance, you really should try her, Kostya, she's the dirtiest fuck you'll ever have."'

The tears were streaming now. Silent, unchecked, no longer an adult, but a child. Hopeless and helpless, what was there to say? She opened her mouth to speak. At first, nothing. Then a quivering apology, as pathetic as it was inadequate.

'Sorry?' scoffed Komarov. 'Sorry that he fucked you? Or sorry that I found out?'

'Please, don't do this to me.'

'*To you?*'

'It meant nothing!'

'Not to you, perhaps.'

She raised her head and mustered the remains of her shredded dignity. 'Whatever you think of me, Kostya, I love you.'

It was the first time she'd said it, her voice as fragile as a snowflake. But he didn't seem to have heard.

'You fuck some guy and tell me it's business? Do you know what that makes you?' She wouldn't look at him but she could feel the stare. 'It makes you a whore, Petra.'

I walk along Kutuzovsky Prospekt, too numb to feel the cold. Too numb, for the moment, to feel anything. It's Boris Bergstein who fills my head, not Salman Rifat. The only thing I can think about is the promise I made to myself in Bilbao, after I'd killed Arkan in Belgrade. I really believed I would never kill anyone again. My only chance for a future had been to consign Petra to the past.

An hour later, I let myself into the bolt-hole at Bibirevo. I'm cold and wet. In the bag under my arm, there is vodka. I don't bother to shed my coat or fetch a glass; I drink straight from the bottle. For a while, the confusion in my mind grows worse. Pain fills the cavity where my heart's supposed to be. But then the alcohol dulls my nerves and all the sharp edges begin to soften. By mid-afternoon, I'm slumped on the floor of the living room, my back to the wall. Next door, the television is so loud I can feel it reverberating through me. It's dark when I start on the second bottle.

When I wake up, I'm lying face-down on the bed, still dressed. My head feels as though it's been cleaved in two. The pain adds to the swirling nausea. I'm going to throw up. I get off the bed. The room shifts, I stumble, the bile rises in my throat. I just make it to the toilet. I vomit violently, clutching the rim of the bowl to stop myself from falling completely. One shuddering retch after another, hot tears welling in my eyes.

It's ghastly but it's not enough for the purge I need. I

stagger back to the bedroom and rinse my mouth out with vodka from the second bottle; there's still three-quarters of it left. I spit the bitter, contaminated mouthful into a mug and then drink from the bottle again.

The next time I wake up, my headache is worse. I shrug off the coat I'm still wearing. There are dried droplets of Bergstein's blood on the right sleeve.

I knew from the start that I wasn't Petra Reuter. When Alexander saw me in Provence, he must have suspected it too. He only had to look at me to see something he'd never seen before: a physical ripeness, peace of mind, a life in balance. My softness was corporal and emotional, in equal measure. It was arrogance on both our parts to assume I could ever claw back the brutality I once had.

I carry on drinking, then pass out.

There's an incessant thumping in my head. And outside it, too. When I open my crusty eyes, they sting. There's daylight coming through the window.

Thump, thump, thump.

I'm not in bed. I'm on the floor. An appalling smell assaults me. I've thrown up over myself. I can feel it on my face, around my mouth, in my hair, on the ground beneath me.

Thump, thump, crack!

That one wasn't in my head. When I try to turn to see the source, the room sways. I close my eyes. When I open them again, a blurred figure towers above me. My throat is raw, my voice a rasp. 'Go away. Leave me alone.'

Kostya looks down at me and says, 'Enough.'

He carried her to the bathroom, ran the taps, peeled away her soiled clothes and lowered her clammy, stinking body into water that was warm, not hot. The bathroom light was a fluorescent tube behind wire mesh. It flickered, making her queasy. Komarov noticed and switched it off. He washed her hair, then cleaned her body before helping her out of the bath. Wrapped in a towel, she sat on the toilet lid while he drained the bath, rinsed it thoroughly, and refilled it with fresh water. When it was full, he helped her back in. He went to the kitchen and returned with two glasses, one of water, one of steaming tea.

'Drink the water first. Slowly. Then the tea.'

He left her there with just a dull wash of hall light for illumination. She followed him through the apartment with her ears; cupboards opening and closing, water running into a plastic vessel, footsteps, the scrubbing of a floor, more footsteps, more water, more scrubbing. She sipped her tea. It was hot and sweet, and almost too powerful for her tender stomach.

Stephanie wasn't sure how long passed before he returned. He pulled the plug, helped her out, dried her, wrapped the towel round her and led her to the bed. The sheets were cold and brittle against her warm, pink skin. He handed her two pills and another glass of water.

'Take these.'

'What are they?'

'Take them.'

She swallowed both. He made her a second glass of sweet tea and then pulled up a chair beside the bed. He sat down.

'Kostya . . .'

'Not now.'

It was dark when she woke up. He wasn't in the chair. Her head throbbed, her eyes felt hot and blood-shot, her stomach felt bruised. She heard distant sirens;

the window was open, freezing air blowing away the stuffy warmth of the bedroom. She dressed slowly – a pair of baggy, black drawstring trousers made of thick cotton, a grey sweatshirt over a mauve T-shirt, climbing socks. Her clothes, but last seen in her room at the Baltschug. She found Komarov in the kitchen.

He was looking out of the window, his back to her. When he exhaled, cigarette smoke rebounded off the glass. Beneath the aroma of tobacco, disinfectant. There was a pan on the stove, steam rising from the top. She didn't move or speak. Eventually, Komarov turned round. He didn't seem surprised to see her.

'How are you?'

Good question.

Her wet, washed clothes hung from a wooden rail over the sink, each damp garment a flag of humiliation. She sat down at the small kitchen table and shook her head.

'I feel so tired, Kostya. Nobody my age should feel this tired.'

In the pan, there was chicken soup. Komarov gave her a bowl.

'I'm not hungry,' she said.

'Eat it anyway.'

He sounded like Boyd. He tore a chunk of bread from a loaf and set it down beside the bowl. She consumed the food slowly, still unsure of her stomach. Komarov joined her, then made more tea. Afterwards, they went into the living room. The carpet was clean but the damp patches were still dark, the smell of disinfectant stronger. He poured himself a shot of Georgian brandy from a bottle she'd never seen before. He didn't offer her any.

411

'How did you find me?'

'I followed you here. Then left you to it.'

'Why?'

'Because there are no short cuts.'

Apparently not. It transpired that it was the fourth of January.

She'd lost an entire day to the bottle.

They'd finished their food and were sitting at the kitchen table, Komarov drinking, Stephanie disgusted by the very idea of it. In the corridor outside, an argument, a couple shouting, the man drunk, possibly the woman too.

'I'm sorry, Kostya. God, I'm sorry. I thought I could cut myself in two, that it wouldn't matter. I thought it was a price worth paying if it helped us to escape. I thought . . . Christ, I don't know what I thought. Not then, not now. I just know that I'm sorry. And that if I could take it back, I would.'

'But you can't.'

She stared at the table. 'No.'

'I'm sorry, too. Not for the way I felt, but for calling you a whore. That was –'

'I *am* a whore.'

'No . . .'

'Yes, Kostya. I am.' She looked up at him. 'At least . . . I *was*.'

He squinted at her. 'What do you mean?'

'I don't want to lie to you any more. There's no point.'

'Petra . . .'

'I'm not Petra.'

'*What?*'

412

'I'm not Petra Reuter. I'm not German. I'm not an assassin or a mercenary terrorist.'

Komarov's face was blank but there was confusion in his eyes. He played for time, drawing slowly on his cigarette. 'If you're not Petra, who are you?'

She told him the truth. 'I don't know. But my name is Stephanie.'

'Stephanie . . .'

'I'm too many people to count, Kostya.'

'I only want one.'

'My name is Stephanie Patrick, not Petra Reuter. I'm English, not German. I'm twenty-eight, not thirty-one.'

Incredulity began to make way for anger. 'Is this some kind of joke?'

She shook her head. 'It's the truth. Petra Reuter doesn't exist.'

'I *know* that's not true.'

'Petra Reuter is a legend, Kostya. A myth. Just like Koba.'

'You're lying.'

'She was created for me.'

'By?'

'By faceless people.'

Komarov inclined his head to one side. 'Faceless *government* people?'

'They're beyond government. They're beyond the law. They're even beyond where you are. You and all the others: Vatukin, Rogachev, Kosygin . . . they're beyond all of you.'

'Who are you?'

'We don't exist, Kostya. There is no department. No agency chief answerable to a politician on a committee.

No one to bribe. There is no register of staff, no record of activity.'

'But *you* . . . who are you?'

Stephanie shrugged. 'I'm a technician. That's all.'

Komarov poured himself another shot.

'Why are you telling me this now?'

'Because it's the truth. I've been lying all my life. I'm tired of it. Ever since I met you, I've hated myself for not trusting you. Especially when I saw the risks you were taking to trust me. And now . . . now I can't do it any more. I don't care. I want you to know the truth. And if you decide the truth isn't good enough, I'll accept that. I just want somebody to know who I am, Kostya. One person. That's all.'

Still reeling, he said, 'Tell me, then.'

She painted a childhood – almost idyllic, certainly realistic – brought to an abrupt end at nineteen by the bomb which brought down flight NE027 over the Atlantic, killing her parents and two of her three siblings. She described in excruciating detail her inability to cope with the tragedy, the turn to alcohol and narcotics to ease the pain and the move towards the anonymity of London. Alone in an alien city, with no money to support her increasing chemical dependence, her slide into prostitution had been as inevitable as it had been unoriginal. A spiral of decline followed, hastened by her complete lack of concern for herself. She lived from trick to trick and fix to fix. She could have died – *would* have, and sooner rather than later – had it not been for some unlikely intervention. Then Magenta House.

'Worse than prostitution in a way. More invasive.'

'I don't believe that.'

Stephanie was biting a thumbnail. 'The men who

paid for me only got inside my body. Magenta House got inside my mind.'

She told him about the metamorphosis. From junkie hooker to the terrorist Petra Reuter. Then there was Malta, the breakdown years that followed – when she really *was* Petra Reuter – culminating in the assassination of Arkan in the lobby of the Hotel Inter-Continental in Belgrade. Five days later, her epiphany in a seedy hotel room in Bilbao, leading to her reinvention in the south of France and, finally, to Alexander's catastrophic reappearance.

Once started, her history gushed out of her, reducing her to tears at some points, hardening her at others. Komarov listened, silent and astonished.

'You see now?' she said, once it was over. 'It's the truth. I'm a daughter who lost her parents, a sibling who lost a brother and a sister. I'm a drug addict, a prostitute, an assassin. I've been so many people, I don't remember who I am any more.'

Warm and alone, she heard him next door; the creak of the floor, a cough, a cupboard hinge squeaking. When they'd gone to bed, she'd slid beneath the blankets, naked, and he'd stayed on top of the blankets, dressed. They'd remained awake for a long time but neither had whispered a word. The confession made, silence had seemed safer.

Now, she pulled on her clothes. The last of her hangover was gone. Her first clear head for two days. Or was it three? When she stopped to consider it, she realized it was a lot longer. It was four years, maybe five. And it wasn't about the alcohol in her bloodstream, it was about the burden of truth.

Komarov was in the kitchen. Outside, it was snowing heavily. She crept up behind him, put her arms round him and rested her head against his back.

He said, 'Are you okay?'

'I should be asking you that.'

She felt tired and confused. There was nothing left. Boris Bergstein's greed had seen to that. No Koba, no Tsentralnaya, no inside track. And no assassin, either. James Marshall was no closer to being avenged. As for the trade in New York, maybe it would happen, maybe it wouldn't. There were never guarantees.

Komarov said, 'I'm going back to New York tomorrow. Come with me.'

'I can't,' she whispered. 'Not yet. I need to go to London first. I need to speak to him.'

'And afterwards?'

'Are you sure you want me?'

'I'm sure.'

She squeezed him tighter. 'I'm so sorry.'

'There's no need to be.'

'I wish I could believe that.'

Komarov turned round to face her. 'We are what we are. We can't change it. And what you are is what I love. That's it. Nothing more.'

Stephanie hoped it was true. 'But all the things I told you –'

'It doesn't matter. I want *you*. All of you. The addict, the prostitute, the terrorist. The woman standing in front of me.'

She recognized the turning without difficulty. The Jeep – borrowed from Komarov, who'd borrowed it from a friend, no questions asked – was almost too wide for the narrow track. The lake came into view, flat and flawlessly white, followed by the turquoise house at the ice's edge. Blue icicles hung from the eaves; a row of jagged daggers. Stephanie climbed the wooden steps to the front door and knocked. Inside, the dogs started barking – Alsatians, she remembered – but no one came to answer. She tried again and called out. Then she heard a squeak – a footfall in snow – and turned round. Josef Bergstein was pointing an old Walther PPK at her. He was wearing a heavy jersey, old jeans, felt boots. The cold had reddened his bird-like features, his head and shoulders were dusted with snow. He had to have heard the vehicle long before she'd reached the clearing beside the house; retired or not, it seemed his senses were still acutely tuned.

'Coming here without warning can be a mistake.'

'I need to talk to you.'

'I'm not in the mood for company.'

'I know. But I had to come.'

He lowered the gun. 'What do you want?'

'I want you to know what happened.'

'They tortured him, wrapped him in razor wire, put him in the trunk of a car and set it on fire. The police found the Passat at Ramenki. That's what happened.'

'Not quite. He was dead before they put him in the car.'

Bergstein hesitated. 'Go on.'

'I was the one who killed him.' She looked down at the Walther. 'I thought you should know.'

Inside, it was warm. The room smelt of old leather, sweet tobacco and dogs. The brazier grumbled softly.

One of the Alsatians circled her, sniffed her hand, then curled away. She sat on a lumpy sofa with a tartan rug thrown over it. Bergstein began to prepare coffee.

'You're Tsentralnaya?'

'No.'

'But this was Tsentralnaya business?'

'Yes.'

'What's your connection?'

'I'm in the same line of work as you.'

He didn't turn to look at her. 'He told you?'

'He told me you used to work for the KGB, as a paymaster. But I have other sources. He never knew, did he?'

Bergstein shook his head. He took two china cups from a wooden shelf, one with hand-painted red roses, the other plain white.

'Have I heard of you?' he asked.

'Probably.'

'Tell me.'

'Petra Reuter.'

Now, he turned round, raising an eyebrow. 'Really?'

'Yes. But Boris never knew.'

'I don't think the name would have meant anything to him.'

'Probably not.'

'What was your business with Boris?'

'I'm afraid I used him. He never knew what my business was.'

Josef Bergstein smiled sadly. 'That I can believe. Borya thought he was something he could never be. His dreams were always too big.'

'I came to like that in him.'

'So did I. But it was a weakness.'

'It was what got him killed.'

Bergstein asked how and she told him, as he poured coffee for both of them. He handed her the cup with the roses.

'Who were you looking for?'

'Two people. Although they could be the same person.'

She described the killing of Rogachev and Marshall in Paris and her search for their killer.

'And the other one?' Bergstein asked.

'Koba.'

A grunt of something. Not quite laughter but close to it. 'Koba . . .'

'Yes.'

'To kill Koba, you'd have to kill a lot of people.'

They talked for an hour. When the coffee was finished, Bergstein produced bread, sausage and cheese. Stephanie asked how Maria Bergstein was coping. She wasn't, Josef said. Not really. Boris had been her only child. He'd spared her the awful details but still she wanted to know *why* it had happened. He'd had to lie to her because she had never fully understood the life that Boris had led. That, he told Stephanie, was the myopic naivety of a doting mother for you.

'Can I ask you something? Being an independent . . . how is that?'

'You mean, doing it for money?'

'Yes.'

'Didn't the government pay you?'

'Sometimes.'

'So what's the difference? It's a job.'

'You know what I mean.'

Stephanie considered Petra. 'It's better.'

'How?'

'It's cleaner. There's no hypocrisy because there's no attempt at justification.'

Bergstein nodded. 'That's what I always imagined.'

'Has that been a problem for you?'

'From time to time.'

'In what way?'

'I worked for the First Chief Directorate of the KGB before the reorganization, then for SVR. For five years, my boss was a man called Furmanov. I don't know how many orders he handed down to me in that time but it was plenty. And where is Furmanov now? Living in Geneva with a nineteen-year-old Argentine girlfriend. He's negotiating a deal with American publishers for his memoirs. As for me – the one who had to do all his dirty work – I'm supposed to be retired. Last week, though, I got a call from Petrov, Furmanov's replacement at SVR. He's handing down an elimination order. Wants it to go outside the department. He offers me more money than I used to make in five years. Says he thought of me straight away because Furmanov is the target. Thought I might find that appealing. In truth, I don't know if the contract is SVR or Mafiya. What I do know is that Furmanov will be dead before he writes so much as the title of his book, whether I take the job or not. I used to think my work meant something; it was unpleasant but justified. Now? I don't know. The government changes, the targets change, but nothing really changes at all.'

They talked into the early afternoon. When Bergstein showed her out, the wind had died. The snow fell gently. As Stephanie opened the Jeep door, he put a hand on her shoulder and said, 'By the way – what you did to Boris – it was the right thing.'

'Are you sure?'

He nodded. 'The end was never in doubt. You saved him the agony.'

24

Valentina Rudenko led Stephanie from the kitchen into the living room. *Samson and Delilah* by Camille Saint-Saëns was playing on a cheap Samsung, Olga Borodina and Dmitri Hvorostovsky singing. On top of the small round table by the window, there was a large manila envelope, the bulky contents in the bottom half. The top half had been folded over and the package had been secured by three thick elastic bands.

'Sergei called,' Rudenko said, placing the tray she was carrying on the sideboard.

'He's agreed to see me?'

She shook her head. 'He said he had to leave Moscow.'

'He's here?'

'He never left. But now he needs to go. He asked me to get some things for him. Some dollars, his second identity . . .'

'Second identity?'

'About a month before he disappeared, he told me he'd bought a new passport from a forger in Birjulevo. He asked me to hide it for him because he was nervous about keeping it in his apartment.'

'What else is in the package?'

Rudenko looked away. 'A gun, some computer disks.'

'What's on the disks?'

'Information about his work – past and present. Currency for a foreign country, he calls it.'

'I thought Sergei disapproved of selling secrets.'

'For commercial gain, he does. They're not for money. They're for sanctuary.'

Stephanie peered out of the window. Late afternoon and it felt like it had been dark since September. On the opposite side of Red Army Street, there was a dilapidated truck. From the back of it, a farmer was selling potatoes, onions and carrots. Next to the truck was the Jeep. She'd been on her way back to Moscow when she'd turned on her mobile phone; a message from Rudenko – could she come and see her as soon as possible? Stephanie almost hadn't bothered. What was the point? It made no difference now. Still, Rudenko had gone out of her way for her. She was contributing. That counted for something, Stephanie supposed.

'When are you taking it to him?'

'I'm not. You are.'

'Did you tell him that?'

'No.'

'Is that going to work?'

'You'll have to make it work. You'll have the package. Without it, he can't go anywhere. It's his life's work. You'll have to make him talk and then decide how much of what he's telling you is the truth. And how much of the truth he has to tell you before you let him go.'

'When's the rendezvous?'

'Tomorrow morning.'

Leaving her plenty of time to catch her afternoon flight to London. 'Where?'

'Luzhniki Market.'

* * *

They turned off Murmansky Prospekt and the road vanished into snow. It was falling again, strangely magical in the headlights. Street lamps stained the smoke from the factory chimney a dirty orange. Stephanie could just make out the Ostankino TV tower in the distant Moscow night.

Down the steps, back into the subterranean warmth. In the dormitory, most of the beds were unoccupied; it was still early. Komarov unbuttoned his coat and led her into the dining area; the concrete cellar, the building's network of pipes at ceiling level, trestle tables beneath, benches on either side. Food was being served from a table at the far end. A stew with dumplings and vegetables, dispensed from a large steel vat by Ludmilla. The recipients formed a ragged queue and shuffled past her, taking a chunk of bread from the basket at the end of the table.

Ludmilla had two helpers, Max and Andrei. Max was a doctor, Andrei worked in the Moscow Stock Exchange. They spent several nights a week helping at the refuge. They were young, well-educated, altruistic; Stephanie found their idealism naively evangelical. And completely refreshing.

'Kostya's different to the others,' Andrei said, just after midnight, as he, Ludmilla and Stephanie drank tea in a damp storeroom that had been converted into an administrative office.

Komarov was talking to Max in another part of the refuge. It was quieter now. The food had been cleared away, the basement had been cleaned and many of the homeless were asleep.

'What others?' Stephanie asked.

'The new Russians.'

'That's because he's not a new Russian,' Ludmilla said. 'He's an old Russian. A pre-Revolutionary Russian, in love with the country and its people. And not in love with the people who run the country. Or own it. Which is how it always was.'

'Not just here,' Stephanie said.

'The new breed aren't that new. They behave the way the aristocrats used to behave. They make fortunes out of the misery of others and then flaunt it in front of them.'

'It's true,' Andrei said, rolling a slender cigarette. 'Even the great American robber barons gave fortunes away. They bought respectability through charity. That hasn't happened here. The new Russians don't care about anybody but themselves. They take as much as they can and the rest of the world can fuck off.'

'But not Kostya.'

Ludmilla shook her head. 'He comes from a tradition that used to rob the rich to help the poor. The new Russians rob everybody – especially the poor – and keep it all for themselves.'

'Maybe that will change.'

'Not any time soon.'

'One day,' Andrei said, 'when they've bought everything else, it might occur to them to spend some money on a lasting legacy. But not yet. They're not ready. They think philanthropy is something dirty their girlfriends do to them.'

'But if one of them offered you a million rubles tomorrow . . .'

'We'd take it. And it wouldn't have to be a million. Anything would be better than nothing. Frankly, we don't care *why* the money is given. No ruble is too dirty for us.'

'Which is why you look the other way when Kostya pays for this place and the others. Because beggars can't be choosers.'

'Exactly. But like I said, he's not like them. Ask the people next door on the camp beds. They wouldn't piss on a new Russian if he was on fire. But for Kostya, they'd do anything. He doesn't just pay for this. He's *involved*.'

We pull away from the refuge. The snow insulates us against the sound of Moscow. Kostya looks deep in thought as we turn left onto Murmansky Prospekt.

'What are you thinking?' I ask.

'Nothing.'

'That's not true.'

'It doesn't matter.'

'It does now.'

From Murmansky Prospekt we join Mira Prospekt and head towards the city centre.

'I was thinking about the woman you used to be.'

It's not the answer I expected. And it's not hard to guess which woman he means. 'The prostitute?'

Kostya nods.

'What about it?'

'I was trying to think what that must have been like.'

'It wasn't like anything.*'*

'You know what I mean.'

'Have you ever had sex with a prostitute?'

Strangely, I know the answer the moment I've asked the question.

'Yes,' he replies, without pause. It's a statement of fact and a fact of life.

'And what did you feel?'

'Would you like me to tell you I felt some guilt?'

'I'd like you to tell me the truth.'

'I felt nothing. It was purely physical.'

I consider the parallel. 'Well, that's how it was for me, too.'

We drive on for a while, before he says, 'There was no emotion at all?'

'None. You have to kill it before it kills you.'

'And how do you do that?'

'The same way you learned to survive in the east. You adapt. You close yourself down, you don't think of the future, the past, anything at all. You don't think of the man inside you. You don't feel him, no matter what he does. You go numb and wait for it to finish. At the start, you think it's a question of minutes. In the end, it turns out to be years.'

Kutuzovsky Prospekt. He's cleaned the place but some of the evidence of his rampage remains. The television sits in the corner of the living room, the ripped flex snaking across the carpet. The broken picture of Irina lies on the table. We talk for a while, then I go to bed. I can't bring myself to be completely naked yet so I keep my T-shirt on. Beneath the sheets, I lie still and listen to him pacing next door.

I feel his fingers first, between my thighs, then inside me. His tongue follows. I do nothing at all. I remain on the verge of sleep, every part of me relaxed, and it feels as though I'm imagining it. When he takes off my T-shirt, rolls me onto my front and enters me from behind, I enjoy the weight of him pressing down on me, the sound of his breathing, the feel of it on my skin. Tonight, it feels good to be used.

Afterwards, neither of us says a word.

The next sense to be aroused is smell. Coffee. I open my

eyes and see daylight through a crack in the curtains. A blue
sky, not the customary pewter. I catch a glimpse of Kostya, a
towel wrapped round his waist. His hair is wet. He's carrying
two clean shirts; he's packing for New York. My heart sinks
a little, then soars a little; I feel tender, warm and sticky. It
might have been a wonderful dream, so I'm grateful for the
evidence between my thighs. He notices that I'm awake, brings
me a cup of coffee and kisses me. He tastes fresh.

'When will I see you again?'

'Soon. I'll sort something out in London. One way or
another.'

'And if he won't let you go?'

'We'll have to decide.'

He sits on the edge of the bed. 'A life on the run?'

'Yes.'

'Sounds exciting.'

'It won't be. Not after a while. It'll be boring.'

'But worth it.'

'God, yes.' I run my fingers over the tattoos on his stomach.
'At least we'll be together.'

'And truly free.'

'Yes.'

'For the first time. For both of us.'

A small city of narrow alleys created by hundreds
of stalls, Luzhniki Market stood inside the black iron
railings that fenced the Lenin stadium complex. It
was close enough to the 95,000-seater stadium to fall
under the blanket of its colossal shadow. Inside the main
gate, there was a statue of Lenin, his face turned to the
wind, a billowing overcoat draped around his shoulders.
From where Stephanie stood, the stadium seemed
to hover above the market like some enormous fly-

ing saucer. Snow sparkled on the glittering gold roof.

At the edge of the market, the security: charmless characters in black, armed with attitude, militaristic badges, batons and two-way radios. The paramilitary look, courtesy of the Lipetsk gang. It was an open secret that they ran the market, taking a cut from everybody.

The channels were packed; Luzhniki's reputation as the cheapest market in Moscow attracted shoppers not only from the city, but from far further afield. Around the stadium's southern edge, there were rows of decrepit buses, all displaying their points of origin; Mahachkala in Dagestan, Nizhny Novgorod, Stavropol. Sharing the costs of the journey – including the bribes paid out en route – the traders travelled endlessly, arriving empty, leaving laden, hoping for a slim profit back home and that the wheezing, creaking bus would get them there. The cycle complete, it was then repeated. Close to the parked vehicles, there were stalls selling sandwiches, pies, tea and beer.

Valentina Rudenko had described Luzhniki as a counterfeiter's paradise. Stephanie saw stalls offering Adidas sportswear, Wrangler jeans and Calvin Klein underwear at a fraction of a legitimate price. Traders sold tights, toothpaste, blouses, jars of Nescafé, fur hats, polyester sheets and French perfumes from Poland. The more valuable goods, like fur coats, were hung on rails high above the stalls, well out of a thief's reach.

It was a freezing morning, not a cloud in the sky. Packed snow on ice made footing treacherous. Men and women, young and old, all barged past one another. Some shoppers loaded their goods onto small trolleys or into brightly-coloured nylon laundry bags. Stallholder accents came from the Ukraine, Azerbaijan, Moldova,

Uzbekistan. Many Muscovites, Rudenko had said, felt that working at Luzhniki was beneath them.

Portable radios played music: Britney Spears, Mahler, the latest sensation from Tashkent. Occasionally, an announcement over the stadium's public address system swamped everything: Svetlana, aged six, was looking for her mother, or, perhaps, a belated birthday greeting for Yuri, a cigarette vendor from Minsk.

Stephanie reached the end of an aisle and checked her watch. Five to eleven. A group of tough Caucasians had gathered around a metal turnstile at one of the stadium's gates. Dark-skinned, dark-haired, they looked sullen and suspicious, dressed in dirty tracksuits, leather overcoats and tight, faded jeans. She turned up the channel to her right. A stallholder tried to interest her in coats made from polar fox and water rat. A sour-faced woman pushed a cart past her, stacked with grey pies, limp pastries, chocolate, cigarettes. On top, one thermos for coffee, another for tea.

Stephanie began counting the stalls to her left. *You'll see the bags,* Rudenko had said. Indeed. Raised on a series of poles, large plastic laundry bags in a series of check patterns; white with blue, red with black, or any other combination. *Three stalls on,* she'd added, *next to the one-armed Latvian selling Gillette razors and Duracell batteries.*

Blue plastic sheeting covered the stall. Scarves had been draped over the supporting poles. There were jerseys on hangers, each hanger hooked to a pole. The choice was limited; round-neck or V-neck, plain or with horizontal bands, khaki or grey. It didn't look as though any had been sold. Sitting on a stool was a short woman in a quilted coat. She wore a cream headscarf with flowers of scarlet, violet and turquoise.

'Is Sergei about?'

She didn't bother looking up at Stephanie. 'Who?'

'Sergei.'

'I don't know anybody called Sergei.'

'Really? Then you must know fewer people in Russia than I do. If I threw a handful of gravel into the air, I'd probably hit three men called Sergei.'

'If you want to buy something, let's see some rubles. If not, fuck off.'

'Valentina couldn't make it. I've come instead.'

'Valentina who?'

Stephanie stepped forward and lowered her voice. 'Listen to me. See this bag? If I don't give it to him, his life is finished. And if I don't see him in the next ten seconds, I'm walking away and that'll be it. I'll dump the bag in the Moscow river, catch a plane and disappear. By the time the flight attendant gives me my drink, I'll have forgotten who Sergei is. Just like you have. On the other hand . . .'

A man appeared, emerging from behind the plastic curtain at the side of the stall. He looked gaunt compared to the photograph that Rudenko had shown her. His hair was greyer and he had a nervous tic. Stephanie wondered whether it was recent.

'What happened to Valentina?'

'Nothing. She's fine. She sent me instead.'

Sergei Roskov shook his head. 'Why?'

'Because she's a better judge of character than you are.'

He looked at the bag. 'What have you brought?'

'All that you asked for.'

'What do you want?'

''I need to know about Marburg Variant U-13. And

you can skip the "I don't know what you're talking about" routine.'

'How do you know about it?'

'Yevgeny Vlasko told me all he knew when I saw him in London. Biopreparat, M-8389, the Fifteenth Directorate . . .'

'Please. There's nothing to say.'

'I'll be the judge of that.'

'It's not safe to talk here.'

'Well, we're not going anywhere else. The quicker you are, the quicker you can leave. Why are you running, Sergei?'

'Who are you working for?'

'Does it matter?'

He looked over his shoulder. 'Did Yevgeny tell you about the outbreak at M-8389?'

'Yes.'

'About the three cleaners who died?'

'Yes.'

Roskov bit his lip. 'It wasn't an accident. They were sent into the airlock deliberately. It was a controlled experiment.'

'Using humans?'

'Well . . . an Azeri, a Chechen and an Uzbek. In other words, expendables.' When she caught his eye, he said, 'That was the way it was, back then.'

'But as I understand it, the whole of Building 112 was closed down. Vlasko told me they had to seal it tighter than Chernobyl.'

'Because they had to make it look like an accident. To convince the workers at M-8389, to convince the investigators. To convince Yevgeny.'

'And you?'

432

He looked offended. 'I was with Yevgeny. Neither of us knew.'

'When did you find out?'

'Much later.'

'When you took over his job at Biopreparat?'

'After that.'

'At Siberian Star?'

Roskov nodded. He'd begun to fidget, constantly glancing at the stream of human traffic outside the stall.

'How did those at Siberian Star find out about M-8389?'

'They bought the files.'

'Bought?'

'Siberian Star bought Department 17 of M-8389.'

'What was Department 17?'

'The archive division. It was based in a fortified warehouse on the outskirts of Almaty. It contained all M-8389 files, including those relating to Marburg Variant U-13 and the infection of the cleaners. The Department was formerly under the control of the Fifteenth Directorate.'

'How can you buy a department?'

Roskov smiled coldly. 'This was in the mid-Nineties. You could buy anything with hard currency. Anything at all. If you'd offered enough, you could have turned the Kremlin into a Sheraton. CNN in every room . . .'

'Where did the money come from?'

'From the parent company. Weiss-Randall. It's an American firm.'

'Alexander Kosygin.'

'Yes.'

'He was a member of the Fifteenth Directorate at the time of the M-8389 infection?'

'Yes.'

'So he knew . . .'

'Knew? He was in charge of it. There were three of them.'

'And the other two are dead.'

Roskov stamped his feet against the cold. 'Please, the bag . . .'

'Why are you running?'

'Please . . .'

'*Why?*'

'Some of the Department 17 information went missing. Either lost or destroyed, no one knows. A lot can happen between Almaty and Moscow. Kosygin took me into his confidence because he knew I'd helped to develop Marburg Variant U-13.'

'And what did he want?'

Roskov fell silent.

'What, Sergei?'

'A device.'

'What device?'

'A delivery device.'

'For aerosol?'

Roskov nodded. 'But I couldn't. I was there at M-8389. With Yevgeny.' His fear temporarily cast aside, he said, 'I *saw* what happened to those three.'

'Do you know who's in the market for U-13 now?'

'Serbs. That's what I heard.'

'Do you know who?'

He shook his head. 'But it makes sense.'

'Why?'

'Kosygin was always involved with Tsentralnaya and Tsentralnaya was always the organization with the strongest Serb connections. These days? I don't know. But back then . . .'

'What kind of connections?'

'The right kind. Rogachev and Milosevic were close. Vatukin knew him too. Milosevic made millions from Tsentralnaya. In return, Tsentralnaya ran concessions throughout Serbia. Arms, prostitution, drugs, money-laundering. Anything and everything.'

It came full circle. As she knew it would. There were no surprises any more. She handed the bag to Roskov, who asked if he could go. Like a pupil in class. Sure, she said, why not? He looked relieved. Then terrified.

Stephanie looked over her shoulder. Two men were separating themselves from the throng: one large, one short, both in dark zipped jackets, one with a hat, one without. Roskov was gone. Half a second's opportunity and he'd taken it, slipping out of the stall the way he'd come in. The woman on the stool was sliding away from Stephanie, melting into the market. One of the men was reaching inside his jacket. Stephanie turned and followed Roskov past the flap of blue plastic. She squeezed between the backs of stalls, stepping over boxes, pressing against frames and tarpaulins, until she came to a narrow break. She glanced left and right. No sign of Roskov any longer. She glimpsed movement to her left, figures breaking from the sluggish motion of the crowd. She headed right.

Sheer ice beneath and suddenly she was on the ground, clattering into legs. Three people fell with her. On her hands and knees, she scrambled to her left, then rose to her feet by a stall selling kitchenware. A thug stepped forward with a punch. She ducked it, saw the second thug out of the corner of her eye, spun on her right foot and clattered her left into his jaw. The blow sent a shudder through him. He swayed, then collapsed.

The first was coming back at her. She grabbed a kettle from the stall, stepped outside the arc of a punch and swung upwards, catching him on the chin. The kettle disintegrated in her hands.

There were five new faces focusing on her, coming closer, blunt intent etched on each of them; three from the right, two from the left. She pushed the stallholder out of the way, jumped onto the trestle table, knocking over a set of saucepans. She reached for the aluminium stanchion and the leading piece of metal pipe. The stall lurched. She swung forward, hooked a leg over the top and rolled onto the red-and-white striped plastic sheeting. The structure began to collapse. At the last moment, she jumped, crashing through the tarpaulin canopy over a stall in the neighbouring alley. She fell to the ground in a cascade of fur coats. The astonished stallholder was knocked to the ground. Stephanie found herself splayed on top of him. He lay on his back, panting, blinking, not moving.

She flashed him a smile. 'Honestly, I'm not that sort of girl.'

Then she was gone, running without a plan. *Keep moving, never stop.* Carving through the crowd, faster, fitter, stronger. She was within sight of the black railings at the edge of Luzhniki Market, within sight of Lenin himself. That was the last thing she remembered with any clarity.

25

It felt as though someone had kicked her heart. Explosive, the shock wave ripped through her, scrambling muscles and mind. She collapsed and they were onto her. Men in black leather coats pushed the crowd back. Two of them were armed. They flashed badges in front of startled faces. She would have screamed but there was no air in her lungs, no blood in her muscles. She was jelly. Hands grabbed her arms, a fist clutched her collar. They dragged her. In her mind, she lashed out at them with her feet. In reality, she could feel her limp legs trailing behind her.

Now, they were in a car. A saloon. The paralysing sensation was beginning to wear off. She was on the floor beneath three pairs of heavy boots. The men above her were squashed together on the back seat. Someone switched off the blue flashing light in the rear window. The driver, Yuri, was arguing with the man in the passenger seat. She closed her eyes. The car was going fast, swerving sharply, accelerating, braking, a hand hammering the horn.

An electric stun gun of some sort, she guessed. She hadn't seen who it was. A face in the crowd, only moving forward at the last moment.

Don't move. Make them believe you're in worse shape than you are.

The car slowed, swung into a long curve and turned

onto a rougher road, the suspension creaking from one pothole to the next. Stephanie allowed herself a narrow slit of vision through the window above. A dark sky, snow, a fence, a gate with a sign over it. She couldn't read what was written on it. Soon, she didn't need to because she saw the tips of rusting yellow cranes poking over the tops of turquoise cabs. They passed one lorry after another.

The Automarket at Stroguino.

The car halted inside the works shed. Mentally, Stephanie tried to pull herself together. With five of them, there would be only a fraction of a chance at best. She closed her eyes as the engine died. The back doors opened. Hard rubber boots scuffed her as the men scrambled out of the vehicle. She forced her breathing to slow, relaxing her muscles to limpness.

One man per arm, then the pull. The left shoulder burnt, an aggravation of the New York injury. She let her neck soften. Her head drooped. A third man clutched a handful of coat. Where were the other two? She opened her eyes and saw an upside-down world. They were several yards ahead, talking. She knew she couldn't let them take her too far inside.

Go on, Boyd whispered into her ear.

She snapped her head forward and sank her teeth into the thick wrist of the hand on her coat. The man gasped, then stooped, pulling the other two off balance. She gripped the hands holding her own hands and yanked as hard as she could. The men staggered backwards. She fell to the ground and swiped her right leg to the right, catching one of them behind the knee.

Get up. You can't do it on the ground.

There was no break in what followed; she threw

438

punches, ducked punches, deflected kicks and had kicks deflected. She was quicker than any of them. She struck two of them in the balls and was vaguely aware of one of them sinking to his knees. She poked another in both eyes. He wheeled away, his hands covering his face. The pair in front joined the struggle.

She could have taken the five individually but, collectively, they were too many. One of them had a knife. She felt the first cut as a dart of hot pain across her back. The second ran down her left biceps. As she spun away from a third, somebody landed a kick in the small of her back and that was it. Once she was on the ground again, they set about her; punching, scratching, swearing, kicking, spitting. Her lip split. So did the skin over her right eyebrow. One of them held her entire throat in his huge, filthy hand and squeezed. She gagged. It felt as though his fingers would break through the skin. He shifted his body so that he was kneeling on her arms, pinning them to the ground. Her jacket ripped open, she felt hands tearing at her clothes, heard the whisper of a knife slicing through her shirt. Two hands fumbled with the top of her trousers. She bucked furiously. Two punches to the pit of the stomach blasted away the rest of her fight. She felt buttons popping, fingers tugging at the black cotton. One boot was already gone.

She looked up at the face above her. Brown stumps for teeth, a purple birthmark on his left cheek, small grey eyes, a grin that was getting wider. The air was soured by his foetid breath and rancid body odour. The second boot was off. Her trousers followed, dirty nails scratching her from hip to ankle. She felt rough palms on her thighs, fingers tugging at her knicker-elastic.

'Get off her.'

The command carried authority. It was Yuri, the driver, his authority reinforced by the nine-millimetre automatic in his right hand. Later, he told them.

Two of them hauled her up a metal staircase and into a supervisor's office. Under Yuri's supervision, they stripped her down to her bloodstained T-shirt and knickers, bound her to a chair, her wrists tied behind her back, each ankle taped to a wooden leg. Yuri opened both the windows. Snow blew in. He didn't want her to be too comfortable, he said. Then he told one of them to drive the man with the injured eyes to a clinic. That left three: the two who were sent back to the shed floor and Yuri, who settled himself in front of a television in the next-door office. A partition window allowed him a complete view of Stephanie. She saw him warming his hands over a gas heater. Hers had lost all feeling. She couldn't tell whether it was the cold or whether the binding around her wrists had cut off the blood supply.

She looked around. A desk with an old typewriter and two telephones. A coffee mug with pencils and biros standing in it. A calendar on the wall with a team photo: Spartak Moscow, 1998. A grey metal cupboard in one corner, packing boxes in another. The floor was a wafer-thin brown carpet laid onto bare concrete.

She managed to ignore the cuts and bruises but the cold chewed its way through skin and flesh, heading for the bones, and for the marrow inside. She closed her eyes and sent herself somewhere hot. An island, a beach, a dazzling sun overhead. She felt herself in warm water, the salt on her skin, the sun burning her, luminous coral beneath her and, surrounding her, fish of every colour ever imagined.

*   *   *

Much later, she heard approaching engines. They echoed as they entered the shed. Outside, the sky was darkening. Stephanie was shivering uncontrollably, her arms and legs now a greyish blue. The engines ceased, replaced by slamming car doors, voices, footsteps on concrete, then on the metal steps. Yuri moved out of his warm office to greet them on the gantry. A group appeared on the other side of the window. Six, seven, eight . . .

The door opened. The first man into the office was Vatukin. His breath froze around his head, which was partly hidden beneath a black wool cap pulled low to the brow. His quilted jacket made him look comically inflated. He clapped his hands together vigorously.

'It's colder in here than it is outside. Shit, it's colder in here than it is in Vorkuta.' Unpleasant laughter from those behind him. 'You should watch out, Petra. Dressed like that, you're going to catch something nasty.'

More laughter from the sycophants. Stephanie watched him come close. Yuri was behind him, to the left.

'The great Petra Reuter.' He turned his back on her. 'We'll see . . .'

He spun round and punched her, catching her on the right cheek, just below the eye. Her head snapped back, hitting the top slat of the chair. More jokes for his audience, more amusement. On such a cold evening, he told them, it was important to take some exercise to keep the blood flowing. He punched her again and broke her nose. Her hot blood steamed as it spilled over her mouth and down the front of her T-shirt.

'So, are we ready now?'

He worked the fingers of one hand against the other, stretching the leather over his knuckles. Then he asked about Komarov. What was their relationship? Personal, she mumbled. The answer earned her a slap. Was Komarov a target, a dupe, or a conspirator of some sort? She shook her head at every choice and suffered the consequences. Vatukin changed tack.

'What about Roskov? How did you find him?'

Stephanie imagined Valentina Rudenko in her place and felt sick. She lied, was punished, and lied again. Vatukin was careful not to hit her too hard. She was aware of that and clung to it: *he needs answers to his questions.* That was what she told herself. But in the back of her mind she knew that it was a hope, not a certainty.

'What did Roskov talk to you about?'

'Nothing.'

'You were seen.'

'He didn't have time. Your people turned up . . .'

'When we find that stinking harridan who runs the stall, we'll get every fucking word of it. So do yourself a favour and earn some goodwill. What did you talk about?'

Stephanie shook her head.

'Maybe you need some encouragement?'

She didn't move.

'My nuts are freezing into ice cubes. Somebody give me a cigarette.'

Yuri handed over the one he was already smoking. Vatukin took it and crouched in front of Stephanie, balancing himself by holding onto her left thigh.

'Even with a glove on my hand, I can tell that you're frozen.' He blew on the tip of the cigarette. It glowed a fierce orange, shedding tiny sparks. 'Feel like talking yet?'

Stephanie clenched her teeth. Vatukin pressed the tip of the cigarette against her right elbow. Her nerves erupted. She tried not to cry out. But did. Her whole body in spasm, the local fire spreading through every part of her. The contact seemed to last for ever. She could hear it, she could smell it. And then it was over. Vatukin stood up, took a casual drag from the cigarette and passed it over his shoulder without bothering to look round.

'Thanks, Yuri. Don't smoke it all at once. I might need it again.'

There was no more hitting. Vatukin milked the greater threat of the burns instead. Through the white noise raging in her brain, Stephanie found herself thinking how slick he was. No fumbling novice, this one. Quite the professional. He stretched four burns over an hour, three on the elbow, one on her side. At one point, he'd lifted her T-shirt and held a fresh cigarette close enough to her left nipple for Stephanie to feel the heat. He'd let her imagine the pain. The best work was always done in the head. To begin with, at least.

'You really should speak to me, Petra. There's no point in trying to protect yourself. Or anybody else, for that matter.' The softer his tone, the more sinister he sounded. 'Kostya doesn't need protecting. Not by you, not by anyone. How do you think he's managed to survive? If either of you needs protecting from the other, it's you from him.'

He's lying.

'I know things about you, Petra. I know about Koba.'

How? It doesn't matter how. Don't fall for it.

'But you don't know who Koba is, do you? Or have you chosen not to look too hard? Maybe that's it. Maybe you're beginning to suspect. Maybe you've suspected right from the start.'

He clutched her left shoulder. Then squeezed, gently at first, then harder, pushing and pulling, digging his fingers into her frozen flesh, finding the damaged nerves. She wanted to give him nothing but failed. At first a gasp, then a whimper, finally a sob. She was squirming for him.

Vatukin shook his head. 'There's still a lot of damage. It must have been painful at the time. But if you jump into a lift shaft, what can you expect?'

The first time they'd made love, Komarov had guessed. Now Vatukin. What did that mean? Did it mean anything at all? She was too confused to work it out. Which was part of the strategy, she was sure. She tried to blank the idea from her mind, but the possibility, once imagined, could not be erased.

'You were after the disk, naturally. The disk that Salibi acquired. There's no point in denying it. Everyone was after the disk. Kostya knew that, of course.'

Despite everything, surprise. And it must have showed because Vatukin looked thrilled.

'You didn't know? It's true. He was the one who killed Rogachev in Paris, and that British SIS officer. I forget his name but Kostya took the disk from his coat pocket. Made it look like an accident and bumped into him as they were leaving the brasserie on the rue du Faubourg Saint Honoré. Rogachev never even noticed him.'

Stephanie refused to believe it.

'Kostya had his reasons. As for the disk, he didn't

444

know where it had come from or what its true value was. But Salibi did. As for poor old Oleg . . . well, Tsentralnaya was going nowhere under his leadership. We had Kazaks screwing up our business in Yekaterinburg and Novosibirsk, we even had Chechen dogs interfering here in Moscow. Can you imagine? Anyway, he's no longer around and those fuckers have been put back in their place. So it's business as usual. But you know what this means, don't you?'

Stephanie's head was swimming.

'There is no Koba. Which brings me to the last thing. You know Marcel Claesen? Of course you do. And he knows you. He identified you on New Year's Eve. That's why he was there. I needed to be sure. And now I am. You took the Arkan contract, didn't you?'

What point was there in denying it? She shrugged a little.

'Who hired you?'

She shook her head.

'*Who hired you?*'

'I don't know.'

'Yuri, light me another cigarette, will you?'

'I don't meet my clients.'

'That's shit.'

'It's true. It's better for them, better for me.'

'So how do you get work?'

'Through Stern.'

'Who the fuck's Stern? Sounds Jewish.'

'He's an information broker. Works over the Internet. He's never been seen.'

'That's shit too.'

'It's true. No one knows who he is. That's why it works.'

Vatukin's temper was fraying, the sinews popping in his jaw. 'Tell me who hired you to assassinate Arkan.'

Struggling for breath, Stephanie whispered her reply. 'I told you, I don't know.'

Vatukin lowered himself so that she could see his face. 'I'm going to make you a generous offer. If you tell me who hired you, I'll shoot you in the head. If you don't, I'll leave you to these bastards for a couple of hours. And then one of them will shoot you in the head.'

She didn't bother to say anything. Vatukin stood up and reached into his jacket pocket. She expected a gun. Instead, he withdrew a device with a metal claw at the end. He pressed something with his thumb and the device fizzed loudly, electric blue light dancing between the sharpened points of the claw.

'Remember this morning at Luzhniki? I'm going to give you one more chance. Who hired you to assassinate Arkan?'

'Get lost.'

Vatukin lifted her T-shirt and planted the prod between her breasts. She screamed, then passed out. When she came to, she was trembling. Her eyes were blurred by tears. The saliva that dribbled from her lower lip was a rosy pink.

She heard Vatukin say to Yuri, 'I want her dead by eleven. Use one of the Trabbies and dump it at Ramenki like last time. You got that?'

'Sure.'

'We're going to White Square. You come by when you're finished. I want you there by eleven thirty. That gives you a couple of hours with her here before you head out to Ramenki.'

'Okay.'

'And Yuri . . .'

'Yes?'

'You boys can fuck her as much as you like, but I want her alive when that car goes up in flames.'

Alone in the office, she could still see them through the grimy glass. They were on the gantry, talking. The immediate effects of the electric shock were passing, the cold taking over where the pulse had left off. A wave of nausea swept over her.

How many of them were there in total? Seven at least, maybe eight or nine. Vatukin disappeared, taking three with him. She watched more silent conversation. Yuri made a call. She heard engines starting – one vehicle, then two – then fading away once they were clear of the shed. Several minutes passed before Yuri opened the door and sauntered back into the office. Two brutes wandered in after him.

'Which one of you ugly bastards wants to warm her up for me?'

Dread pooled in her stomach. She tried to partition body and mind. As a prostitute, it had been a trick performed daily, hourly, half-hourly. At any time of the day or night. After a while, it had become instinctive. To keep a part of herself to herself, locked away, protected and private. Divorced from her body, it had mattered less what anonymous strangers did to it. It had made it easier to cope with the pain, the disgust, the humiliation. The alternative was panic, then hysteria. From her own experience, and from the experience of others, that was worse.

The stillness started in the head and then, like an

447

anaesthetic, spread through the rest of her. The body was reduced to matter and nothing more.

She saw a shadow moving along the gantry towards the office door. Another man. After a while, the numbers would cease to matter. Some small part of her was thinking ahead – past the ones in the room and all the others – to a moment where she might break free. As long as there was hope, she would tolerate anything.

The door opened. The man closest to her unfastened his belt buckle. It sounded unreasonably loud, like a hearty thump. And then he was falling forward, knees buckling. The second man began to turn. Another thump, then a third. He, too, started to crumple. Yuri's eyes widened. A fourth shot propelled him back across the desk. The partition window was splattered crimson.

Josef Bergstein stepped over the first body. In one hand, a Browning with a silencer attached, in the other, a knife with a short blade.

'We don't have much time.' He knelt on the floor and cut away the tape binding her ankles to the chair legs. 'I had to wait until there were fewer of them. Before, there were too many.'

'Before?'

'When Vatukin was here.'

'How did you . . .'

'I wasn't following you. I was following him.'

'I don't understand.'

He offered her a glimpse of a smile. 'Retirement doesn't suit me.' When she shook her head, he said, 'You didn't really think I'd do nothing, did you?'

Her feet free, he moved behind her and took the knife to the cord round her wrists.

'There are six more downstairs, all armed to the teeth.'

'How did you get up here?'

'You may have the speed of youth on your side but I have years of experience on mine.'

She tried to stand but her legs gave way. Bergstein caught her. She put an arm round his shoulder, he hooked an arm round her back. Her hip flexors were cramping. She tried to stretch. Her thighs and calf muscles creaked. She couldn't feel her feet at all.

'Cold and inertia,' he said. 'It'll pass. Let's go.'

On the gantry, they turned right. Below, three men huddled by a black Land-Rover, one of them on a mobile. At the end of the gantry, there was an emergency exit. Bergstein tried the handle. Locked.

'I'm going to shoot it open,' he whispered. 'Once I do, we've got seconds, nothing more. Do you think you can run?'

Stephanie nodded. 'Somehow.'

He pointed the gun, raised a hand to shield his eyes and was about to fire when Stephanie grabbed him by the wrist. She pointed to the frame of the door. It was welded shut. Bergstein blanched and, for the first time, Stephanie was truly scared. Before, there had seemed little point.

They headed for the steps at the other end of the gantry and descended as quietly as they could. They were halfway down when they were spotted.

'Back!' Bergstein barked at her, pushing her up the staircase.

From below, she heard shouts and the sound of running feet. There was a single shot, then a volley. Bergstein retaliated, the silencer damping each crack.

449

Someone cried out. She heard a gun hitting concrete. Then she heard a dull cough directly behind her.

Through the metal beneath her feet, she felt the reverberation of his falling body. She spun round. Bergstein was clutching his stomach, blood leaking from between his fingers. But his mind was still working. He fired back and Stephanie saw two men throw themselves behind a large drum of coiled steel.

She held out her hand. 'Come on!'

A bullet passed overhead, a window shattered.

'No . . .'

'Give me your hand!'

'You go.'

'No.'

He let loose another round. '*Go!* Find them. Make them pay.'

'I'm not leaving you.'

He shot her a look, part anger, part plea. 'Do it for Boris. For his mother. Do it for me.'

Stephanie was paralysed.

'Contact Stern,' Bergstein gasped. 'He has something for you.'

'*What?*'

'What's the matter with you? Have you forgotten who you are?'

No. I know who I am. For the first time since Belgrade, I'm Petra Reuter.

Bullets ricochet off metal, splintering concrete. At best, Bergstein can buy me seconds. We look at each other for the last time. Then I turn round and sprint towards a rectangular window halfway between the steps and the sealed emergency exit. I hurl myself through the glass, twisting to one side, trying to gather myself into a ball. Just as I was taught. I'm on Central Park West again, leaping into the unknown. I explode into the night, shrouded in thousands of glass fragments. I start to drop, then hit the wall. My left shoulder erupts. Again. Concrete rubs skin from my left thigh and arm. I fall onto the fire escape, tumbling to the landing below.

I'm aware of my injuries but adrenaline drives me on. I'm at the bottom of the fire escape before my mind catches up with my body. The first priority is to clear the area. The second is warmth.

I run barefoot along the side of the shed. The soles of my feet don't hurt yet – they're too numb to feel anything – but they will. The ice is as sharp as broken glass. More gunfire means he's still alive. For the moment. There are four cars parked outside the shed. Two of them have keys in the ignition. Left there, no doubt, by men who jumped out of their cars at the first sound of shooting and ran to investigate the source.

I choose the Mercedes. My frozen fingers fumble with the ignition. It's an automatic. I select 'drive', release the handbrake and hit the accelerator. My lifeless naked foot slips off the pedal. The vehicle lurches. I try again and the wheels spin beneath me. A man staggers out of the shed through a side door, clutching his ribs with his left hand, a gun in his right. There's no time to pull away. Instead, I veer towards him. He fires. The passenger wing mirror shatters. The bumper clips him, then the passenger side of the vehicle mashes him against the corrugated concrete wall. I feel his body ripple through the fabric of the car.

Through the main gates and onto the rough road without checking for oncoming traffic. It's only now that I realize I'm driving in darkness. I switch on the lights. There are virtually no road signs but I know roughly where I am. I head away from central Moscow. Within five minutes, I'm on the outer ring road, travelling north. I can't afford to draw attention to myself so I keep my speed down and try to drive smoothly, which becomes increasingly difficult as my body temperature starts to rise and the shaking begins again.

This is the golden hour. I look at the clock. Ten past nine. I subtract the five minutes that have elapsed since I got clear; I have until five past ten. The golden hour is the first hour, the hour of advantage, the hour in which others are trying to assess damage and formulate a plan. In a crisis, you have to make the golden hour count.

It's twenty-five past nine when I peel off the outer ring road, half past by the time I kill the engine outside the entrance to the block in Bibirevo. I see no activity in the hall but there are two well-clad figures in the distance, scuttling from one sheltered door to another. I switch off the lights and take a deep breath. There's no alternative.

I get out. The cold feels worse now that I'm marginally warmer. In the boot, I find the puncture repair kit and take out the jack. Then I lock the car and head for the building. A couple step out of the lift. The sight of me stops them in their tracks. A filthy woman wearing a bloodstained T-shirt and knickers, holding a car jack in her right hand, with three blistering cigarette burns at the elbow. They see bruising, blood, a broken nose, a black eye, a swollen mouth and a riot of matted dark hair. They're too stunned to say anything. They don't even ask if I'm all right.

I step past them, take the lift and pray that it won't break down. There's no one along my corridor, which is a relief. I don't have my keys. Summoning all my strength, I swing the jack at the fragile lock on the front door. It fractures at the second attempt and I creep into the flat. If anyone is waiting for me, this will be the end of it. I don't have the strength for a fresh opponent.

I wedge the front door shut behind me. I've got a list in my head that needs a tick in every box. The kitchen clock says it's nine thirty-four. In the bathroom, I run my head under a tap, rinse my face clean of dirt and blood, then wash my hands. Most of my body can wait but the nose can't. It's too crooked. I take the tip between thumb and forefinger and move it. It seems so soft, almost liquid. I can feel the grate of the connecting tissue. There's a pronounced bump on the side. I secure it between the fingers of both hands, take a deep breath and then press. Short and sharp. There's a gross crack, a bolt of pain through my sinuses, a squirt of blood from both nostrils.

It's not perfect but it's better. I clean away the blood with more cold water, dry myself, then hastily smear foundation over the worst of the facial bruising. I dab Vaseline onto the cut over my right eye. In the bedroom, I take the holdall out of the cupboard and dress: two T-shirts, a pair of jeans, two pairs of socks, boots and a thick navy-blue Polartec fleece. I grab the mini Mag-Lite and then go back to the bathroom, where I sweep everything into the holdall. Time to go.

Back in the Mercedes, I drive fifty yards to the locked garages. The car clock says it's nine forty-four. I get out and run to the pigeon hut. Behind it, I brush the weeds aside and cast the torch over the ground. I sweep away the snow. When the tiny mound reveals itself, I use the jack to scratch through the frozen dirt. The skeleton key is where I left it. I unlock the padlock and enter the hut. Grouped tightly together, the pigeons stir, cooing to me. At the back of the hut, the Mag-Lite finds the grille. I lift it clear of the drain and release the black cord from an iron strut. At the end of the cord hangs the plastic pouch containing the identity that Cyril Bradfield created for me.

Irene Marceau, a Swiss woman.

I dump the Mercedes outside Kazansky Station at eight minutes past ten. The golden hour has elapsed. What is Vatukin doing about it? As I cross the street to Leningradsky Station, I can barely walk. I'm running on empty.

Into the booking hall and up the stairs to the small office where they sell tickets for Tallinn and Helsinki. At last, a small stroke of luck. It's not busy. I pick a window with a woman server. Puffy-faced with badly peroxided hair, she looks tired.

'The Tolstoi. Am I too late?'

She stares at my cuts and bruises. Then she glances at her watch. 'Not yet.'

'A single.'

'To Helsinki?'

I nod. 'Is it full?'

'Quite.'

'Is there any chance of a compartment to myself?'

She consults her computer. 'Not in second class. But there are three first-class compartments that . . .'

'I'll take one.'

'It's two berths.'

'I don't care.'

She begins to process the ticket. I unzip the nylon pouch and bring out a roll of rubles. She arches an eyebrow. The part of me that is Petra sees what's going on behind her eyes and decides to make a pre-emptive strike.

'I'm finally leaving the bastard,' I mutter.

She looks up at my battered face again. 'Are you all right?'

From somewhere, I find theatrical tears. 'I will be.'

I board the Tolstoi at ten fifteen, ten minutes after the golden hour has elapsed. At ten seventeen, precisely on schedule, the train pulls away from Leningradsky Station.

26

The train crawled through the city, heading north-west. Stephanie closed the sliding door to her compartment and secured the latch. It was warm and stuffy, with two equally uncomfortable berths. She looked at herself in the mirror on the back of the door and wanted to cry. Not because of her appearance but because of the reasons behind it. Boris Bergstein, Josef Bergstein, Salman Rifat, Marcel Claesen and all the others, all brought together through her.

The darkness outside her window lent a sense of security. Clear of Moscow, the last of her adrenaline burnt, her injuries began to hurt again. She checked her nose in the mirror. Not great but good enough. Around her nostrils, the blood had dried black. In the holdall, there was half a tube of Savlon. She rubbed some onto the cigarette burns, which stung furiously, and onto her cuts and grazes. Then she took off her boots and socks to examine the soles of her feet – lacerated and filthy; she plastered them with the rest of the cream.

She lay down and heard the carriage attendant moving up and down the corridor outside. A cart from the restaurant car passed through. There was a knock on the door. *Anything to eat or drink?* Nothing, she replied.

Very slowly, the metronomic bang and clatter of the train lulled her to sleep. Later, she was woken by raised voices from another compartment. It was two thirty-five, wherever she was, and early evening in Manhattan, where Komarov was. Cocktail time, she imagined, in some skyscraper bar with a pianist playing Cole Porter or Sinatra. She ached all over and was cold, despite the heating. Outside, the pitch black was emphasized by the infrequency of any other light; an occasional pinprick – a weak yellow spot from some distant farm marooned in the middle of nowhere – or the flash of some passing trackside lamp.

Josef and Boris Bergstein, uncle and nephew, one killed by her, the other killed while saving her, both in the same location. She felt it ought to mean something but knew better; death was rarely significant. Almost always, it was routine.

When she next woke, her muscles had seized. It took twenty minutes of painful stretching to work some blood round her body. During the on-board customs inspection at Vyborg, she played the Swiss tourist, pretending to speak no Russian. The officials regarded her with suspicion, then concern. One of them spoke broken German. She'd been mugged, she explained, but it had all been dealt with in the proper way by the police in Moscow. Now, she just wanted to forget about it and to visit her friends in Finland.

The Tolstoi pulled into Helsinki station on time at eleven thirty. It was a beautiful morning; not a cloud in the sky, minus fifteen Celsius. Before leaving the terminus, she called Magenta House from a pay-phone.

'Good morning, this is Adelphi Travel.'

'I need to speak to Alexander.'

'There's no one of that name –'

'For God's sake.'

'I'm sorry. You must have the wrong number.'

'Market-East-one-one-six-four-R-P.'

'One moment, please.'

It was Rosie Chaudhuri who came onto the line. 'Stephanie, where are you?'

'Helsinki. Look, I need you to give him a message. It's urgent.'

After the call, she crossed the station square and made her way up Vilhonkatu. On the three floors above the Hamlet restaurant, there were three separate hotels, each occupying a single floor. Stephanie took the stairs to the Station Hostel on the second floor. The reception desk was a table with a strip of old Formica tacked to the front. Behind it sat a skeletal man with a greasy ponytail, in black leather trousers and a lilac long-sleeved T-shirt with a fading image of Robert Plant on the front. Stephanie guessed he was in his fifties. He glanced at her over a pair of incongruous half-moons.

'A room, please. Number four.'

The request for a specific room caught his attention. Her bruises intensified it. 'Four?'

'At the back, overlooking the courtyard.'

He consulted the keys on the board to the left. 'It's already occupied. You can take five. That overlooks the courtyard.'

'I want four.'

'I told you . . .'

She'd already begun to peel some of Irene Marceau's dollar bills from the roll. 'I'll pay extra, of course.'

A quarter of an hour later, the transaction complete, she was installed. The previous occupant had been relieved to be relocated at no extra expense when he'd learned that his room had a rodent problem that needed immediate attention. Stephanie locked the door and opened the window. The courtyard was gloomy, an airless well created by the grey backs of four unloved buildings. To the left, the old metal pipe leading down from the gutter. And there it was, attached to the back of the pipe, nearly touching the wall. A small pewter case that was almost invisible in the pipe's shadow. Stephanie checked the ledge. No packed snow or ice. She climbed onto it and, clutching the frame for support, reached across. The case was hooked onto two small screws. It was a little stiff. Not surprising, really. It had been there for three years. But it came away easily enough. Back inside her room, she prised the case apart to reveal a small key on a chain.

It was a ten-minute walk to the twenty-four-hour University Pharmacy on Mannerheimintie, where she bought a selection of disinfectants and dressings. Back in her room, she picked the grit and dirt out of the soles of her feet, cleansed them and washed them with antiseptic. When she'd finished attending to herself, she rested for an hour, then walked to the Senaatintori branch of the Merita-Nordbanken on Aleksanterinkatu. The bank's lobby was cavernous and warm with a stone floor, a high ceiling and a huge, solid stretch of green marble from behind which the staff served. Stephanie presented her key and was shown to the vault containing the safe-deposit boxes. Alone, she removed all the contents of the box and placed them in the holdall. Back in her room at the Station Hostel, she spread the contents across her bed.

Franka Müller, the most complete identity Petra Reuter had ever had available to her. When she'd been living in the south of France as Stephanie Schneider, she'd regarded the Müller alias as her ultimate insurance policy. In her mind, she'd felt that all she ever needed was a window of twelve hours to get her to Finland. She'd always believed that once she was in Helsinki – once she was Franka Müller – she would be safe.

On her way back to the Station Hostel, she stopped at the Lasipalatsi Multimedia Centre, where she had to wait for half an hour for an Internet terminal to become available.

Hello, Oscar. I believe I've been sent something.

By a former KGB hit-man, too. Consorting with the enemy, Petra? Frankly, I'm shocked.

I doubt that. I have a suspicion that the two of you were acquaintances.

Were?

I'm afraid so. Yesterday, in Moscow.

Not by you, I hope.

No. He died saving me.

That doesn't surprise me. I always felt he was too human for his profession.

What did he leave me?

Stephanie entered the Strindberg Café on Pohjoieses-planadi at five thirty, as agreed. She joined the queue at the counter. The place was busy, the clientele a broad mix: middle-aged men in tweed jackets and grey flannel trousers, women in fur-trimmed coats and make-up, students with pierced nostrils and henna rinses. Behind the glass, there were salads, sandwiches and pastries, but Stephanie couldn't think about food so asked for hot chocolate instead. As she collected her change, she saw that Alexander was already there, sitting at a table in the corner, his back to the window. The most secluded spot in the café, naturally. His gabardine rain-coat was neatly folded beside him, a cup of coffee in front of him.

'Jesus Christ . . .'

'It's not as bad as it looks.'

'If it was, you'd be dead.'

She sat down. 'You really know how to make a girl feel special, don't you?'

'My flight got in early. I tried to call you but your phone wasn't on.'

'It's somewhere in Moscow. Along with everything else. How long have we got?'

'I'm booked on the last plane back. It leaves at seven thirty. I've got a car waiting so we have an hour, maybe a bit more.'

'Rosie told you everything?'

'Everything that you told her, yes.'

'That's all there is. There is no Koba.'

'So you say.'

'But the trade goes ahead the day after tomorrow in New York.'

He took a small notepad out of his jacket pocket. 'Details?'

Stephanie shook her head. 'No.'

'We need to alert the US authorities.'

'There isn't time. Not for them to get it right. They'll screw it up. I'm the only one who stands a chance.'

'You don't look as though you could stand up, let alone stand a chance.'

'I'll manage.'

'Holding out on me is a bad idea, Stephanie.'

'So's screwing me.'

He frowned. 'I'm not with you.'

'That's why you're here. This is the last time we'll see each other. I don't want it to be like last time. I want us both to know in advance what's going to happen. After New York, we're even. When it's over, I'm going to disappear again. And this time, I'm retiring.'

'What if you can't stop the trade? You're playing with lives, Stephanie.'

'Guess what? I'm past all that. I don't care. This is the only way it works. Eventually, I'll get the information to you. You might have to wait a month or two but . . .'

'Well, you've got it all sorted out, haven't you?' The tone in his voice made her nervous. He took a sip of coffee. Alexander wasn't the sort to fight battles he knew he couldn't win. Instead, he'd shift the territory until they were fighting a battle he knew he could win. Which was why he said, 'Now tell me about Konstantin Komarov.'

Coming from his mouth, the name sounded corrupted.

Stephanie struggled with a sense of dread. 'What about him?'

'How does he fit in to all this?'

'He doesn't.'

'Really?'

'He did a lot of business with Oleg Rogachev and now he's doing a lot of business with Vatukin. But they're not that close.'

'What about you and Komarov? Are you that close?'

It was a question asked only because the answer was already known. But she still couldn't tell him the truth.

She shook her head. From beneath the folded rain-coat, he produced the portable DVD player that Rosie Chaudhuri had taken to Zurich. He opened it, pressed play and slid it across the table to her.

'I don't think you'll need the headphones. I think the image speaks for itself.'

In flickering colour, a room she recognized, the vantage point high in one corner. Where, she now remembered, there was a vent. Just above the door. Painted white like the walls. It was her bedroom at Old Court Place. She saw herself straddling Komarov, the white duvet cast aside, crumpled on the floor. Her head thrown back, her breasts quivering, Komarov's fingers digging into her buttocks as they pressed themselves against each other. Despite the marginal clarity, their hunger was self-evident. She pressed stop and snapped the lid shut.

'Is there no end to you?' she whispered.

'Do you behave like that with all the men you're not that close to?'

'You recorded me? In my own home? *How could you?*'

All too easily. She knew that. He let his silence work on her. Despite some spectacular competition, Steph-anie had never hated anyone more than she hated Alex-ander at that moment. Her fury was so incandescent, she couldn't bring herself to speak. For the first time in her life, she felt she could have killed for pleasure.

'Let's talk about him.'

'I've got nothing to say to you, you festering bastard. It's none of your fucking business.'

'Really?'

'He's not Koba and that's all there is to it.'

Alexander smiled icily. 'A semantic distinction, at best.'

'I'm as much Koba as he is.'

'I don't doubt it for a moment. But were you in Paris? Did you kill Oleg Rogachev? Did you shoot James Marshall in the back of the head? Did you steal the disk and sell it to Salibi?'

Stephanie was stunned. 'We had a deal. We *have* a deal. You made a promise. Koba and then you'd let me go.'

'From the start, avenging Marshall was a priority.'

'Only because you believed Koba was responsible.'

'As far as I'm concerned, Komarov is Koba. Just like everyone else.'

'No. Rogachev was the target. Marshall was . . .'

'A mistake? Come on. Komarov is a *threat*.'

'Vatukin is the threat. He's the one talking to Serb renegades.'

'Are you blind? Vatukin is a puppet. Komarov is the key to Vatukin. He speaks to Tsentralnaya, he speaks to all of them. He's the one thing they all have in common.'

'Christ, you *promised*!'

'Grow up, Stephanie.' Simultaneously, Alexander managed to look bored, amused and annoyed. 'Besides, what were you going to do with Komarov? Plan a future, get a mortgage and buy a Volvo? You're no different from anybody else in our world. You take comfort where you find it because relationships are an impossibility.'

'Not true.'

'Tell me of one relationship you've had that's worked.'

'This one.'

A mistake and she knew it the moment she said it.

'You're screwing a rich criminal whom you meet in hotel rooms for a night here, two nights there . . . and you think that's a relationship that's working?'

I could argue with him – I could throw the rest of my hot chocolate over him – but what would be the point? I don't want to associate Alexander with any sense of pleasure on my part, no matter how transitory.

'Men like Komarov don't go to trial,' he says.

'Not if you shoot them.'

'They bribe judges, intimidate jurors, destroy evidence. They murder witnesses. And once they're back on the street, it's business as usual, with all the suffering that goes with that. In any case, we don't necessarily want them to go to trial, do we? Who knows what kind of dirty secrets might be exposed to the light of day?'

I picture the refuge and the children's home in Izmailovo.

'You're wrong,' I tell him, even though I know it's pointless to try to explain.

'Well, it doesn't matter one way or the other. It doesn't concern you. I'm sending someone else.'

'You can't.'

'It's not a matter for discussion, Stephanie.'

'If you kill him, I'll let the trade take place.'

Alexander wags an admonishing finger at me. 'You know, I don't think you would. But even if you did, it wouldn't change anything.'

'You bastard.'

'You don't understand. I'm making a concession. You take care of Vatukin and it's as we were. You walk away.'

'You *don't* understand!'

'Stephanie, they're both already dead.'

'It's not as simple as that.'

'Yes,' he replies, 'it is as simple as that.'

I want to scream but I don't. Because he's right. In his world – the real world – complicated things can be made simple. That's what he does. He provides clear-cut solutions to complex problems. It's what Petra does too.

'Then let me do it.'

There's a long, incredulous silence before he responds. 'You can't be serious.'

Our eyes meet. 'I am.'

'No chance.'

'Please.'

'Leave it alone, Stephanie. Let's keep it anonymous.'

'You owe me this.'

'I don't owe you anything.'

I lean forward and keep my voice lowered but there's no mistaking the force in it. 'You want him dead? Fine. If it has to be done, there's no reason not to let me do it. I know you'll be watching us anyway, just in case. What have you got to lose?'

'I'm afraid you're too good . . .'

'Bullshit.'

'It's true. And we both know it.'

'I give you my word.'

Which raises a sardonic smile. 'That's not really my idea of a cast-iron guarantee.'

'What does it matter to you who does it? You'll still get what you want. A life for a life. After all, that's what this is really about, isn't it?'

I wake up and look out of the window. At first, all I see is cloud. Gradually, though, I see that it's not cloud. It's ice.

465

Greenland, vast and unblemished, an astonishing white expanse as far as the distant horizon. I see a tiny speck speeding across this amazing screen: a Finnair MD-11 bound for New York.

'Can I bring you something? A cappuccino, maybe? Or some water?'

A female flight attendant is looking down at me, smiling pleasantly.

'A cappuccino would be nice.'

Under the blanket, I draw my legs up onto the seat and hug them close to my aching body. The business-class cabin is less than half-full. Most passengers are asleep, one or two are watching movies. I look at my watch. I've been dozing for three hours, which is three hours more than I managed last night at the Station Hostel in Helsinki.

There are twenty-four hours to the trade. Komarov is safe until then because Alexander needs me. Afterwards, we'll try to run, of course. But we won't succeed. Alexander knows my word is worth nothing, which is why I know that Kostya is already under surveillance. A team of four or five, most likely. If they weren't already in place, Alexander would never have agreed to this. We won't see it coming. They'll know all about me and they'll be ready. At the first suspicious sign, they'll kill us both. I can't even rely on being better than them because they'll be good. Boyd will have made sure of that. What a perverse irony. He'd be mortified, I think. I hope. If only he knew . . .

I'm part of Alexander's equation and it's a delicious prospect for him. Do I save myself and kill Kostya? Or do I die with him trying to run for it? Alexander won't be under any illusion about my intention. We know each other too well for a deception as blunt as the promise I made him.

*The flight attendant returns with my cappuccino and I'm
still flying over the blank canvas of Greenland.*

There were two men arguing outside the Seven Joy Coffee Shop. Stephanie crossed Mulberry Street and headed
down the narrow steps to the basement. The corridor
smelt of damp coats, cheap cigars and aniseed. There was
no one in the waiting room at the Wu Lin Dental Practice. She opened the door without knocking. Wu Lin was
on the other side of the room, alone, hunched over a
counter, an Anglepoise lamp illuminating a small dish.

'We closed.'

'Perfect.'

He spun round, frowned at her, then recognized the
face and was alarmed.

'What you doing here?'

She gave him her coldest smile. 'Let's just say, I'm
not here for any root canal work.'

'You don't come here like this. Telephone first.'

'Sorry. No time.'

Which was true. Finnair flight AY005 had touched
down a little late at twenty past four. It had taken
Franka Müller almost three hours to negotiate the for-
malities at JFK and the traffic into Manhattan. Not a
record, she suspected, but not good.

'What you want?'

'A gun.'

'When?'

'Now.'

'I got no gun here.'

'Really?'

Wu Lin shook his head. 'Not safe.'

Stephanie stepped forward, he edged back.

She said, 'Somehow, I get the impression you'd feel a lot safer *with* a gun. Given the lines of business you're in, who knows who might want to take a pop at you. A patient with a poor filling, perhaps. Americans do love to complain. Or maybe someone you sold some hardware to.'

He wasn't sure, she could see that; he recognized her but couldn't remember the exact details of their deal.

'One hour . . .'

'Now.'

'Not possible.'

There were dirty instruments on the tray attached to the dentist's chair. Wu Lin saw Stephanie looking at them and began to cower in the corner. Stephanie said, 'The last time we met, I warned you that cheating me was a mistake.'

It didn't take much. A few veiled threats and out it came, from the back of the drawer beneath the workbench. A Colt Delta Elite, chambered for a ten-millimetre Auto Pistol cartridge. A 1987 US Government model with a blued forged-steel slide and frame, and a black neoprene wraparound grip. She slipped the gun into the rucksack that she'd bought at the Stockmann department store in Helsinki that morning. Which was where she'd also bought a complete set of clothes; in her room at the Station Hostel, she'd discarded all traces of Irene Marceau before heading for the airport at Vantaa.

It was just before nine when Stephanie got out of a cab on Fifth Avenue. Komarov took her into his apartment, closed the door, kissed her on the mouth, then held her face in his hands.

'What happened to you?'

She shook her head. 'Hold me.'

He did, crushing her body against his. 'Is it over?'

'Almost.'

27

Komarov's jacket was folded over the sofa, his tie laid on top. The sleeves of his shirt were rolled to the elbow, a blue Russian Orthodox cross protruding from one, a band of greyish green from the other. He offered her a choice of two chilled Cristall brands, Moskovskaya or Gzelka. Stephanie dumped her rucksack on the floor.

'Moskovskaya.'

He poured a couple of fingers into two tumblers and handed one to her.

'We have tonight and tomorrow night,' she said. 'After that, we run.'

'What about tomorrow, during the day?'

'Nothing out of the ordinary.'

'That *will* be something out of the ordinary.'

'I'm serious, Kostya. They're watching you.'

His smile evaporated. 'Me?'

'I'm not the reason we're running. You are.'

She watched him fail to understand why.

'The Uzbek who was murdered in Voronezh. Was that you?'

He narrowed his eyes. 'You mean, am I really the Don from the Don?'

'Yes.'

'No. I'm not.'

'But he cheated you.'

'And I rewarded the man who killed him.'

470

'You hired someone?'

'He was a bounty hunter. I'd put a price on the Uzbek's head.'

'And what about Oleg Rogachev? Did you kill him?'

Komarov took his time lighting a Chesterfield. 'Who told you that?'

'Is it true?'

Of course it was. He nodded.

'And James Marshall, the SIS officer?'

'They were together. It was the only way to be sure.'

'Christ.'

'Is that what this is about? A British intelligence officer?'

'For you, yes.'

'Why?'

'Rogachev gave Marshall the disk, then you stole it.'

'That's right.'

'What was on it?'

'Information to destroy rivals. Details of their business operations. How they were laundering money. The corporate networks they'd established. Personal bank details. The names and addresses of potential informers. All their points of vulnerability. It was very detailed.'

'And you sold the disk to George Salibi?'

He frowned. 'Of course not. I destroyed it.'

'So what was in his safe?'

'Whatever you found.'

'I found nothing.'

'Exactly. There was a rumour that I sold it to him. I don't know how it started. As for Salibi, I guess he thought there was currency in the rumour. That if people believed he had it, he could use the idea as leverage.'

'But he underestimated the value of the information that was supposed to be on it?'

'Yes. Which was why it became a target for retrieval, not a bargaining chip.'

'Why were you involved in the first place?'

'Oleg and I were quite close. He wanted us to be closer. He wanted me to work for Tsentralnaya and not for myself. I said I wouldn't but he wasn't convinced. He thought I could be persuaded. He told me about the disk and the trade, and I told him I thought he was insane. I said it would lead to a criminal war fought on many fronts and that everyone would lose. But he said that couldn't happen if nobody knew the source.'

'He trusted you enough to tell you this?'

'Why not? I never gave him a reason not to. I made Tsentralnaya a fortune. But I made fortunes for others, too. They trusted me as much. It was an impossible situation. I tried to stop him – I told him it was a cheap shot – but his mind was made up.'

'So when he went to Paris, you followed.'

'If I'd let him go ahead with it, there would have been chaos. And after the chaos, recrimination. That sort of thing never remains a secret. And once his name was out, mine would have followed. Either directly, or by association.'

'And James Marshall?'

'I had the disk but I didn't know what Rogachev had told him.'

'God, what a mess.'

'It could have been a lot worse.'

'I was forced out of retirement to prove that Petra

didn't kill Marshall. And in doing that, I've condemned you.'

'That wasn't your fault. Or even mine. It was really Rogachev's.'

She couldn't be bothered to argue the point. 'There was nothing nuclear on the disk?'

'Like what?'

'Details of smuggled Plutonium-239.'

Komarov shook his head, drained his glass and poured some more. 'Is that why I'm a target?'

'You're a target because they want a life for a life. And there's no way around that.'

'So . . . ?'

'If they suspect you're about to run, they'll kill you. That's why you have to have a normal day. Just go to the office in the morning and return here in the evening. Nothing happens until the day after tomorrow.'

'Why will they wait?'

'Because that's the arrangement I have with them.'

He looked puzzled. 'You?'

'The people out there are back-up.' Stephanie finished her Moskovskaya. 'I'm the one who's supposed to kill you.'

There was no anger. At first, he just looked stunned. She didn't try to explain because she knew that anything she said would only make it worse. She refilled her glass, then handed him the bottle. They drank in silence for a while. When he broke it, he never asked her for details. When they kissed, she could taste the vodka on his tongue. Or was it hers? They held each other, then sat on the sofa, fingers interlocked, knees touching.

'All the things you told me in Moscow,' he whispered. 'All the details of your childhood – where the

473

dogs slept in the kitchen, how the wind sounded in winter, the smell of a late summer evening rising off the fields – they've been going round and round in my head. I've been thinking about the places we visited over Christmas. Places from your past. Your *real* past. There's so much I want to ask you.'

'The day after tomorrow, we'll have all the time we need.'

'Maybe.'

'We will,' Stephanie insisted.

'I don't want to wait that long.'

It's after two. Over four hours, I've peeled away layer after layer of myself. I've resurrected my family, my memories, and I've rediscovered a version of Stephanie Patrick. Not the prettiest girl in her class but the brightest. And the most difficult. The one most likely to succeed but also the one most likely to endure the greatest frustration. I wanted to write. To be a journalist, a foreign correspondent in a place where there was something to fight for. I wanted to be far away from the complacent and feeble public. I wanted to be an actor, or marry a crofter, or join NASA. I wanted to be respected, ignored, loved, reviled. I wanted to be whatever my parents didn't want me to be.

This is the way I was. Kostya's questions and my answers remind me of what I might have become. There is an alternative me and it's impossible to say which of us is real. Perhaps we both are. Just as Petra, in her own way, is real.

Now, I'm not just exhausted, I'm intoxicated. We finished the Moskovskaya and drank a bottle of Saint-Estèphe. More than the alcohol, though, it's the past that has gone to my head.

Kostya leads me into the bedroom where we first made

love. This is where I removed his clothes and saw his tattoos emerge for the first time. That moment has left me with a tattoo of my own. It's on my memory. As he begins to undress me, it occurs to me that he's about to experience something very similar.

My colours reveal themselves gradually. I don't do anything and we don't speak. The scratches are black flakes. Parallel lines from dirty fingernails, down my left thigh, at my throat, encircling my wrist like a bracelet. Bruises of purple, black and blue across my stomach, ribs, breasts, around my eye, down my left arm and over the shoulder. The three cigarette burns on my elbow and the one on my side are purple blisters that sting to look at, let alone touch. When I'm naked, I feel cloaked by him. Gently, he runs the tip of a finger down my crudely set nose.

'Was it Vatukin?'

'He was one of them.'

'Did they . . . ?'

'No.'

He nods grimly but I'm not sure he believes me.

'If I see him again, I'm going to kill him.'

The fingertip reaches my split lip. I kiss it.

'You won't see him again.'

The Somerset Hotel on West 54th Street. According to the information that Josef Bergstein had left her, the rendezvous was at three. Stephanie arrived just after one. On Stern's recommendation, she approached the hotel from the rear. The loading bay had been filled by concrete blocks. So had all the ground-floor windows. Just above the centre of the bay was the bottom of the fire escape. It was out of reach. Stephanie dragged a tea chest out of the alley and placed an upside-down dustbin on top of it. Perched on top of the bin, she remained a foot short of the lowest rung. It was a small jump but large enough to send a jolt through her shoulder. A cloud of pigeons swooped past her. She climbed to the fourth floor before breaking a window and entering the building.

Between the World Wars, through the Fifties and well into the Sixties, the Somerset had been a particular favourite of British visitors to New York. They liked its large rooms and faded grandeur. They were used to the starched, inefficient service. For many, it was home from home. A victim of neglect, the hotel's reputation faded through the Seventies and Eighties; both building and staff had been in need of a renovation that never came. In 1994, the Somerset closed. And nobody noticed.

The Ellington Suite was an expanded version of the suite in which she'd stripped for Anatoli Medayev. Two of the rooms had balconies, one looking onto West 54th Street, the other onto the Museum of Modern Art. Stephanie scoured the dilapidated rooms, found a place to hide, checked the Colt Delta Elite and settled down to wait. It was cold and damp, icy water trickling down one wall. She could see her breath. The air tasted of mould. Outside, the rain cushioned the noise of Manhattan's traffic.

Vatukin and Alexander Kosygin arrived at half past two with three armed bodyguards. Kosygin was wearing an overcoat with a felt collar and a glossy sable hat. With his patrician features and fine clothes, it was hard to picture him as a Soviet Red Army lieutenant-general in Afghanistan. These days, he looked as though he'd regard a drive through the Bronx as a dangerous detour to the Third World.

One of the bodyguards returned to the ground floor. Vatukin smoked a cigarette by the shutters, Kosygin paced anxiously. At ten to three, Vatukin received a call. When it was over, Stephanie heard him tell Kosygin that Bukharin was on his way with the client, who had two men for protection. She recognized the name: the disfigured KGB Alpha veteran who had escorted her to the Somerset for her meeting with Anatoli Medayev. At five past three, there was a muted thump that was barely audible over the rain.

Vatukin said, 'Did you hear that?'

Kosygin shrugged. 'I didn't hear anything.'

Vatukin looked at the two remaining bodyguards. 'Either of you?'

The shorter of them looked sheepish. 'Maybe. I thought . . . I don't know.'

Vatukin sent him to investigate. Stephanie took the Colt out of her pocket. Ninety seconds passed before there was another thump. Louder, closer, everyone heard it.

Kosygin stopped pacing. 'What was that?'

Vatukin called out after the shorter bodyguard. 'Gennadi?'

Nothing.

'Bukharin?'

The silence persisted.

'*Gennadi?*'

Stephanie's heart rose into her mouth. She reversed across the neighbouring reception room, tiptoeing across creaking floorboards. She stepped into the corridor, which was very dark, but where she felt safer, since she was no longer boxed into the suite. Vatukin and Kosygin were arguing, their rising panic evident in their voices.

There was a quiver in the gloom to her right. In a single, fluid movement, she released the Colt's safety-catch, spun round, raised the gun, took aim, squeezed the trigger and . . . hesitated.

It was Natalya. Eyes wide with alarm, mouth open.

For a moment, neither of them moved. Stephanie thought Natalya looked more shocked by her presence than by the gun. She eased the Colt's safety back on and lowered it to her side.

'Petra!' Natalya whispered. 'What are you doing here?'

She was drenched, raindrops sparkling on her long leather coat, her dark red hair dripping.

'What are *you* doing here?'

'What's going on? Where's Vladimir?'

Stephanie was mired in confusion and didn't notice Natalya's hand coming out of the right pocket of her overcoat. Not until it was too late. She was clutching a Glock 21 with a silencer attached. Before Stephanie could react, Natalya had pressed the tip of the silencer against the bridge of her nose. She smiled, then held out her left hand. Carefully, Stephanie surrendered the Colt, grip first.

'Now turn around and go in.'

The moment they saw them, Vatukin and Kosygin stopped talking. The bodyguard looked to Vatukin for guidance but he was looking at Natalya, then at Stephanie, who saw the brushed aluminium attaché case on the floor beside Kosygin. A prototype from Yevgeny Vlasko's original design? Natalya shifted away from Stephanie so that she had a clear view of everyone in the room. And so that Stephanie was outside of any immediate striking range.

It wasn't clear to Stephanie which of them Vatukin was more astonished to see. 'Natalya? What are you doing here?'

'Perhaps you should ask Petra.'

'I'm asking both of you! And what's happened to Gennadi?'

'The same thing that happened to Dmitri.'

For a man who had once headed the mighty Fifteenth Directorate, Kosygin looked completely stunned. He seemed to have stopped functioning.

Natalya said, 'I guess you're waiting for Bukharin to turn up. But then you probably thought he was in that coffee shop on Union Square a little earlier.'

'What are you talking about?'

'The call he made ten minutes ago. That was from a diner on Broadway. I was with him . . .'

Which is when I get it. The first time I saw Natalya, I thought I might have seen her before. It was at the Trump Taj Mahal in Atlantic City. She was in Salibi's enclosure, I was with Boris Bergstein. I remember thinking that she looked vaguely familiar. I thought she might have been a model.

Vatukin is still talking – and getting angrier by the word – when I murmur, 'Belgrade. The Inter-Continental.'

Suddenly, Natalya's no longer interested in what her lover has to say. She looks at me, eyes aflame. 'What was that?'

'You were there. Just behind him.' She was wearing a long raincoat that day, too. Dark grey, I think, not black leather. 'I saw you.'

'Go on.'

'Arkan.'

'Very good.'

Vatukin falls silent.

'Who are you?' I ask.

Kosygin finally finds his voice. 'Vladimir, what is this?'

He might as well not be in the room. In fact, she and I could be alone.

'You're not Natalya Markova, are you?'

She shakes her head.

'I'll bet you're not from Omsk, either.'

In German, she says, 'I'm not even Russian.'

'But you're not German. Your accent . . .'

'My name is Dragica Maric.'

'You're a Serb?'

'Yes.'

Vatukin's mouth opens but nothing comes out.

I make another leap. 'Central Park West?'

'Right again.'

'So the authorities really were *looking for a woman . . .'*

'For two. They caught me on CCTV going in. This raincoat, a beret, sunglasses. And then there was you. They assumed we were the same person.' She smiles and, this time, there's genuine affection in it. 'Which, of course, we are.'

How true. Wasn't that what we said – what we felt – at Vatukin's dacha?

The bodyguard panicked but Dragica was far too quick for him. Two suppressed rounds from the Glock. The first caught him in the knee, the second in the chest. His weapon spiralled clear of his hand. As he fell, Vatukin reached into his coat pocket. Without a blink, Dragica killed him. First shot. But she added two more for good measure. Which left Kosygin, who was clearly un-armed, to judge by his quivering terror. Rather patheti-cally, he raised his hands.

Dragica said, 'If only his old friends at the Fifteenth Directorate could see him now.'

'Is this the way it was supposed to be?' Stephanie asked.

'Apart from you, yes.'

'All the way back to Rogachev?'

She nodded. 'Tsentralnaya was the organization with the closest links to the Fifteenth Directorate and to Serbia. And Rogachev was the head of Tsentralnaya. So . . .'

'And when he turned out to be harder to manipulate than you thought, you earmarked Vatukin. So then there was the disk. And you needed an outsider for that. Komarov was perfect because he was close but not on the inside. All you then had to do was ensure that he – along with everyone else – suspected what was on the disk.'

'All those details about Rogachev's rivals – they *were* on the disk.'

'Which he destroyed. But the rumour needed to be fuelled, hence Salibi.'

'Correct. We don't have the money to buy what's in that aluminium case.'

'We being?'

Dragica's smile was crooked. 'Do you want the name of an organization? I could make up one for you, if you like.'

'What are you going to do with the Marburg Variant U-13?'

Her shrug was offhand. 'Something . . . *spectacular*.'

Stephanie felt her pulse slow. 'You're actually going to use it?'

'Yes.'

'No threats, no leverage?'

Dragica looked unrepentant. 'No.'

'What will that achieve?'

'In my country, the damage is done. It doesn't matter any more. All we can do is show that an action has a consequence.'

'Have you seen what the weapon will do?'

'Yes.'

'And that doesn't make a difference to you?'

'My family were killed by a missile fired from an American aircraft during the bombing of Serbia. That didn't make a difference. To them, to me, to the men who murdered them. The result is the same. I'm the only one left now. Do you know how that feels?'

She did but she said nothing. The more she learned, the closer they were to one another. When Stephanie looked at Natalya, she saw Petra looking back at her. Behind the eyes, she knew, there was no compassion, just cold logic. And hurt.

Dragica looked across at Kosygin. 'Bring me the case.'

He glanced at Stephanie as though she might have some influence.

'*Now!*'

He picked it up and started to walk towards her. 'You need to be shown how to –'

'I may have good legs and a pair of nice tits, Kosygin, but I'm not an idiot.'

He reached for one of the catches. 'All the same, I think it would be better . . .'

'Leave it.'

The first catch released.

'*Leave it!*'

He fumbled with the second and she fired. One shot

to the throat. His head snapped back, his body sagged, the case clattered to the floor. In Stephanie's mind, a fragile glass container shattered, dispersing invisible particles into the cold, damp air. She looked at Dragica and saw the same thought. Which then passed. Nothing so lethal would be carried in a container so flimsy. Surely . . .

Dragica pointed the gun at Stephanie to keep her in place. Then she stepped forward, crouched, released the second catch and opened the case. It wasn't possible to see the contents from where Stephanie stood but they were reflected in Dragica's expression. Blankness at first, then amazement. Then . . . *amusement?* Not of the comic variety. It looked bittersweet.

She stood up and shook her head. Then she turned the case round with one foot so that Stephanie could see. Foam blocks and a Smith & Wesson. The two of them stood there for what seemed like a long time with only the sound of the rain for company.

Then Dragica said, 'It seems I wasn't the only one with robbery on my mind. You can't trust anyone these days.'

'How did you work both ends?'

'Bukharin is a sympathizer. He feels Russia has betrayed Serbia. And that the leaders of Russia have betrayed their own people. He feels Russia needs to take a step back in order to move forward.'

He was not the only one. Stephanie recognized Bukharin's brutal line of logic: a biological terrorist incident, appalling casualties, global reaction, the inevitable finger of blame cast towards Moscow. And then what? A time of uncertainty. Which for men like Bukharin meant a time of opportunity.

Dragica said, 'Mikhail was the anonymous interface for the end user. Vladimir trusted him, so when Mikhail said the clients wanted to go through him, Vladimir agreed. Mikhail spent plenty of time in the Balkans when he was with KGB Alpha so it felt right to Vladimir. Which was how we persuaded him there'd be cash and diamonds coming today.'

'And you trusted Vatukin to deliver his end of the deal?'

She shrugged in an offhand way. 'I thought I knew Vladimir completely. It seems there was more to him than met the eye.'

'And without you on the inside, Bukharin couldn't have played this end.'

'No.'

'You had it all worked out.'

'All except Vladimir's greed.'

'That should have been the easy part. He was a new Russian, after all.'

Back through the Somerset, Stephanie leading, Dragica a safe distance behind her. They started down the main staircase. Water was cascading through a hole in the ceiling into the lobby, its echo filling the empty space.

'Tell me about Arkan. Who hired me?'

'Who do you think?'

'I assumed it was Milosevic.'

'Correct. Which was why we had to contract out. He was supposed to be close to Arkan. It was an uneasy alliance between two believers in the expansion of Serbia. In truth, Milosevic was scared of Arkan.'

'Why?'

'The profile of his paramilitary Tigers was too high.

There was money coming in from abroad, especially Russia and Italy.'

'Italy?'

'Criminal syndicates looking to the future. They pictured concessions in the Balkans. Money-laundering, organized prostitution, narcotics, arms smuggling. There was talk of casinos . . .'

'I thought those were some of the reasons Tsentralnaya was close to Milosevic.'

'They were. It was Rogachev who suggested that Arkan might become an insurmountable problem unless measures were taken.'

'But Milosevic couldn't risk using one of his own people.'

'No. And he couldn't risk it going wrong, either. Which was why he gave the order to bring in an outsider. The best, he insisted. In other words, you.'

'Why were you at the Inter-Continental? That was a risk . . .'

Dragica smiled. 'You wouldn't believe me if I told you.'

'Try me.'

'I wanted to see you.'

'See me?'

'In the flesh. I wanted to watch you.'

Even though Dragica was behind her, Stephanie knew it was true. It was in her voice. More than admiration, it sounded closer to devotion.

'I'd always wondered about you,' she continued. 'About the woman behind the name.'

'Now you know.'

'Yes, I do. And I was right about you, Petra. We're the same.'

They reached the ground floor, crossed the deserted lobby and headed through a series of service passages down one side of the building that were darker, colder and muskier.

'Stop.'

It was a narrow corridor; Stephanie could have touched both walls. Ahead, lines of perspective dissolved into darkness. The wall to her left was an outer wall; she could hear the rain nearby.

'Get on your knees.'

Stephanie was adrift; Petra was not inside her. There was nothing to grab, nowhere to run to, nothing to say.

'On your knees.'

She sank to the ground.

'Hands behind your head.'

'Am I going to be a trophy?'

Dragica ignored the question. 'Tell me something, Petra. What's Kostya like?'

The last question she would have expected under the circumstances. Or wanted, now that she considered it. It was not an easy one to answer, either.

'How do you mean?'

'What sort of man is he? All the time I was with Oleg – and then Vladimir – I watched him and wondered. To be honest, when I saw the two of you together, I was jealous.'

'You knew about us?'

'Naturally.'

'Vatukin knew too?'

Dragica laughed. 'Of course not! Don't be stupid. Vladimir was a typical man. A typical Russian man. But I could tell. When we were at Café Pushkin, it was obvious what the two of you were trying to hide.'

'Let me guess. You shoot me, he's overcome with grief, you step in to console him. Is that the idea?'

'I hadn't thought of it but it's not bad. Thanks.'

'Don't mention it.'

'Tell me.'

What was there to lose? 'He's wonderful.'

'Do you love him?'

'None of your business.'

'*Do you love him?*'

'Yes.'

'And you say he's wonderful?'

'Yes.'

There was soft laughter in the darkness behind her. 'I thought he might be.'

Dragica fired the Glock.

Stephanie heard it but felt nothing. A second later, the sound of steps, of rushing air, of loud rain and the bang of a door. For a moment, she froze. Then she looked round. She was alone. She jumped to her feet, saw a slice of daylight, pushed the door open and found herself in a narrow alley. She turned right, scrambled over two rolls of fence-wire and a carpet of soggy rubbish.

Erupting onto West 54th Street, she glanced left and right. Through the rain, she saw startled faces, umbrellas, hats, hunched shoulders. But not Dragica Maric.

28

She couldn't go to Komarov straight away. She needed to think. So she walked instead, up through the Fifties, up Central Park West, passing George Salibi's apartment block – the upper floors still stained black by smoke – and through the Park.

By the time she reached the apartment, she was soaked. He didn't ask, she didn't offer. In the bedroom, she peeled off her sodden clothes, wrapped herself in a white towel and curled into a ball on one end of the sofa in the sitting room. Soon, she knew, her body would pay. But not yet. She wouldn't let it.

'Shouldn't we . . . do something?' Komarov asked.

She shook her head. 'Tomorrow, we'll have to look over our shoulders. This is our last day. Let's enjoy it. We'll regret it, if we don't.'

It was the evening she'd always imagined with him. At home, alone, relaxed, no agenda. Somehow, they managed to banish the morning. Komarov suggested they go to Ferrier, their first restaurant. Stephanie said she didn't want to share him. In that case, he'd replied, let Ferrier come to them. Tomato and mozzarella with fresh basil, then grilled tuna in a red pepper vinaigrette and *coq au vin*. To drink, a chilled Meursault, then a Pauillac. They made love on the sitting-room floor and drank the last of the wine from a single glass. Later, ready for sleep, they contrived to make love again, both aware of the silent subtext.

In bed, they whispered in the darkness until Komarov fell asleep, just after three. Stephanie stayed awake, content to listen to the rise and fall of his breathing. At quarter to four, she slipped out of bed, tiptoed into the sitting room, closed the door and made the call. It lasted ten minutes. Then she dressed in the spare clothes bought at Stockmann in Helsinki. In the kitchen, she found a notepad and pen. It took her fifteen minutes to compose a few short sentences. She returned to the bedroom only once, pausing in the doorway until the tears began to well. Then she placed the note on the floor and let herself out.

It was twenty past four when she stepped onto Fifth Avenue. It was still raining. The car was a dark blue BMW. She opened the passenger door and climbed in.

'I thought it might be you.'

Rosie Chaudhuri smiled sympathetically. They drove in silence until after they'd crossed the Triborough Bridge and were on Grand Central Parkway.

'I should have guessed right at the start. You were so different. Not just slimmer and fitter, but more confident. Then when I saw you in Zurich – the bruise on your right cheek, the bandage round your right hand. A karate class, didn't you say?'

'Yes.'

'Some club on the Seven Sisters Road?'

'That's right.'

Stephanie couldn't help her weary smile. 'I can't believe I missed that.'

Rosie, a woman who knew what she did was distasteful but did it anyway. Just as Stephanie had, when she'd been Lisa, the drug-dependent prostitute. The difference was, Rosie believed in something. Stephanie didn't, yet liked and admired her anyway, which seemed to be a contradiction. But so what? She *was* a contradiction.

Rosie said, 'I didn't think he'd go for it.'

'Nor did I.'

'It's not often anyone takes the old bastard by surprise.'

'I wouldn't even have tried, if you hadn't been the one.'

'No?'

Stephanie shook her head. 'I would have risked it and tried to run.'

'I'm glad you didn't. You would have failed.'

'Probably. You're not going to prove me wrong, are you?'

Rosie just smiled.

Eighty forty-two, the departure lounge in the British Airways terminal at JFK. In my hand, my boarding card for flight BA178, due to leave in eighteen minutes. Most of the passengers are already on the aircraft. I've got a lot of memories to compare this feeling to but, in truth, I don't think I've ever felt quite so crushed.

I leave it until the last moment. They're closing the gate. I'm going to be the last to board. I hand over the card and get a portion in return. A final glance over my shoulder, then it's down the umbilical towards the aircraft. The open door comes into view. So does he. I stop. He's flanked by two airport officials. Boris Bergstein once told me that Kostya had a crew at JFK. He never elaborated on that but here is the evidence behind the claim.

'You left me a note?'

There's no hiding his exasperation.

'I didn't know what else to do. I didn't think I could say it to your face.'

The officials give us a little privacy.

'What about the future, Stephanie?'

'There is no future. Not for us.'

'Was there yesterday?'

'Yes.'

'But not now?'

'No.'

'Why not?'

I shake my head. 'There just isn't.'

'Not good enough.'

'I'm sorry . . .'

'We need to talk.'

'No.'

'Take the next flight.'

'I can't.'

'Yes, you can.' He gestures towards the men behind him. 'They can . . .'

'You don't understand. This is part of the deal.'

'What deal?'

'The deal I made this morning, while you were asleep.'

'What are you talking about?'

'This is the only way I can be sure of keeping you alive, Kostya.'

'How?'

'By going back.'

'To London?'

'Yes.'

And then, in growing disbelief: 'To Magenta House?'

'Yes.'

'No!'

491

'There's no other way.'

'You can't. I won't let you. Not after what you told me.'

One of the officials gives an exaggerated cough. 'Excuse me . . .'

Kostya waves a hand at him impatiently. 'One minute, please.'

'We can't run,' I tell him. 'We already know a life in transit doesn't work. We've tried it. You can get away with it for a short while but not in the long term. In the end, you have to stop. So that's what you do. You find a place, you settle, you try to build a life. And then they find you.'

'Not necessarily.'

'Yes, necessarily. You don't know what they're like. They're relentless. They would never stop looking. We might get away with it for a month, a year, maybe five years. But in the end, they'd find us.'

'I'm prepared to risk it.'

'I'm not.'

'Why not?'

My voice is beginning to fail. 'It's just too selfish.' I take hold of him. 'There are people who depend on you. They need you, Kostya. The men and women at the refuge. Ludmilla, Andrei, Max. Mohammed Saev and the children at Izmailovo. And all the others who I've never even met. I can't take you away from them. I'm sorry. I just . . . can't.'

'We can sort something out, Stephanie.'

'No.'

'Take a later flight.'

I shake my head. 'If I don't step off this aircraft at Heathrow, they'll kill you.'

He has no answer to that. Out of the corner of my eye, I see the fidgeting official. He clears his throat again and I tell him that I'm on my way. It's all I can do not to cry.

'I'm saving your life, Kostya. The only way I'm going to get through this is by knowing that. You're too important to waste. They wanted a life for a life. Yours for Marshall. Instead, they get me for Marshall. That's the deal. And it's a bargain.'

'But you can't trust Alexander. You told me that.'

I smile sadly. 'I can now because he knows that he can trust me as long as you're alive. And that's all that matters.'

'This is insane.'

'I know. But that's the world we live in. We're not like the rest. Remember?'

'I won't let you do this.'

'It's not up to you.'

I kiss him for the last time, crushing my mouth against his. I want to immortalize this moment: the feel of him, the smell of him, the taste of him.

My lips brush his ear. 'I love you, Kostya. And I always will.'

Then I break away. I think he says he loves me too. But I can't be sure because I've already gone. I'm biting my lower lip so hard it begins to bleed again. Yet despite everything, there is a small, warm glow at the centre of my chest. I know something about myself that I didn't know before. I'm capable of something that I thought was beyond me and which is far greater than any of the talents that Petra Reuter has amassed.

I stride towards the open aircraft door. The smiling flight attendant is a watery blur to me. She welcomes me on board and directs me upstairs.

I don't look back.

MOSCOW

It was snowing heavily, the latest in a long succession of winter storms. In the former state orphanage once known as Children's Home Number 23, Konstantin Komarov was on the first floor, supervising a team of builders who were installing a row of new showers. The communal bathroom was the second area to be renovated within the building. The dormitories had been completed at the end of January; replastered walls, insulation, new floorboards, wall-to-wall tiled carpeting, pine bunk beds and furniture, double-glazed windows, central heating.

Komarov looked at his watch. Eleven thirty. He'd been up since half past five. Time for tea. He took the back stairs to the ground floor and was passing his office when he noticed the envelope on his desk. And the wet footprints on the floor. He glanced up and down the corridor. The footprints led to the exit; the snow had melted into a series of small puddles. He followed them outside but saw nobody. Back in his office, he picked up the envelope. On the front, a single word. *Kostya.* He opened it. Inside, there were two sheets of headed notepaper. The first contained details of a numbered account at Guderian Maier Bank in Zurich. The second was a letter from Albert Eichner, explaining that the account had been set up for Komarov's use and giving details of the necessary procedures to gain access to it.

There was a third sheet of paper in the envelope. A handwritten note.

Kostya, this is for you. One million and eighty thousand US dollars. The money that Petra earned when she was working for Magenta House. Alexander wanted it back and I told him that I'd given it to a good cause. You should have seen his face; it was worth every cent. I know you'll make the best use of it. I'm afraid these are the most infected dollars in the world. They need the best laundering money can buy so I thought I'd send them to an expert!

By the way, remember what you said to me that night in Aragvi? I've been thinking about it. You were wrong. It's not a mistake to think of you as a good man. You **are.** *As I write this, it's been forty-four days, sixteen hours and twenty-nine minutes since I saw you. There hasn't been a moment in that time when we haven't been together.*